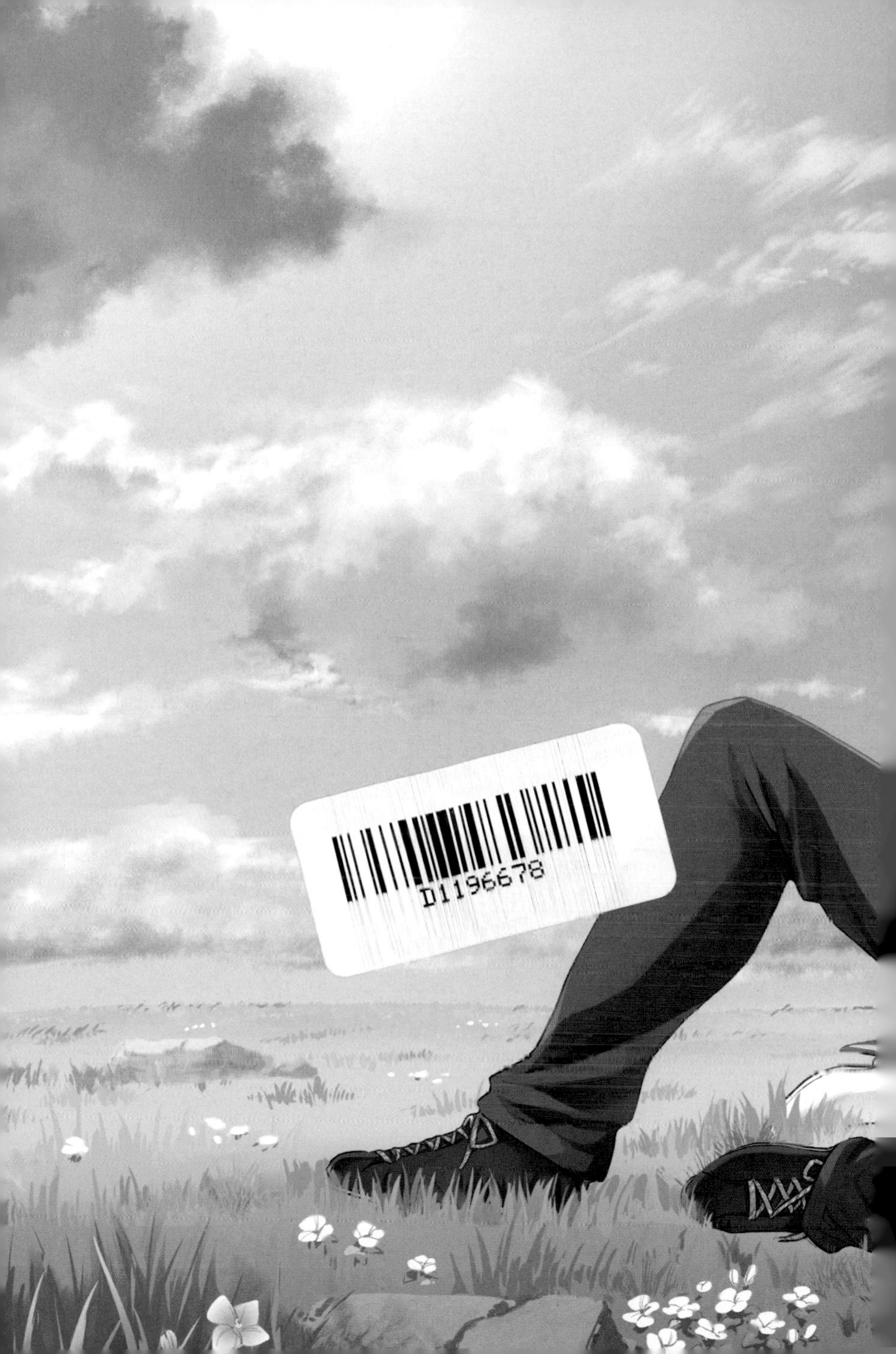

Re:ZERO -Starting Life in Another World-

Chapter 3: Truth of Zero

The only ability Subaru Natsuki gets when he's summoned to
another world is time travel via his own death. But to save her,
he'll die as many times as it takes.

Contents

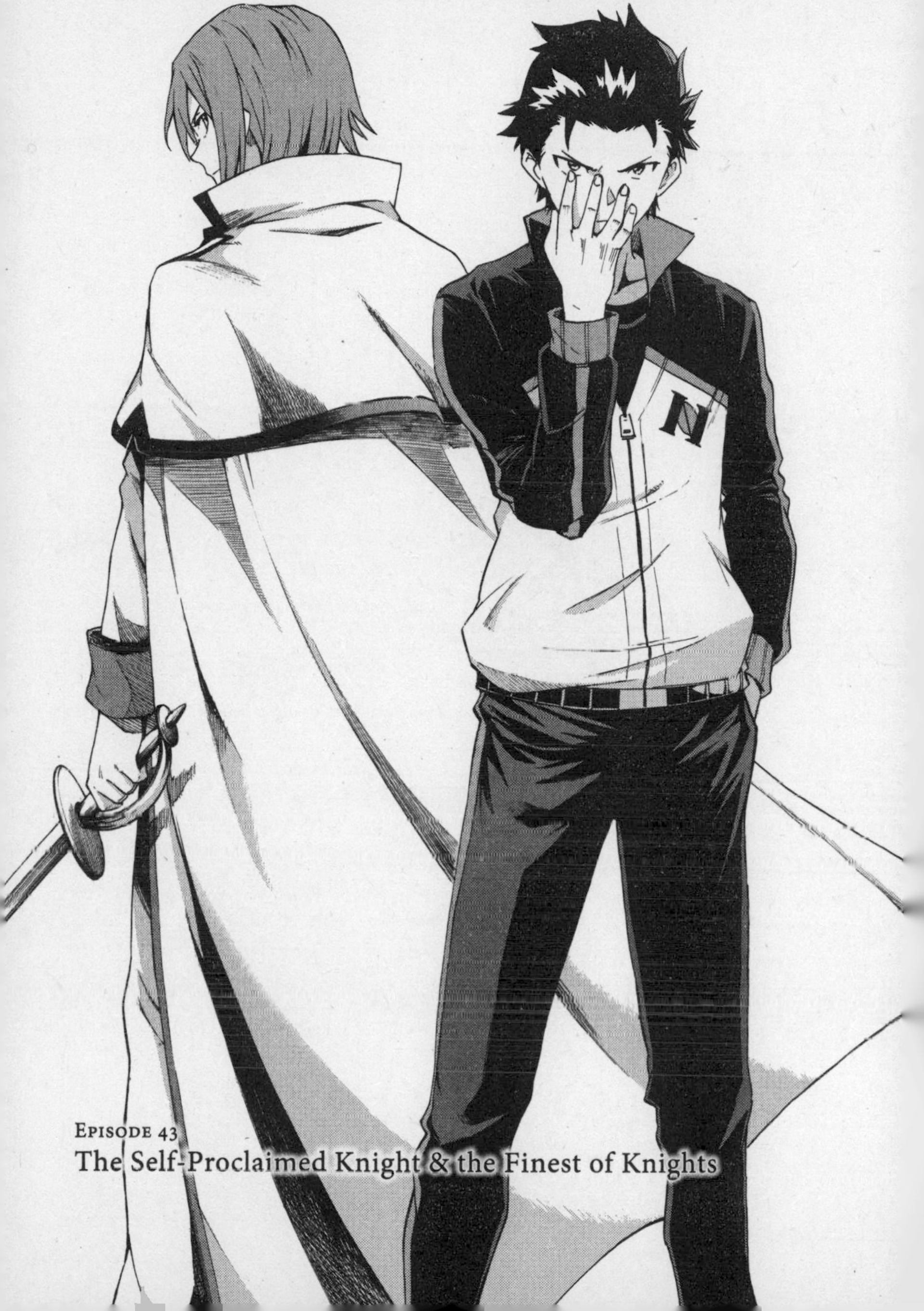

Episode 43

The Self-Proclaimed Knight & the Finest of Knights

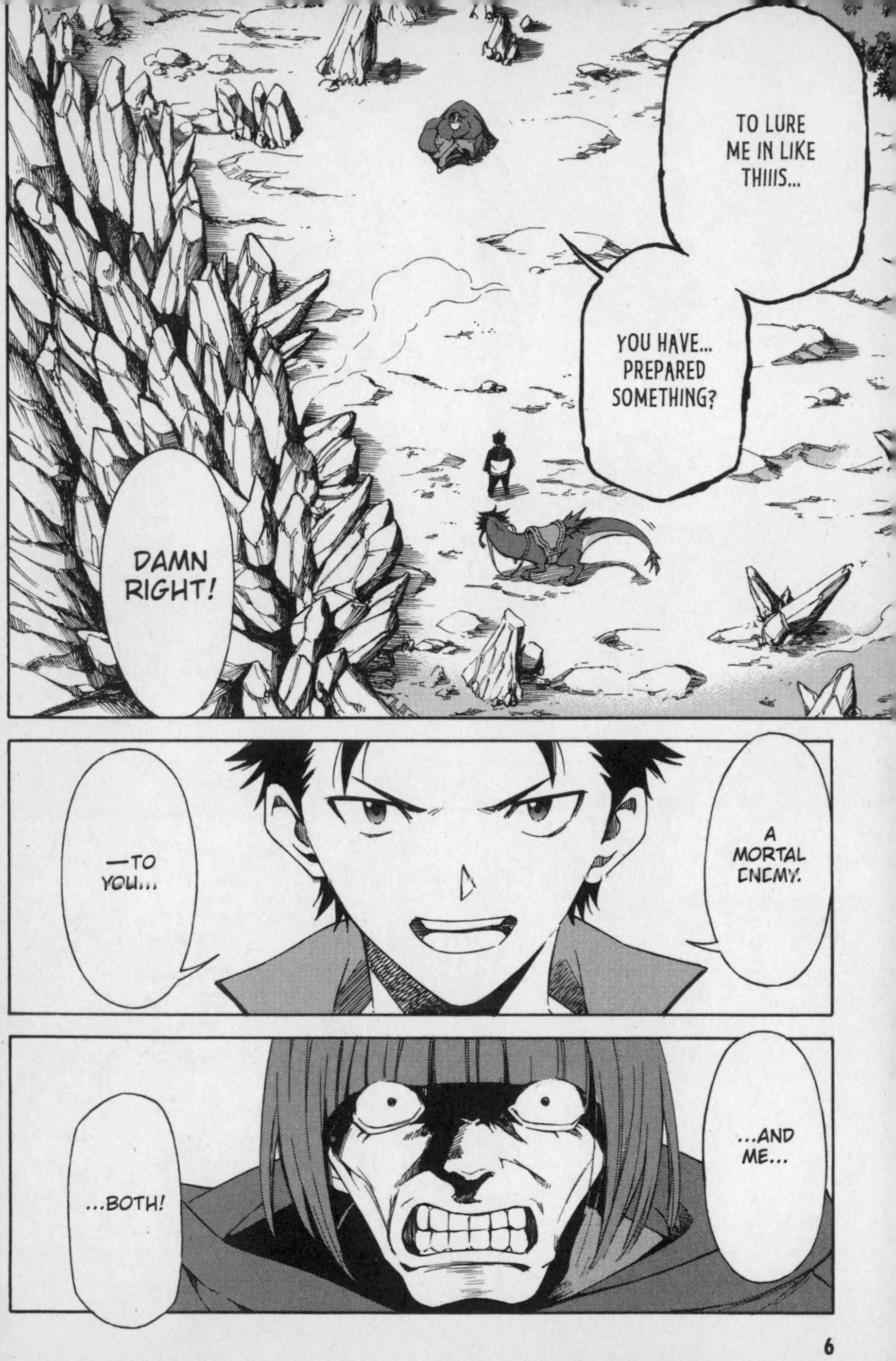
TO LURE ME IN LIKE THIIIS...
YOU HAVE... PREPARED SOMETHING?
DAMN RIGHT!
A MORTAL ENEMY.
—TO YOU...
...AND ME...
...BOTH!

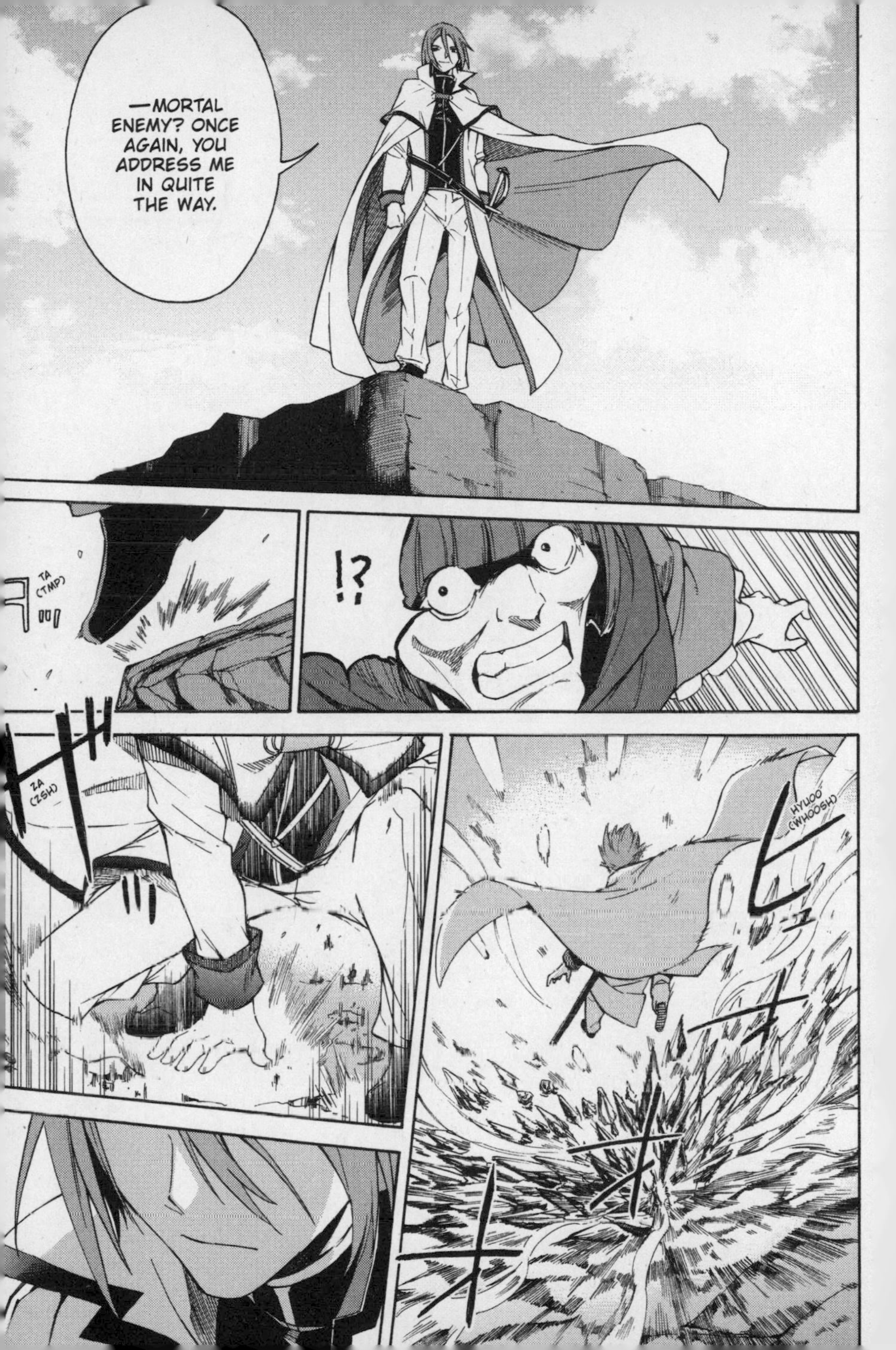
—MORTAL ENEMY? ONCE AGAIN, YOU ADDRESS ME IN QUITE THE WAY.
!?
TA (TMP)
HYUOO (WHOOSH)
ZA (ZSH)

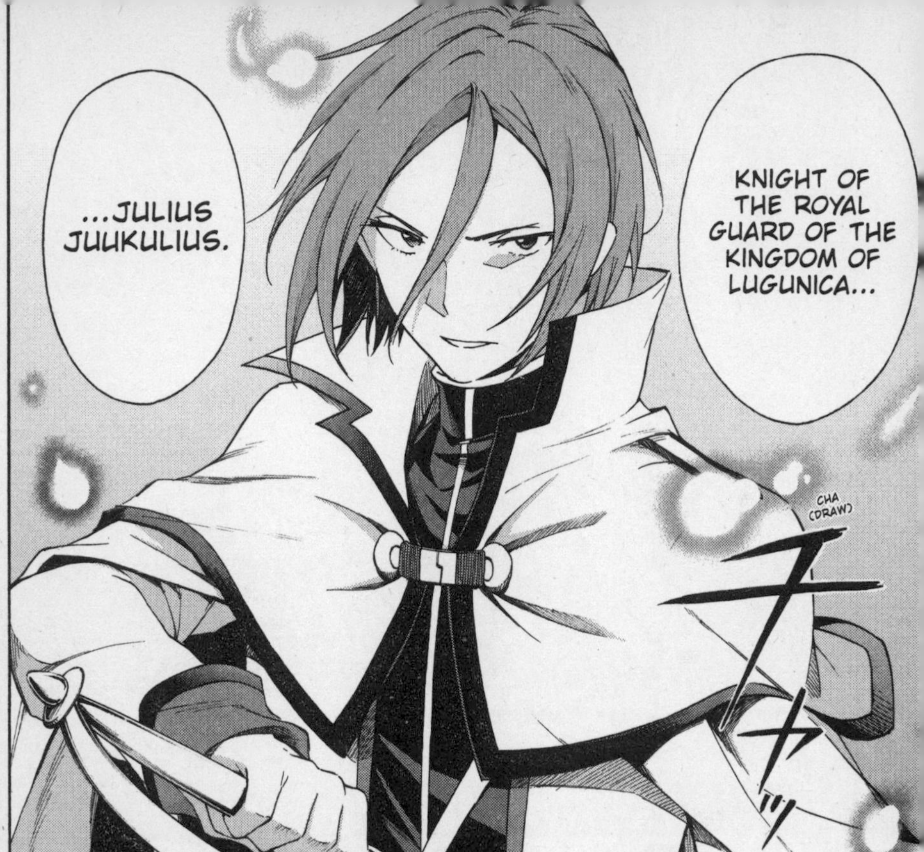
KNIGHT OF THE ROYAL GUARD OF THE KINGDOM OF LUGUNICA...
...JULIUS JUUKULIUS.
CHA (DRAW)

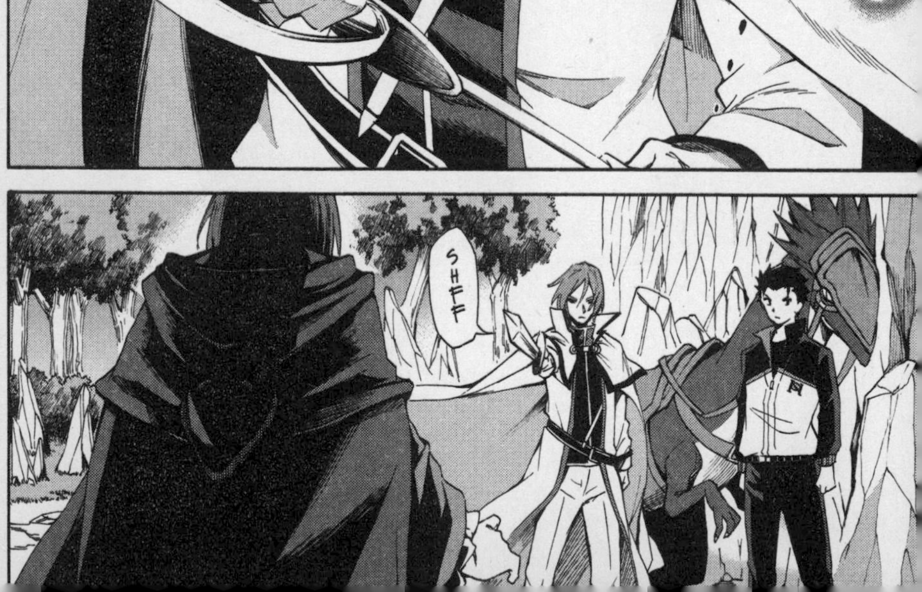
SHFF

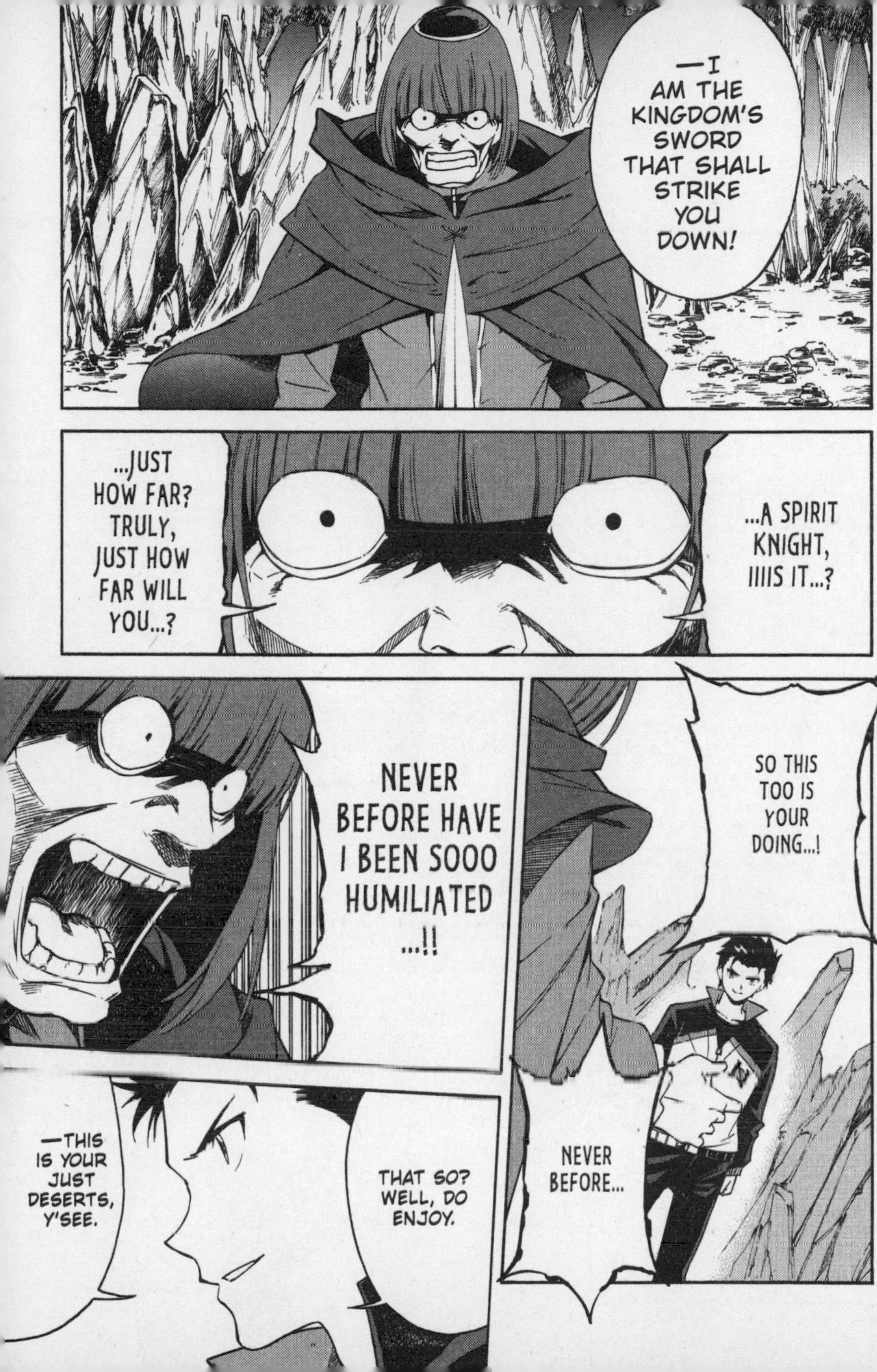
—I AM THE KINGDOM'S SWORD THAT SHALL STRIKE YOU DOWN!
...A SPIRIT KNIGHT, IIIIS IT...?
...JUST HOW FAR? TRULY, JUST HOW FAR WILL YOU...?
SO THIS TOO IS YOUR DOING...!
NEVER BEFORE...
NEVER BEFORE HAVE I BEEN SOOO HUMILIATED ...!!
THAT SO? WELL, DO ENJOY.
—THIS IS YOUR JUST DESERTS, Y'SEE.

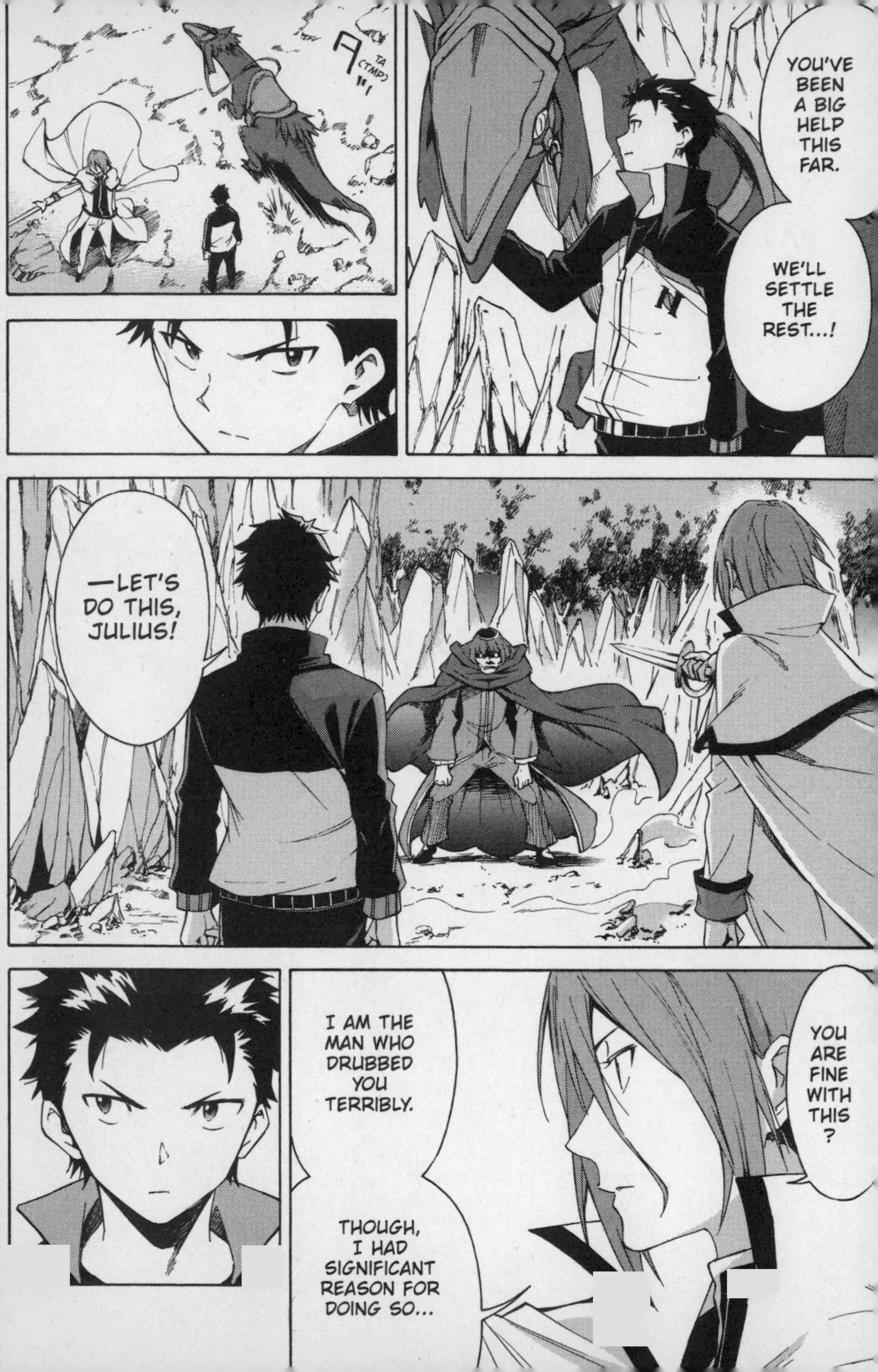
YOU'VE BEEN A BIG HELP THIS FAR.
WE'LL SETTLE THE REST...!
TA (TMP)
—LET'S DO THIS, JULIUS!
YOU ARE FINE WITH THIS?
I AM THE MAN WHO DRUBBED YOU TERRIBLY.
THOUGH, I HAD SIGNIFICANT REASON FOR DOING SO...

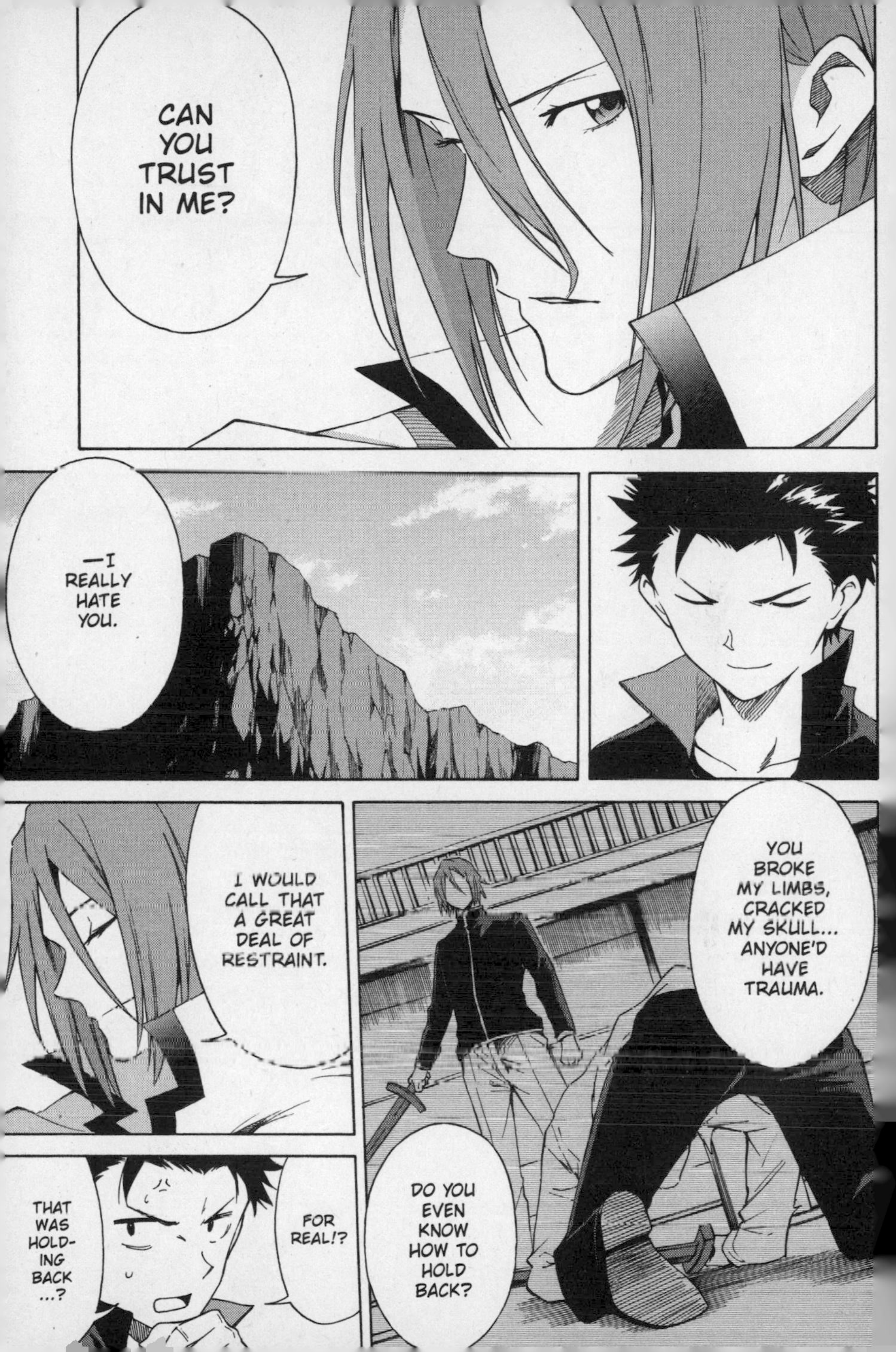
CAN YOU TRUST IN ME?
—I REALLY HATE YOU.
YOU BROKE MY LIMBS, CRACKED MY SKULL... ANYONE'D HAVE TRAUMA.
DO YOU EVEN KNOW HOW TO HOLD BACK?
I WOULD CALL THAT A GREAT DEAL OF RESTRAINT.
FOR REAL!?
THAT WAS HOLDING-ING BACK ...?

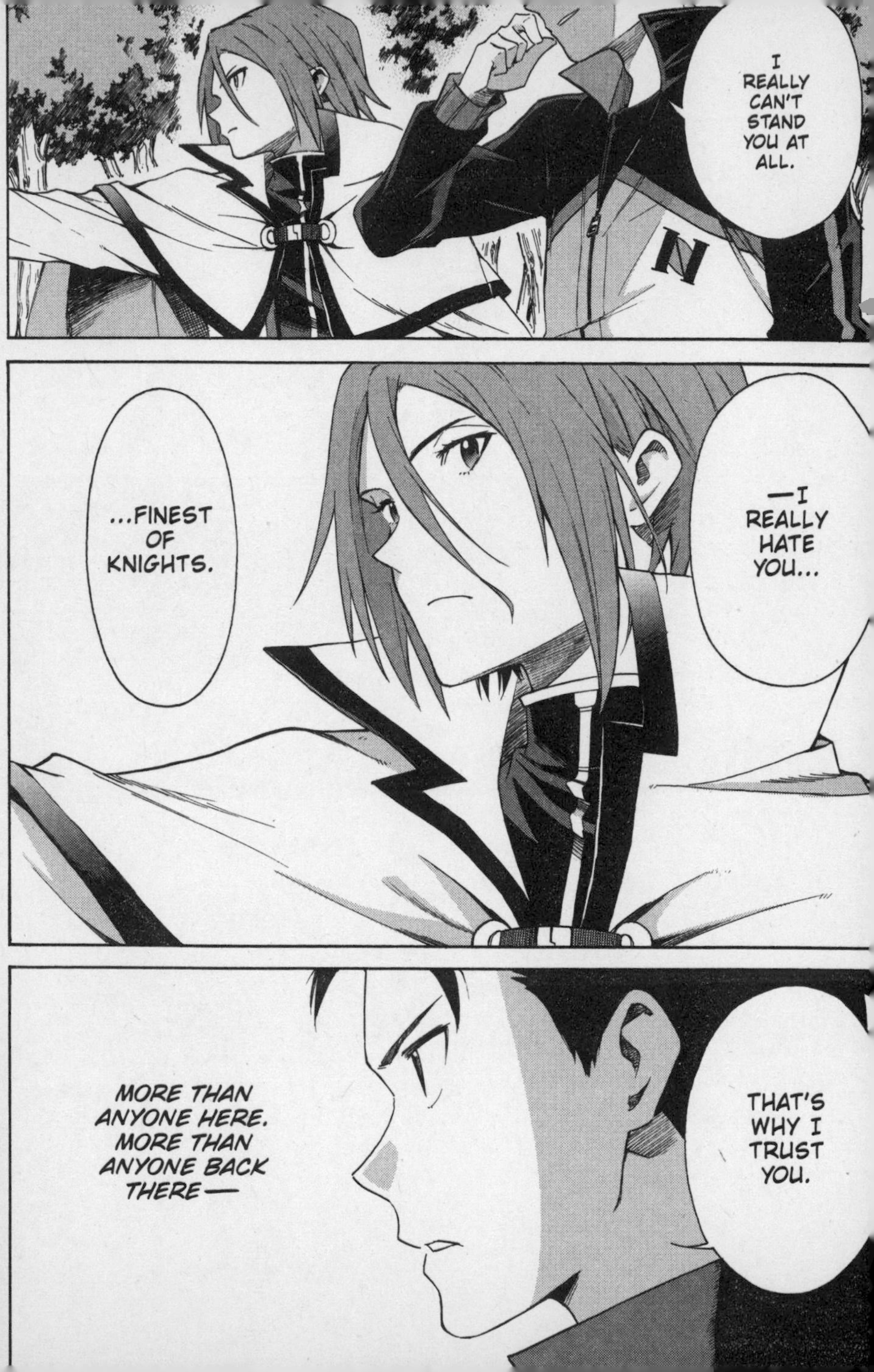
I REALLY CAN'T STAND YOU AT ALL.
—I REALLY HATE YOU...
...FINEST OF KNIGHTS.
THAT'S WHY I TRUST YOU.
MORE THAN ANYONE HERE. MORE THAN ANYONE BACK THERE—

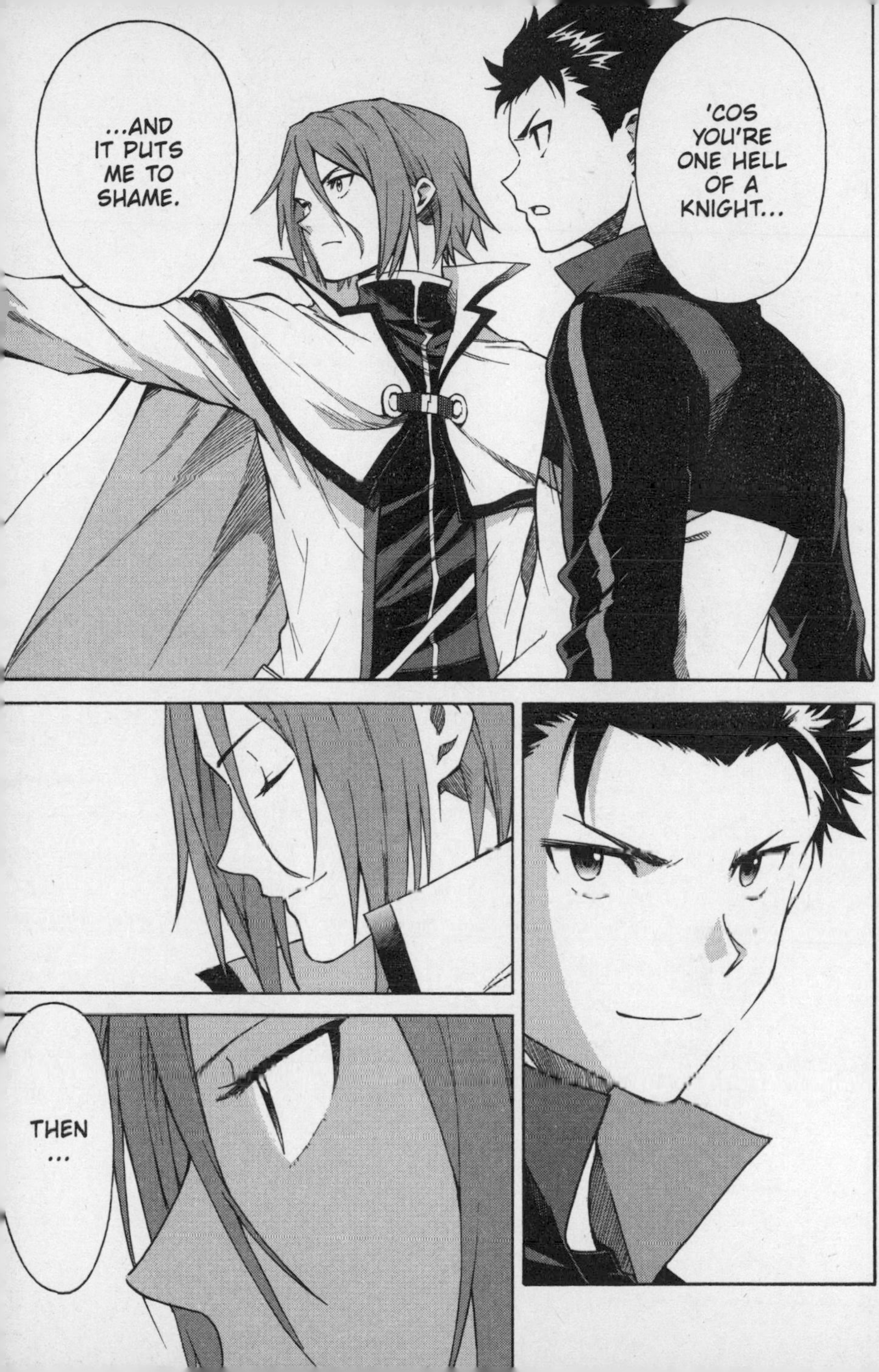
'COS YOU'RE ONE HELL OF A KNIGHT...
...AND IT PUTS ME TO SHAME.
THEN ...

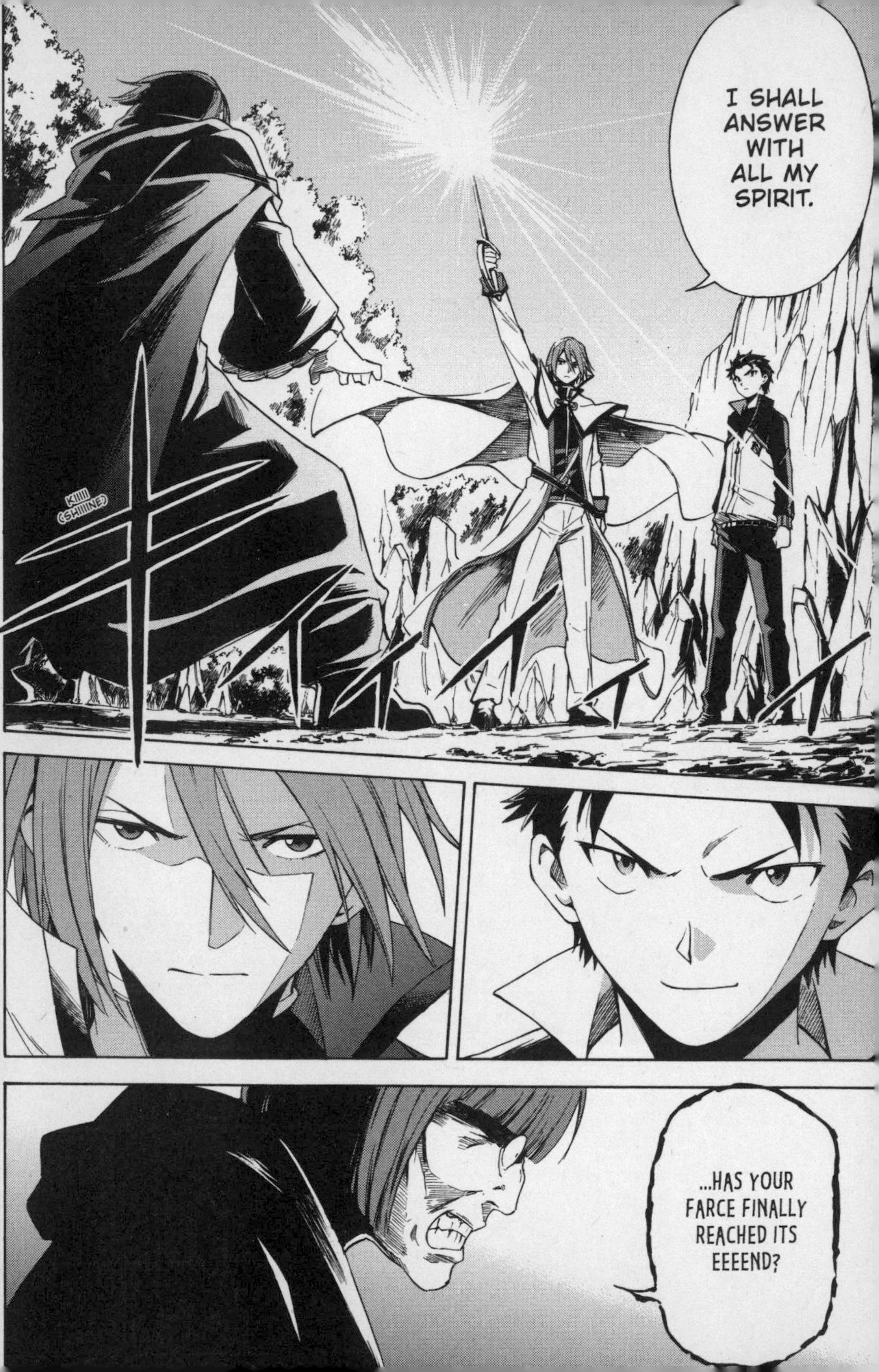
I SHALL ANSWER WITH ALL MY SPIRIT.
KIIIII (SHIIIINE)
...HAS YOUR FARCE FINALLY REACHED ITS EEEEND?

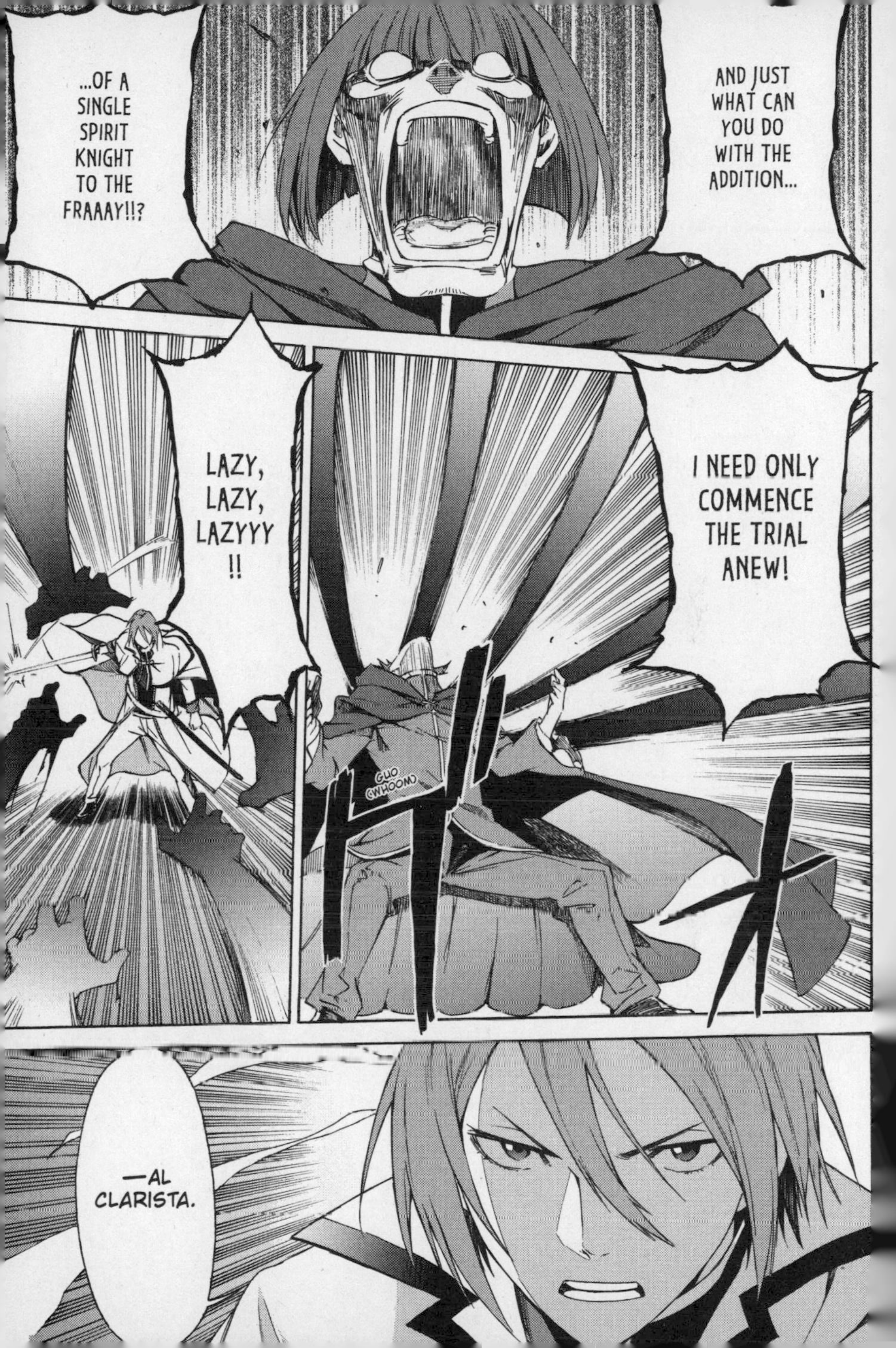
AND JUST WHAT CAN YOU DO WITH THE ADDITION...
...OF A SINGLE SPIRIT KNIGHT TO THE FRAAAY!!?
I NEED ONLY COMMENCE THE TRIAL ANEW!
GUO (WHOOM)
LAZY, LAZY, LAZYYY!!
—AL CLARISTA.

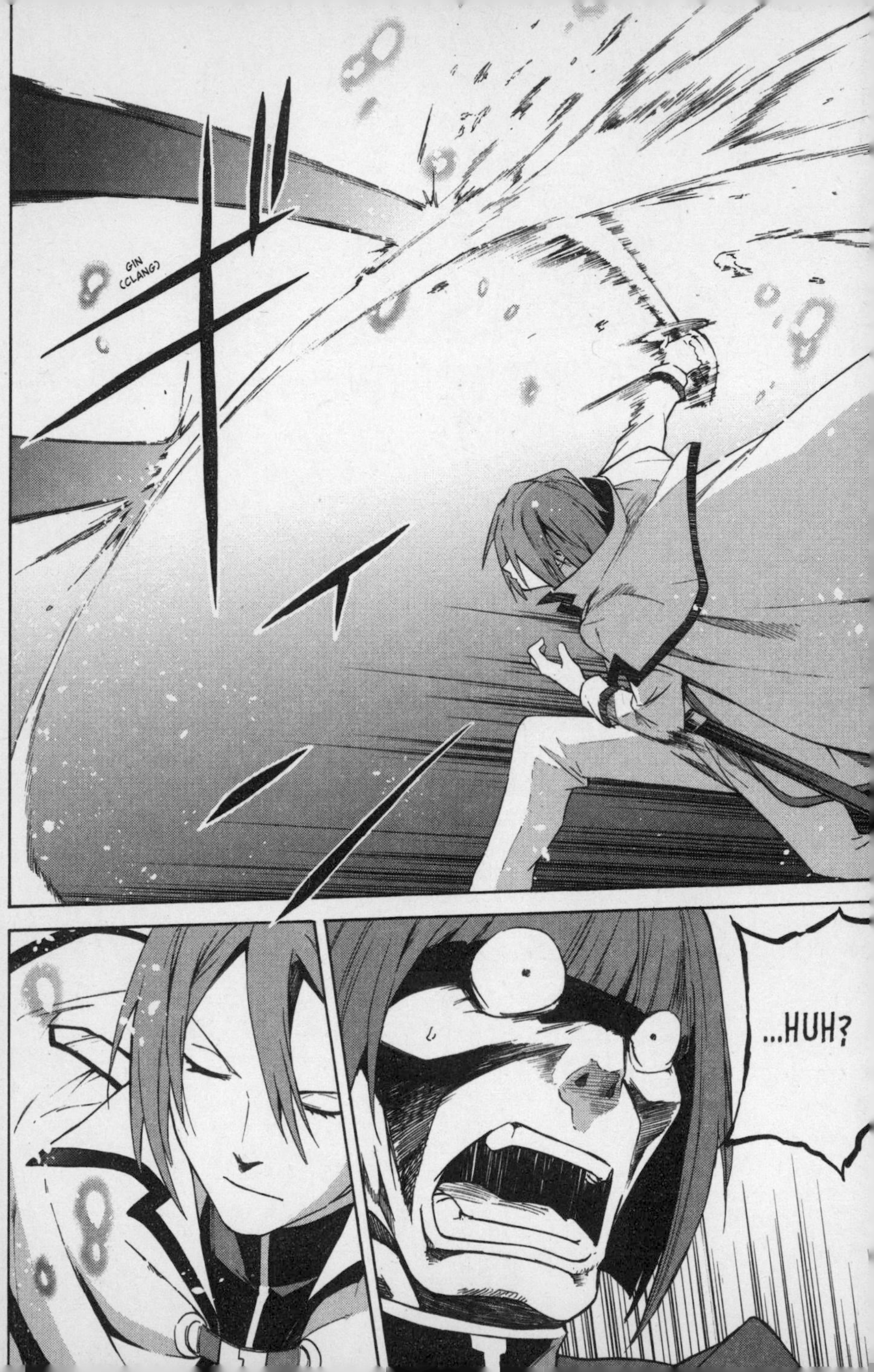
GIN (CLANG)
...HUH?

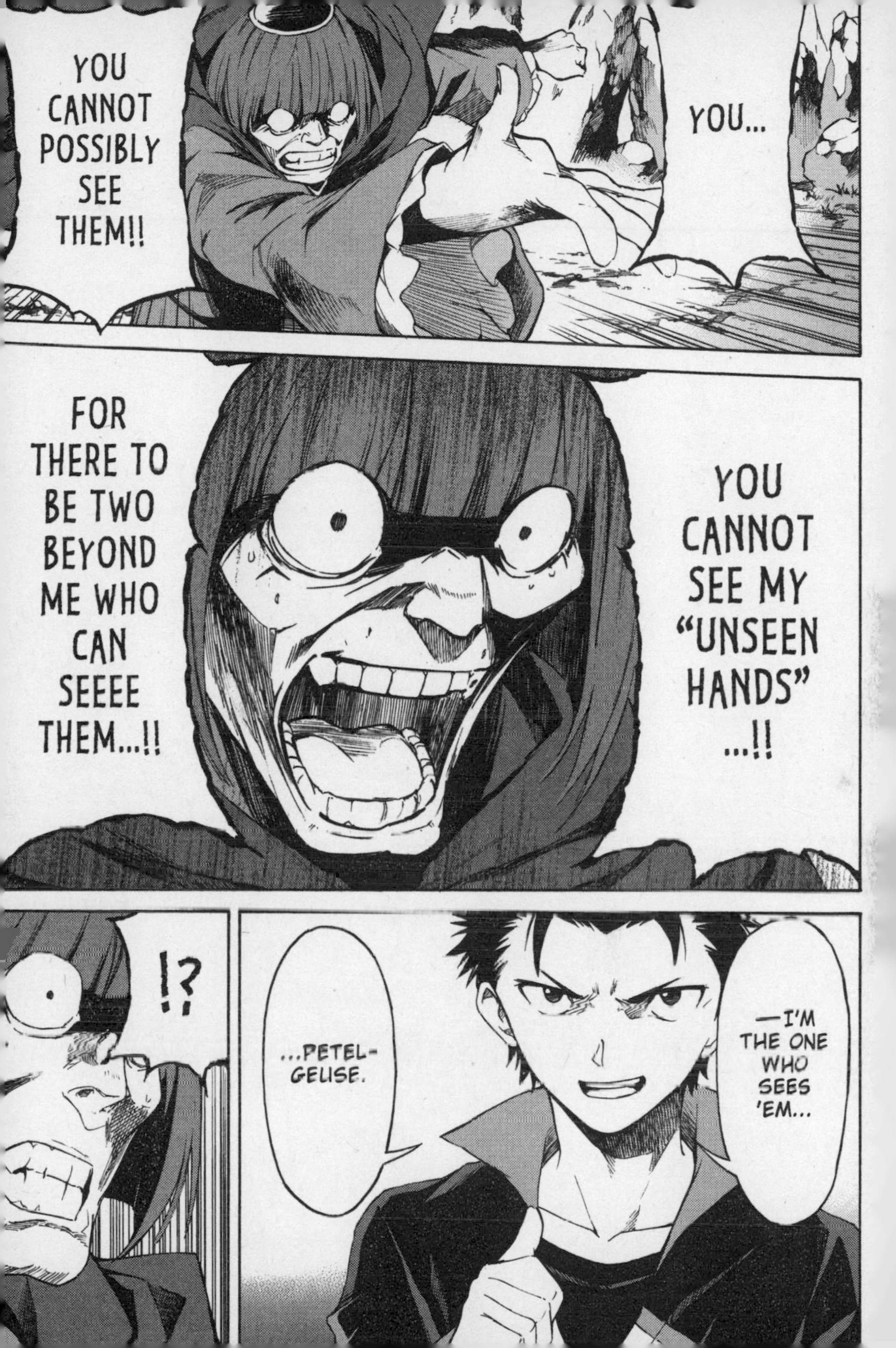
YOU...
YOU CANNOT POSSIBLY SEE THEM!!
YOU CANNOT SEE MY "UNSEEN HANDS" ...!!
FOR THERE TO BE TWO BEYOND ME WHO CAN SEEEE THEM...!!
—I'M THE ONE WHO SEES 'EM...
...PETEL-GEUSE.
!?

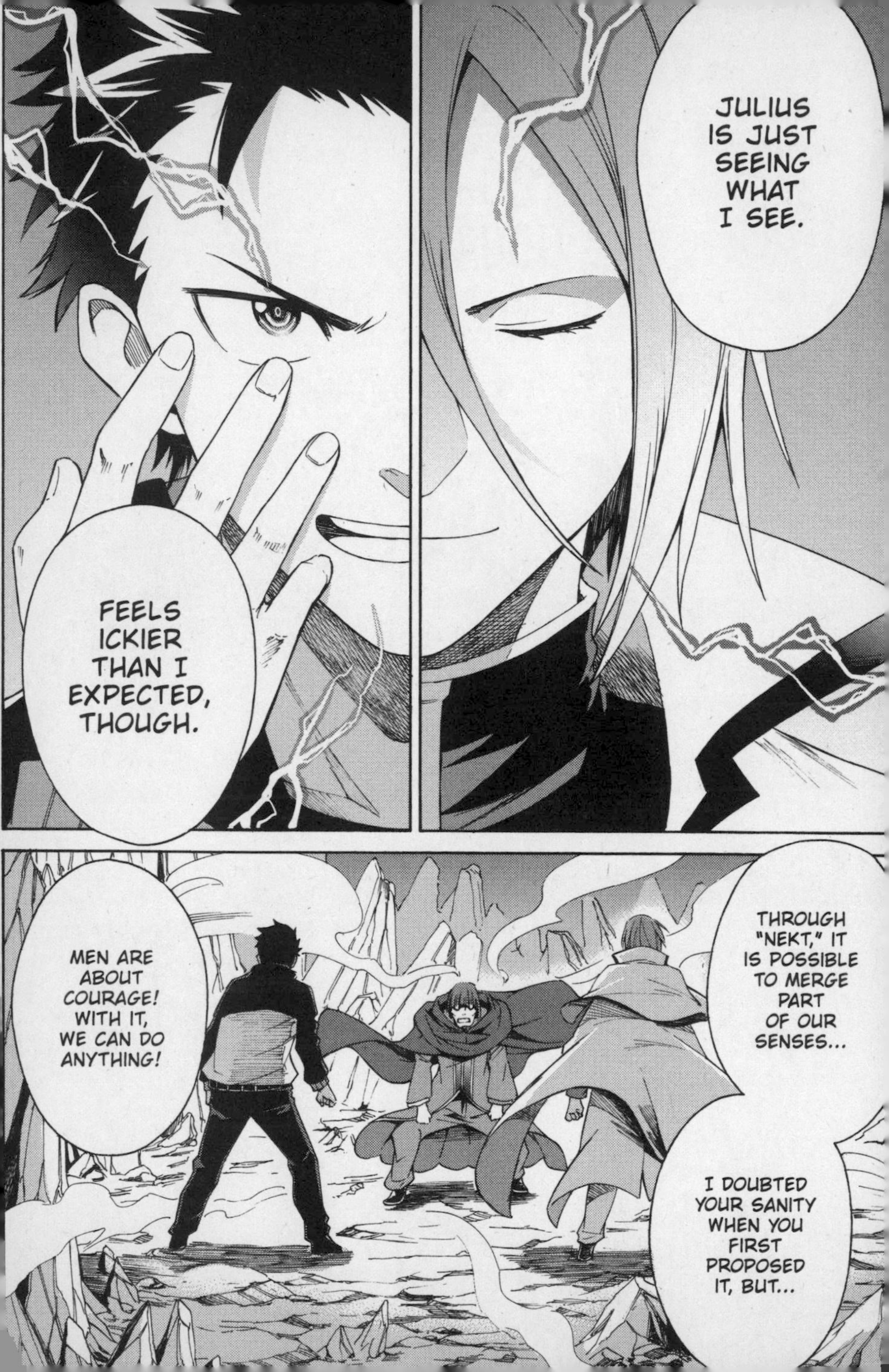
JULIUS IS JUST SEEING WHAT I SEE.
FEELS ICKIER THAN I EXPECTED, THOUGH.
THROUGH "NEKT," IT IS POSSIBLE TO MERGE PART OF OUR SENSES...
I DOUBTED YOUR SANITY WHEN YOU FIRST PROPOSED IT, BUT...
MEN ARE ABOUT COURAGE! WITH IT, WE CAN DO ANYTHING!

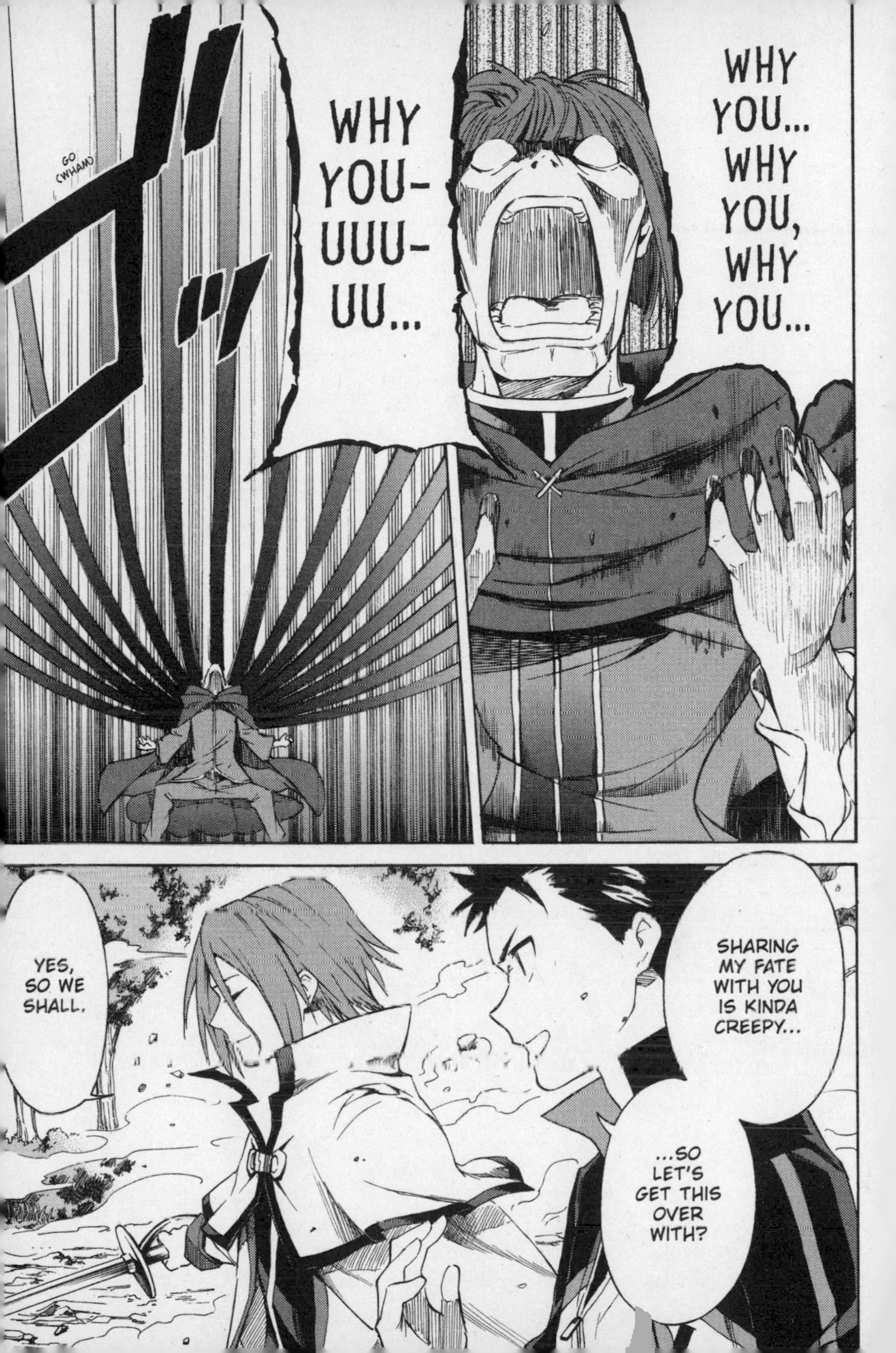
WHY YOU... WHY YOU, WHY YOU, WHY YOU...
WHY YOU-UUU-UU...
GO (WHAM)
SHARING MY FATE WITH YOU IS KINDA CREEPY...
...SO LET'S GET THIS OVER WITH?
YES, SO WE SHALL.

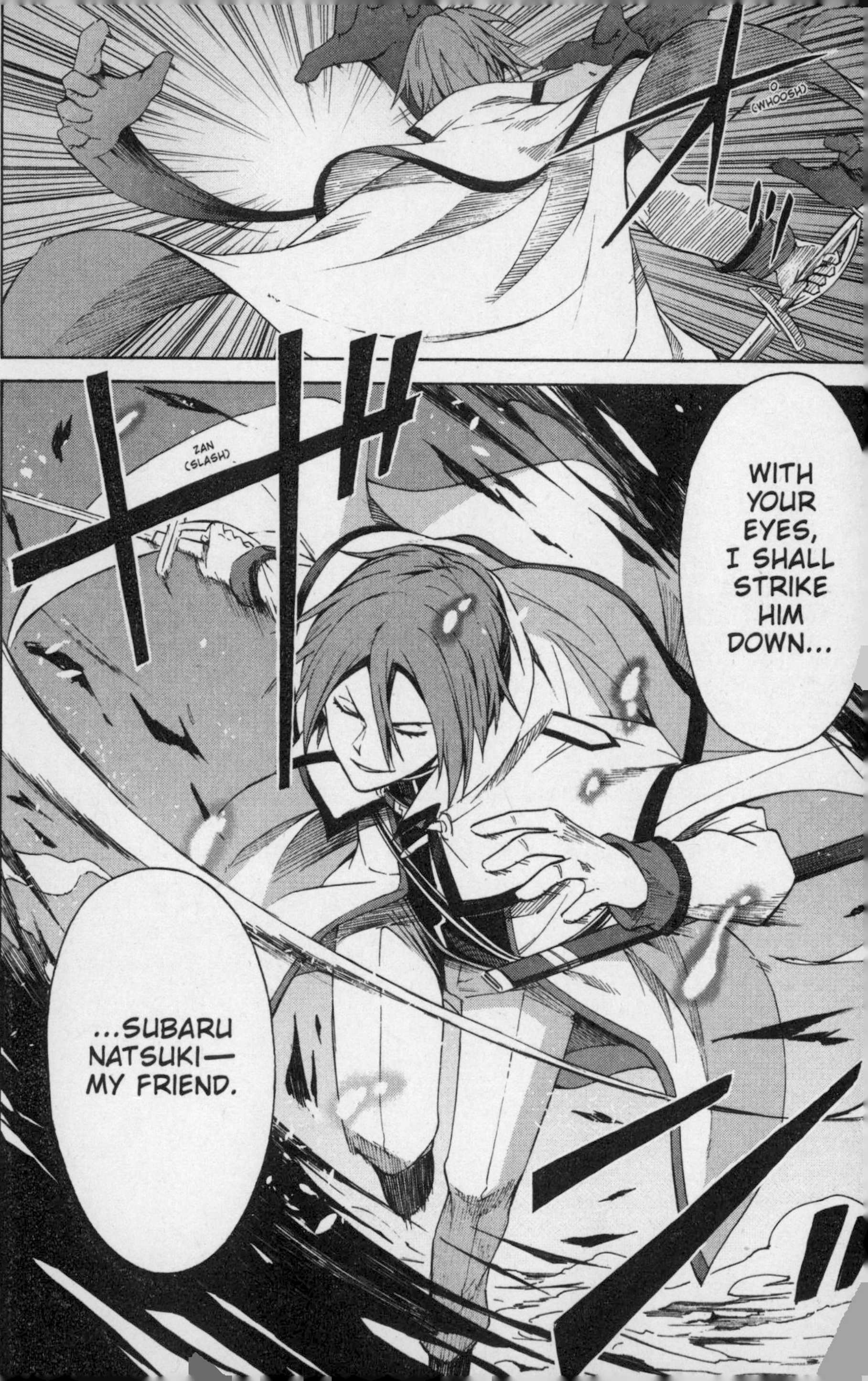
(WHOOSH)
ZAN (SLASH)
WITH YOUR EYES, I SHALL STRIKE HIM DOWN...
...SUBARU NATSUKI—MY FRIEND.

Re:ZERO -Starting Life in Another World-

The only ability Subaru Natsuki gets when he's summoned to another world is
time travel via his own death. But to save her, he'll die as many times as it takes.

The only ability Subaru Natsuki gets when he's summoned to another world is time travel via his own death. But to save her, he'll die as many times as it takes.

Truth of Zero

Re:ZERO -Starting
Life in Another World-

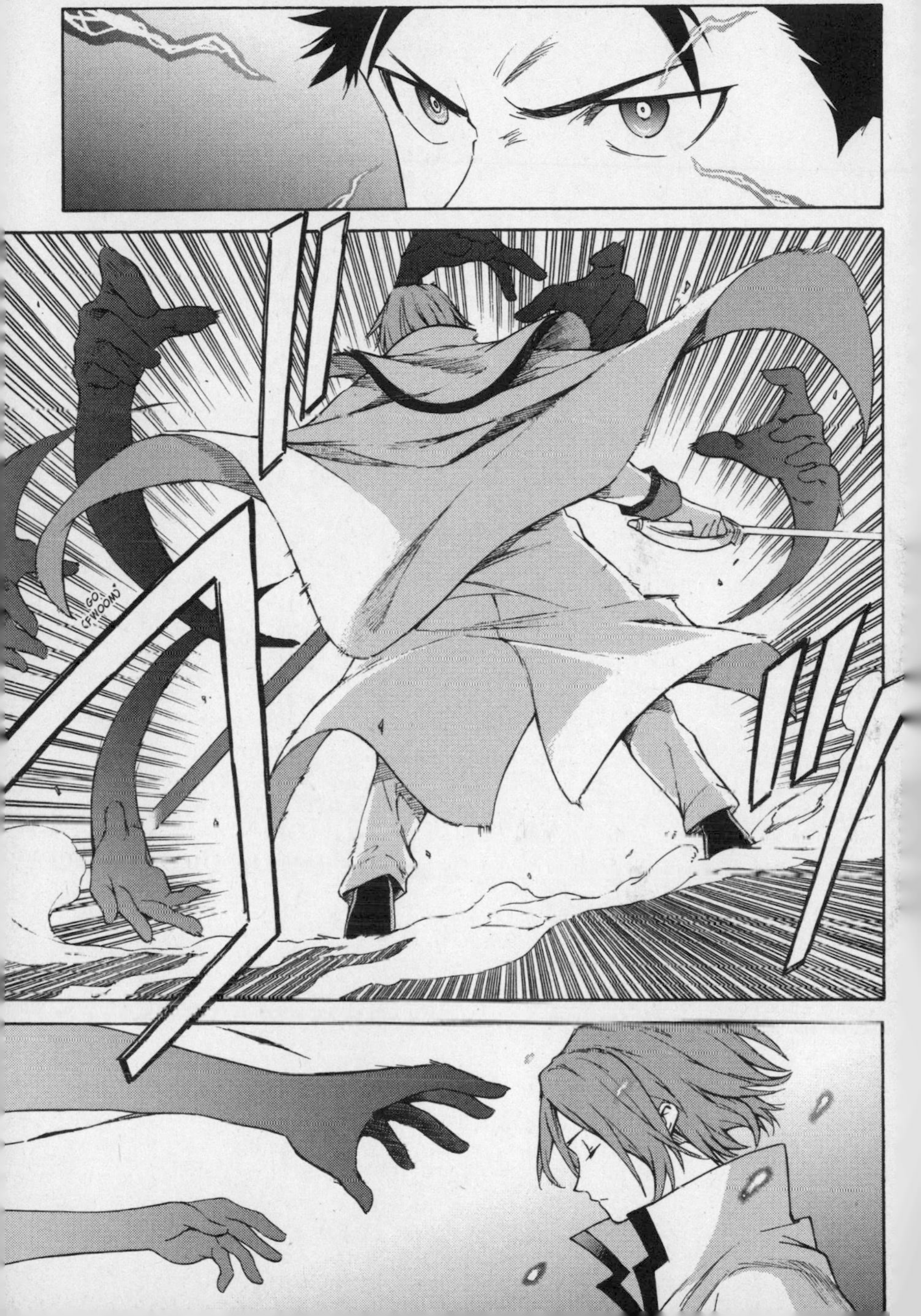
GO
(FWOOM)

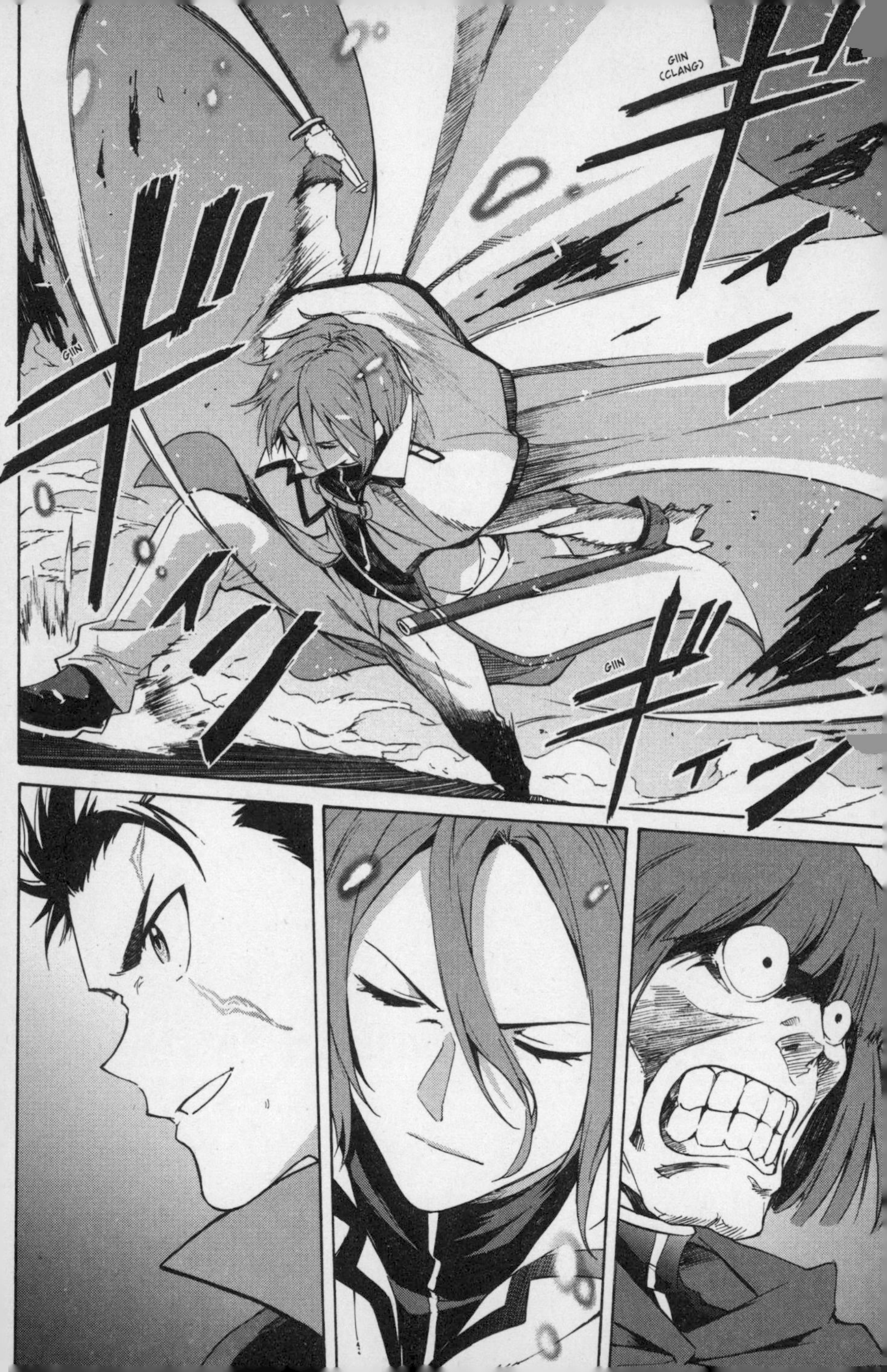
GIIN
(CLANG)
GIIN
GIIN

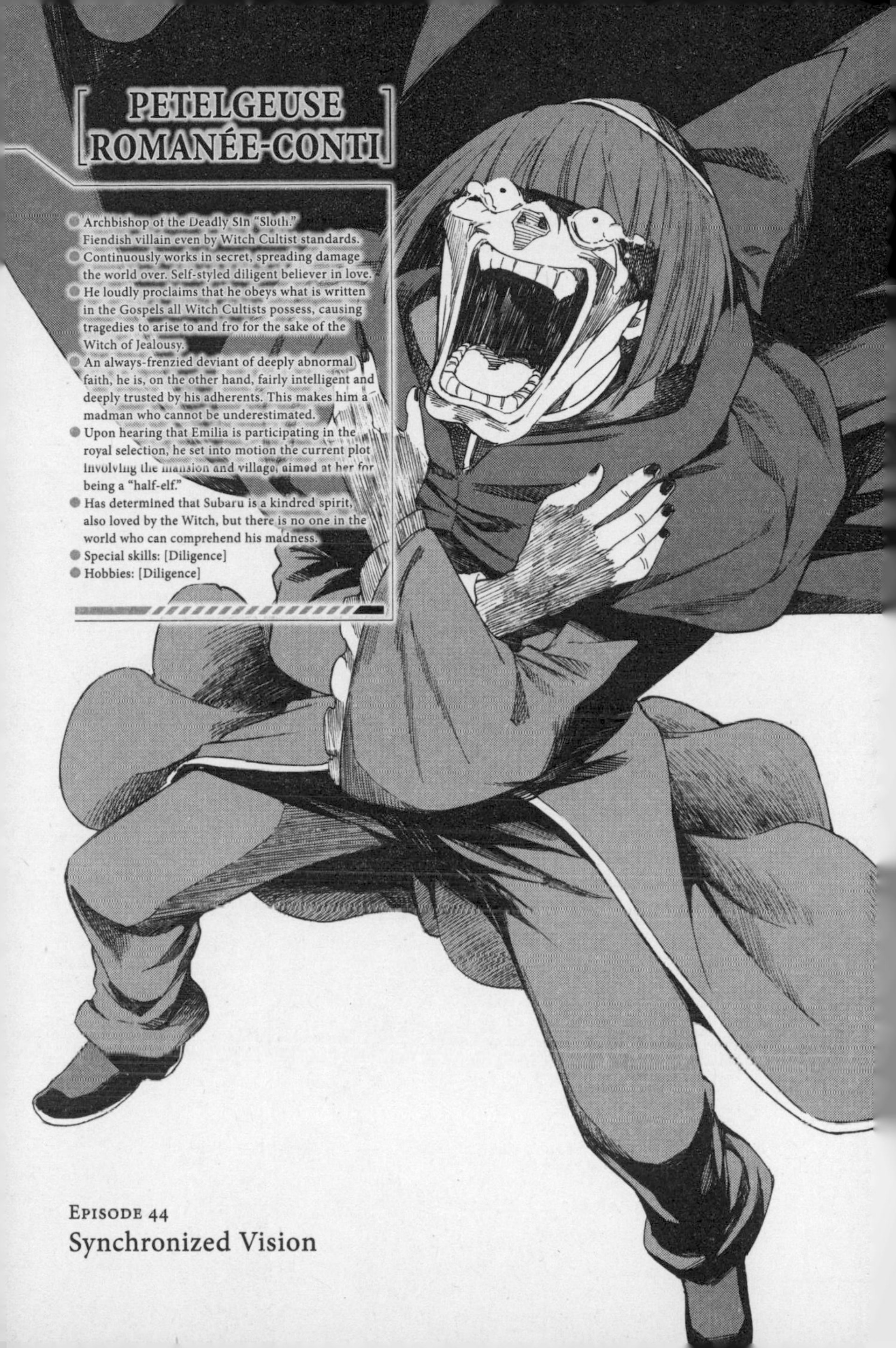
PETELGEUSE ROMANÉE-CONTI
Archbishop of the Deadly Sin "Sloth." Fiendish villain even by Witch Cultist standards.
Continuously works in secret, spreading damage the world over. Self-styled diligent believer in love.
He loudly proclaims that he obeys what is written in the Gospels all Witch Cultists possess, causing tragedies to arise to and fro for the sake of the Witch of Jealousy.
An always-frenzied deviant of deeply abnormal faith, he is, on the other hand, fairly intelligent and deeply trusted by his adherents. This makes him a madman who cannot be underestimated.
Upon hearing that Emilia is participating in the royal selection, he set into motion the current plot involving the mansion and village, aimed at her for being a "half-elf."
Has determined that Subaru is a kindred spirit, also loved by the Witch, but there is no one in the world who can comprehend his madness.
Special skills: [Diligence]
Hobbies: [Diligence]

Episode 44

Synchronized Vision

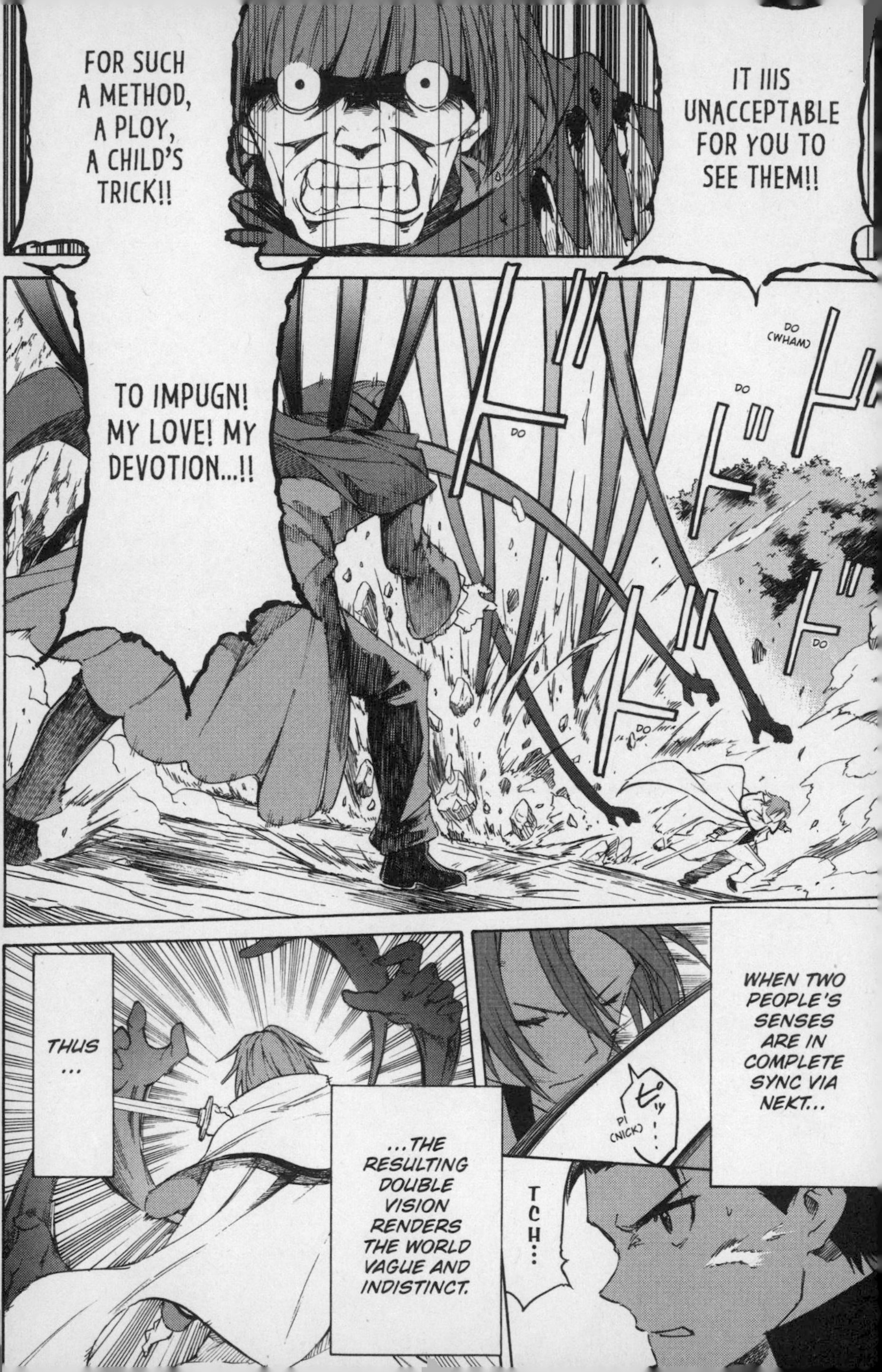
IT IIIS UNACCEPTABLE FOR YOU TO SEE THEM!!
FOR SUCH A METHOD, A PLOY, A CHILD'S TRICK!!
DO (WHAM)
DO
DO
DO
DO
TO IMPUGN! MY LOVE! MY DEVOTION...!!
WHEN TWO PEOPLE'S SENSES ARE IN COMPLETE SYNC VIA NEKT...
PI (NICK)
TCH...
...THE RESULTING DOUBLE VISION RENDERS THE WORLD VAGUE AND INDISTINCT.
THUS...

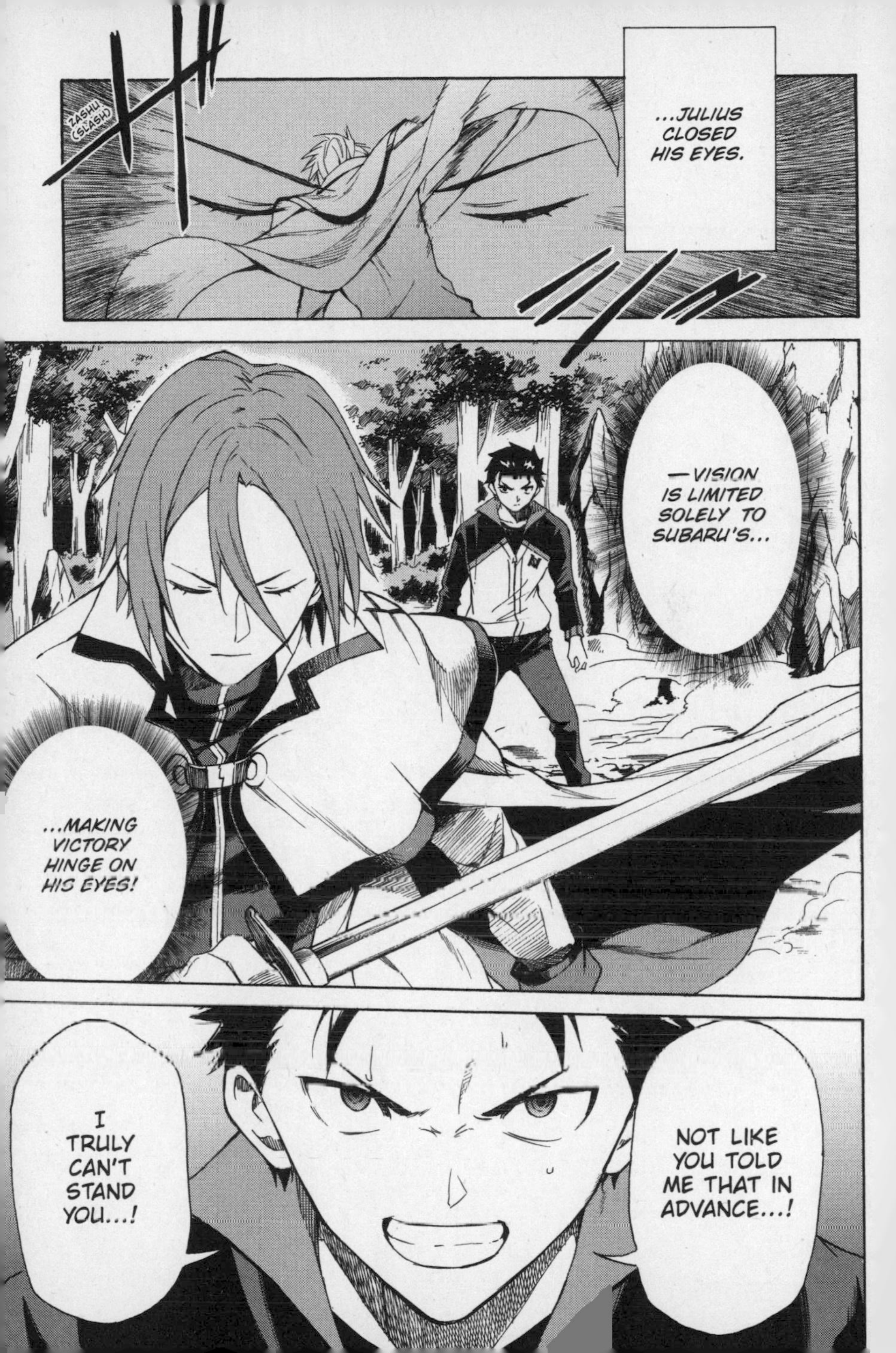
...JULIUS CLOSED HIS EYES.
ZASHU (SLASH)
—VISION IS LIMITED SOLELY TO SUBARU'S...
...MAKING VICTORY HINGE ON HIS EYES!
NOT LIKE YOU TOLD ME THAT IN ADVANCE...!
I TRULY CAN'T STAND YOU...!

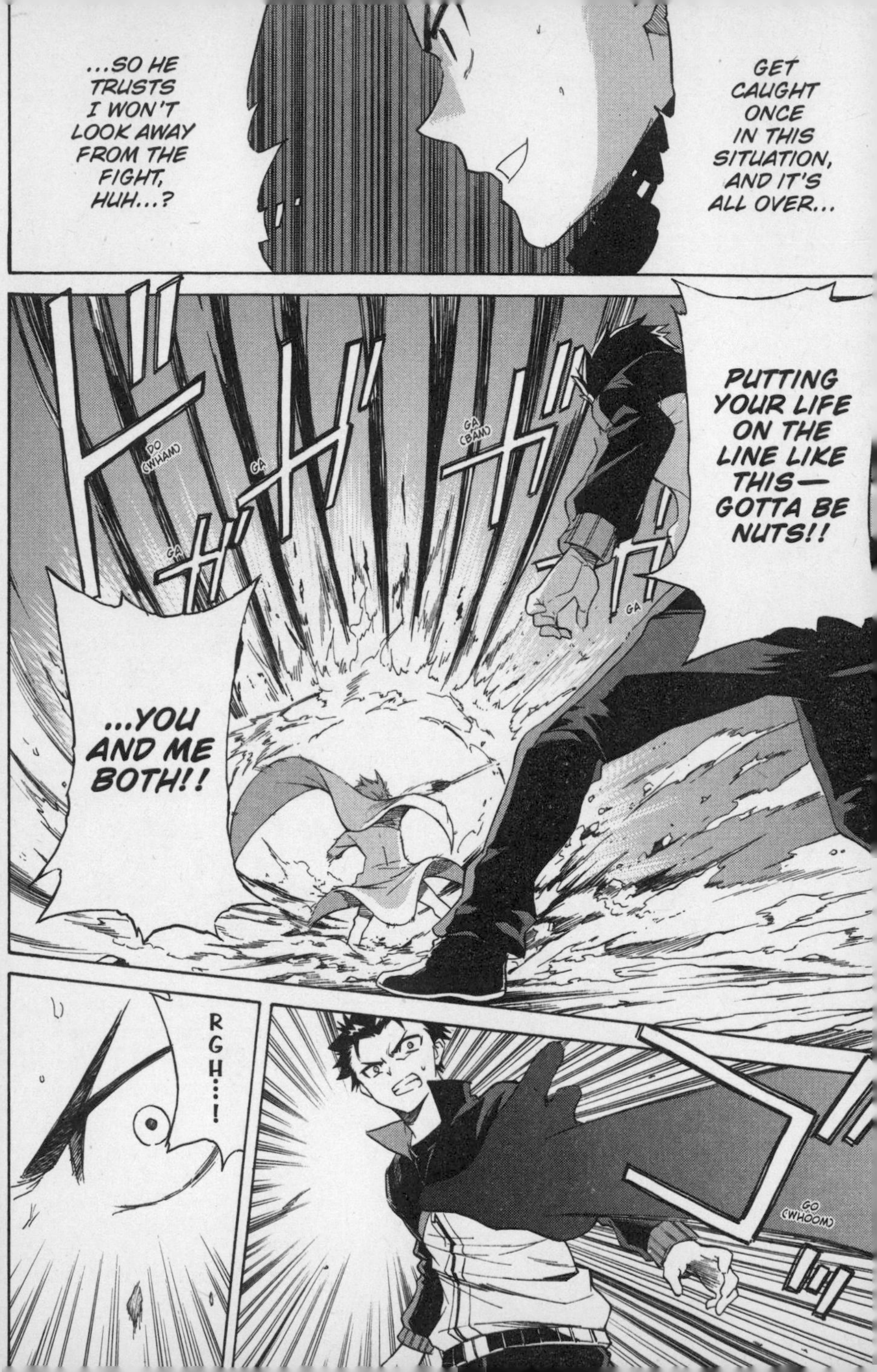
GET CAUGHT ONCE IN THIS SITUATION, AND IT'S ALL OVER...
...SO HE TRUSTS I WON'T LOOK AWAY FROM THE FIGHT, HUH...?
PUTTING YOUR LIFE ON THE LINE LIKE THIS—GOTTA BE NUTS!!
GA
GA (BAM)
GA
DO (WHAM)
GA
...YOU AND ME BOTH!!
GO (WHOOM)
RGH...!

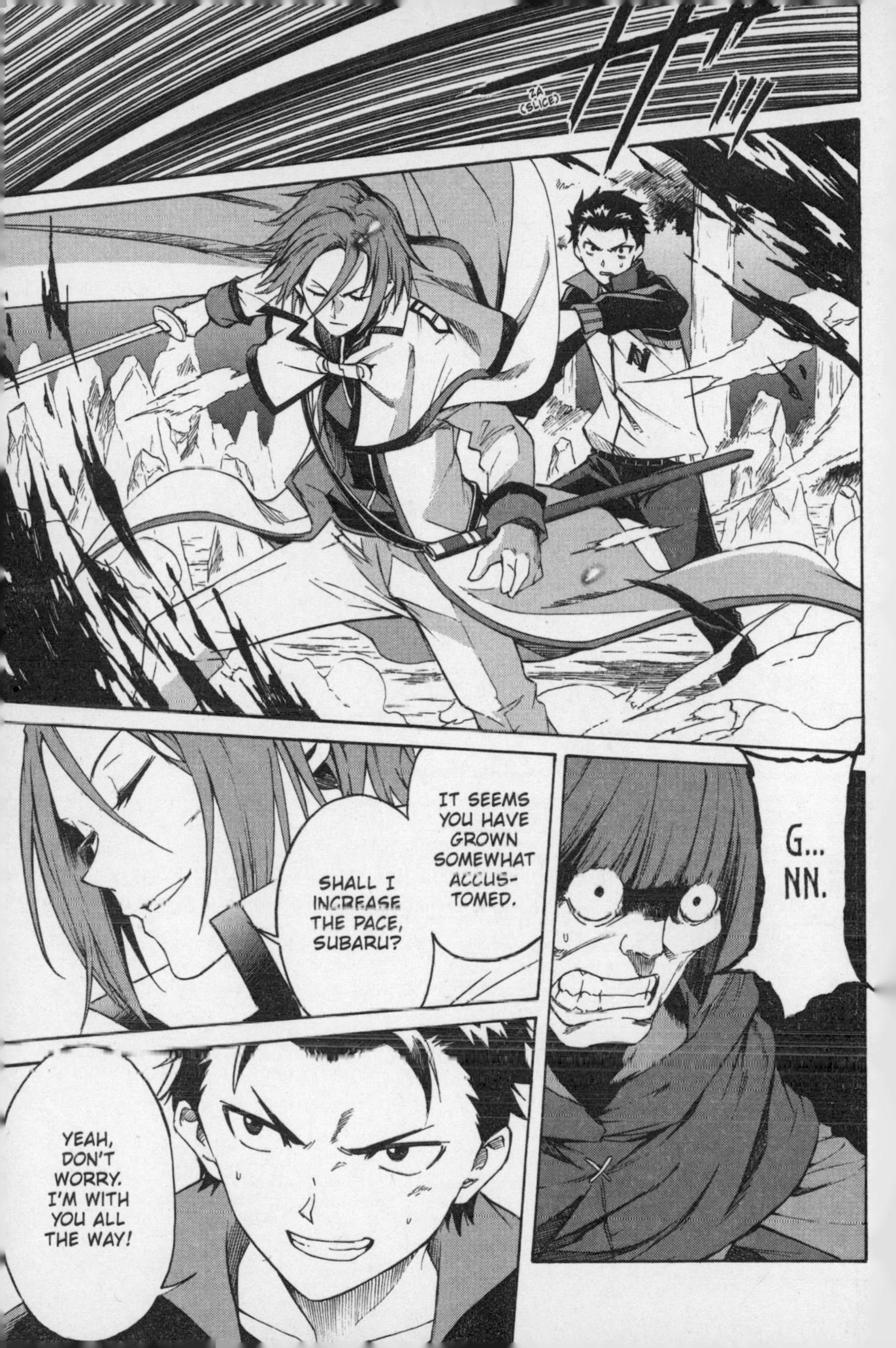
ZA (SLICE)
G... NN.
IT SEEMS YOU HAVE GROWN SOMEWHAT ACCUS- TOMED.
SHALL I INCREASE THE PACE, SUBARU?
YEAH, DON'T WORRY. I'M WITH YOU ALL THE WAY!

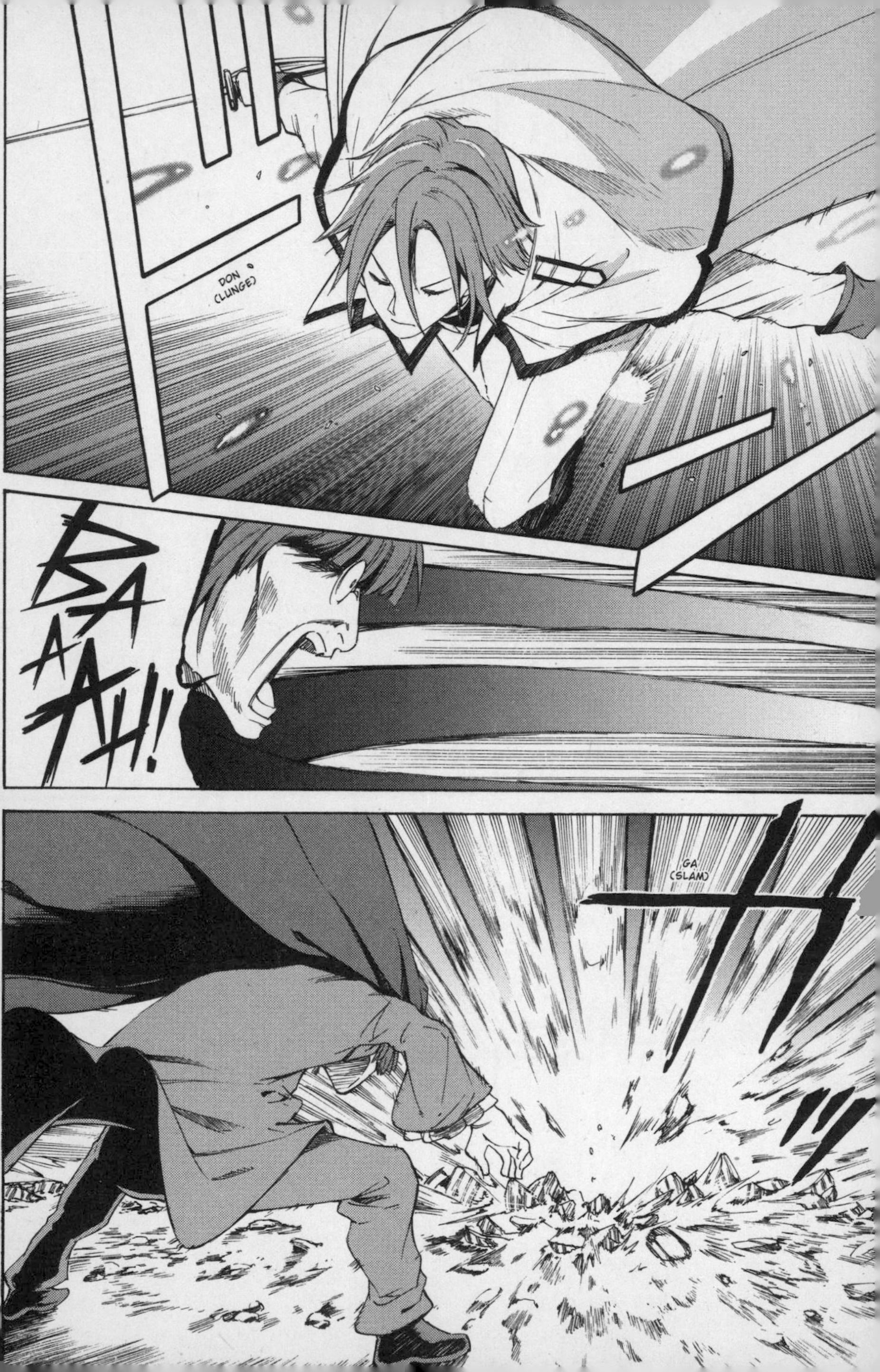
DON
(LUNGE)
BAAAAH!
GA
(SLAM)

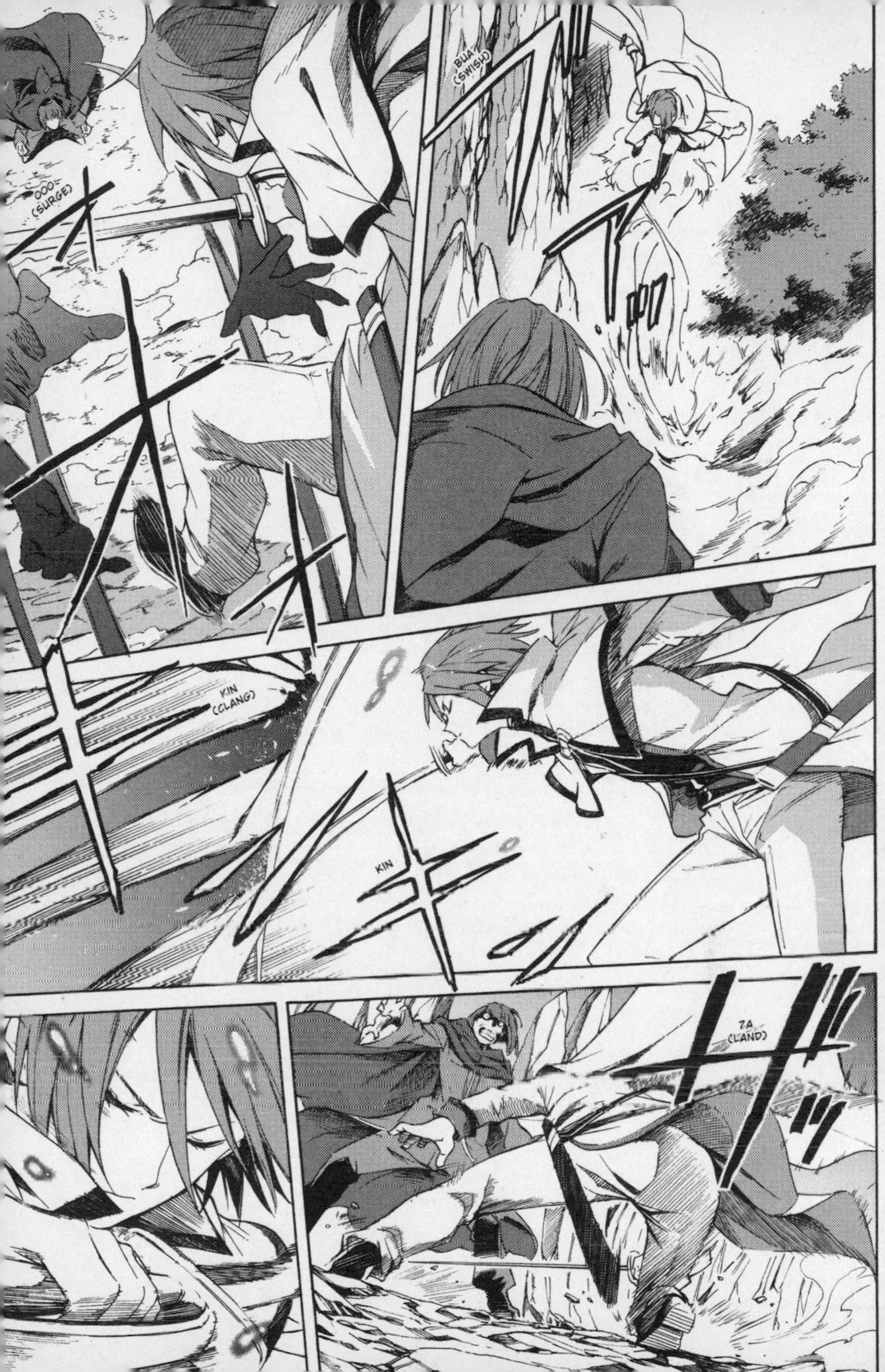
BUA (SWISH)
OOO (SURGE)
KIN (CLANG)
KIN
ZA (LAND)

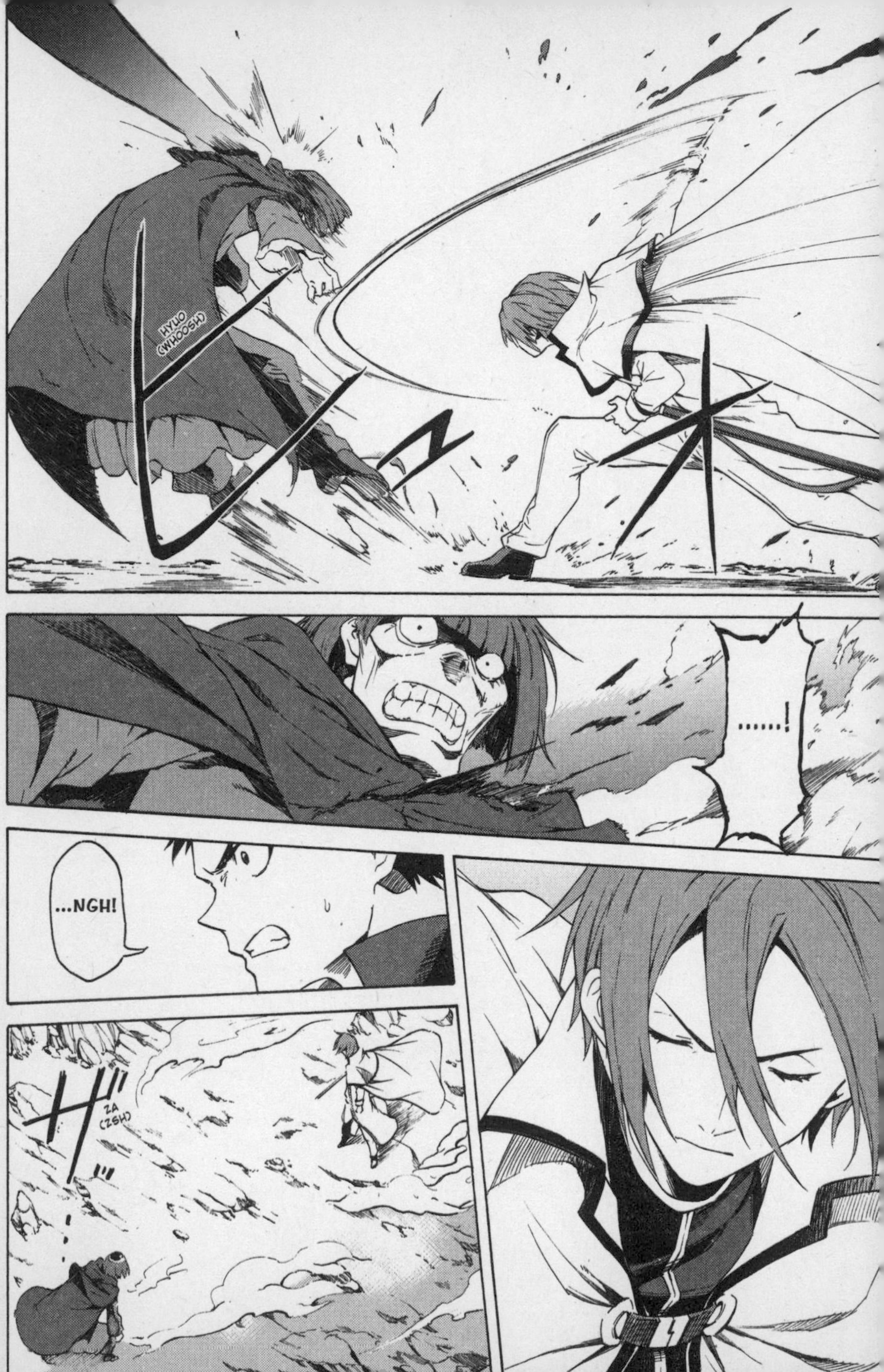
HYUO
(WHOOSH)
......!
...NGH!
ZA
(ZSH)

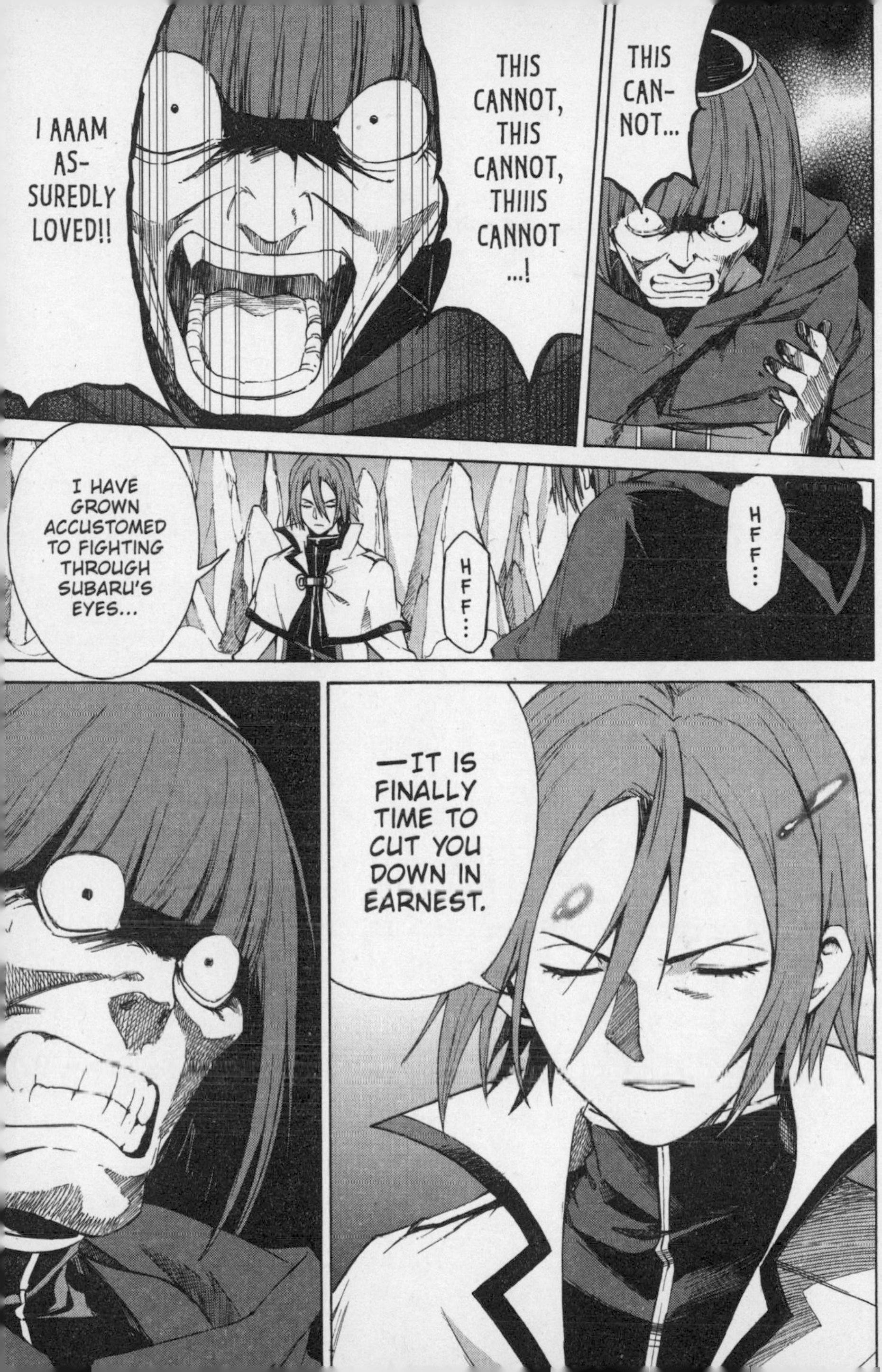
THIS CAN-NOT...
THIS CANNOT, THIS CANNOT, THIIIS CANNOT ...!
I AAAM AS-SUREDLY LOVED!!
HFF...
HFF...
I HAVE GROWN ACCUSTOMED TO FIGHTING THROUGH SUBARU'S EYES...
—IT IS FINALLY TIME TO CUT YOU DOWN IN EARNEST.

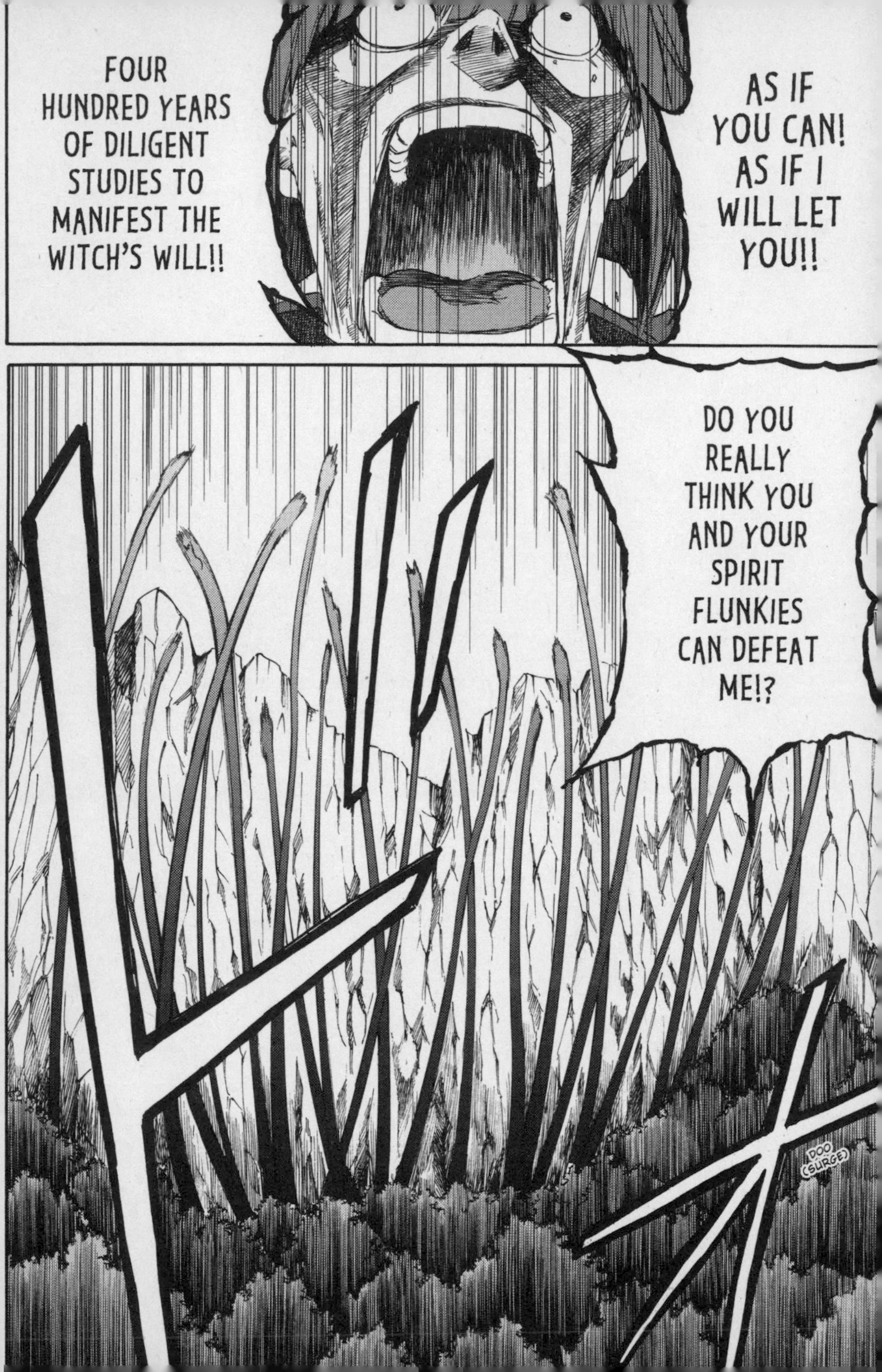
AS IF YOU CAN! AS IF I WILL LET YOU!!
FOUR HUNDRED YEARS OF DILIGENT STUDIES TO MANIFEST THE WITCH'S WILL!!
DO YOU REALLY THINK YOU AND YOUR SPIRIT FLUNKIES CAN DEFEAT ME!?
DOO (SURGE)

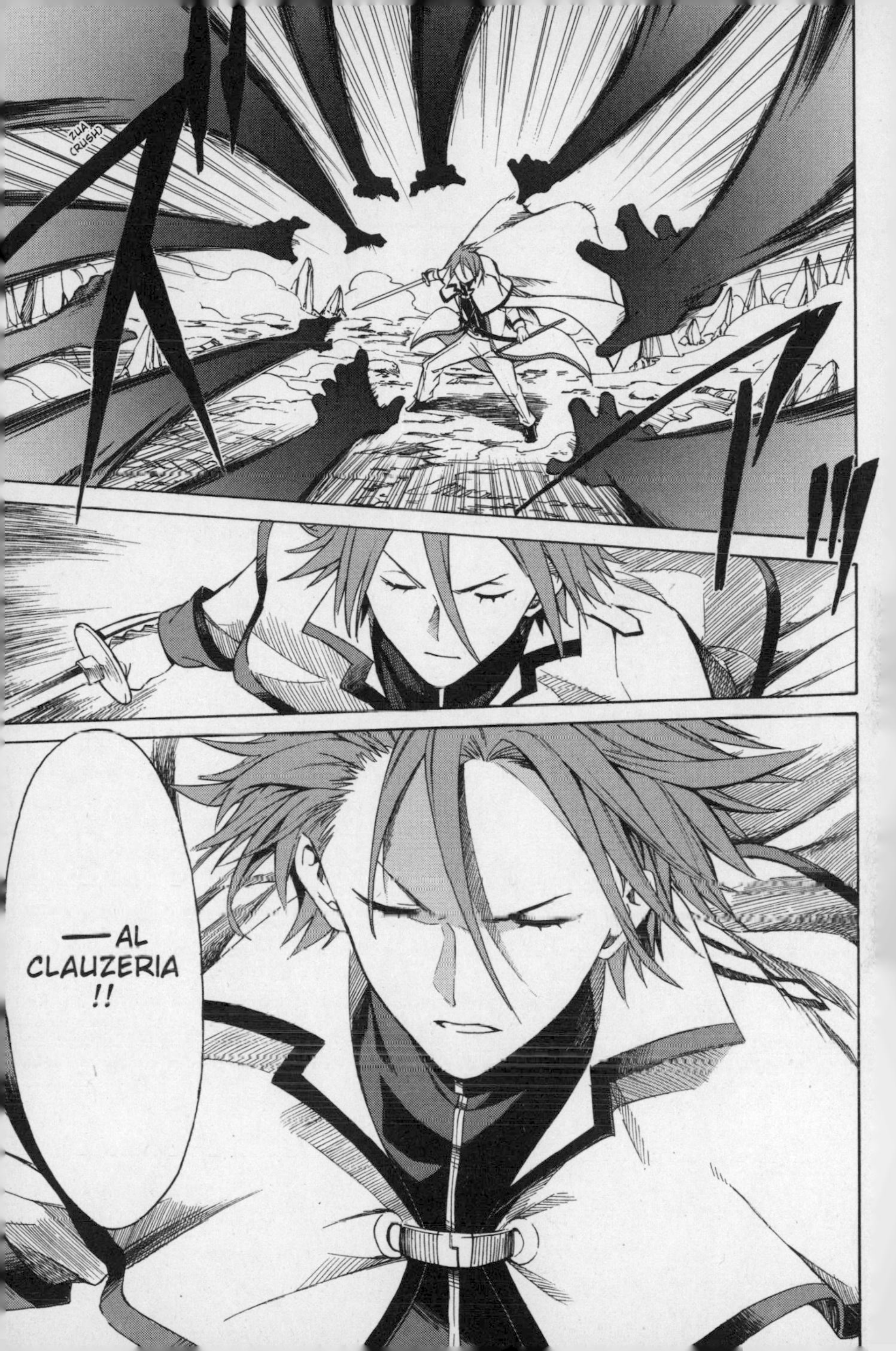
ZUA (RUSH)
—AL CLAUZERIA !!

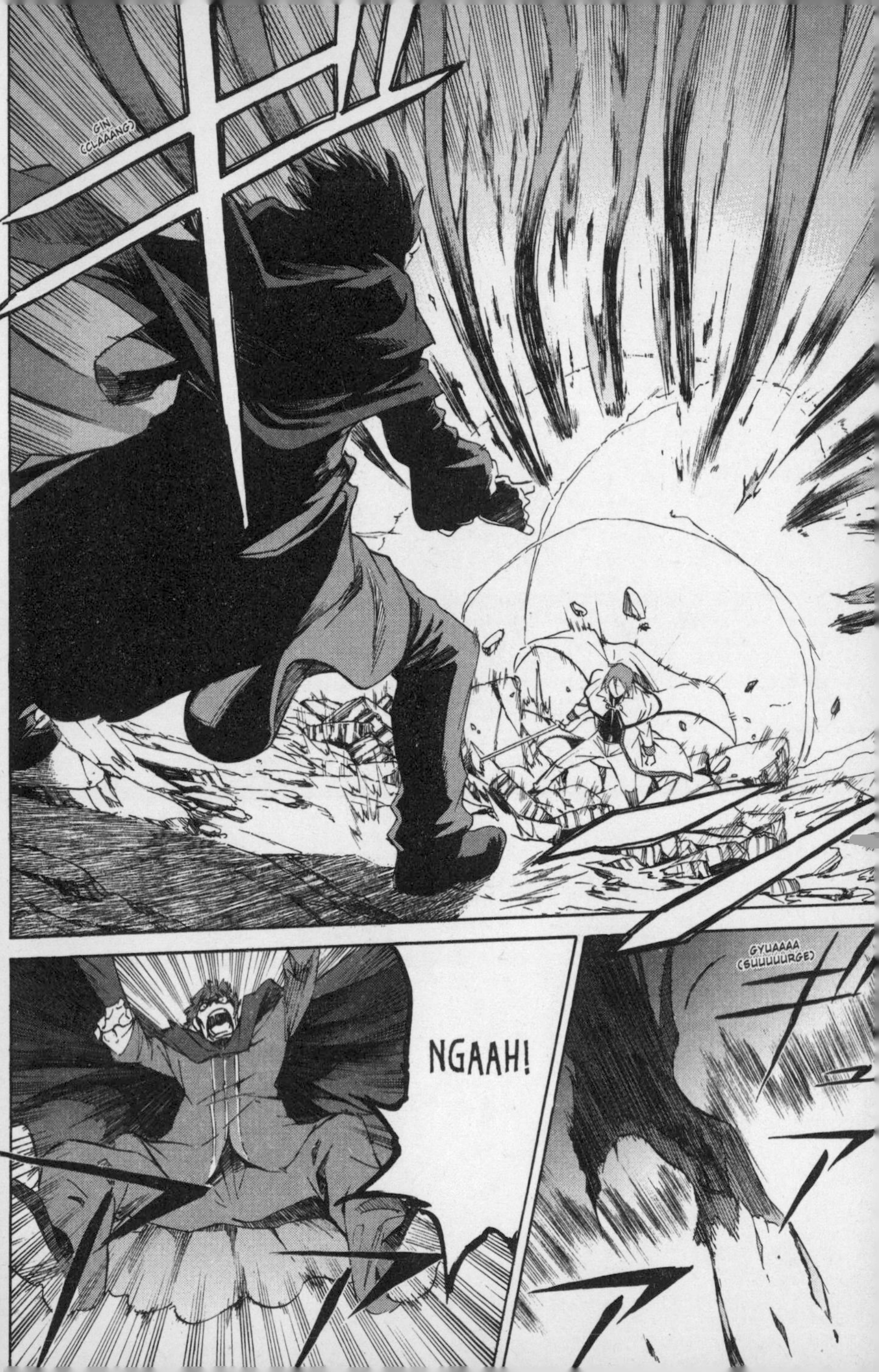
GIN
(CLAAANG)
GYUAAAA
(SUUUUURGE)
NGAAH!

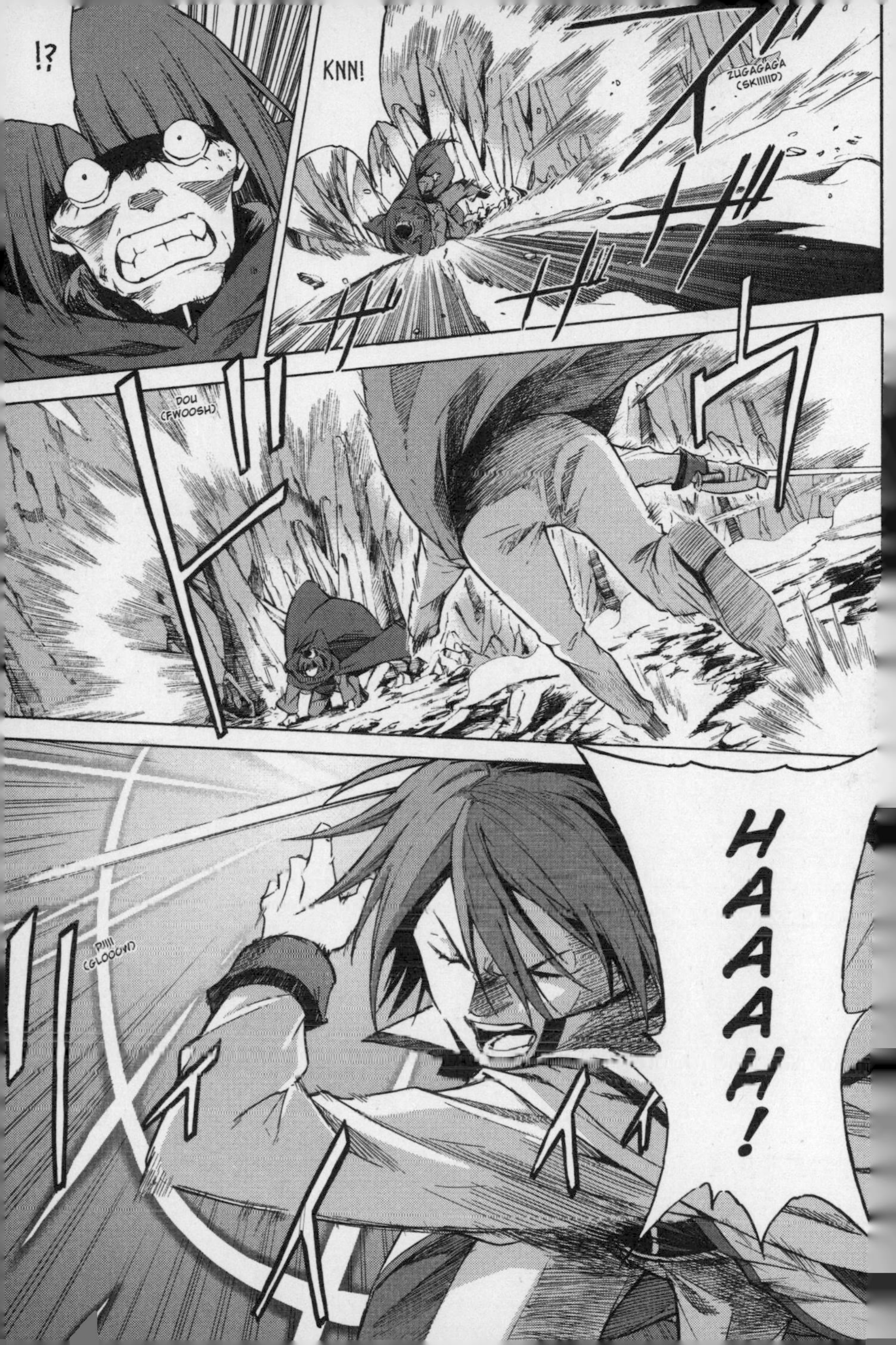
KNN!
ZUGAGAGA
(SKIIIIIID)
!?
DOU
(FWOOSH)
HAAAH!
PIIII
(GLOOOW)

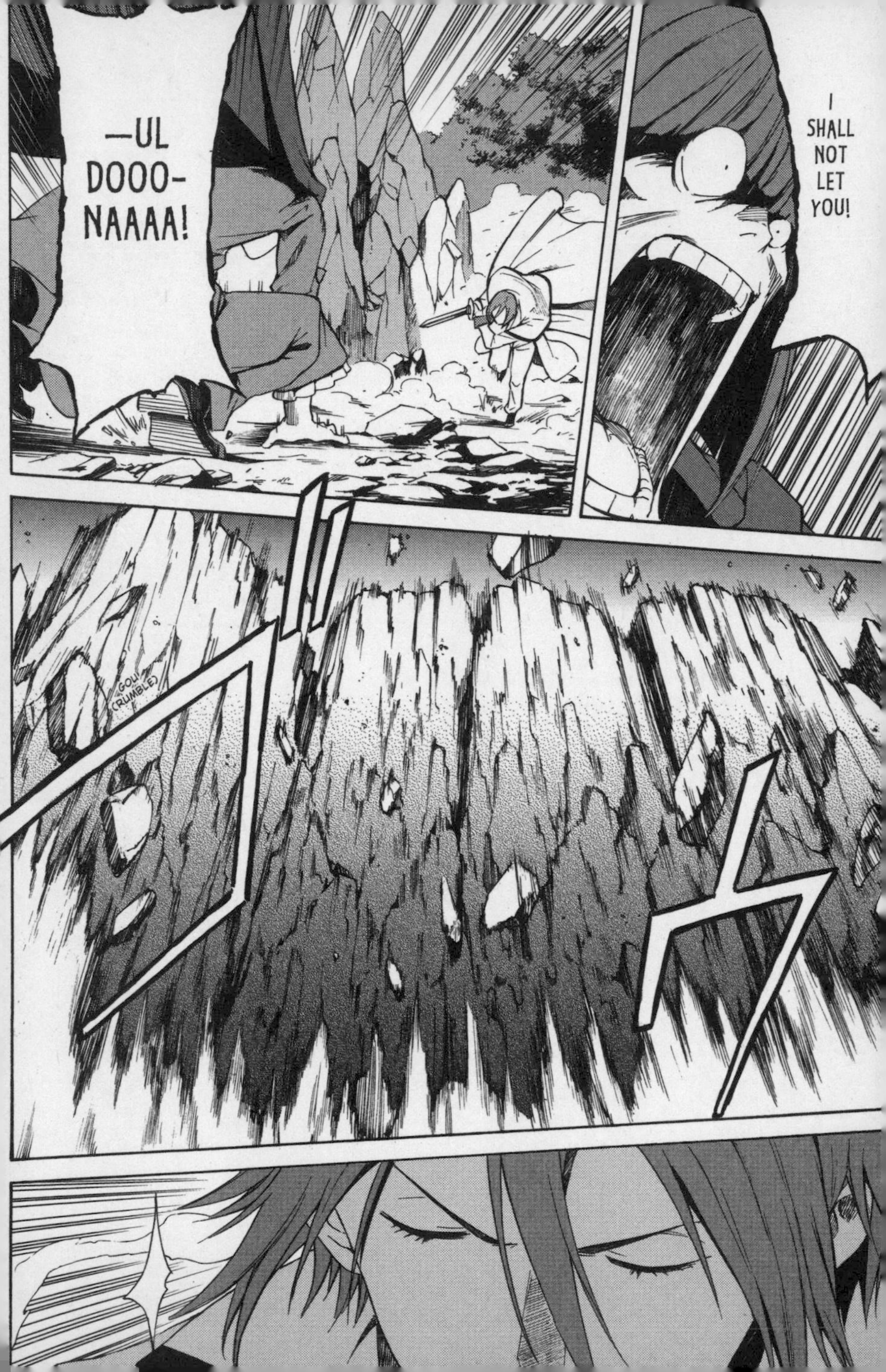
I SHALL NOT LET YOU!
—UL DOOO-NAAAA!
GOLI (CRUMBLE)

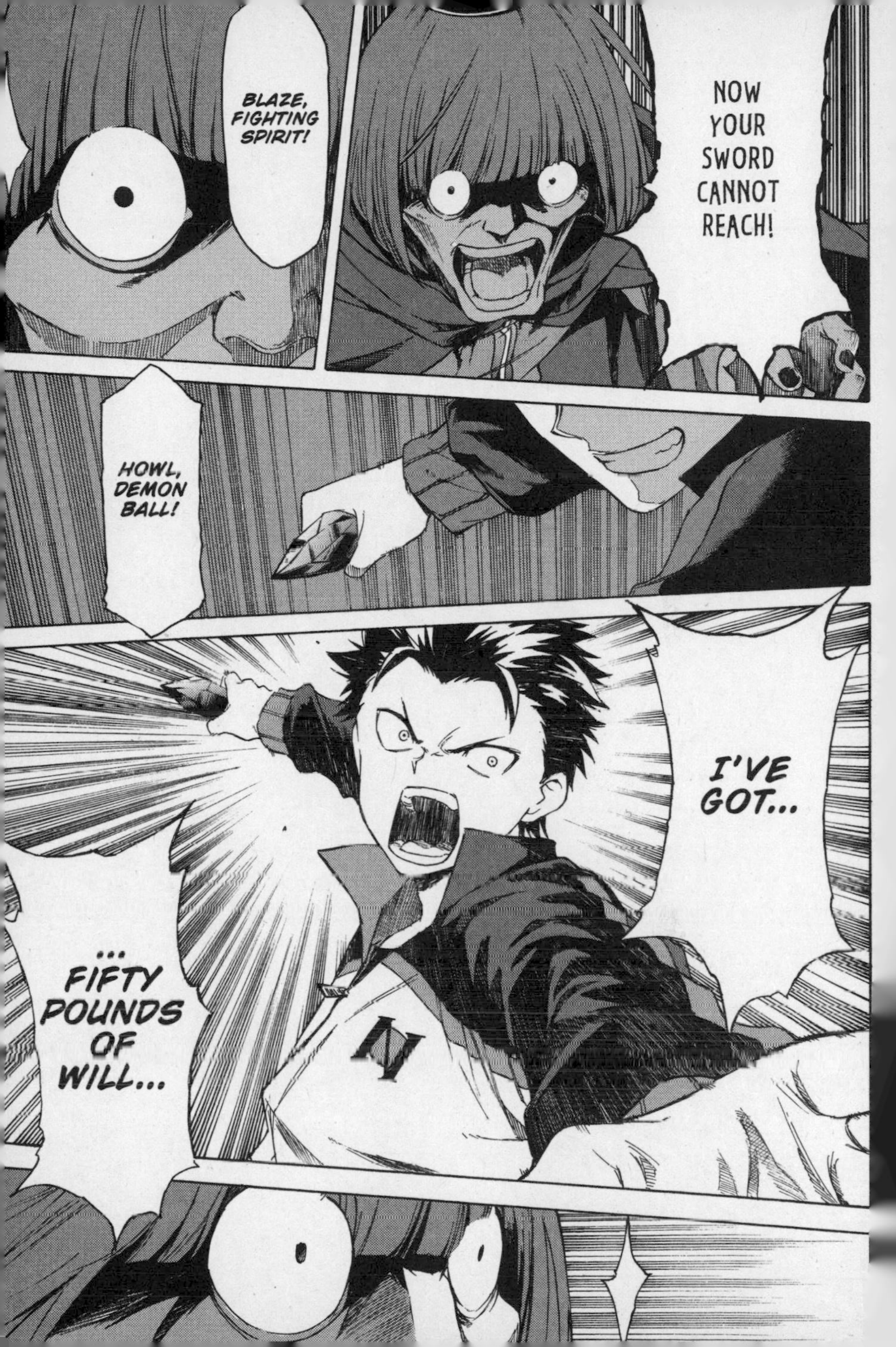
NOW YOUR SWORD CANNOT REACH!
BLAZE, FIGHTING SPIRIT!
HOWL, DEMON BALL!
I'VE GOT...
...FIFTY POUNDS OF WILL...

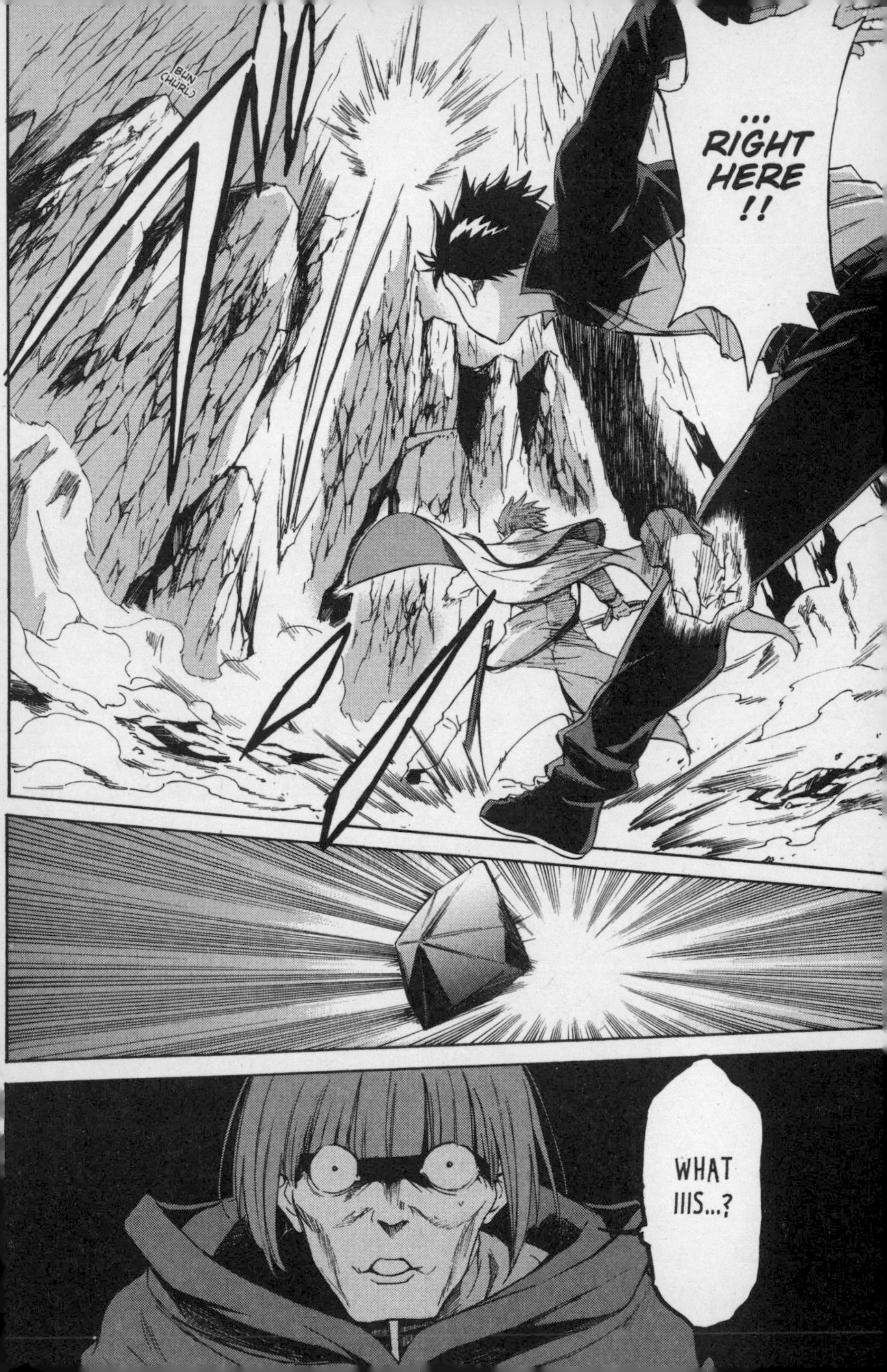
...RIGHT HERE!!
BUN (HURL)
WHAT IIIS...?

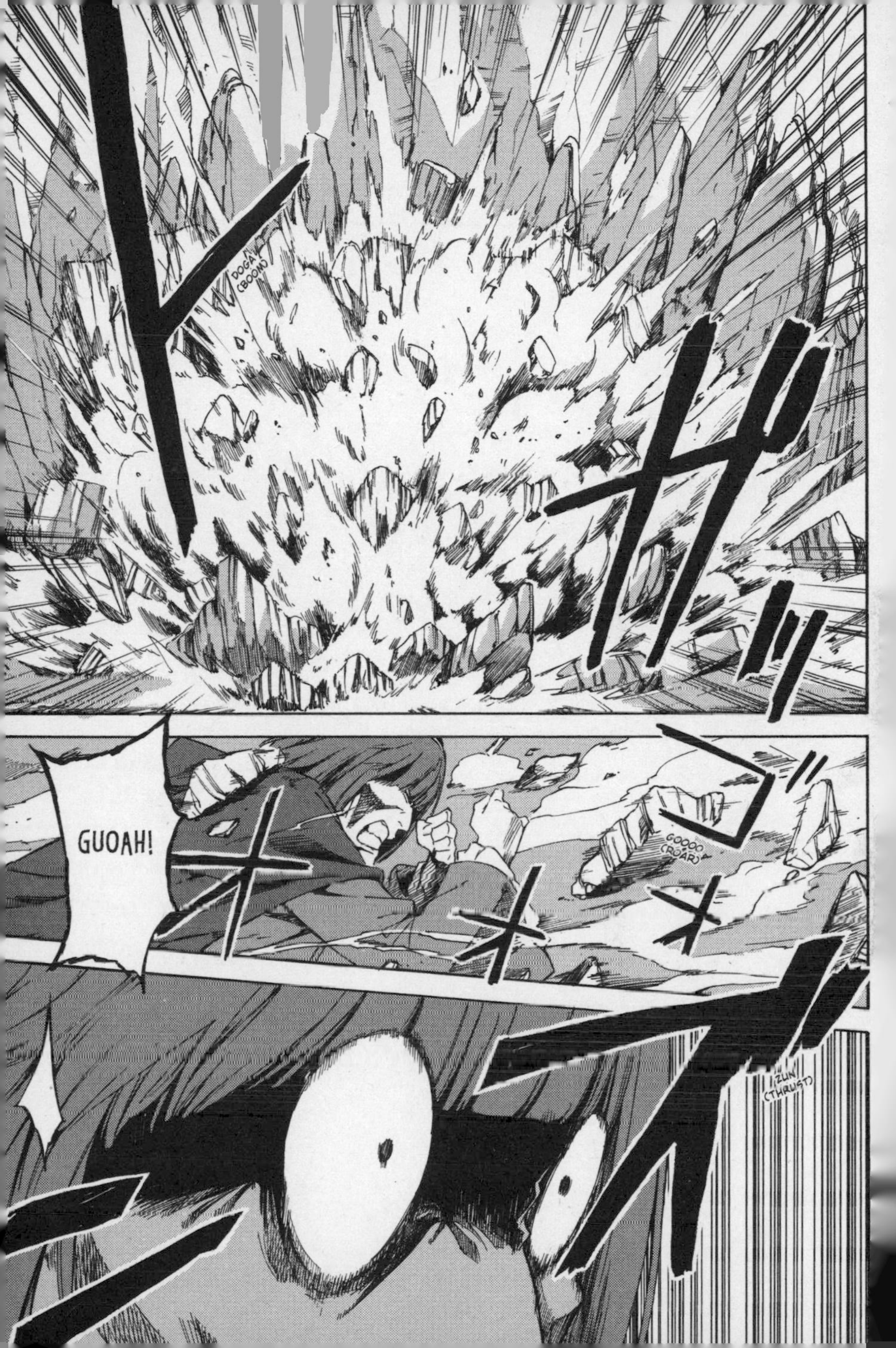
DOGA (BOOM)
GOOOO (ROAR)
GUOAH!
ZUN (THRUST)

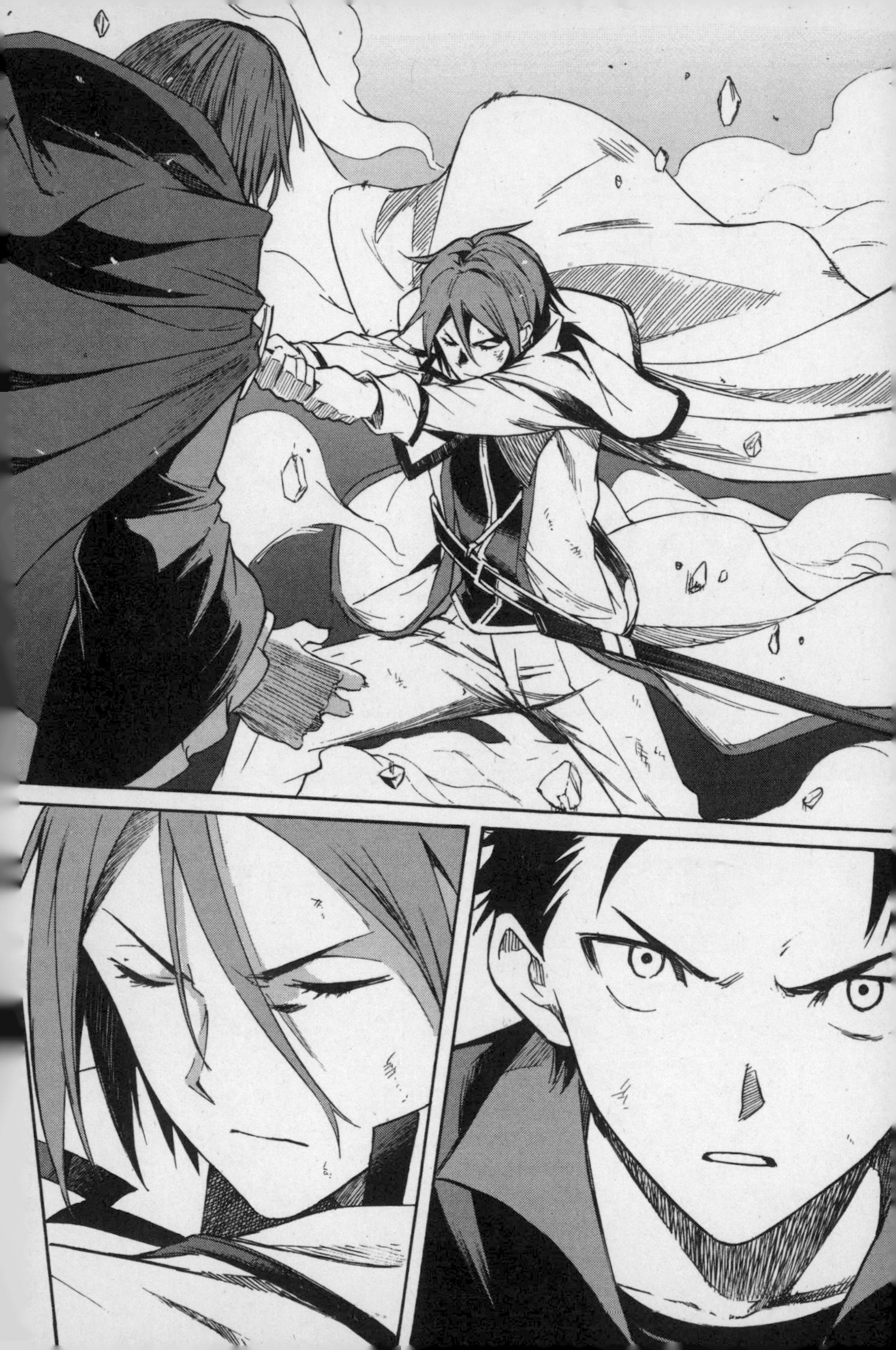

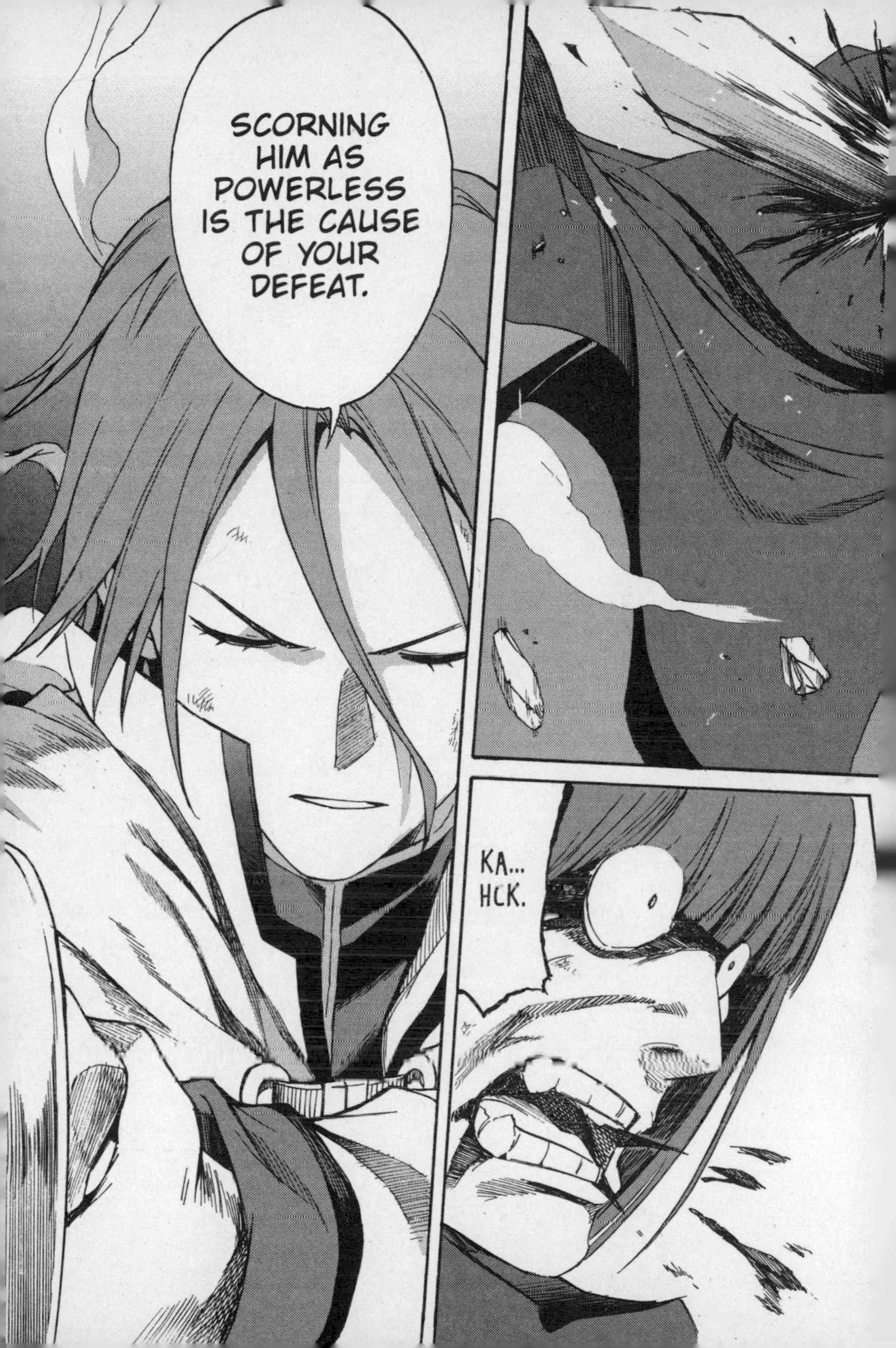
SCORNING HIM AS POWERLESS IS THE CAUSE OF YOUR DEFEAT.
KA... HCK.

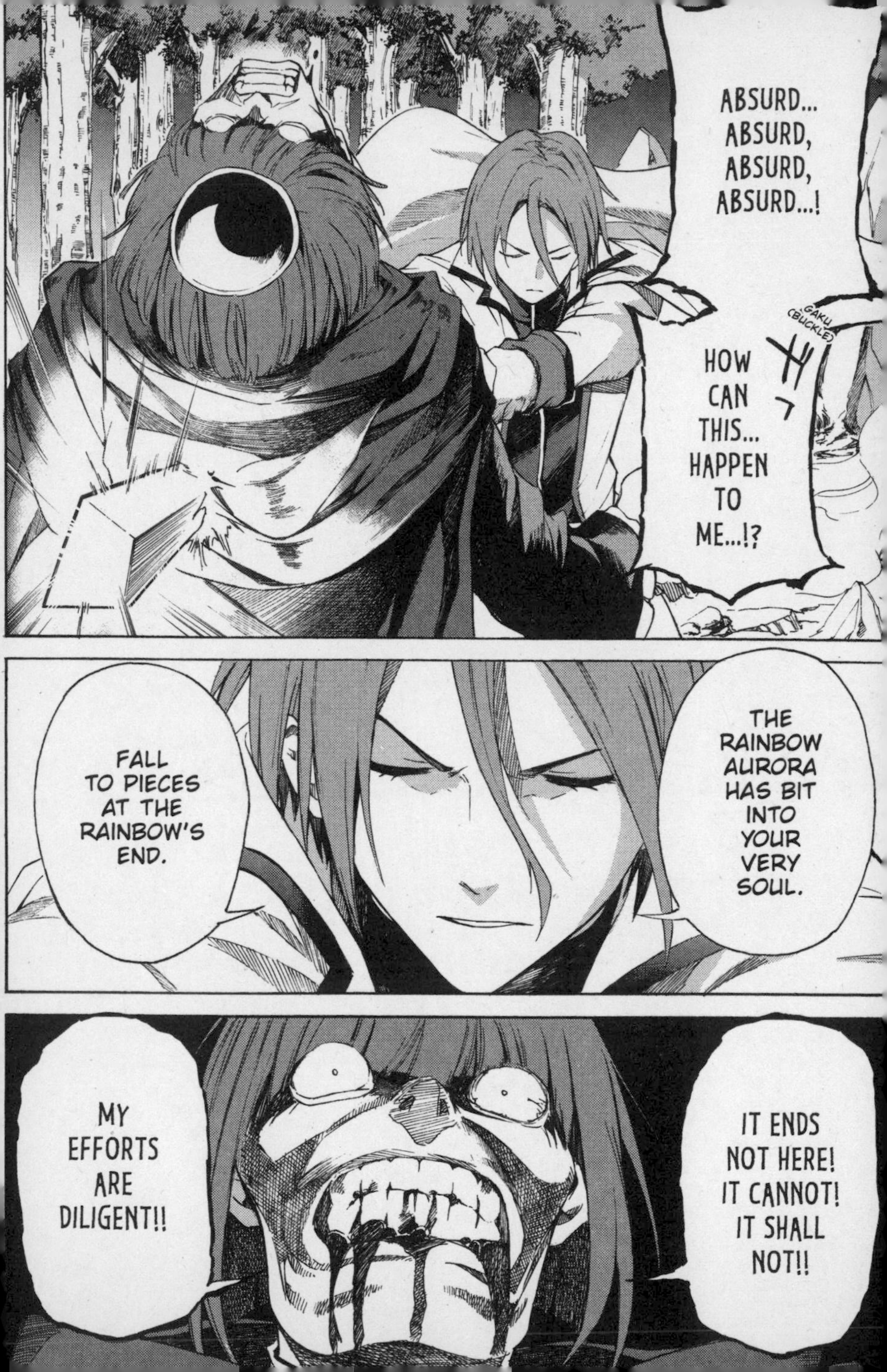
ABSURD... ABSURD, ABSURD, ABSURD...!
GAKU (BUCKLE)
HOW CAN THIS... HAPPEN TO ME...!?
THE RAINBOW AURORA HAS BIT INTO YOUR VERY SOUL.
FALL TO PIECES AT THE RAINBOW'S END.
IT ENDS NOT HERE! IT CANNOT! IT SHALL NOT!!
MY EFFORTS ARE DILIGENT!!

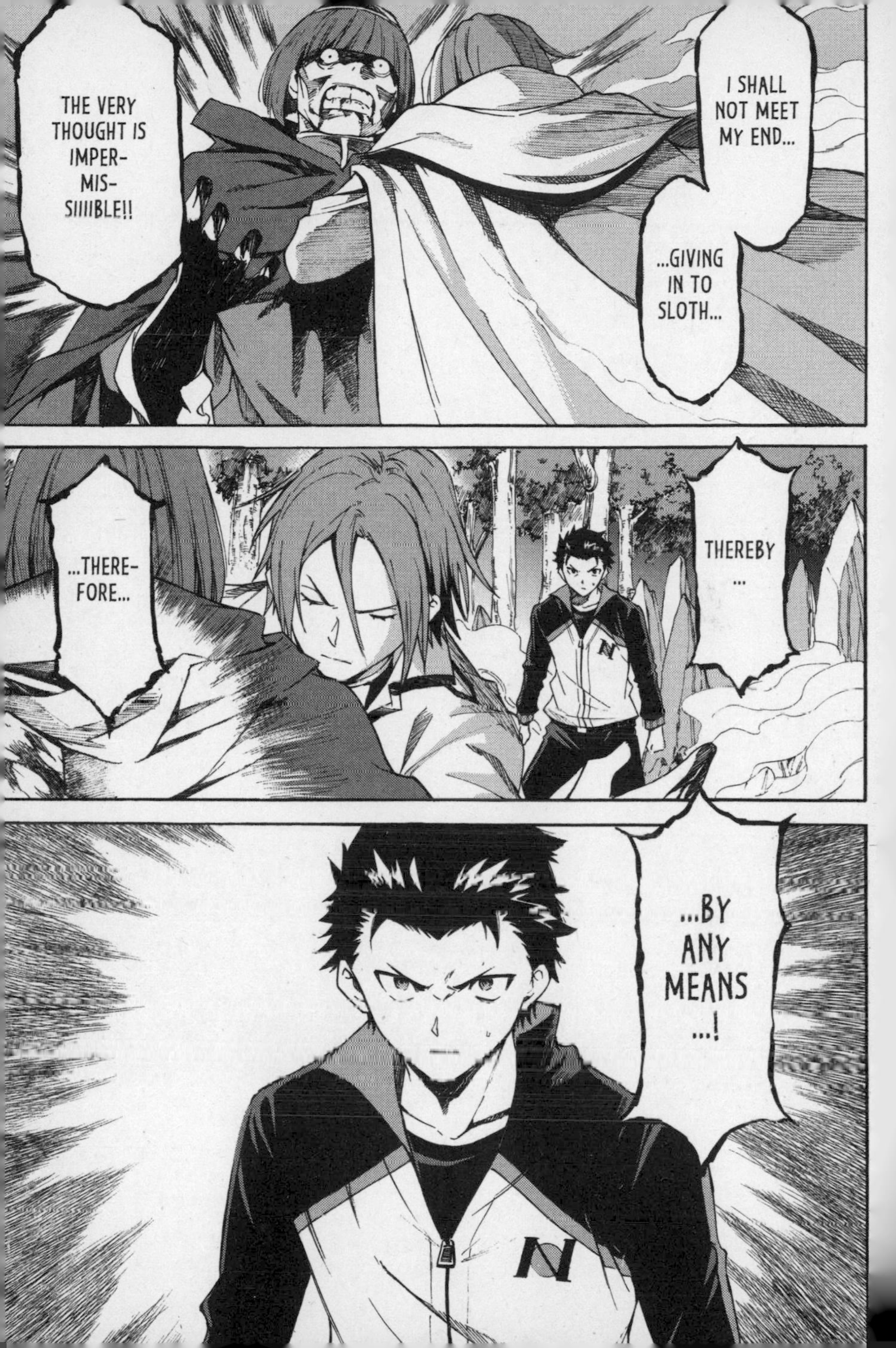

I SHALL NOT MEET MY END...
...GIVING IN TO SLOTH...
THE VERY THOUGHT IS IMPER-MIS-SIIIIBLE!!
THEREBY ...
...THERE-FORE...
...BY ANY MEANS ...!

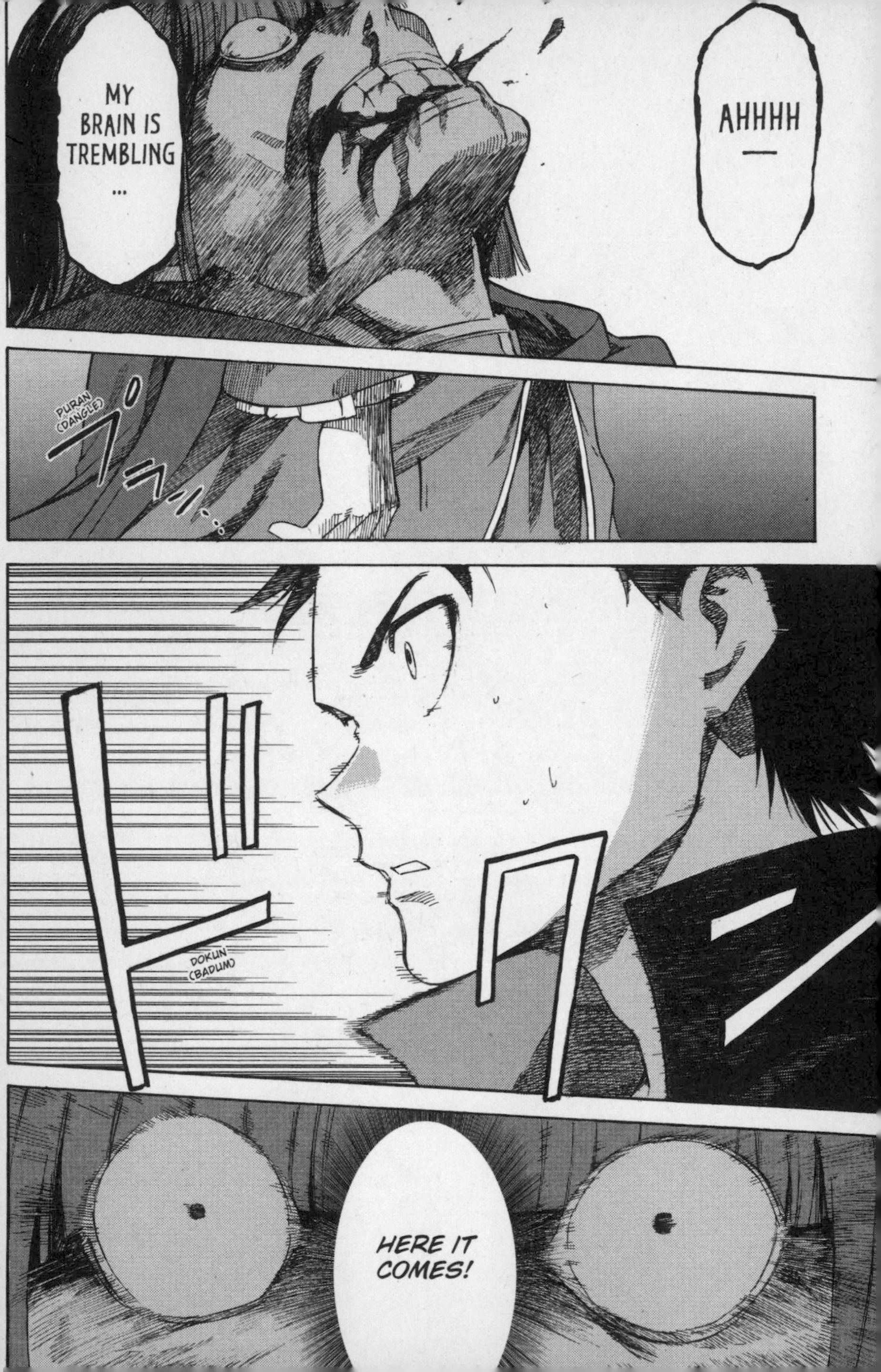
AHHHH —
MY BRAIN IS TREMBLING ...
PURAN (DANGLE)
DOKUN (BADUM)
HERE IT COMES!

Truth of Zero
The only ability Subaru Natsuki gets when he's summoned to another world is
time travel via his own death. But to save her, he'll die as many times as it takes.

Re:ZERO
-Starting Life in
Another World-

Re:ZERO
-Starting Life in Another World-

Truth of Zero

The only ability Subaru Natsuki gets when he's summoned to another world is time
travel via his own death. But to save her, he'll die as many times as it takes.

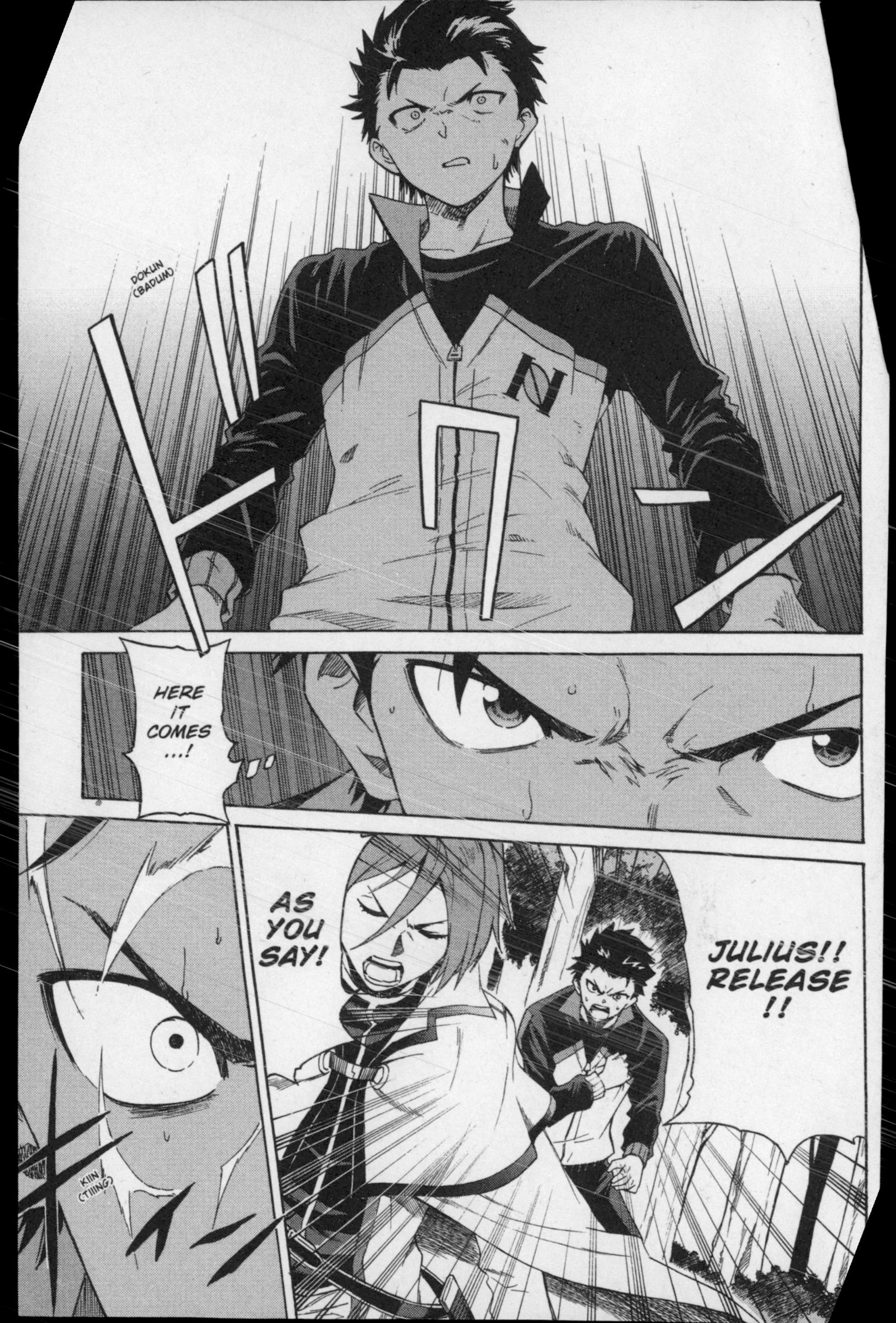
DOKUN (BADUM)
HERE IT COMES ...!
JULIUS!! RELEASE !!
AS YOU SAY!
KIIN (TIIING)

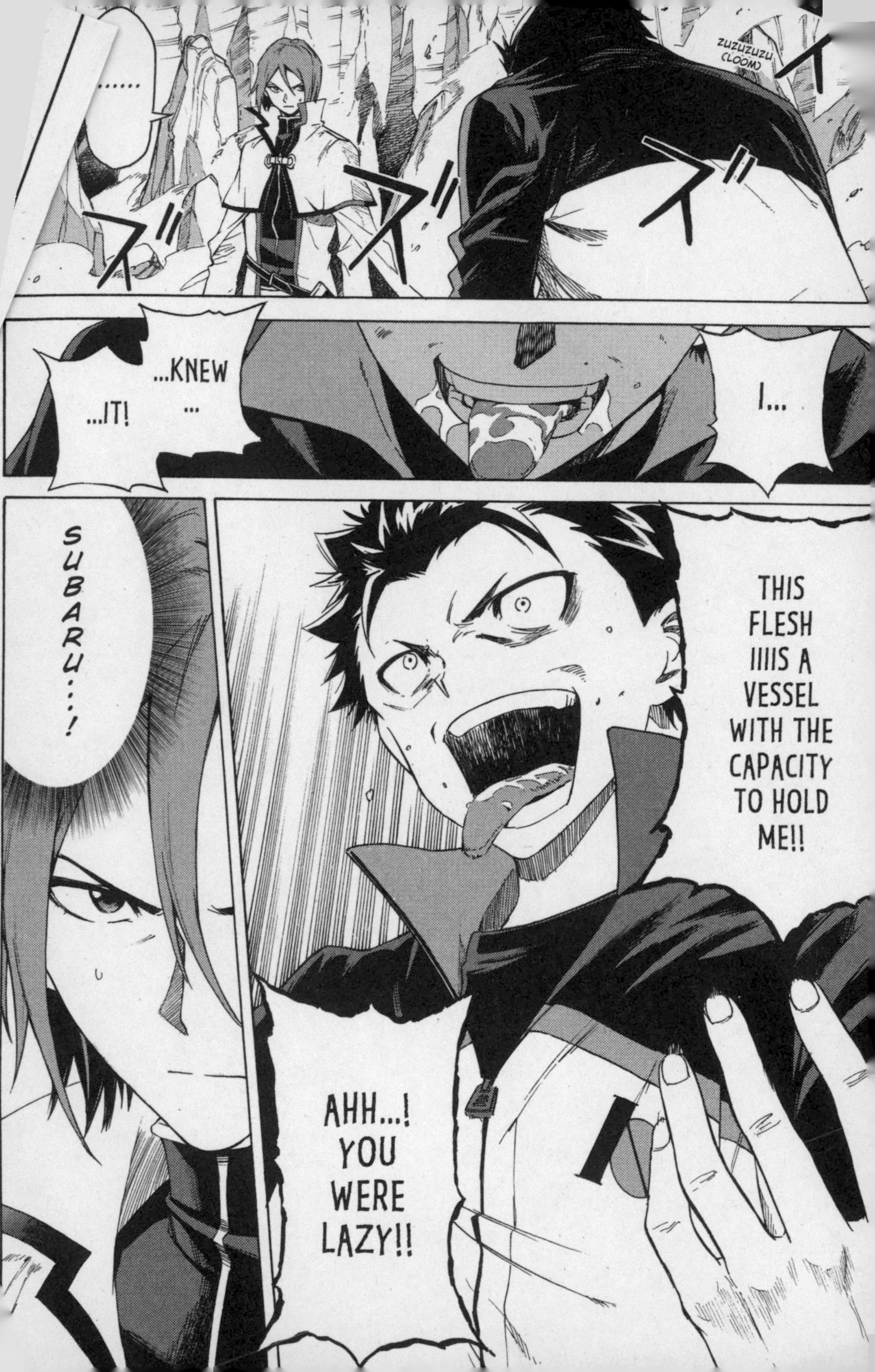
ZUZUZUZU
(LOOM)
......
I...
...KNEW ...
...IT!
THIS FLESH IIIIS A VESSEL WITH THE CAPACITY TO HOLD ME!!
AHH...! YOU WERE LAZY!!
SUBARU...!

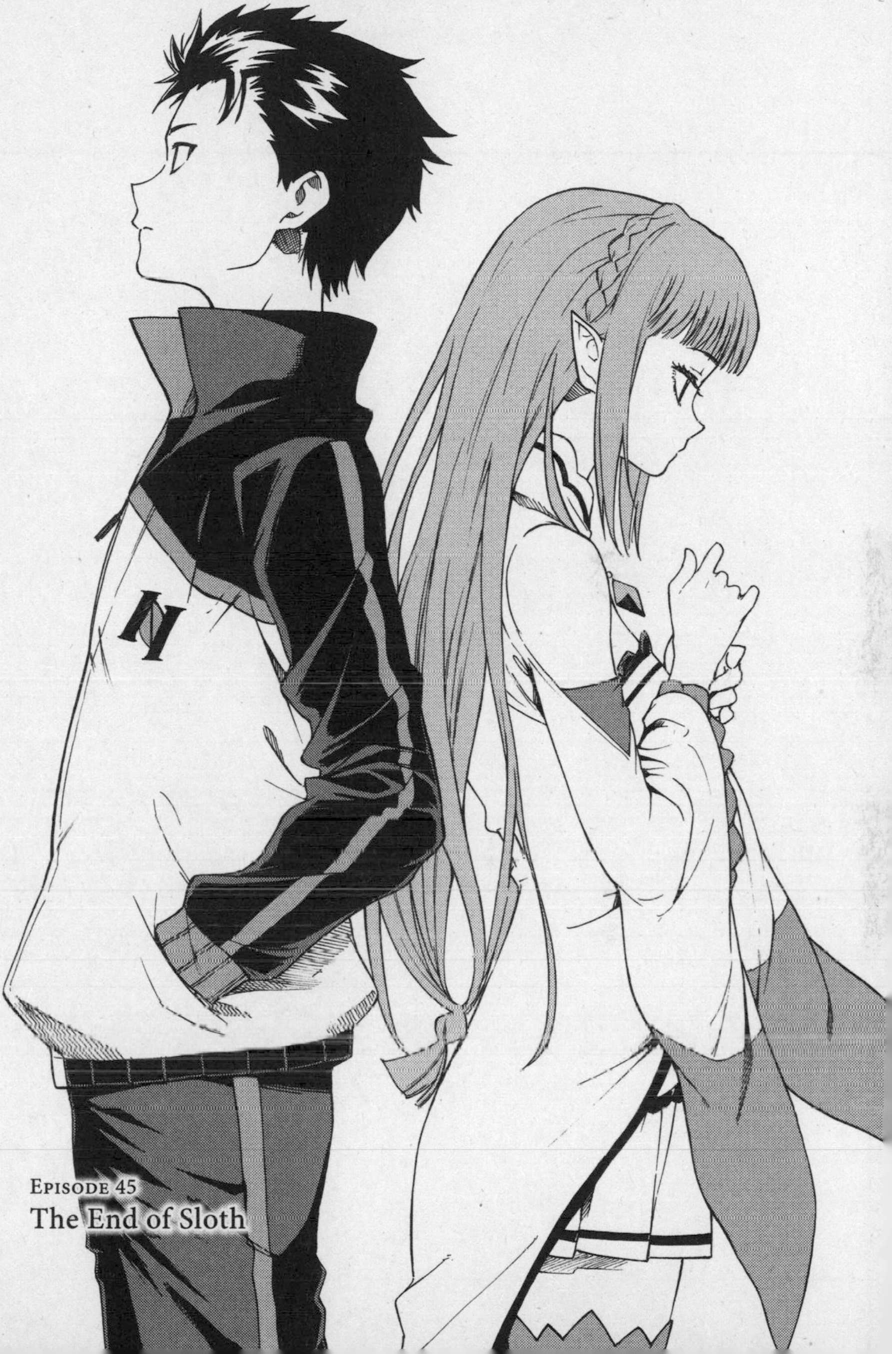

Episode 45

The End of Sloth

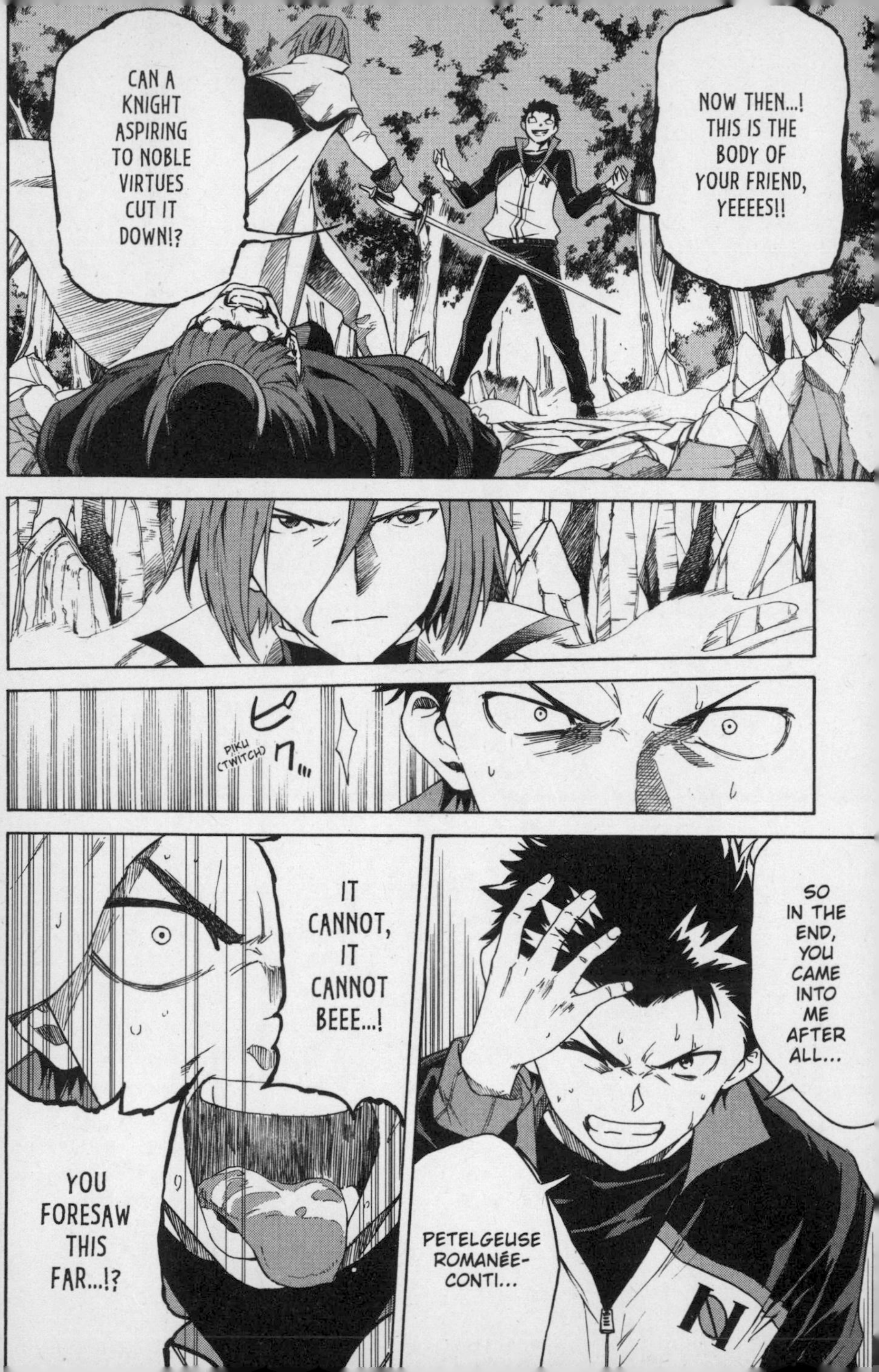
NOW THEN...! THIS IS THE BODY OF YOUR FRIEND, YEEEES!!
CAN A KNIGHT ASPIRING TO NOBLE VIRTUES CUT IT DOWN!?
ピクッ
PIKU (TWITCH)
SO IN THE END, YOU CAME INTO ME AFTER ALL...
PETELGEUSE ROMANÉE-CONTI...
IT CANNOT, IT CANNOT BEEE...!
YOU FORESAW THIS FAR...!?

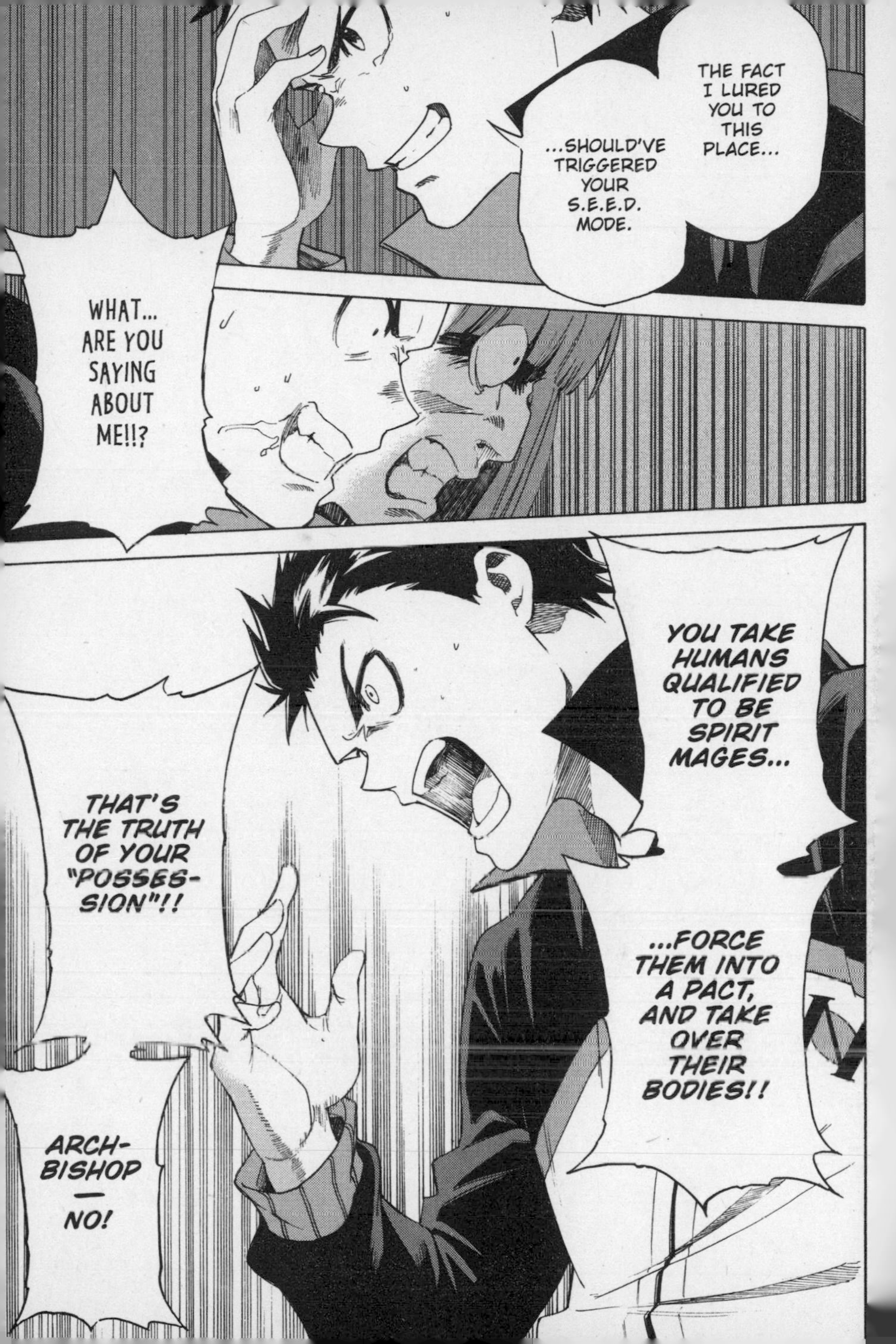
THE FACT I LURED YOU TO THIS PLACE...
...SHOULD'VE TRIGGERED YOUR S.E.E.D. MODE.
WHAT... ARE YOU SAYING ABOUT ME!!?
YOU TAKE HUMANS QUALIFIED TO BE SPIRIT MAGES...
...FORCE THEM INTO A PACT, AND TAKE OVER THEIR BODIES!!
THAT'S THE TRUTH OF YOUR "POSSESSION"!!
ARCH-BISHOP — NO!

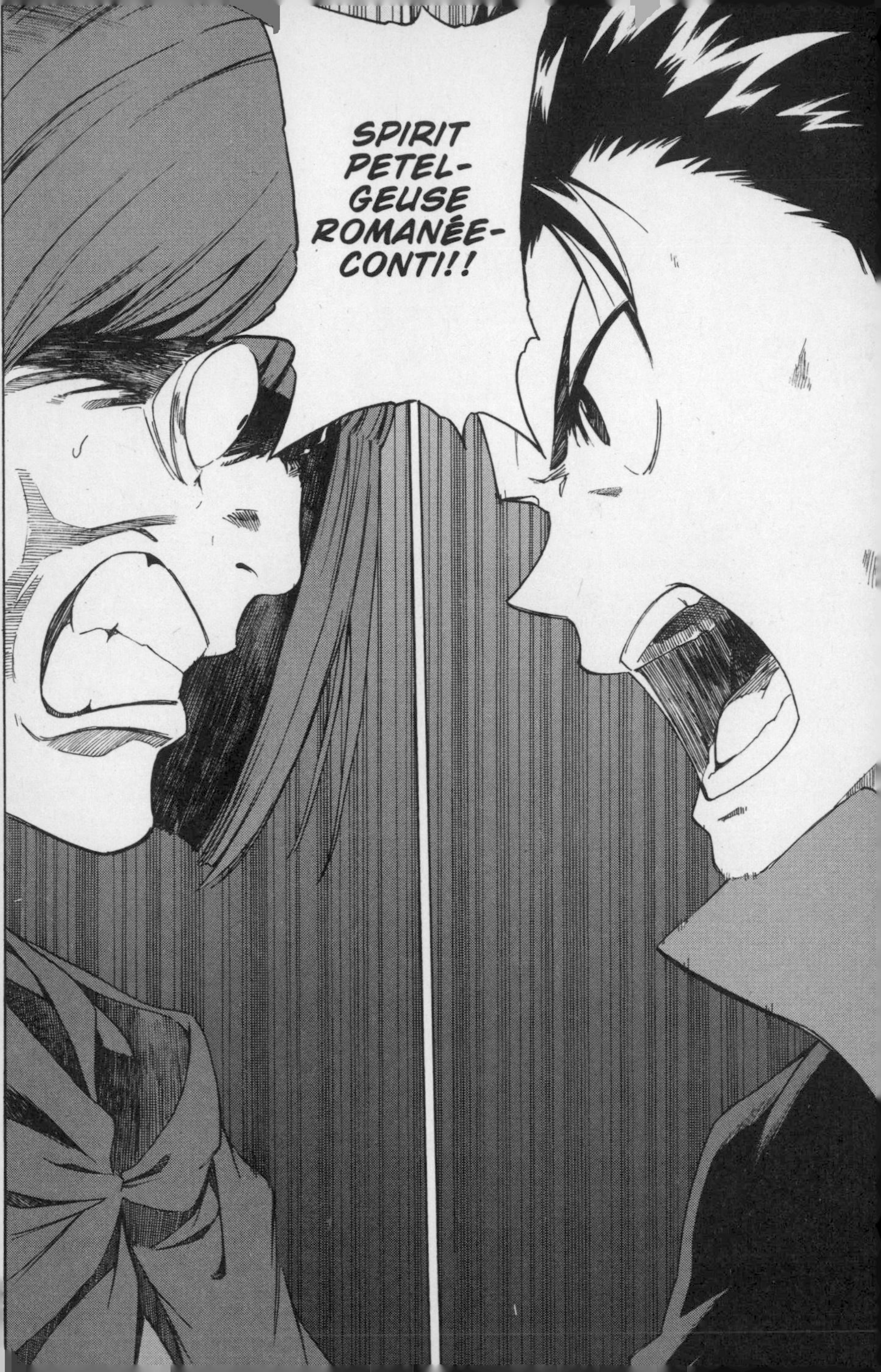
SPIRIT PETEL-GEUSE ROMANÉE-CONTI!!

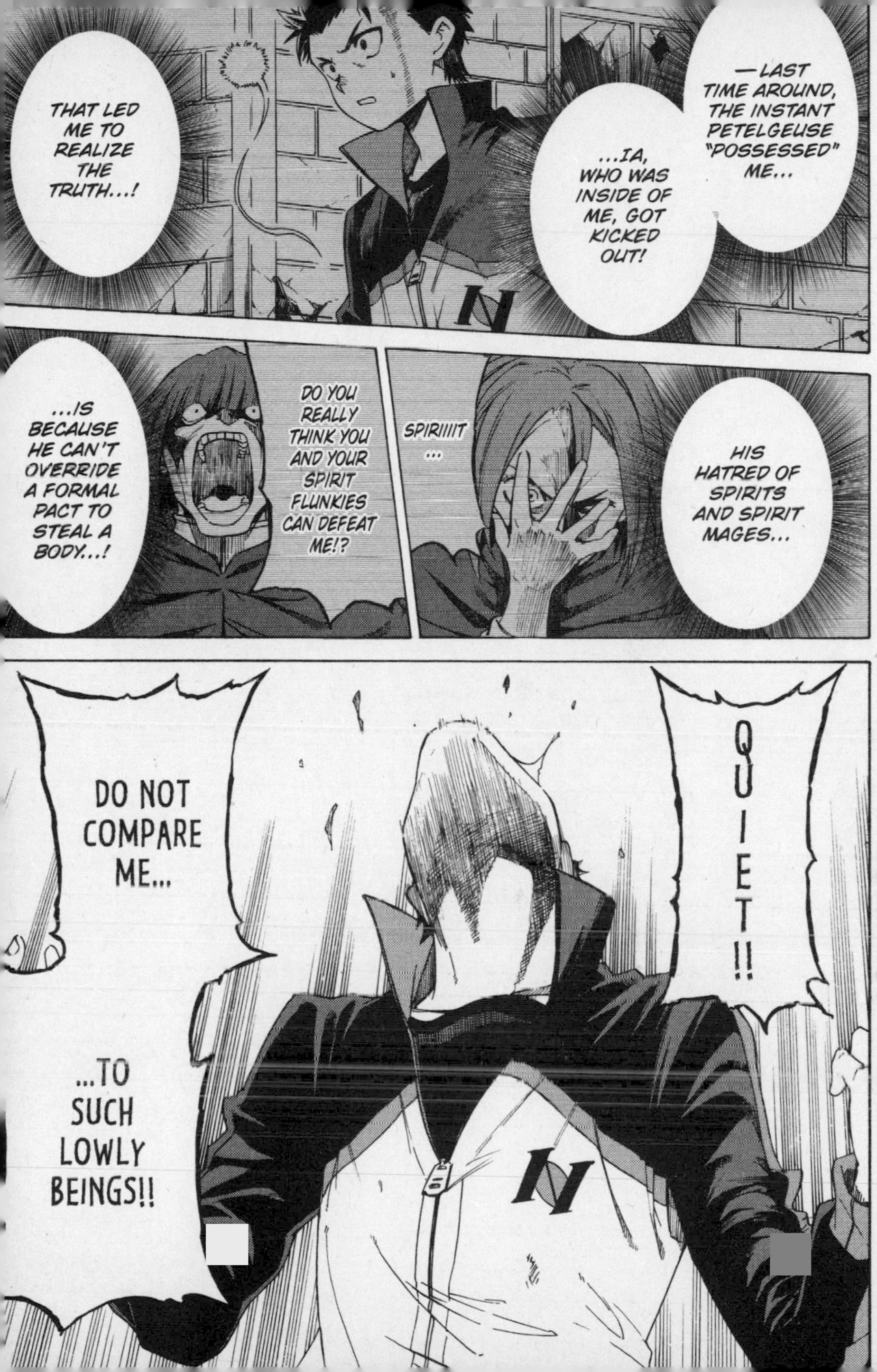
—LAST TIME AROUND, THE INSTANT PETELGEUSE "POSSESSED" ME...
...IA, WHO WAS INSIDE OF ME, GOT KICKED OUT!
THAT LED ME TO REALIZE THE TRUTH...!
HIS HATRED OF SPIRITS AND SPIRIT MAGES...
SPIRIIIIT...
DO YOU REALLY THINK YOU AND YOUR SPIRIT FLUNKIES CAN DEFEAT ME!?
...IS BECAUSE HE CAN'T OVERRIDE A FORMAL PACT TO STEAL A BODY...!
QUIET!!
DO NOT COMPARE ME...
...TO SUCH LOWLY BEINGS!!

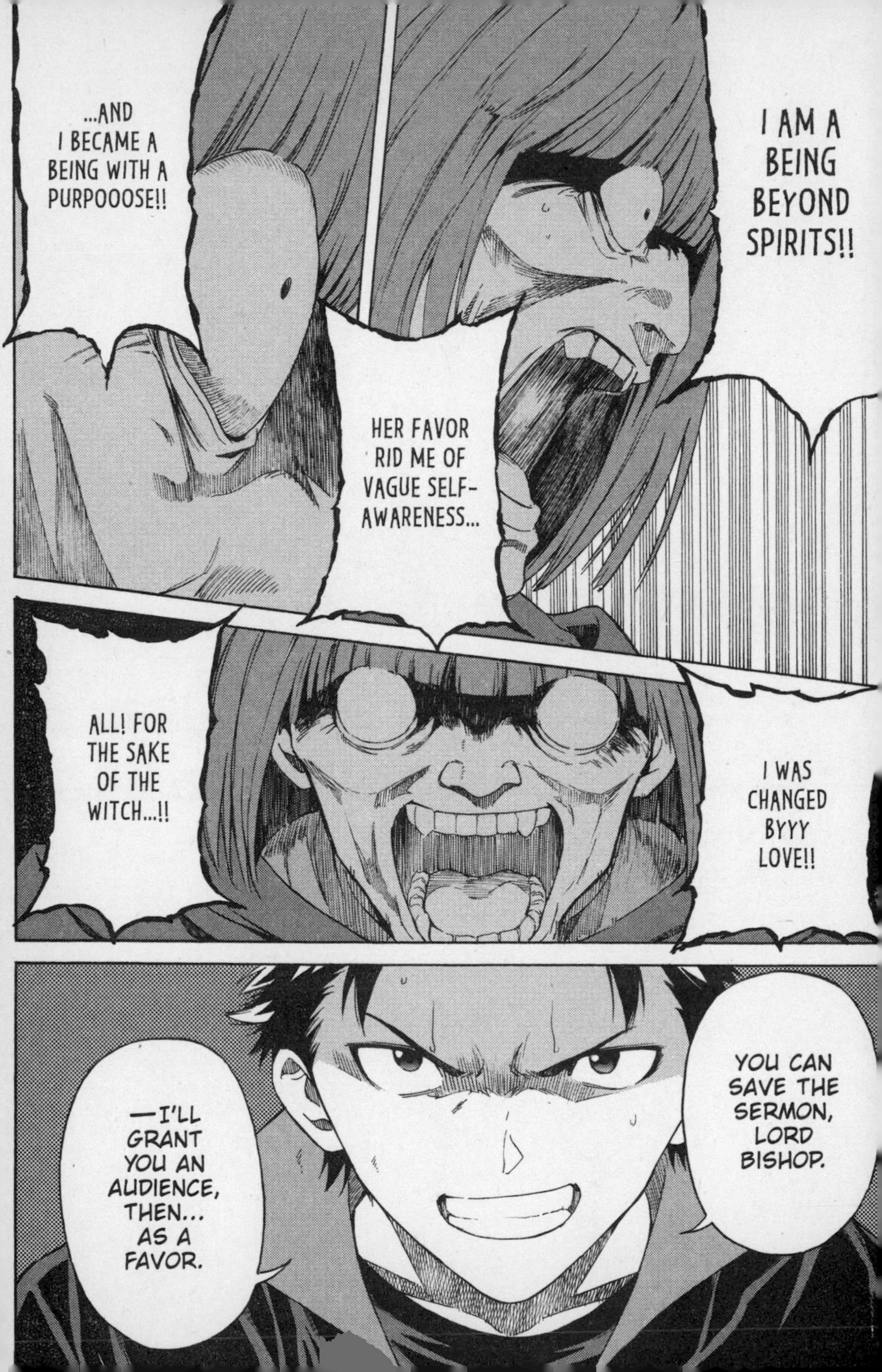
I AM A BEING BEYOND SPIRITS!!
HER FAVOR RID ME OF VAGUE SELF-AWARENESS...
...AND I BECAME A BEING WITH A PURPOOOSE!!
I WAS CHANGED BYYY LOVE!!
ALL! FOR THE SAKE OF THE WITCH...!!
YOU CAN SAVE THE SERMON, LORD BISHOP.
—I'LL GRANT YOU AN AUDIENCE, THEN... AS A FAVOR.

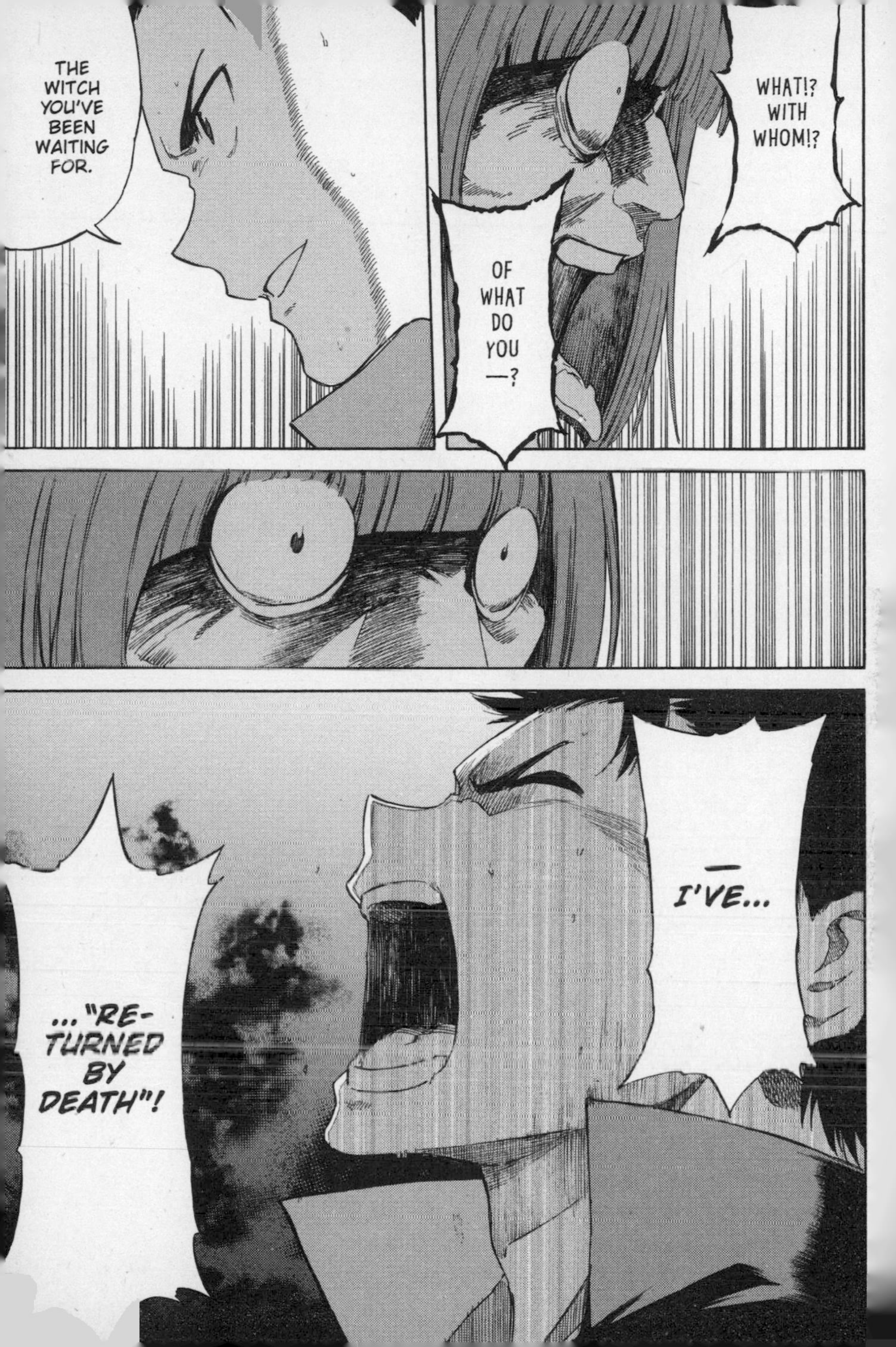
WHAT!? WITH WHOM!?
OF WHAT DO YOU —?
THE WITCH YOU'VE BEEN WAITING FOR.
—I'VE...
..."RE-TURNED BY DEATH"!

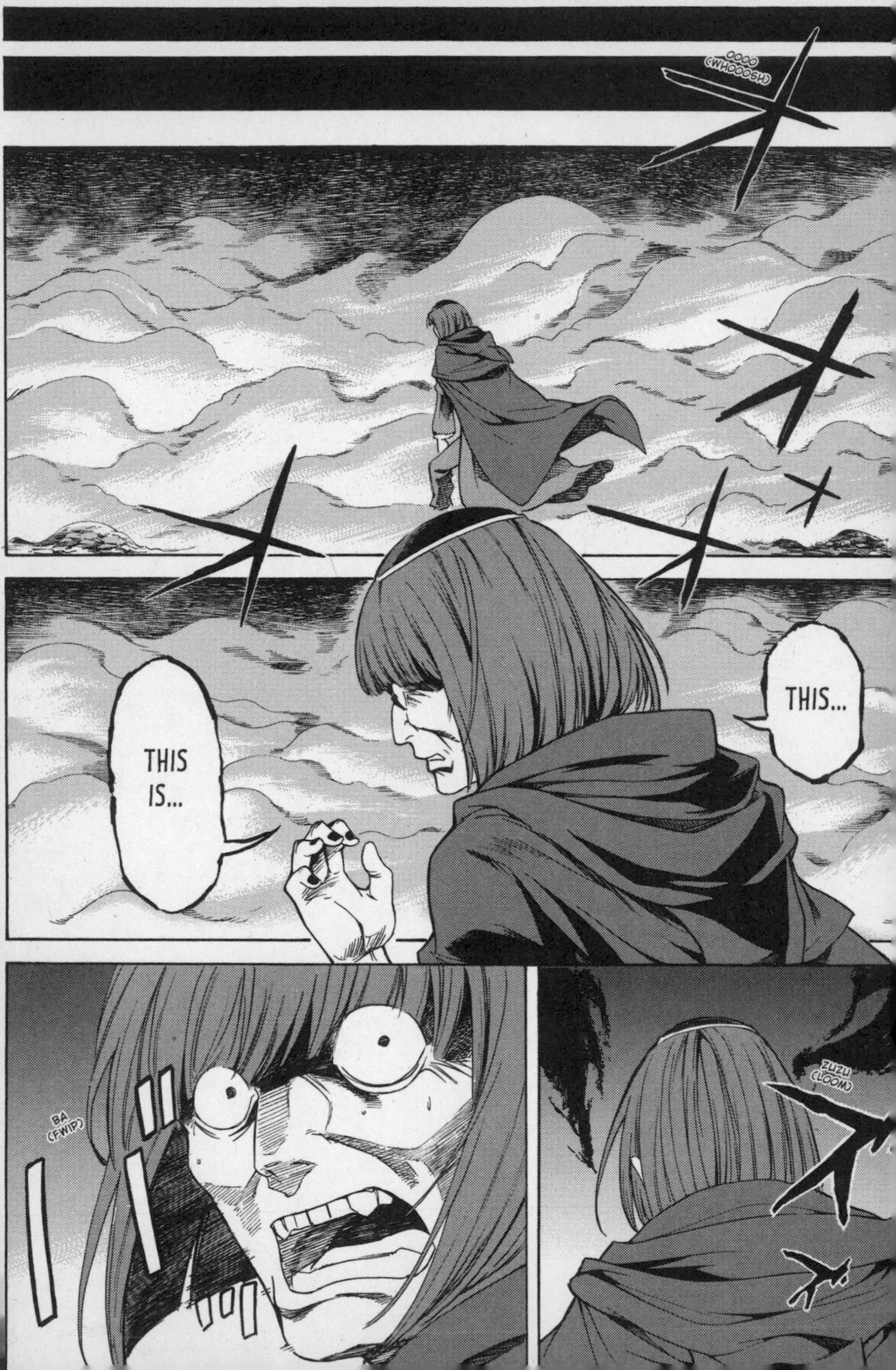
OOOO (WHOOOSH)
THIS...
THIS IS...
ZUZU (LOOM)
BA (FWIP)

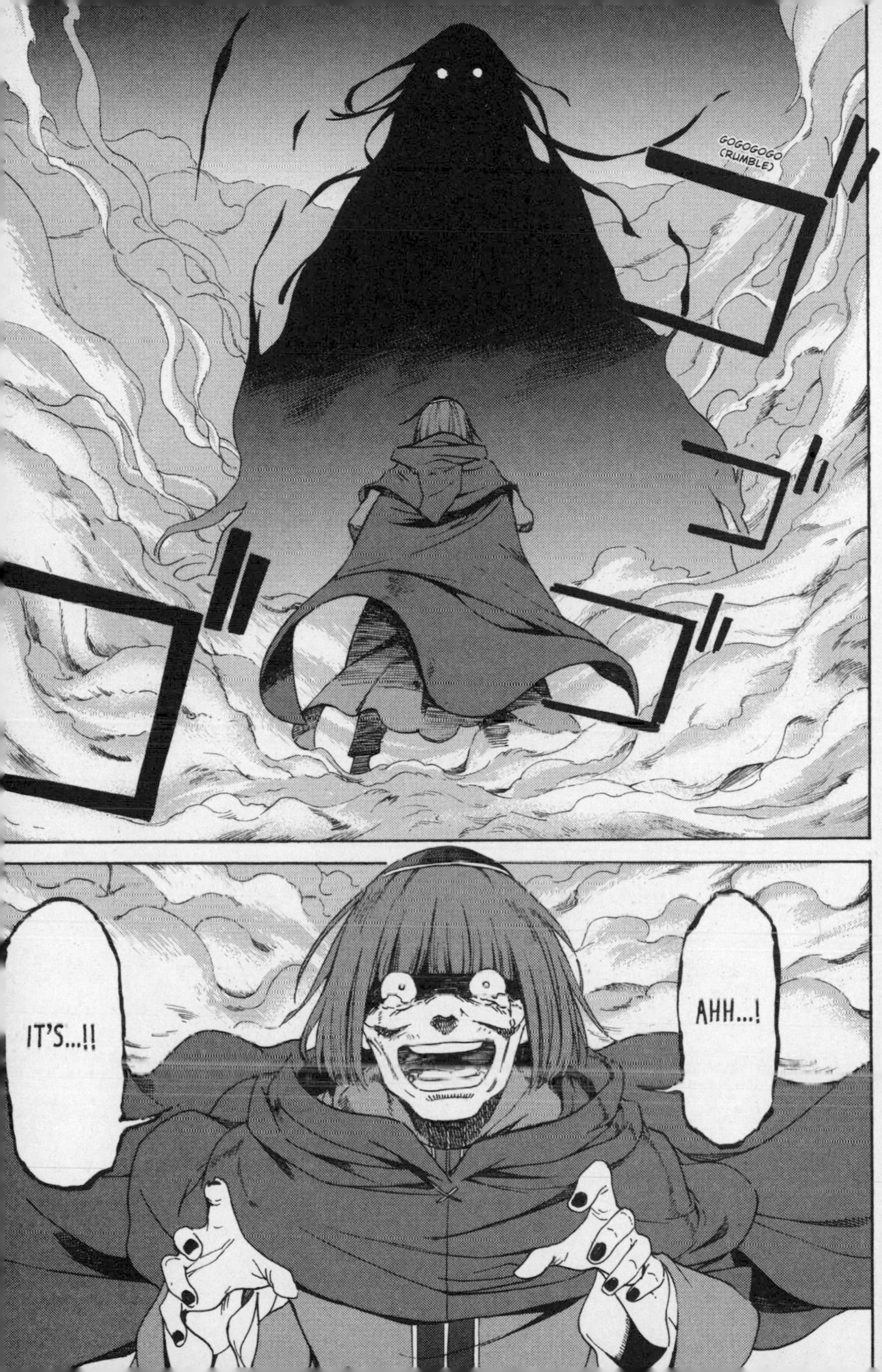
GOGOGOGO
(RUMBLE)
AHH...!
IT'S...!!

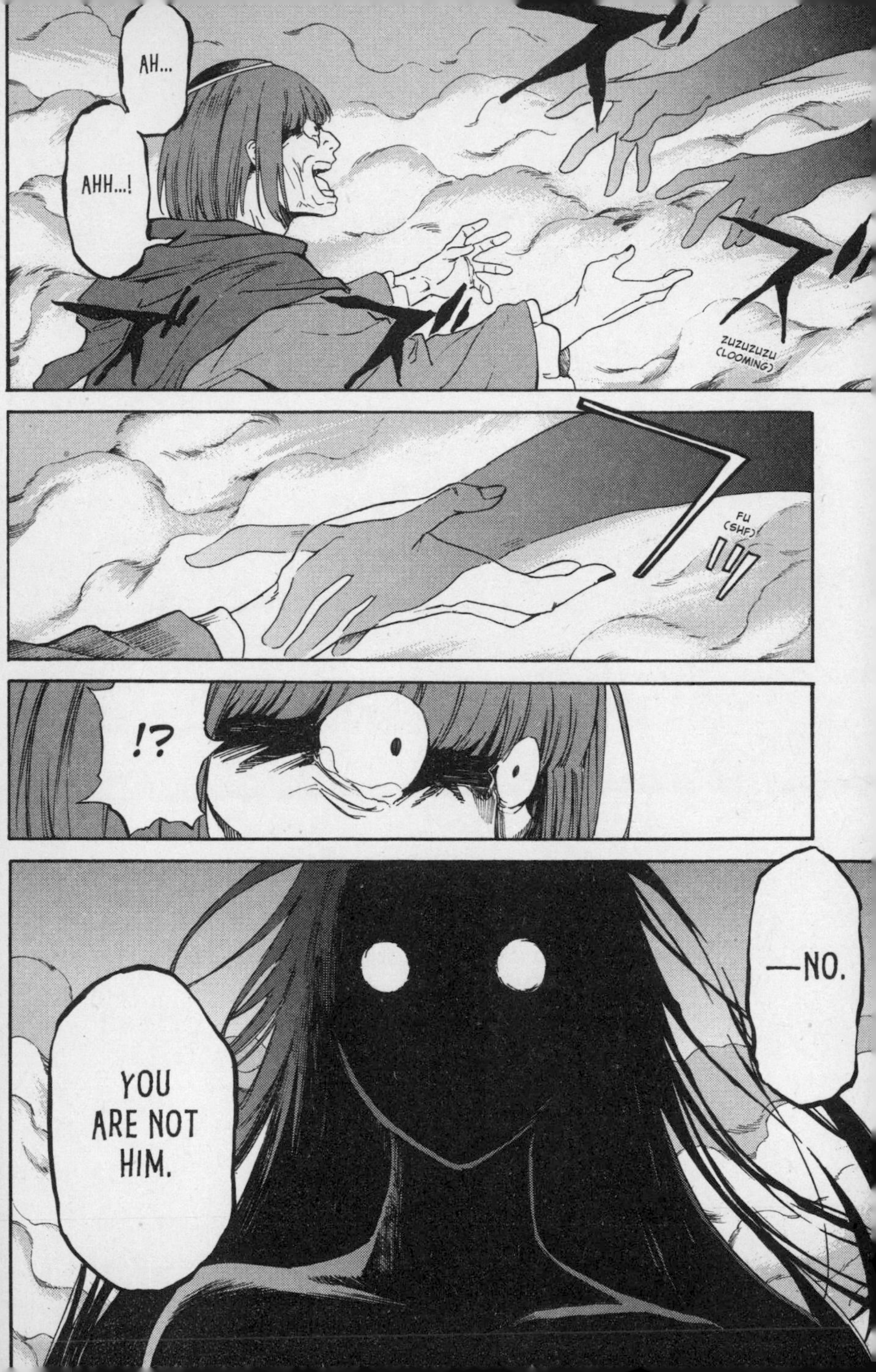

ZUZUZUZU (LOOMING)
AH...
AHH...!
FU (SHF)
!?
—NO.
YOU ARE NOT HIM.

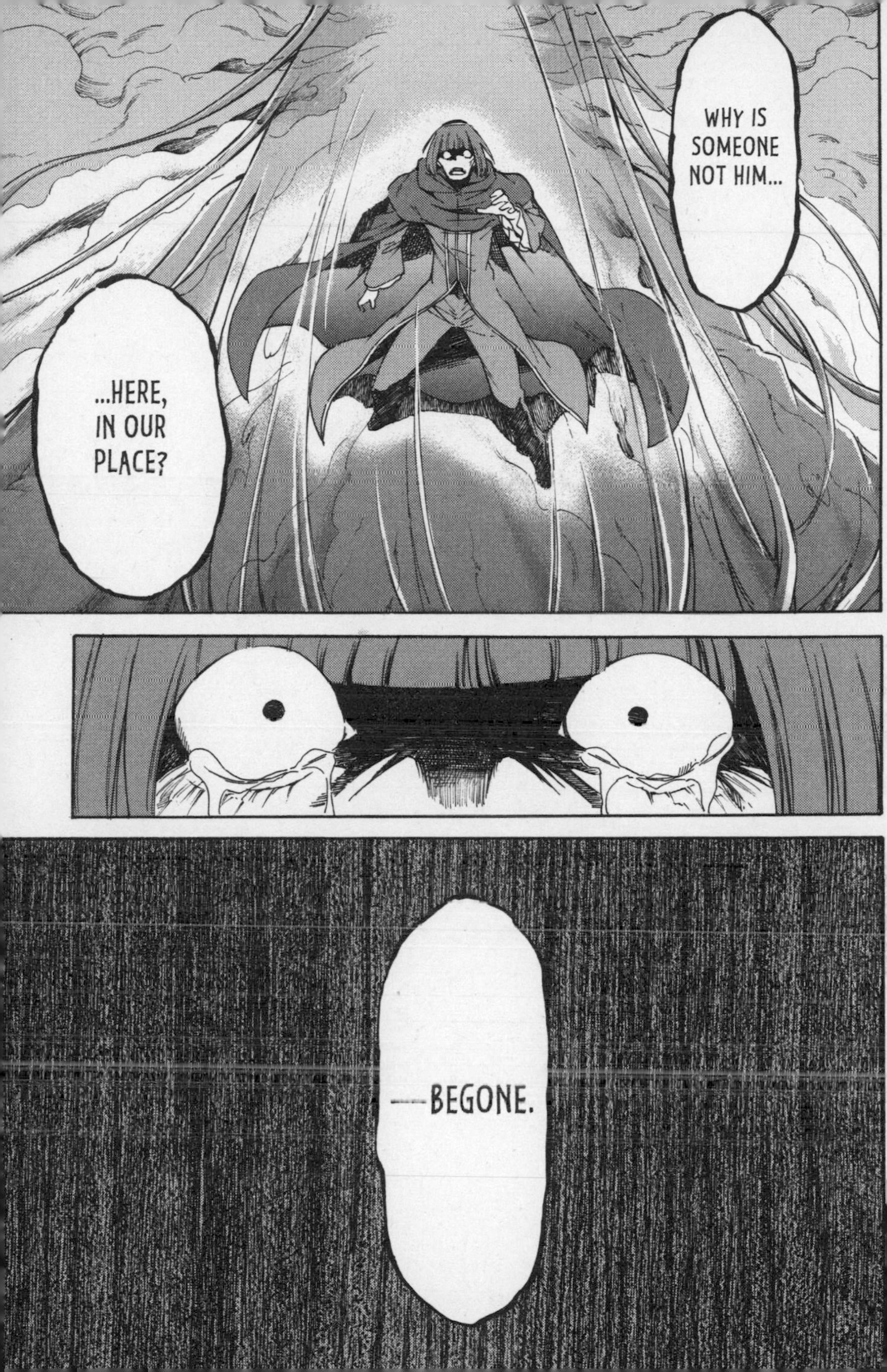
WHY IS SOMEONE NOT HIM...
...HERE, IN OUR PLACE?
—BEGONE.

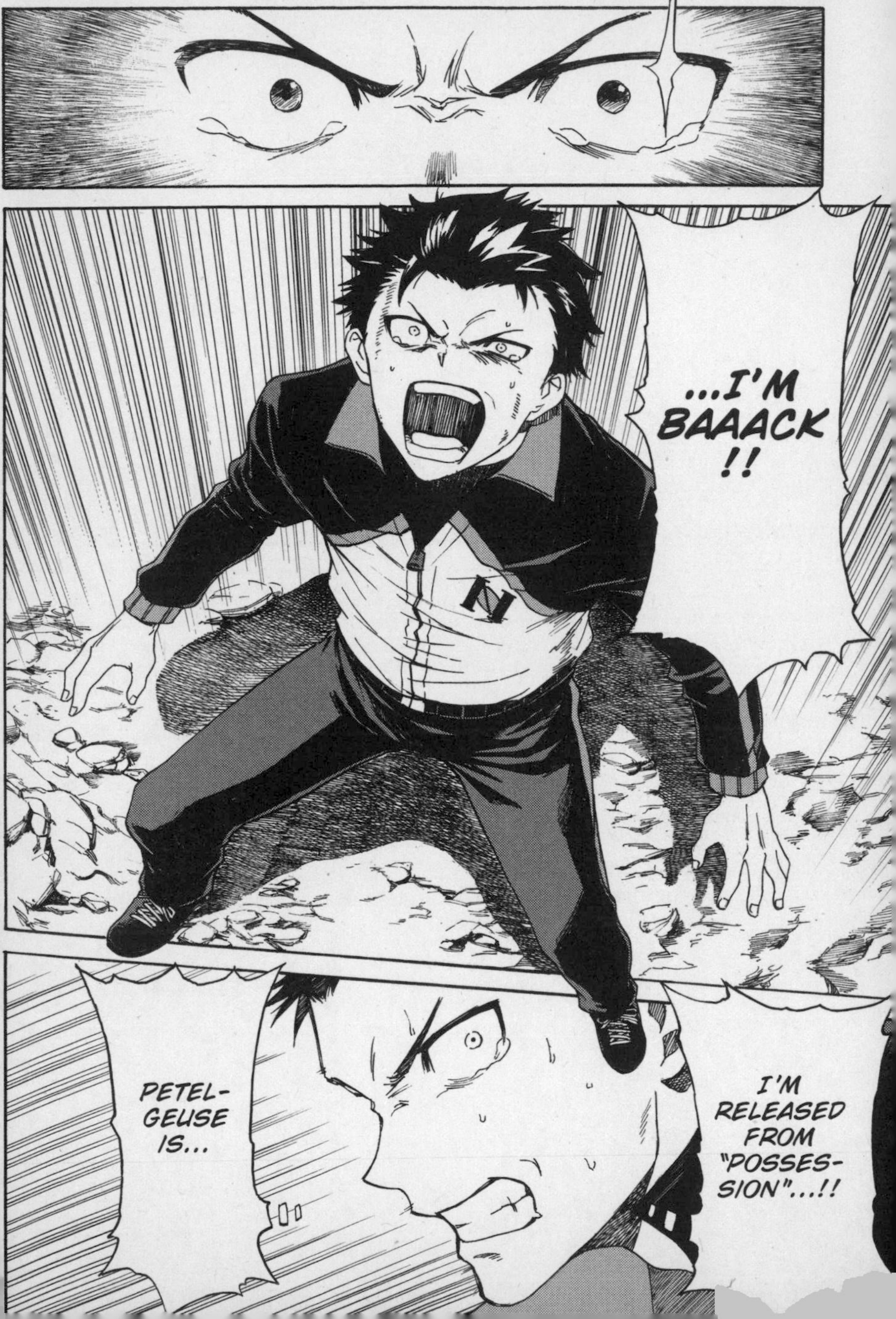
...I'M BAAACK !!
I'M RELEASED FROM "POSSES-SION"...!!
PETEL-GEUSE IS...

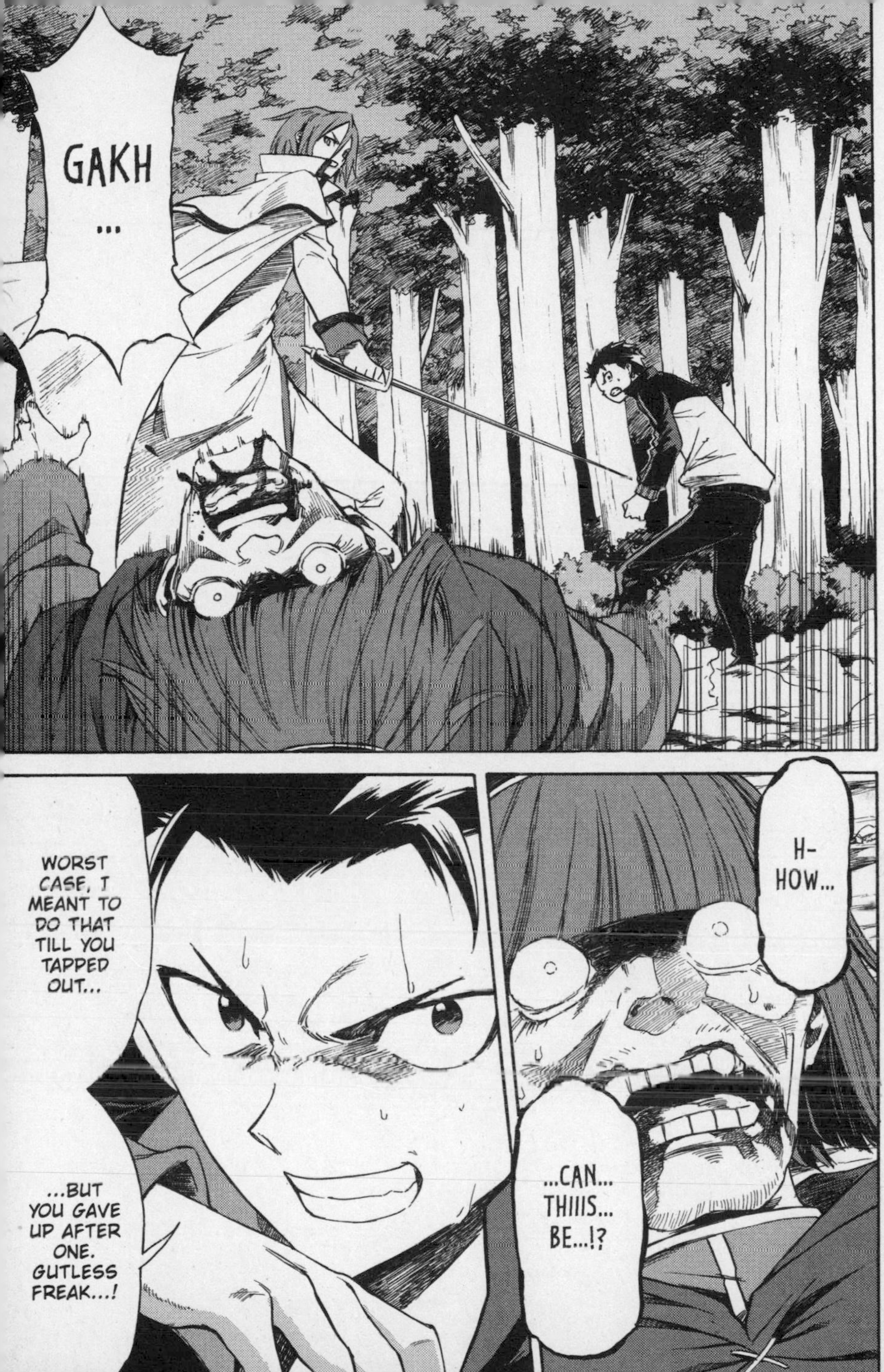
GAKH ...
H- HOW...
...CAN... THIIIS... BE...!?
WORST CASE, I MEANT TO DO THAT TILL YOU TAPPED OUT...
...BUT YOU GAVE UP AFTER ONE. GUTLESS FREAK...!

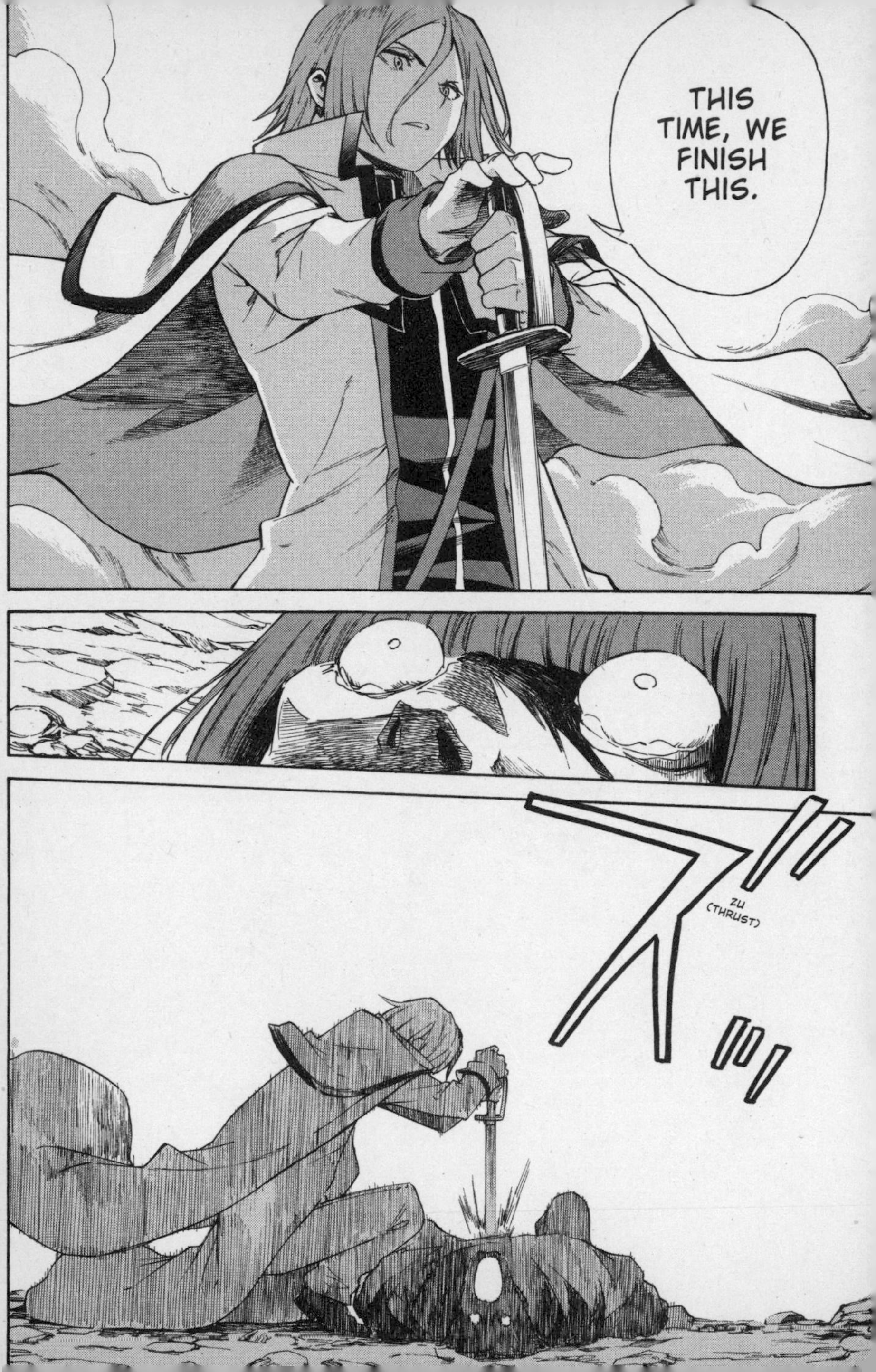
THIS TIME, WE FINISH THIS.
ZU (THRUST)

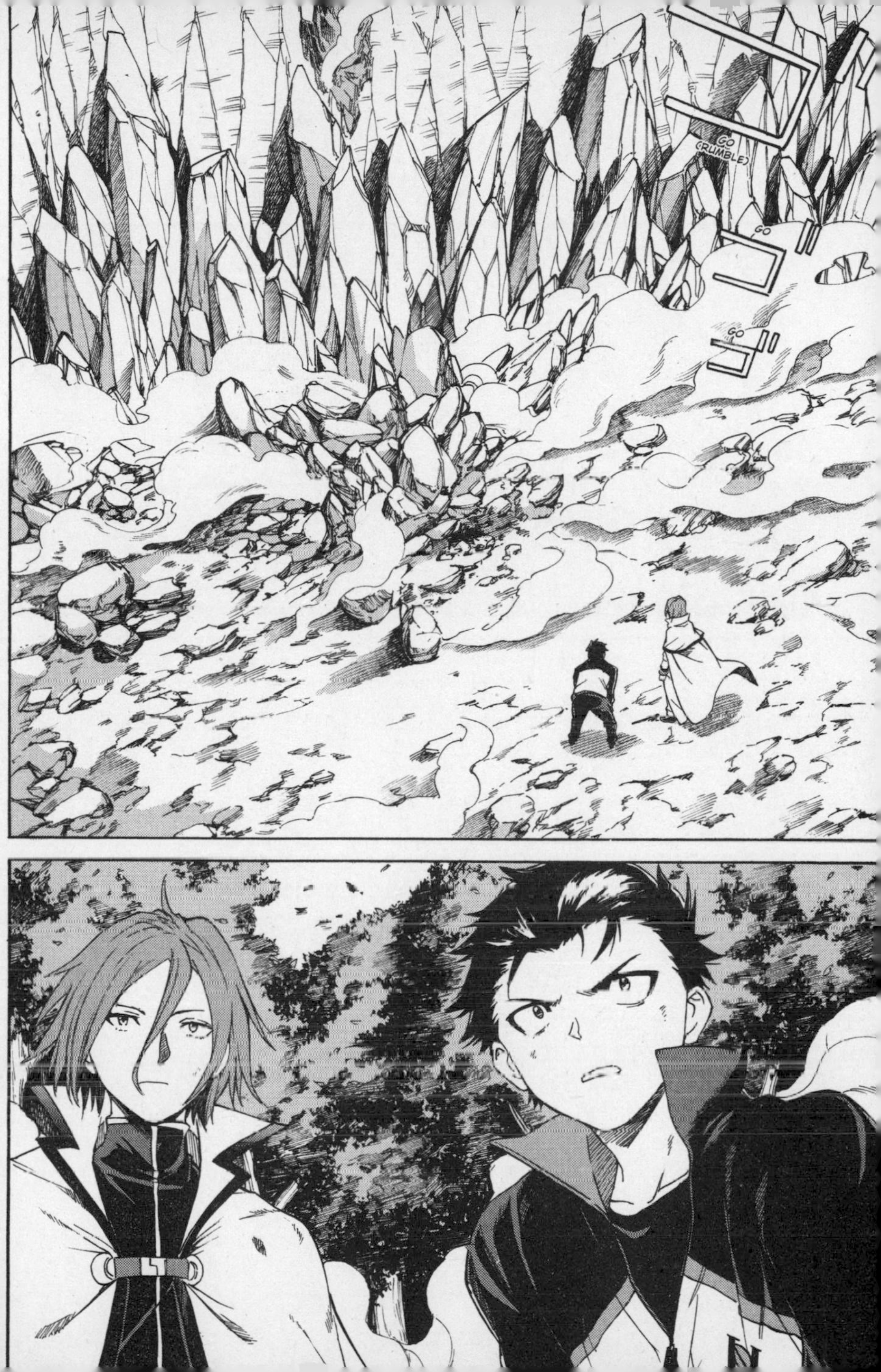
GO (RUMBLE)
GO
GO

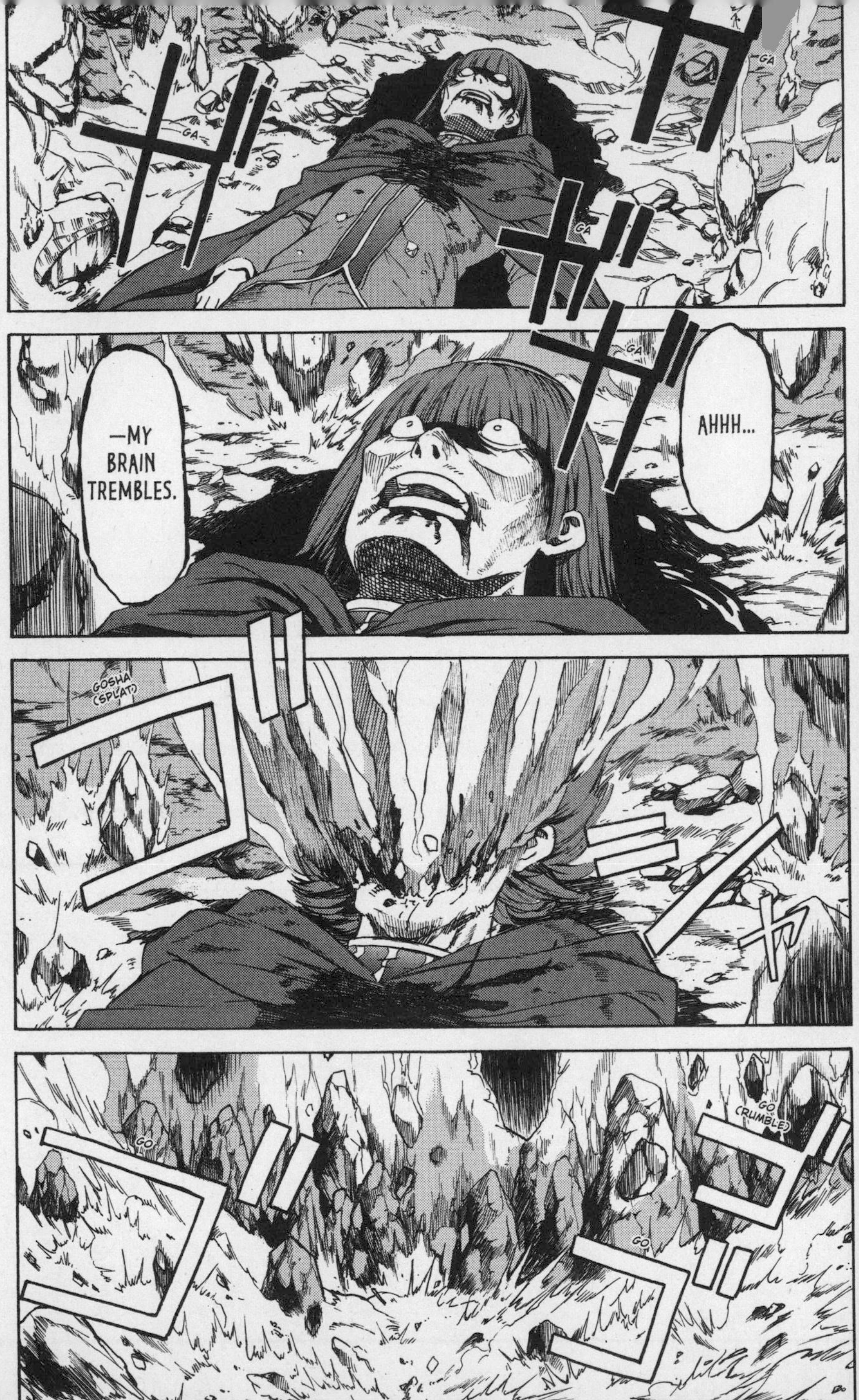
GA
GA
GA
GA
AHHH...
—MY BRAIN TREMBLES.
GOSHA (SPLAT)
GO (RUMBLE)
GO
GO

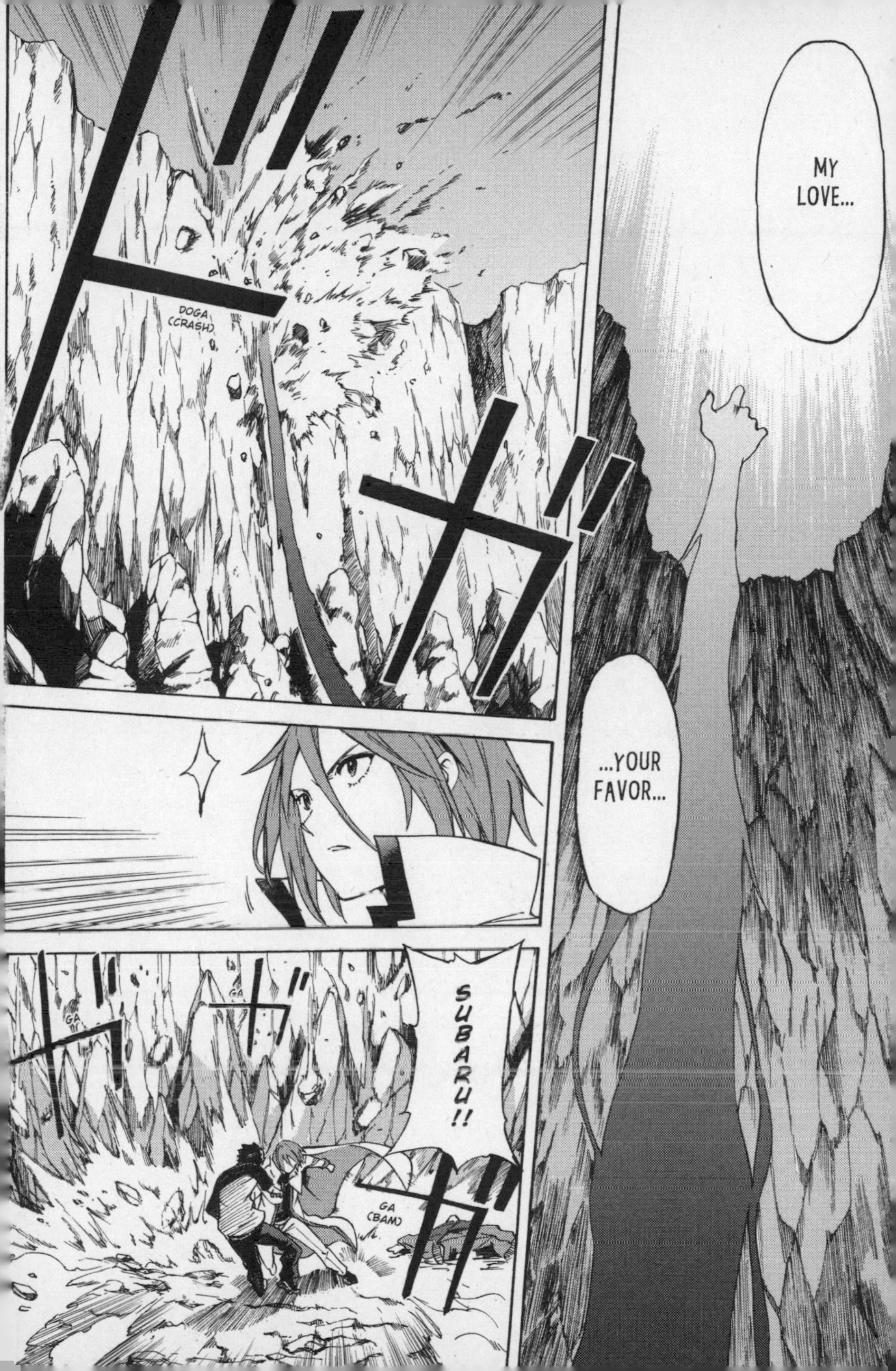
MY LOVE...
...YOUR FAVOR...
DOGA (CRASH)
SUBARU!!
GA
GA
GA (BAM)

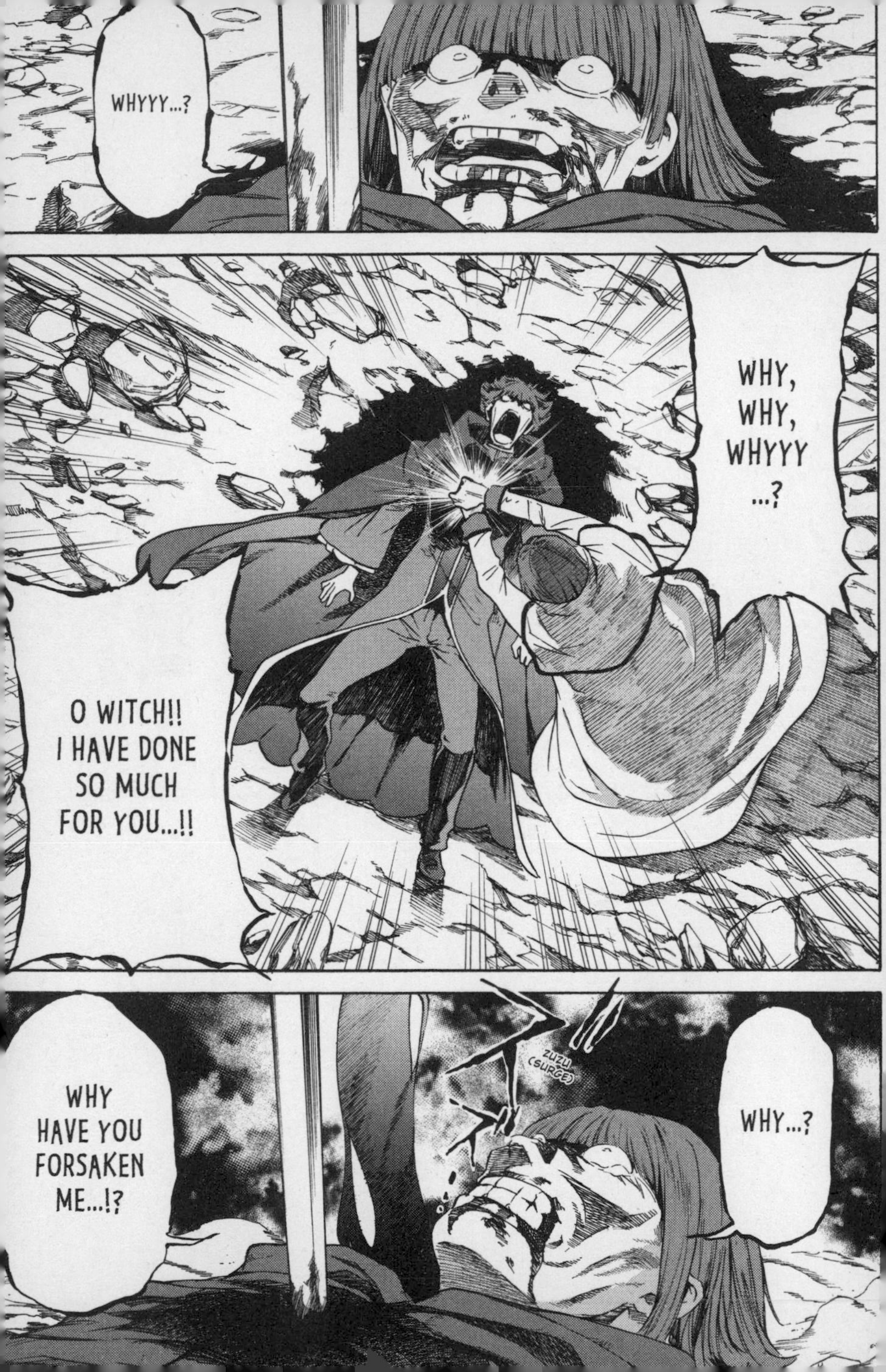
WHYYY...?
WHY, WHY, WHYYY ...?
O WITCH!! I HAVE DONE SO MUCH FOR YOU...!!
WHY...?
ZUZU (SURGE)
WHY HAVE YOU FORSAKEN ME...!?

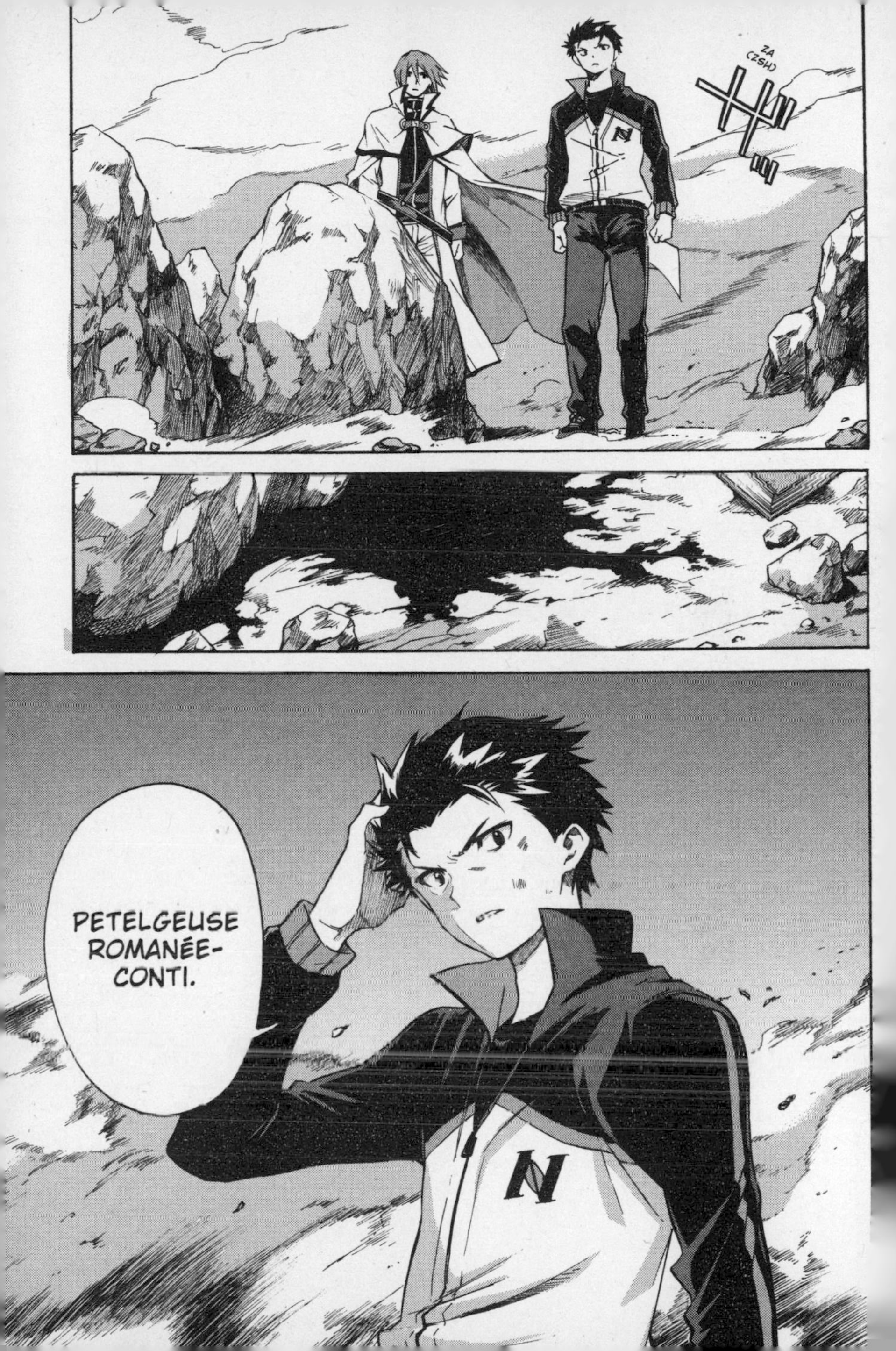
ZA
(ZSH)
PETELGEUSE ROMANÉE-CONTI.

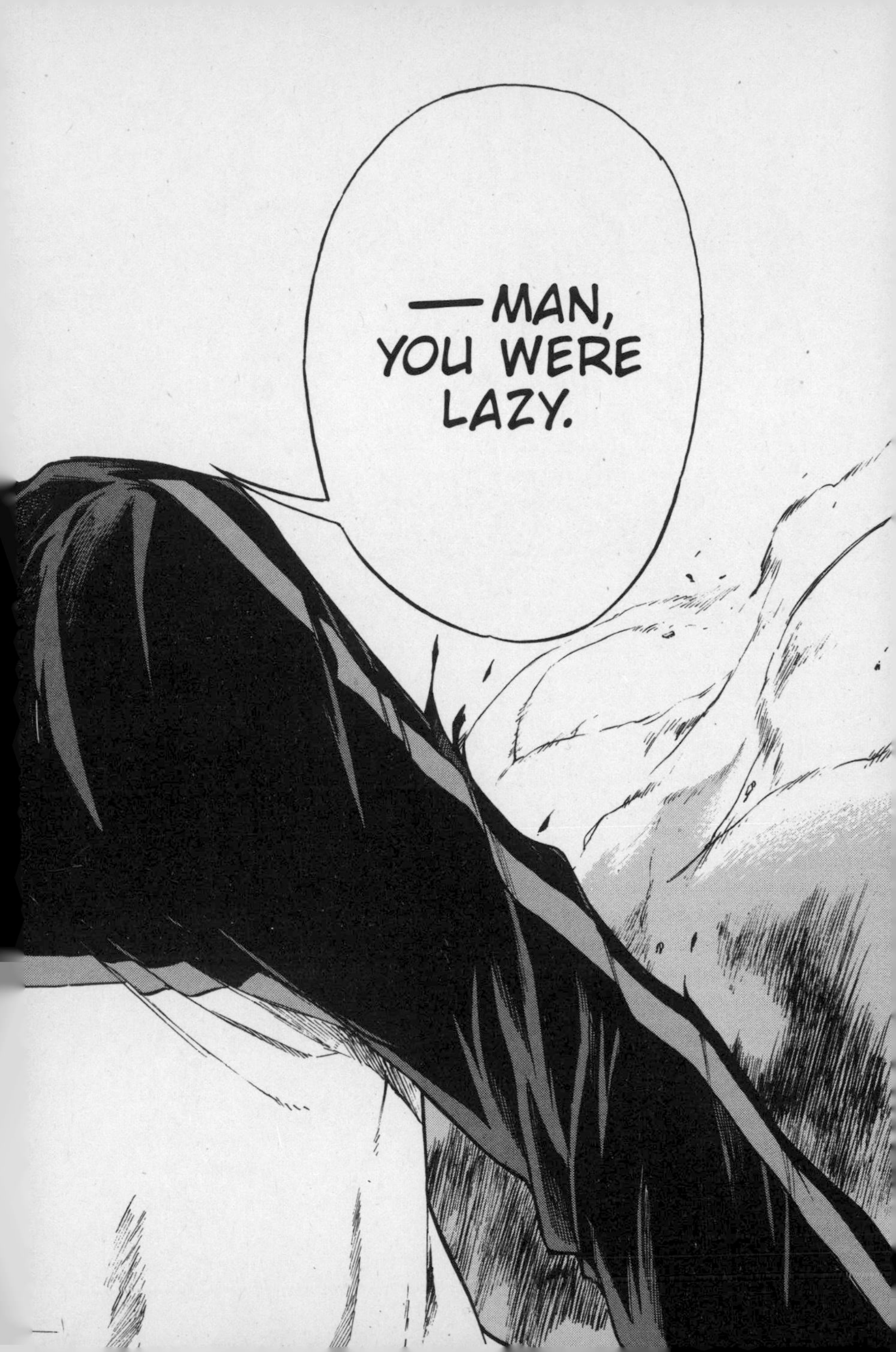
—MAN, YOU WERE LAZY.

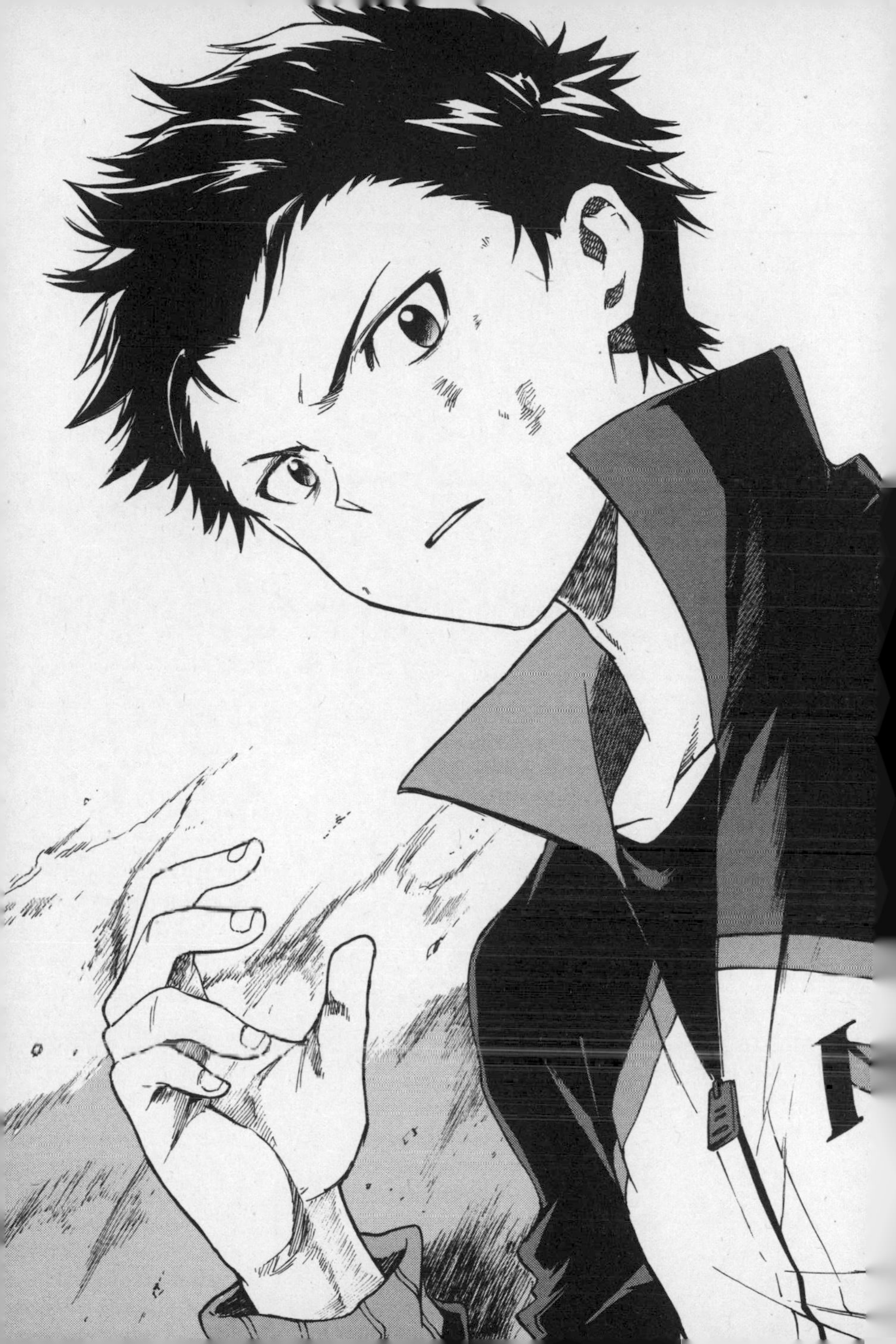

Re:ZERO
-Starting Life in Another World-

Truth of Zero
The only ability Subaru Natsuki gets when he's summoned
to another world is time travel via his own death.
But to save her, he'll die as many times as it takes.

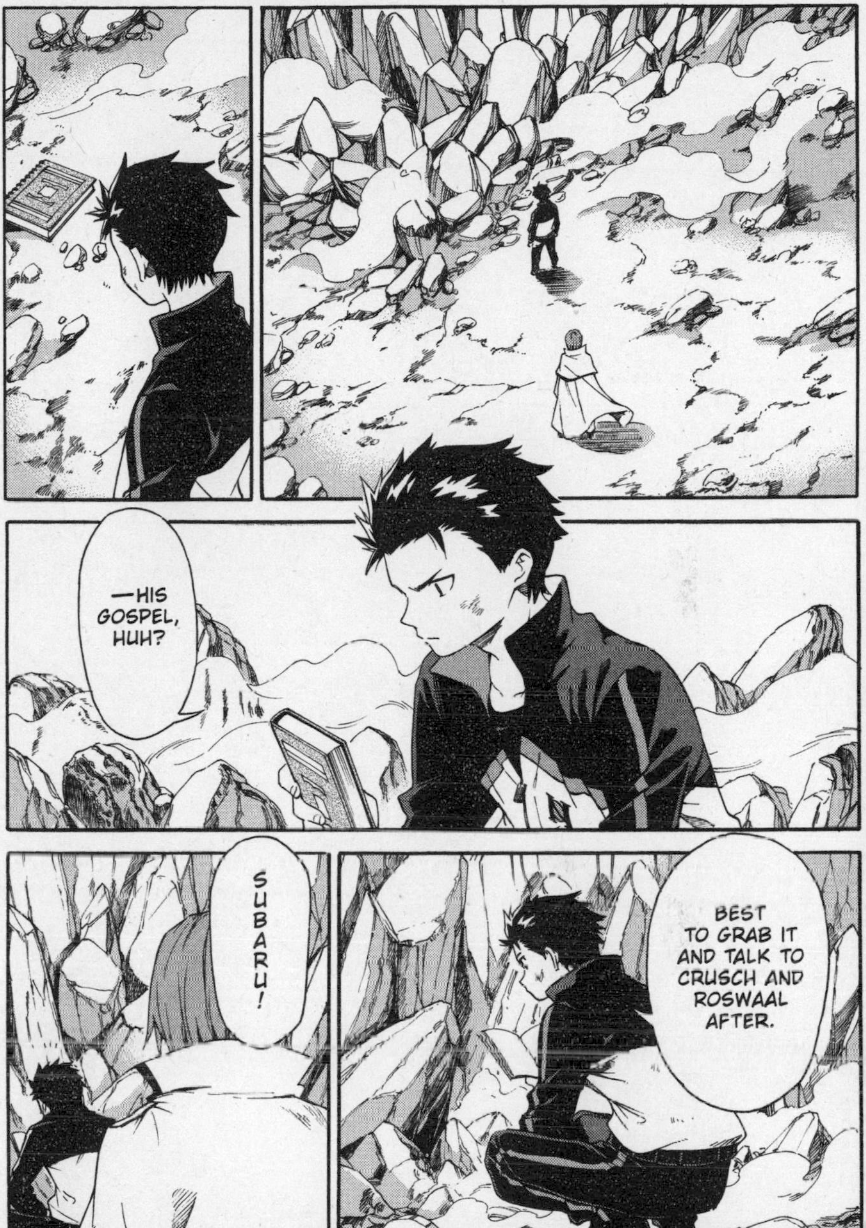
—HIS GOSPEL, HUH?
BEST TO GRAB IT AND TALK TO CRUSCH AND ROSWAAL AFTER.
SUBARU!

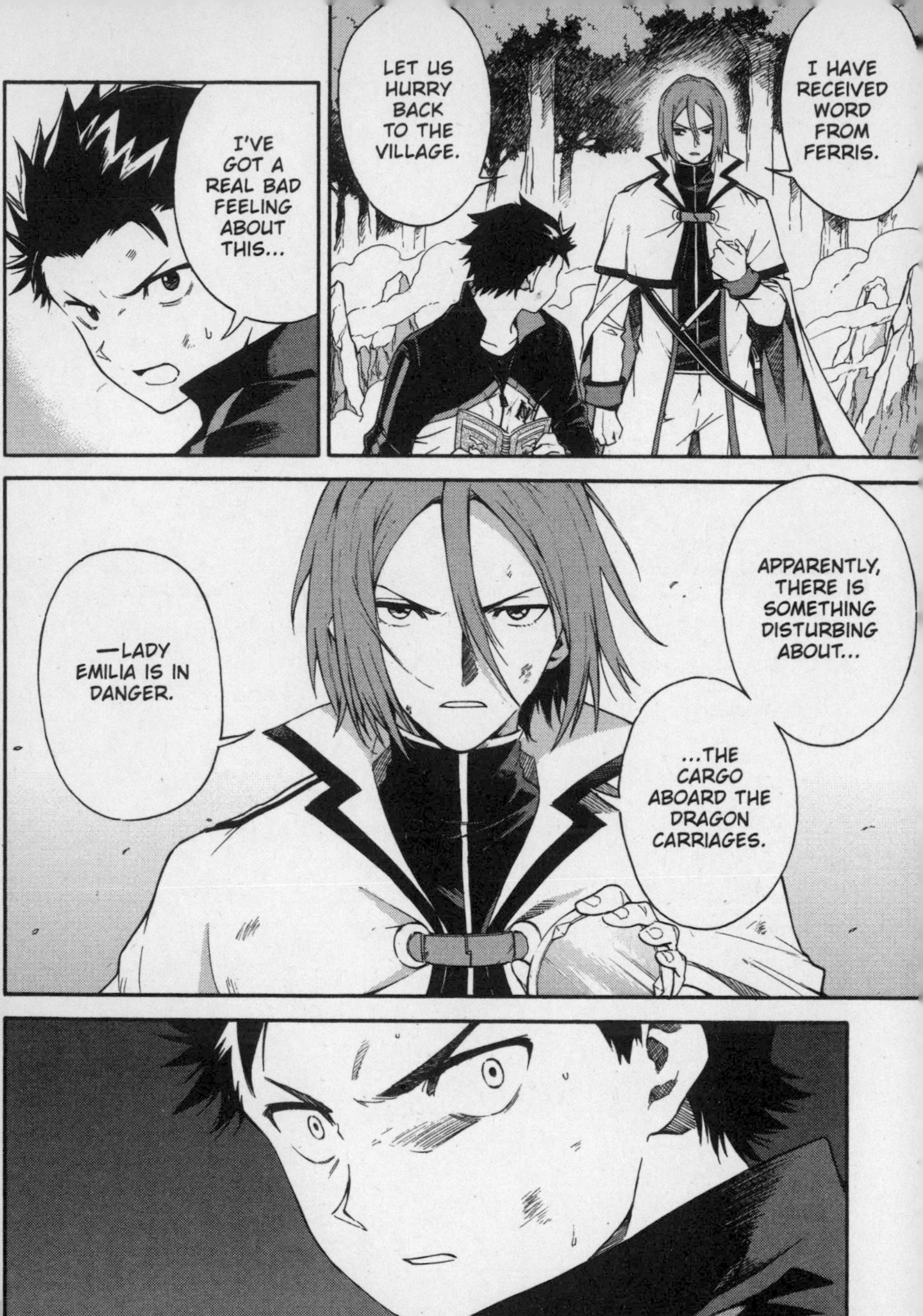
I HAVE RECEIVED WORD FROM FERRIS.
LET US HURRY BACK TO THE VILLAGE.
I'VE GOT A REAL BAD FEELING ABOUT THIS...
APPARENTLY, THERE IS SOMETHING DISTURBING ABOUT...
...THE CARGO ABOARD THE DRAGON CARRIAGES.
—LADY EMILIA IS IN DANGER.

Episode 46
Pursuit

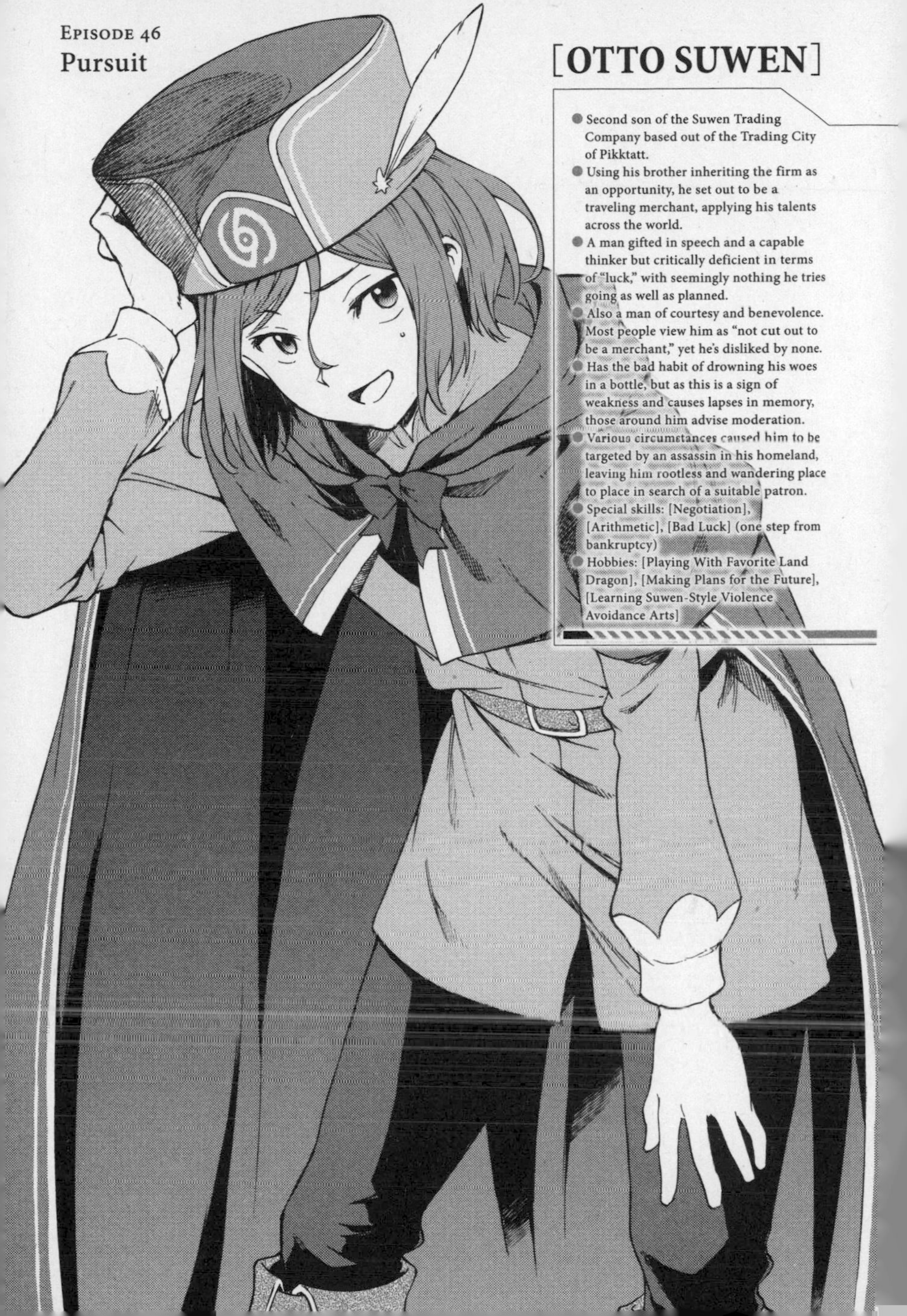

[OTTO SUWEN]

- Second son of the Suwen Trading Company based out of the Trading City of Pikktatt.
- Using his brother inheriting the firm as an opportunity, he set out to be a traveling merchant, applying his talents across the world.
- A man gifted in speech and a capable thinker but critically deficient in terms of "luck," with seemingly nothing he tries going as well as planned.
- Also a man of courtesy and benevolence. Most people view him as "not cut out to be a merchant," yet he's disliked by none.
- Has the bad habit of drowning his woes in a bottle, but as this is a sign of weakness and causes lapses in memory, those around him advise moderation.
- Various circumstances caused him to be targeted by an assassin in his homeland, leaving him rootless and wandering place to place in search of a suitable patron.
- Special skills: [Negotiation], [Arithmetic], [Bad Luck] (one step from bankruptcy)
- Hobbies: [Playing With Favorite Land Dragon], [Making Plans for the Future], [Learning Suwen-Style Violence Avoidance Arts]

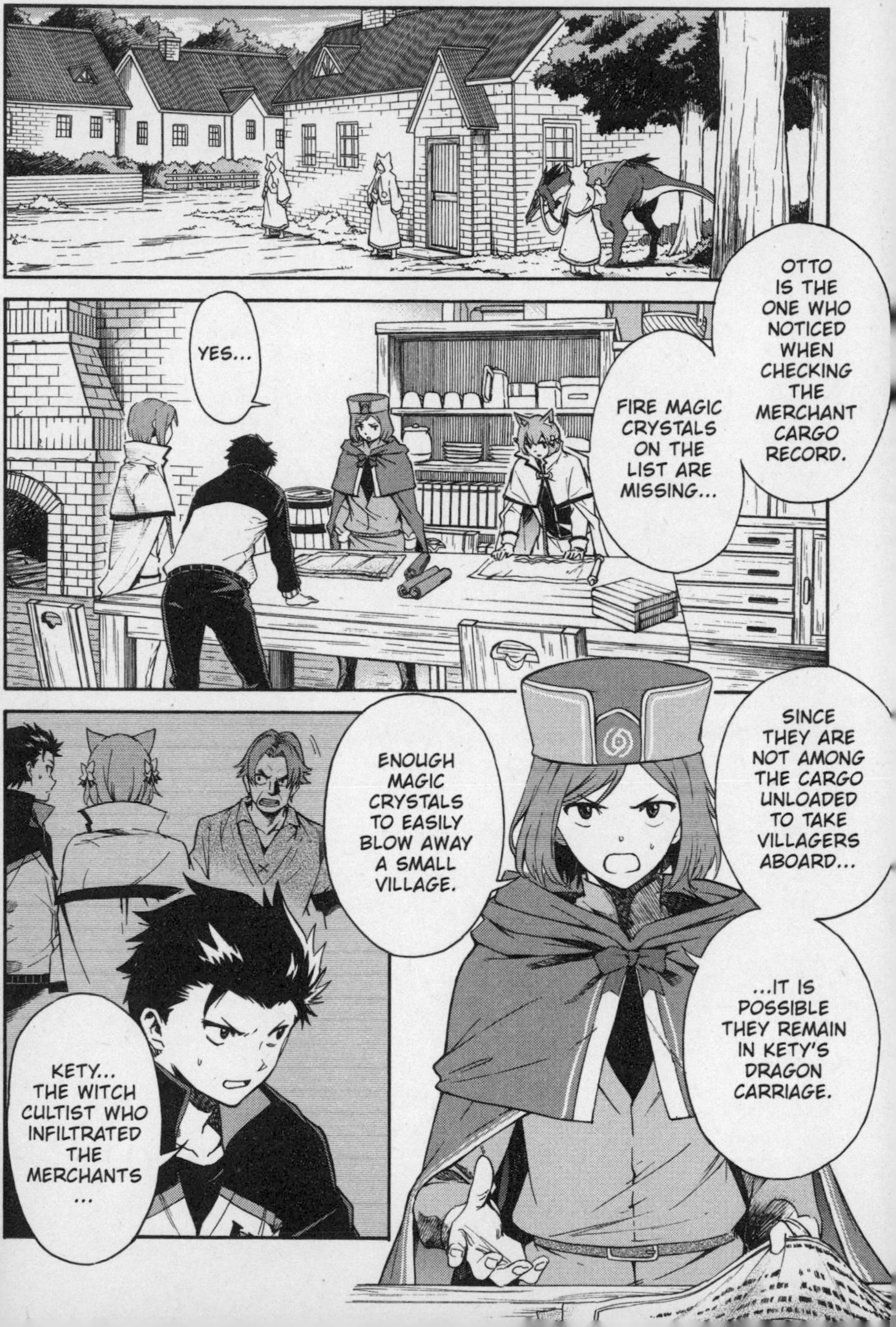

OTTO IS THE ONE WHO NOTICED WHEN CHECKING THE MERCHANT CARGO RECORD.
FIRE MAGIC CRYSTALS ON THE LIST ARE MISSING...
YES...
SINCE THEY ARE NOT AMONG THE CARGO UNLOADED TO TAKE VILLAGERS ABOARD...
...IT IS POSSIBLE THEY REMAIN IN KETY'S DRAGON CARRIAGE.
ENOUGH MAGIC CRYSTALS TO EASILY BLOW AWAY A SMALL VILLAGE.
KETY... THE WITCH CULTIST WHO INFILTRATED THE MERCHANTS...

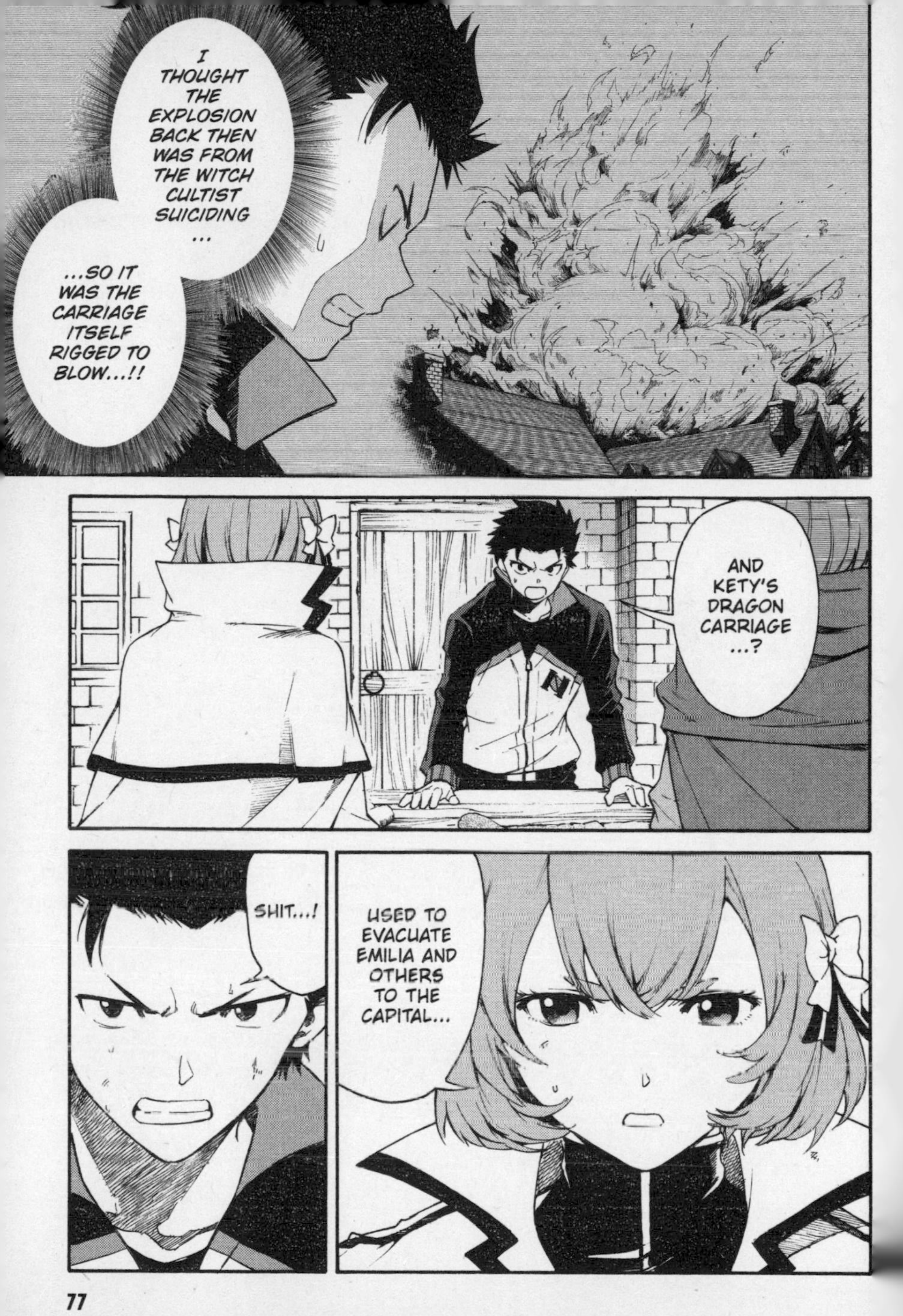
I THOUGHT THE EXPLOSION BACK THEN WAS FROM THE WITCH CULTIST SUICIDING ...
...SO IT WAS THE CARRIAGE ITSELF RIGGED TO BLOW...!!
AND KETY'S DRAGON CARRIAGE ...?
USED TO EVACUATE EMILIA AND OTHERS TO THE CAPITAL...
SHIT...!

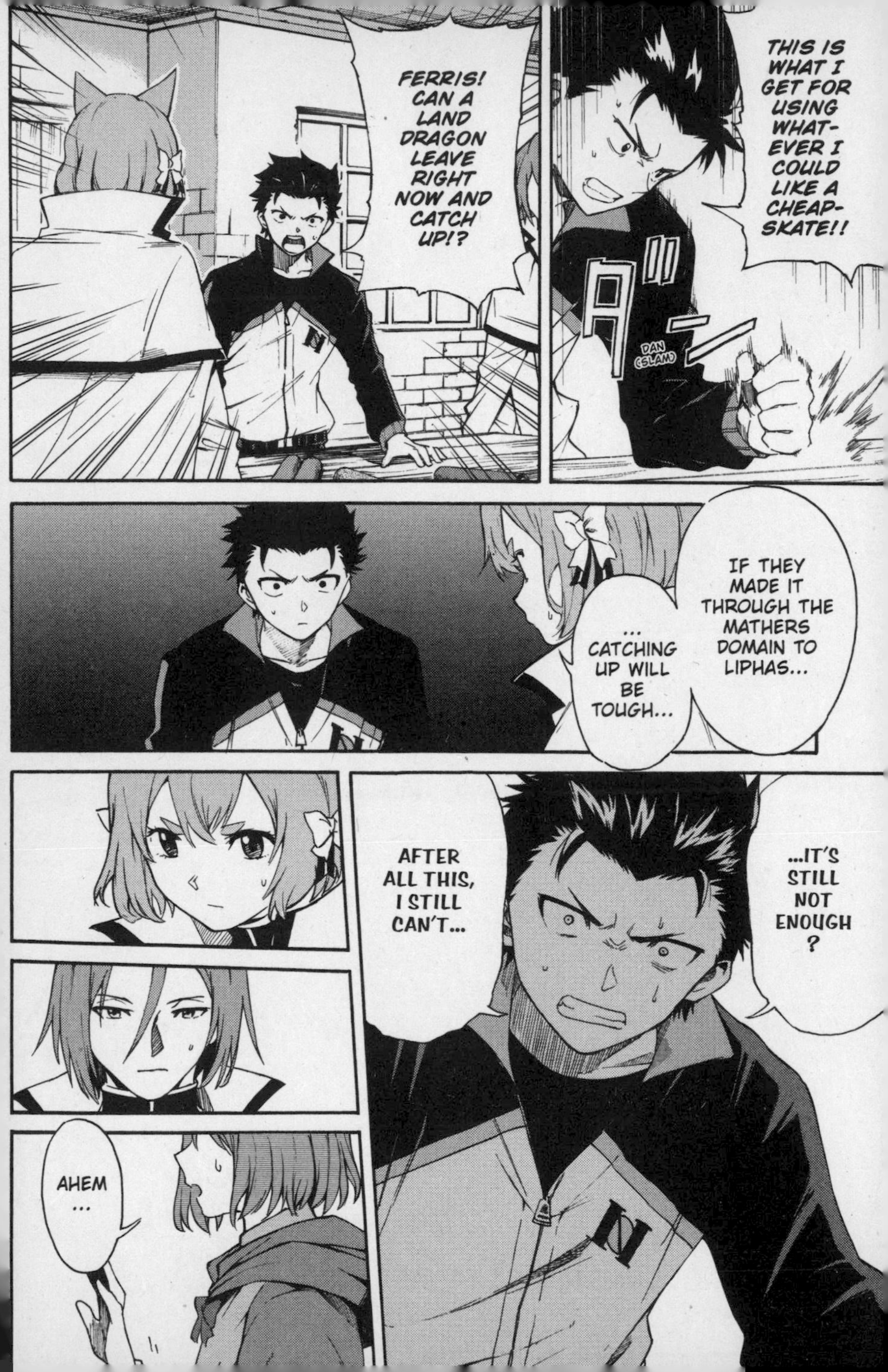
THIS IS WHAT I GET FOR USING WHAT-EVER I COULD LIKE A CHEAP-SKATE!!
DAN (SLAM)
FERRIS! CAN A LAND DRAGON LEAVE RIGHT NOW AND CATCH UP!?
IF THEY MADE IT THROUGH THE MATHERS DOMAIN TO LIPHAS...
...CATCHING UP WILL BE TOUGH...
...IT'S STILL NOT ENOUGH?
AFTER ALL THIS, I STILL CAN'T...
AHEM...

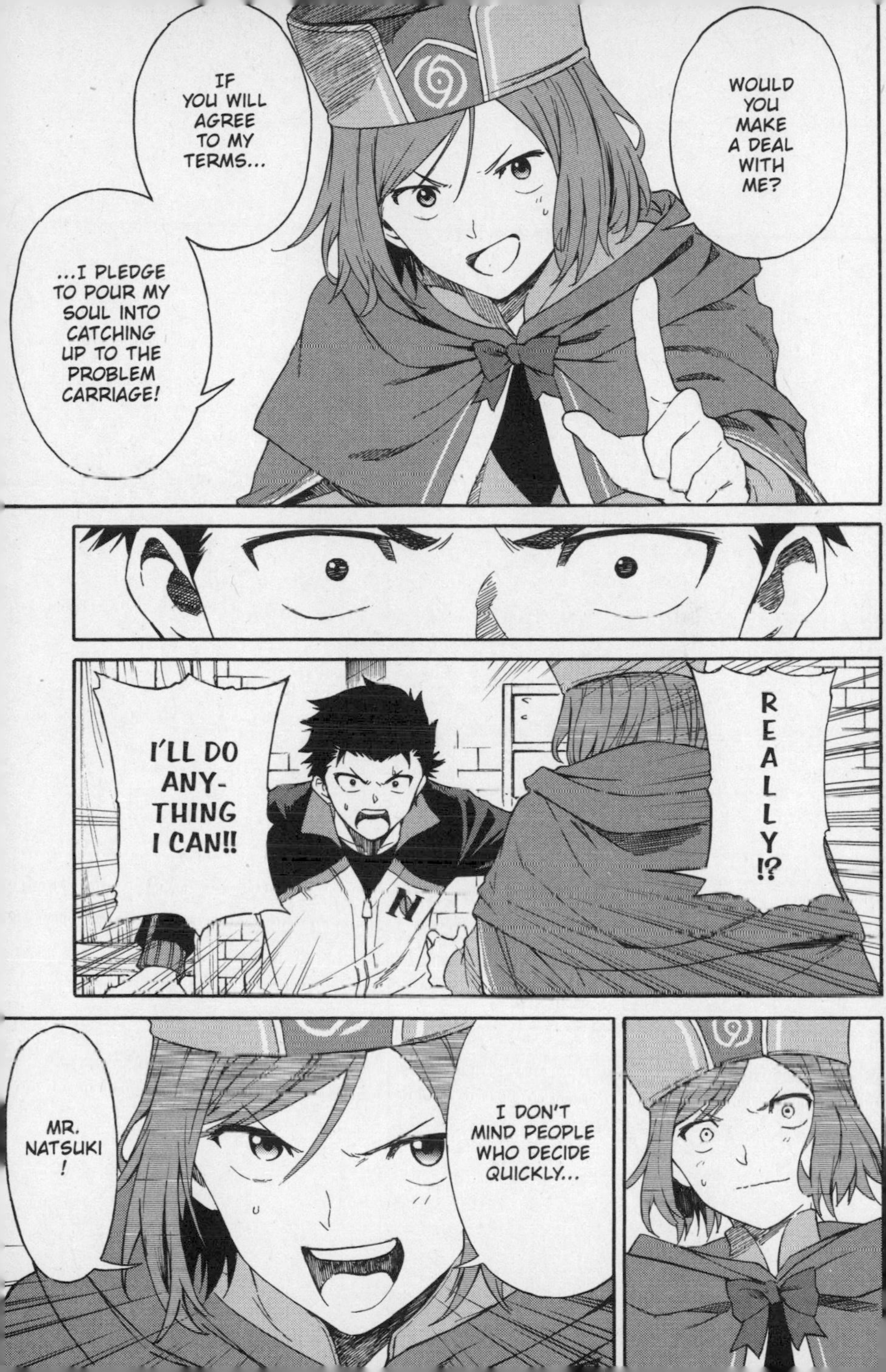
WOULD YOU MAKE A DEAL WITH ME?
IF YOU WILL AGREE TO MY TERMS...
...I PLEDGE TO POUR MY SOUL INTO CATCHING UP TO THE PROBLEM CARRIAGE!
REALLY!?
I'LL DO ANY-THING I CAN!!
I DON'T MIND PEOPLE WHO DECIDE QUICKLY...
MR. NATSUKI!

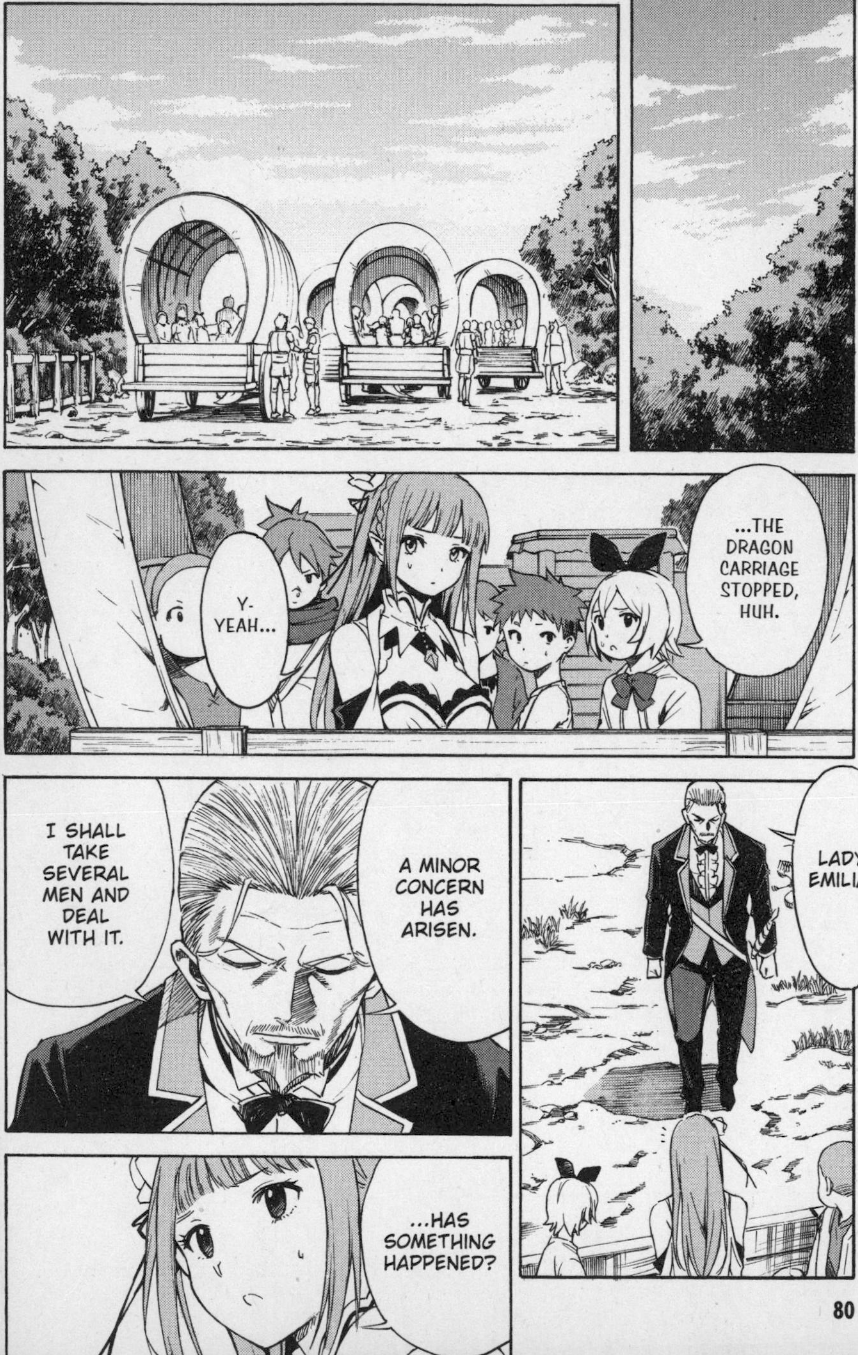
...THE DRAGON CARRIAGE STOPPED, HUH.
Y-YEAH...
LADY EMILIA.
A MINOR CONCERN HAS ARISEN.
I SHALL TAKE SEVERAL MEN AND DEAL WITH IT.
...HAS SOMETHING HAPPENED?

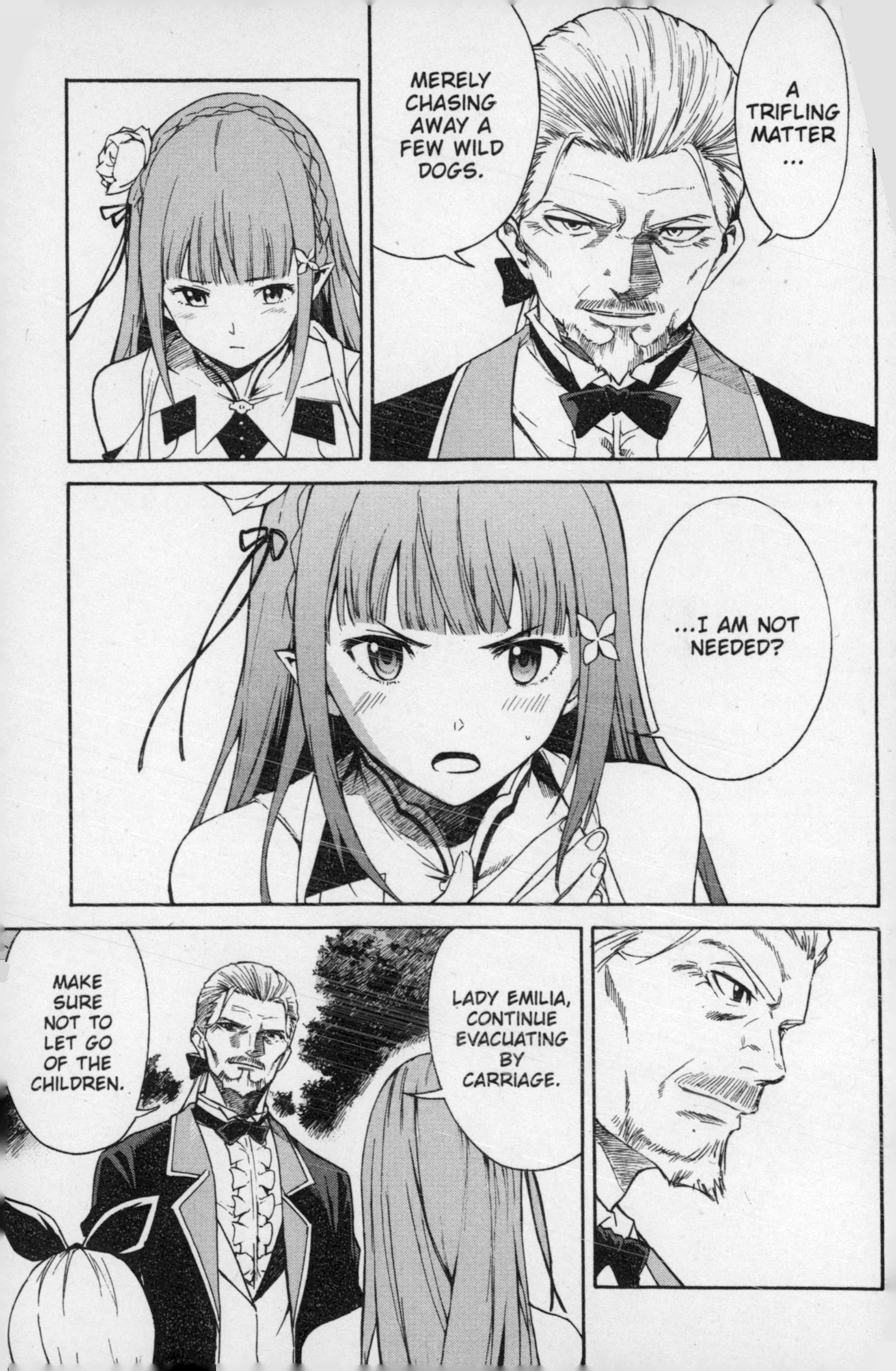
A TRIFLING MATTER ...
MERELY CHASING AWAY A FEW WILD DOGS.
...I AM NOT NEEDED?
LADY EMILIA, CONTINUE EVACUATING BY CARRIAGE.
MAKE SURE NOT TO LET GO OF THE CHILDREN.

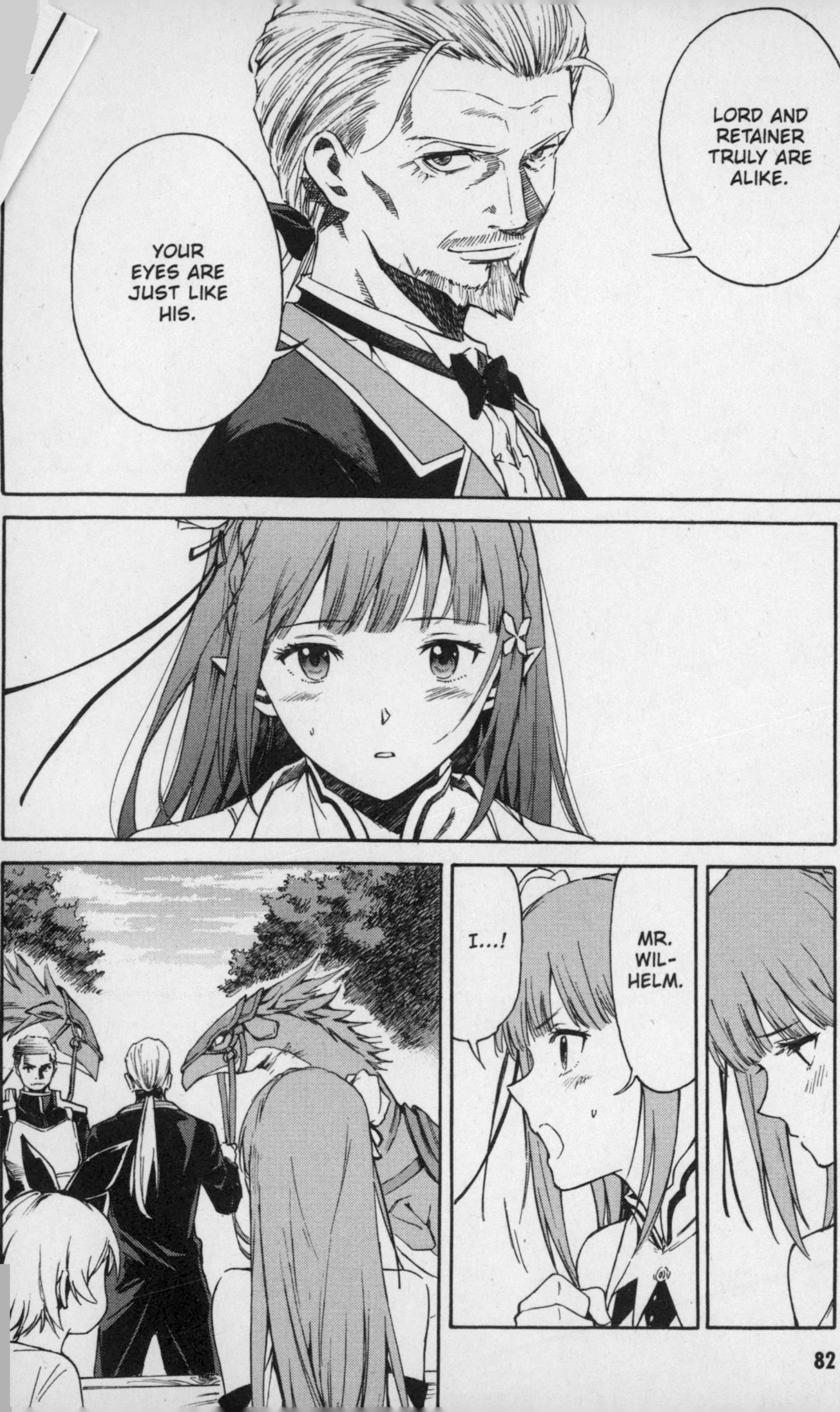
LORD AND RETAINER TRULY ARE ALIKE.
YOUR EYES ARE JUST LIKE HIS.
MR. WIL-HELM.
I...!

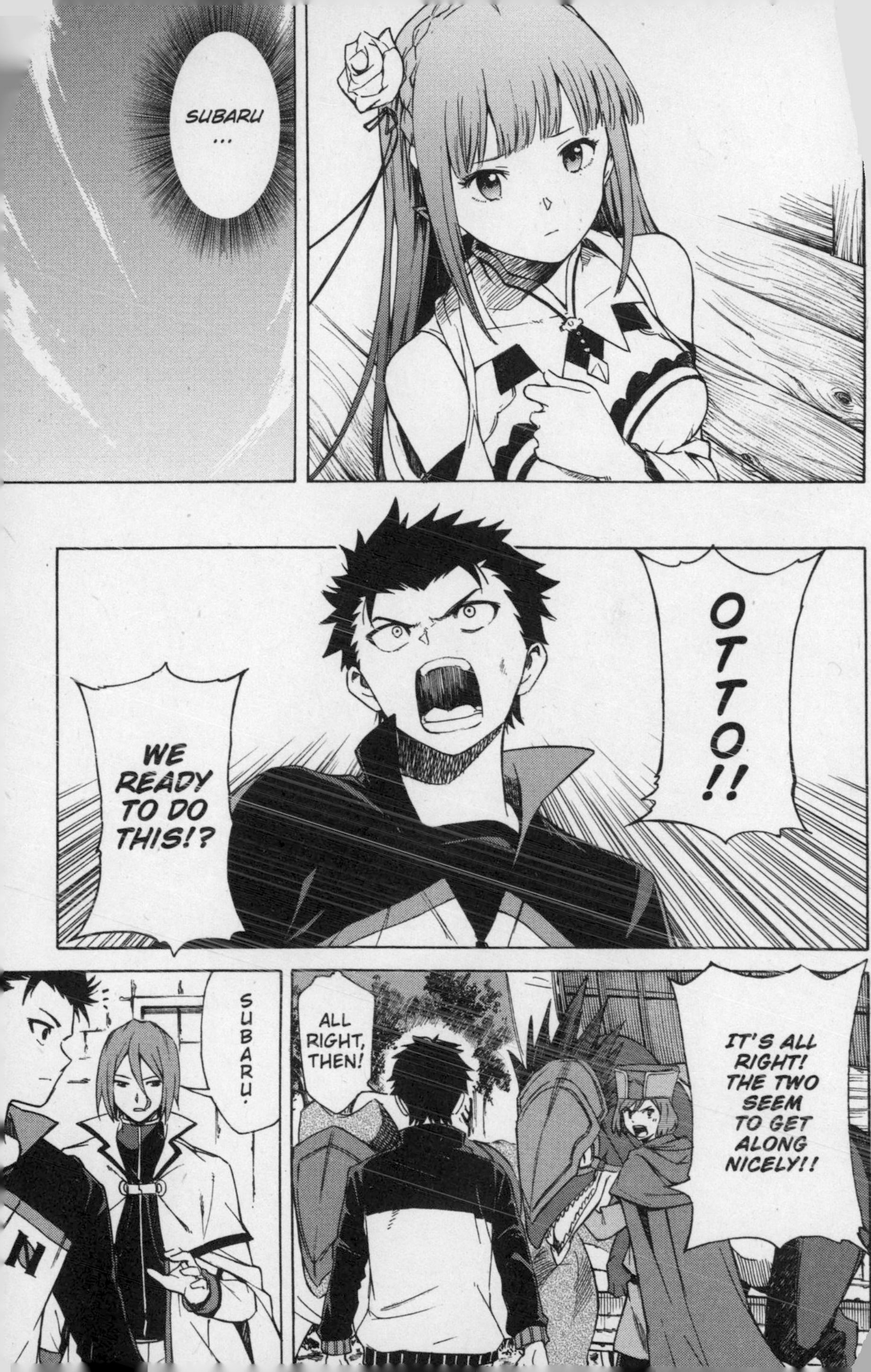
SUBARU ...
OTTO!!
WE READY TO DO THIS!?
IT'S ALL RIGHT! THE TWO SEEM TO GET ALONG NICELY!!
ALL RIGHT, THEN!
SUBARU.

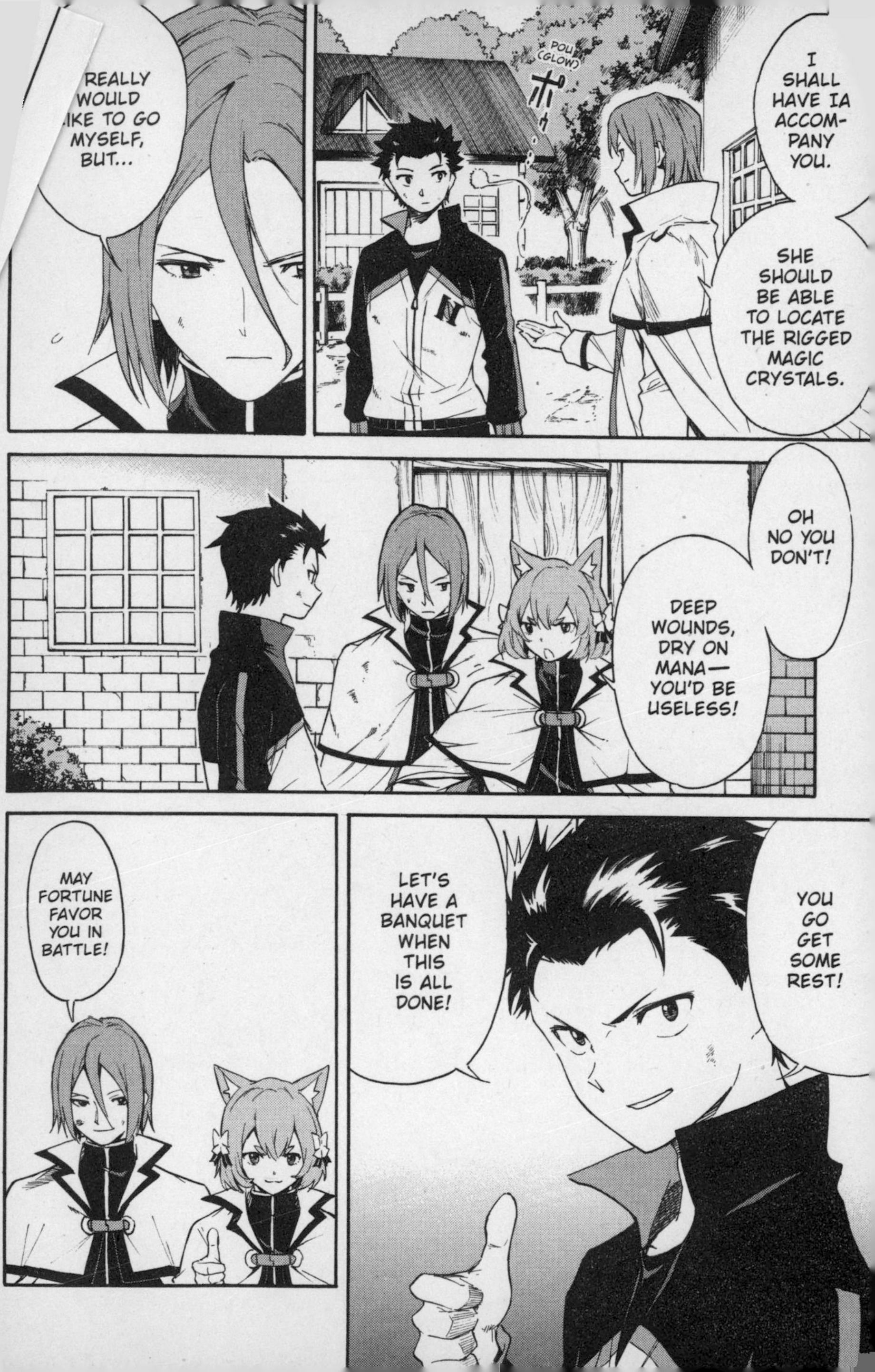
POU (GLOW)
I SHALL HAVE IA ACCOMPANY YOU.
SHE SHOULD BE ABLE TO LOCATE THE RIGGED MAGIC CRYSTALS.
I REALLY WOULD LIKE TO GO MYSELF, BUT...
OH NO YOU DON'T!
DEEP WOUNDS, DRY ON MANA—YOU'D BE USELESS!
YOU GO GET SOME REST!
LET'S HAVE A BANQUET WHEN THIS IS ALL DONE!
MAY FORTUNE FAVOR YOU IN BATTLE!

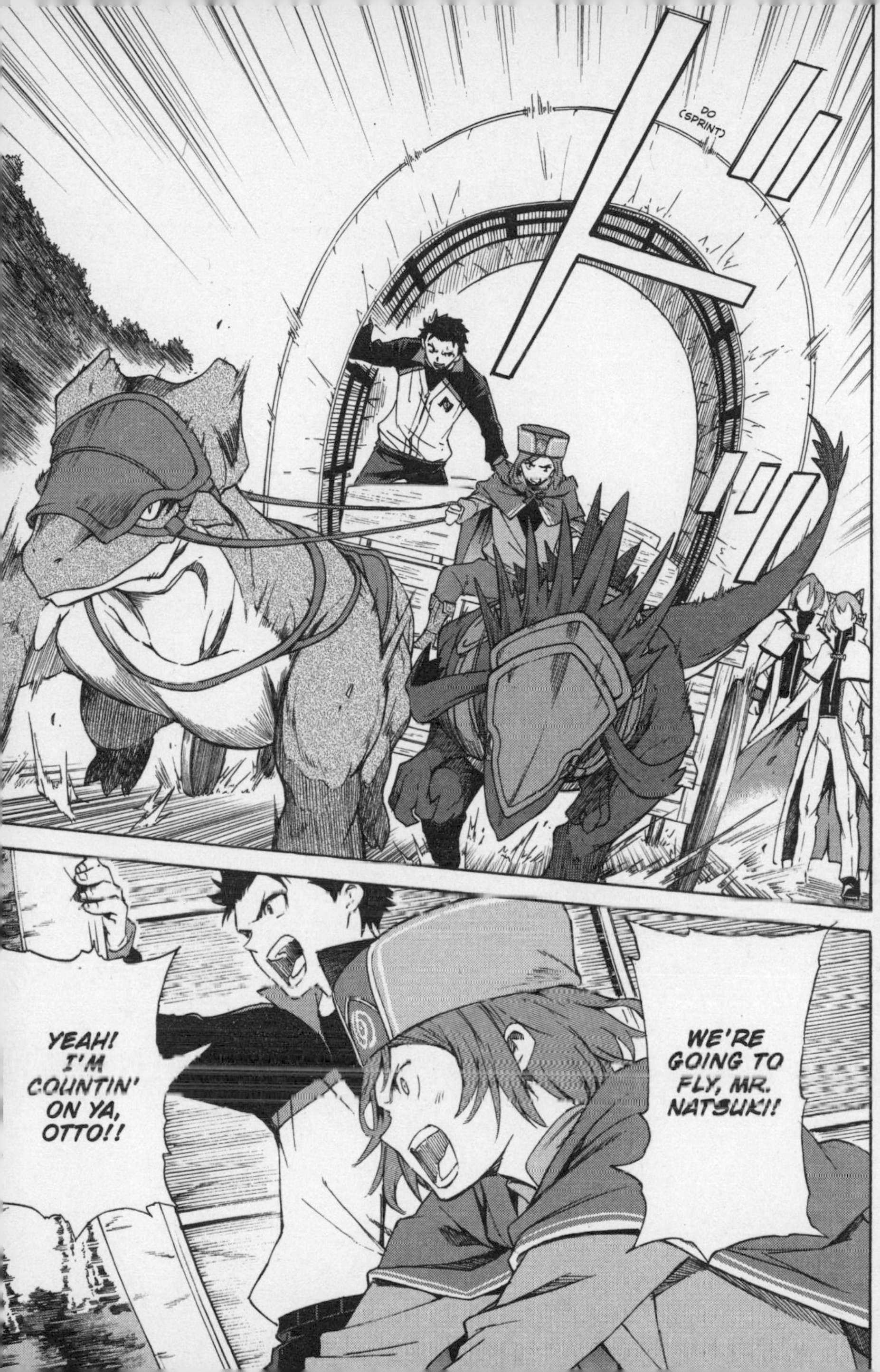
DO (SPRINT)
WE'RE GOING TO FLY, MR. NATSUKI!
YEAH! I'M COUNTIN' ON YA, OTTO!!

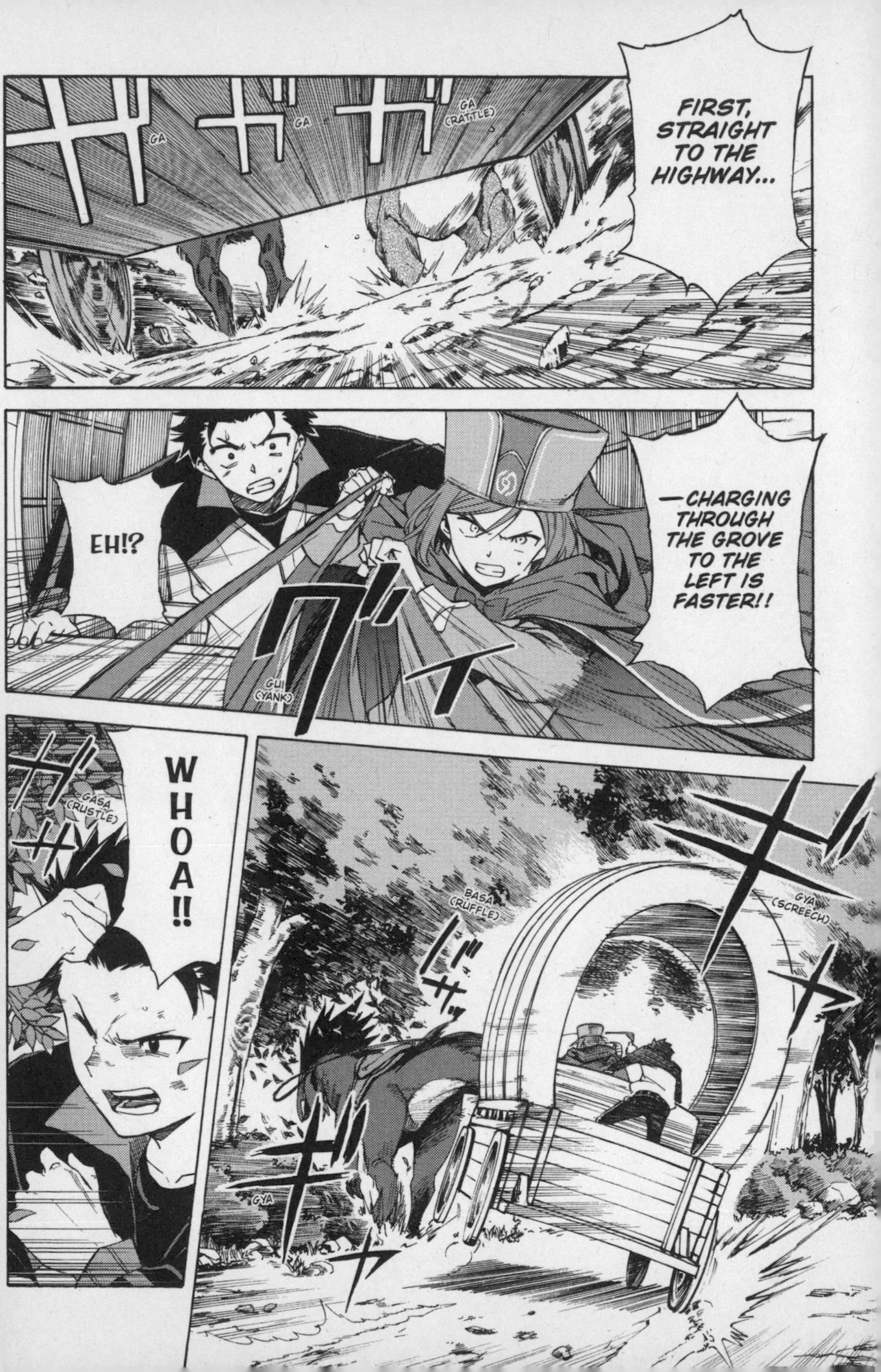
FIRST, STRAIGHT TO THE HIGHWAY...
GA (RATTLE)
GA
GA
—CHARGING THROUGH THE GROVE TO THE LEFT IS FASTER!!
EH!?
GUI (YANK)
GYA (SCREECH)
BASA (RUFFLE)
GYA
WHOA!!
GASA (RUSTLE)

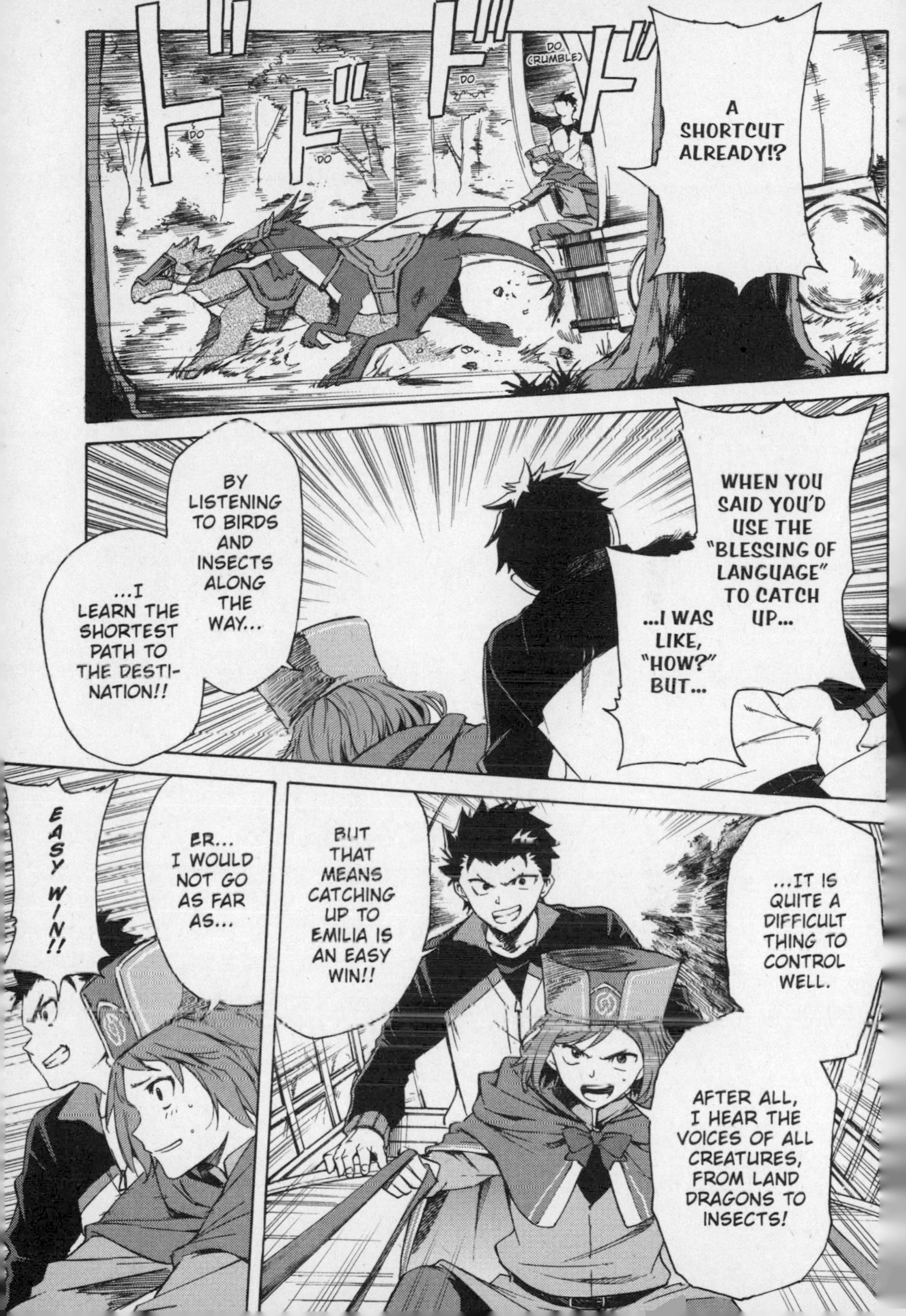
DO (RUMBLE)
DO
DO
DO
A SHORTCUT ALREADY!?
WHEN YOU SAID YOU'D USE THE "BLESSING OF LANGUAGE" TO CATCH UP...
...I WAS LIKE, "HOW?" BUT...
BY LISTENING TO BIRDS AND INSECTS ALONG THE WAY...
...I LEARN THE SHORTEST PATH TO THE DESTINATION!!
...IT IS QUITE A DIFFICULT THING TO CONTROL WELL.
AFTER ALL, I HEAR THE VOICES OF ALL CREATURES, FROM LAND DRAGONS TO INSECTS!
BUT THAT MEANS CATCHING UP TO EMILIA IS AN EASY WIN!!
ER... I WOULD NOT GO AS FAR AS...
EASY WIN!!

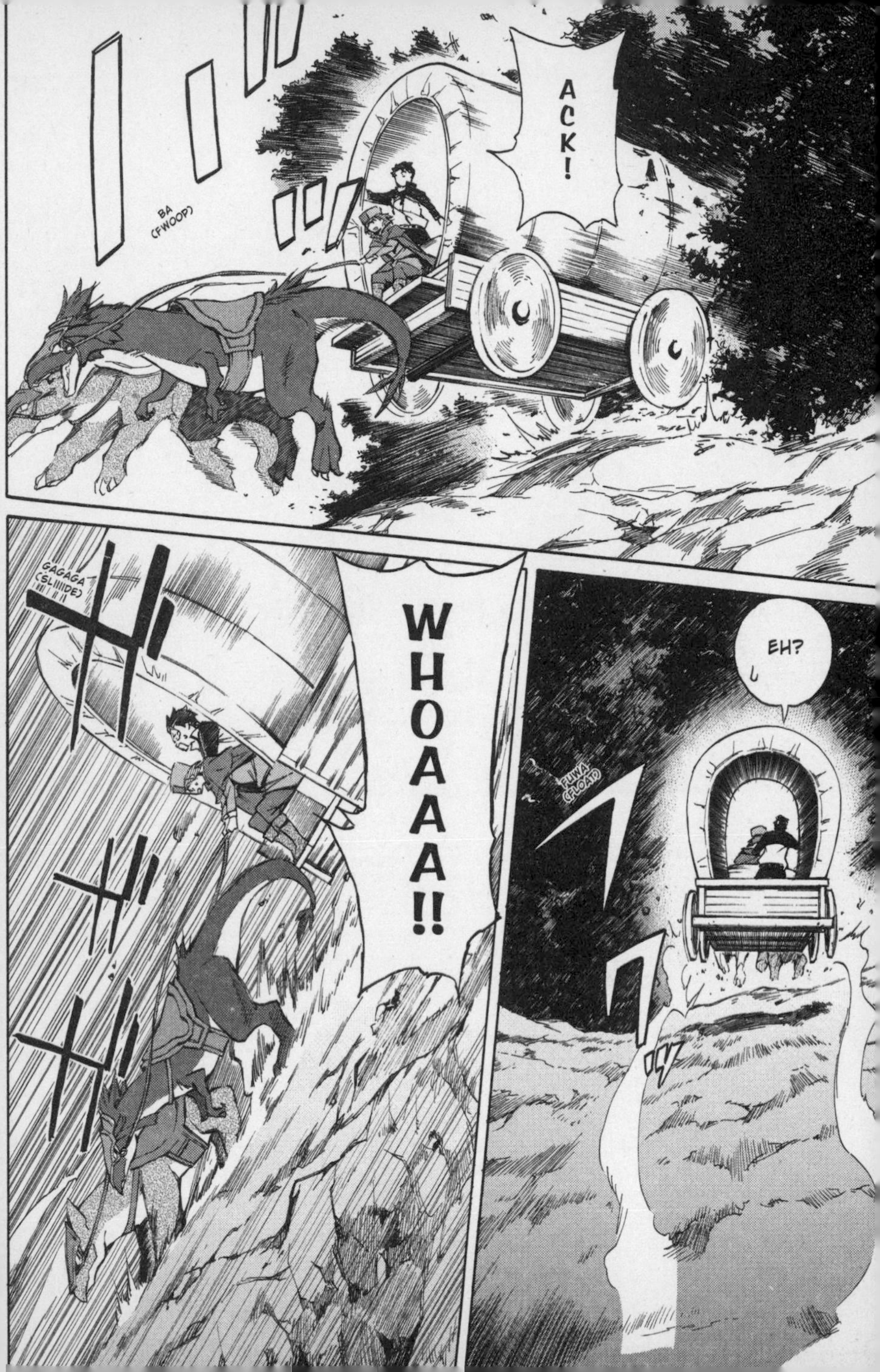
ACK!
BA (FWOOP)
EH?
FUWA (FLOAT)
WHOAAA!!
GAGAGA (SLIIIDE)

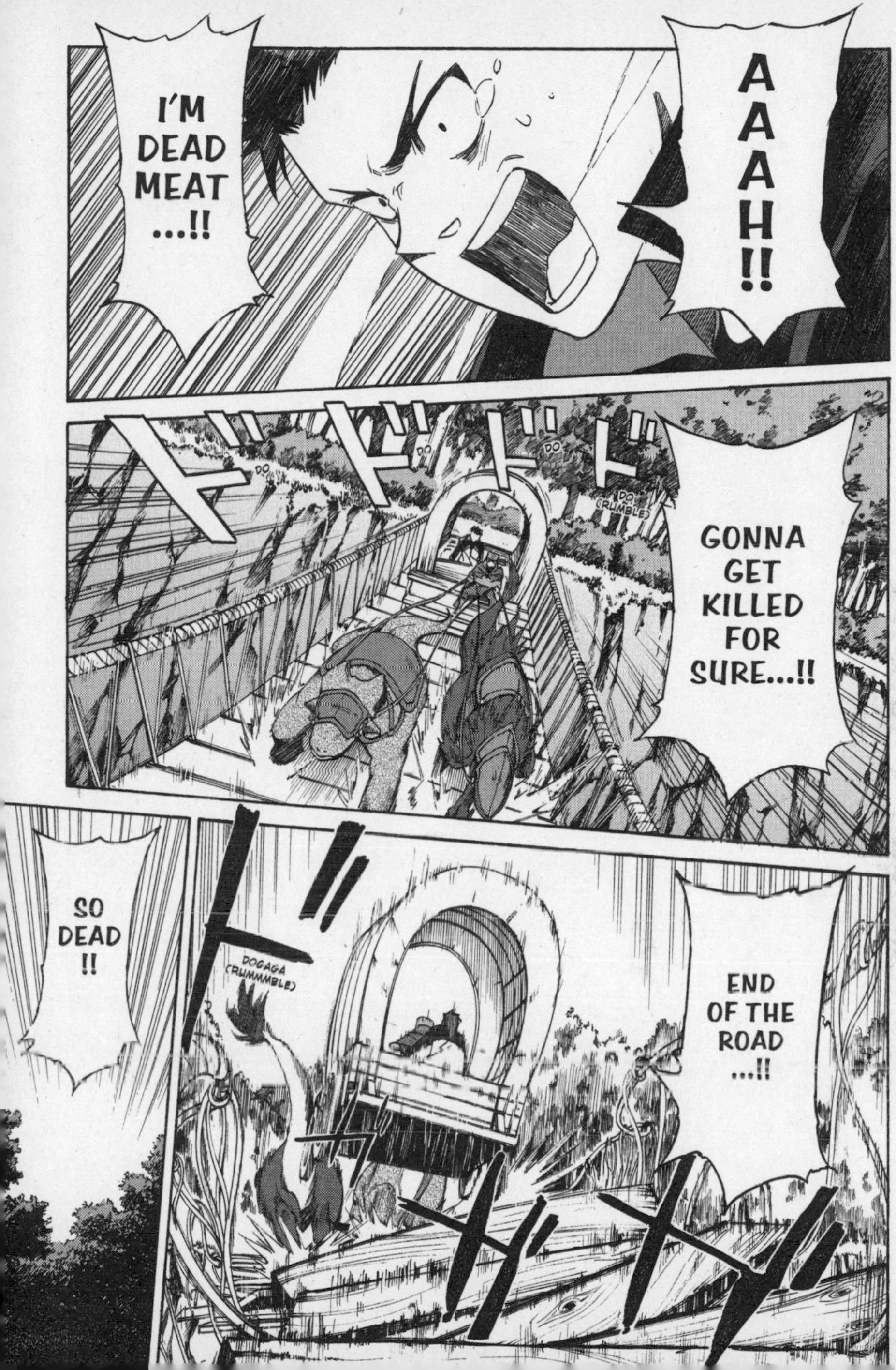
AAAAH!!
I'M DEAD MEAT...!!
DO DO DO DO (RUMBLE)
GONNA GET KILLED FOR SURE...!!
END OF THE ROAD...!!
DOGAGA (RUMMMBLE)
SO DEAD!!

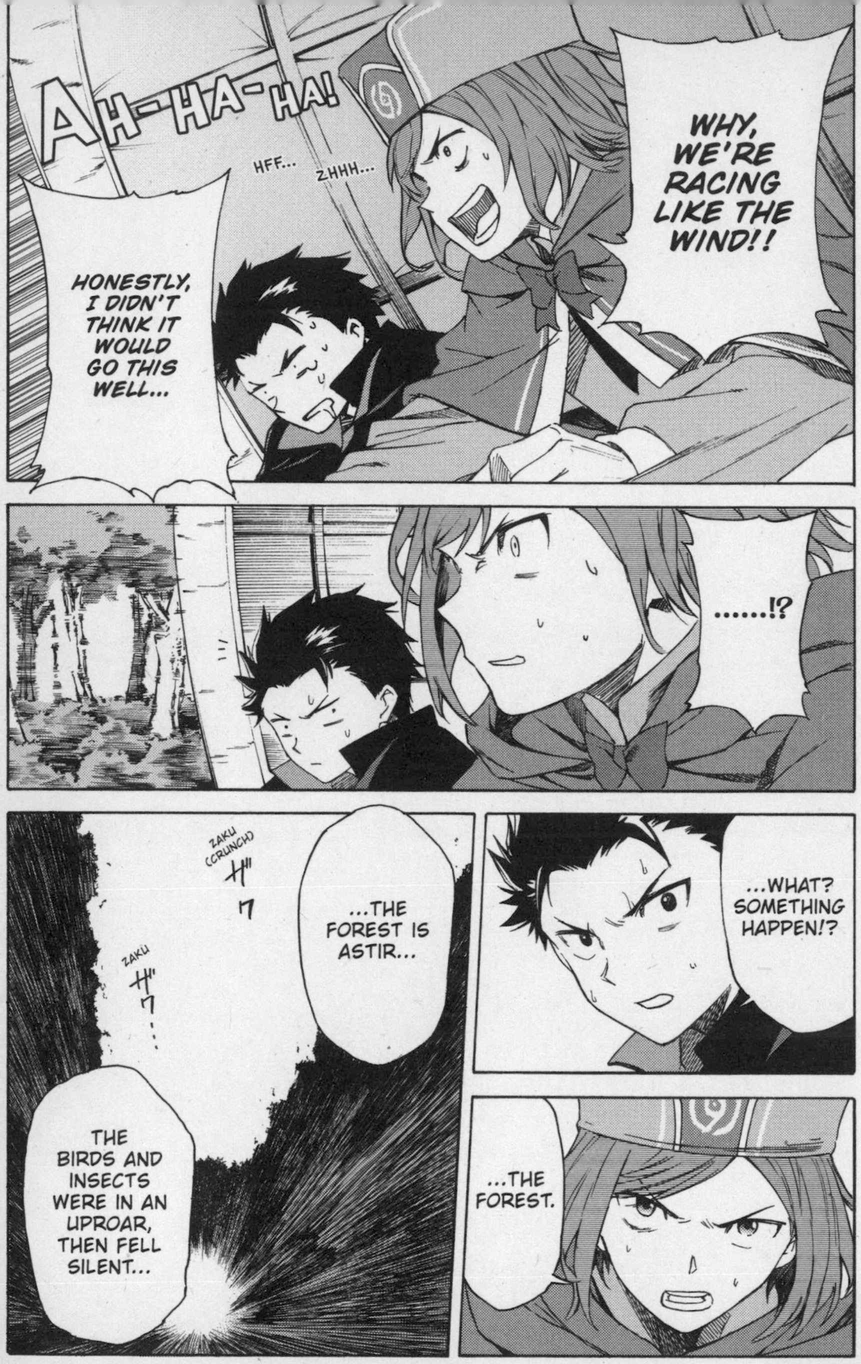
WHY, WE'RE RACING LIKE THE WIND!!
AH-HA-HA!
ZHHH...
HFF...
HONESTLY, I DIDN'T THINK IT WOULD GO THIS WELL...
......!?
...WHAT? SOMETHING HAPPEN!?
...THE FOREST.
...THE FOREST IS ASTIR...
ZAKU (CRUNCH)
ZAKU
THE BIRDS AND INSECTS WERE IN AN UPROAR, THEN FELL SILENT...

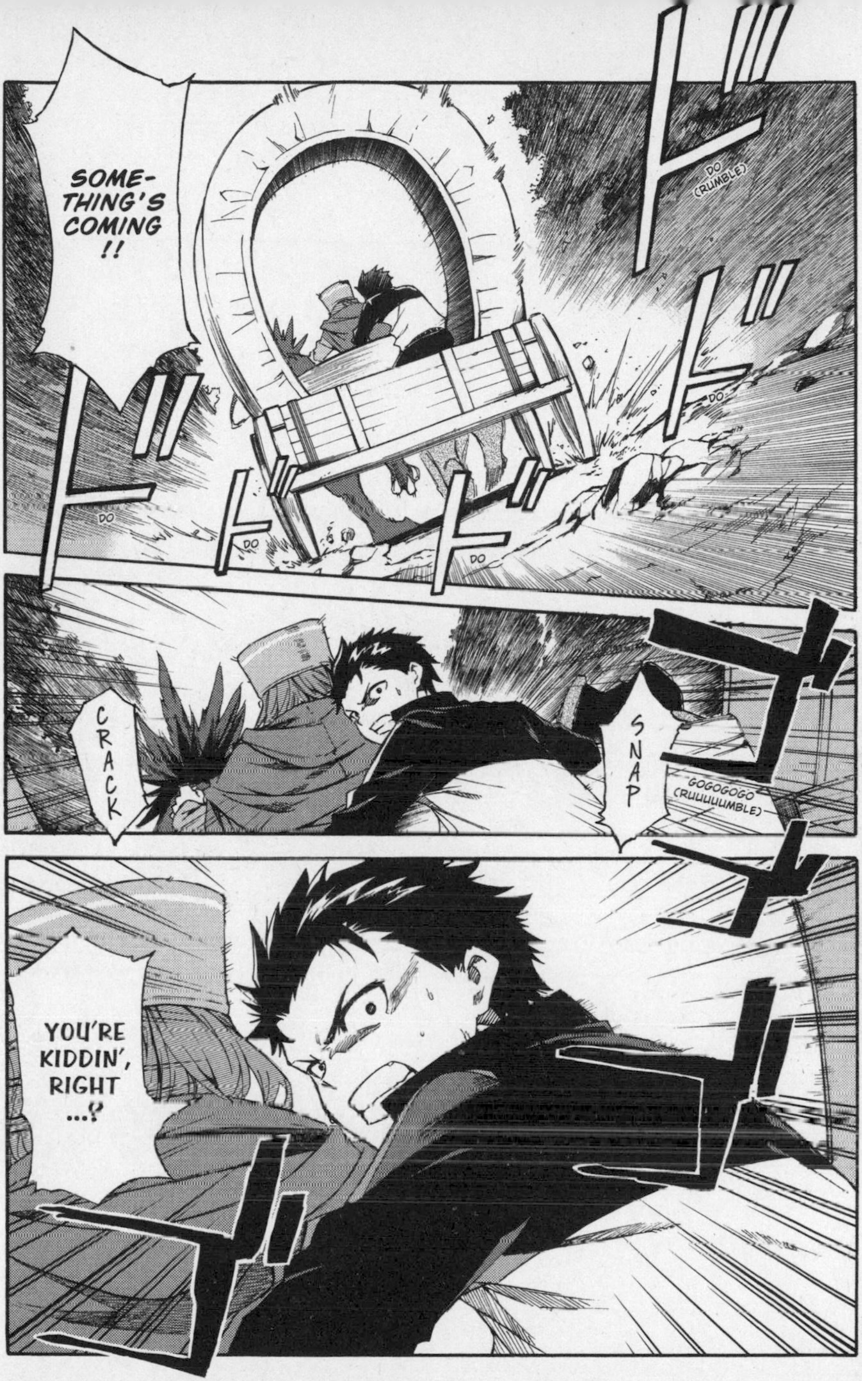
DO (RUMBLE)
SOME-THING'S COMING!!
DO
DO
DO
DO
GOGOGOGO (RUUUUUUMBLE)
SNAP
CRACK
YOU'RE KIDDIN', RIGHT ...!?

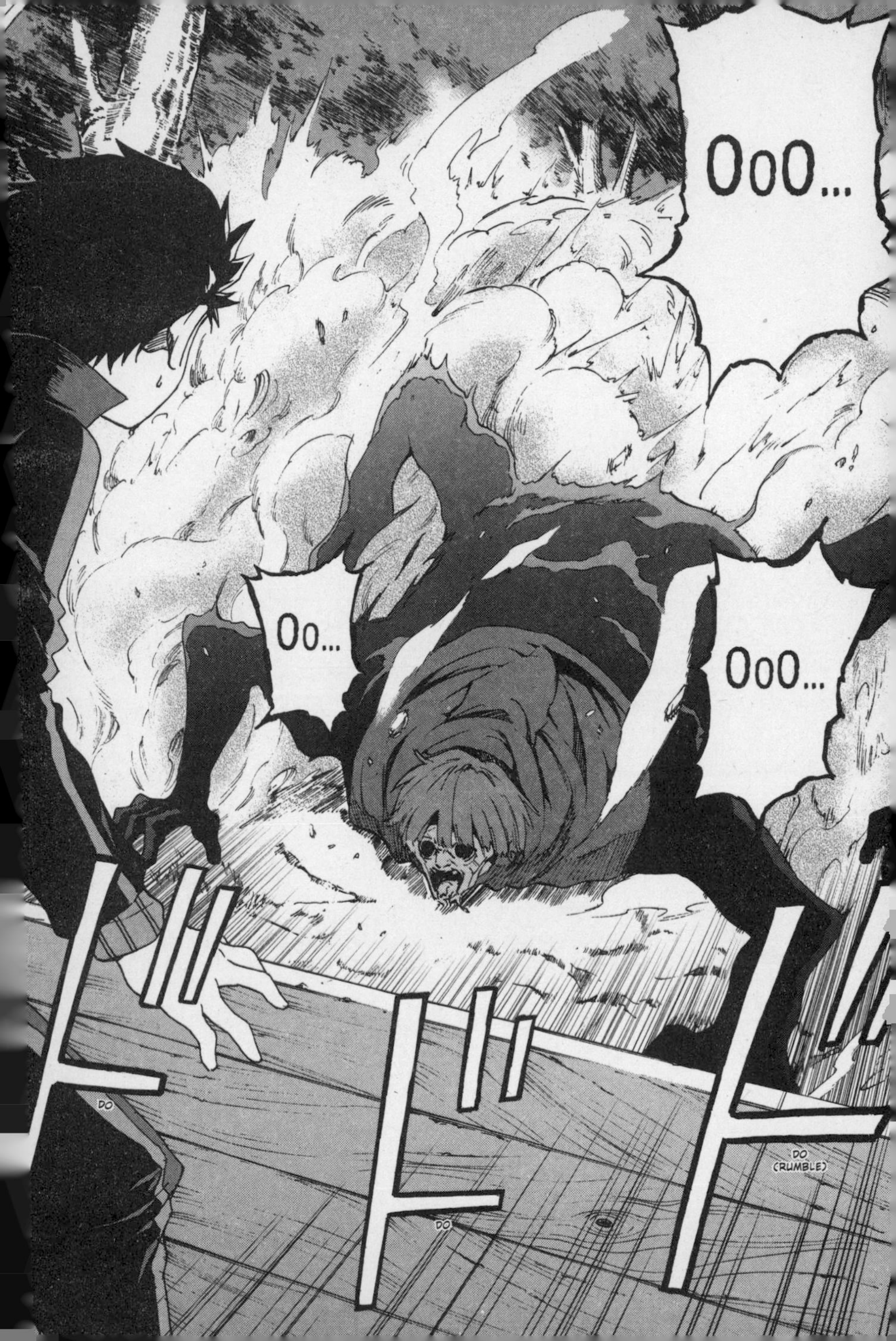
OoO...
OoO...
Oo...
DO (RUMBLE)
DO
DO

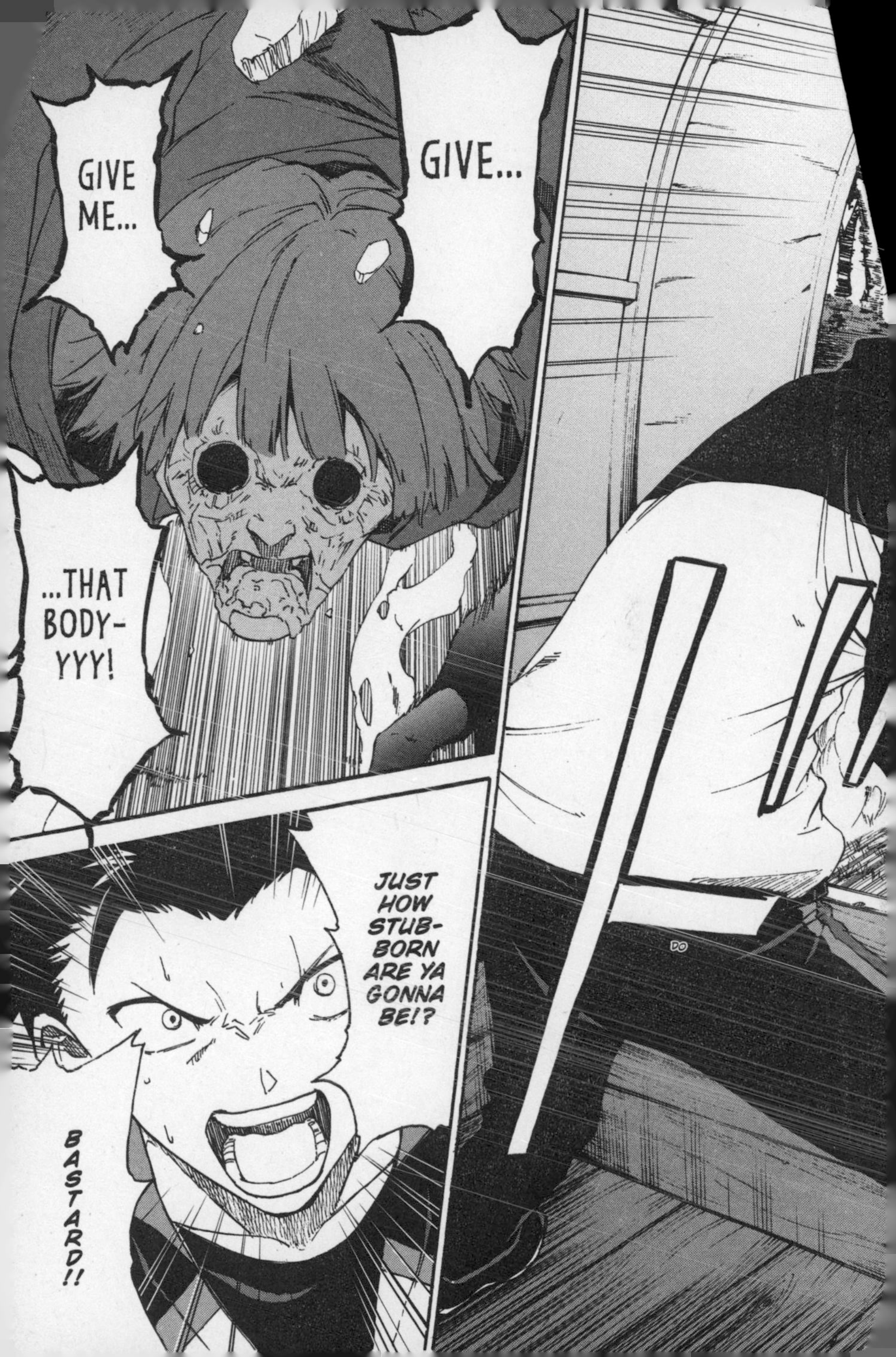
DO
GIVE...
GIVE ME...
...THAT BODY-YYY!
JUST HOW STUBBORN ARE YA GONNA BE!?
BASTARD!!

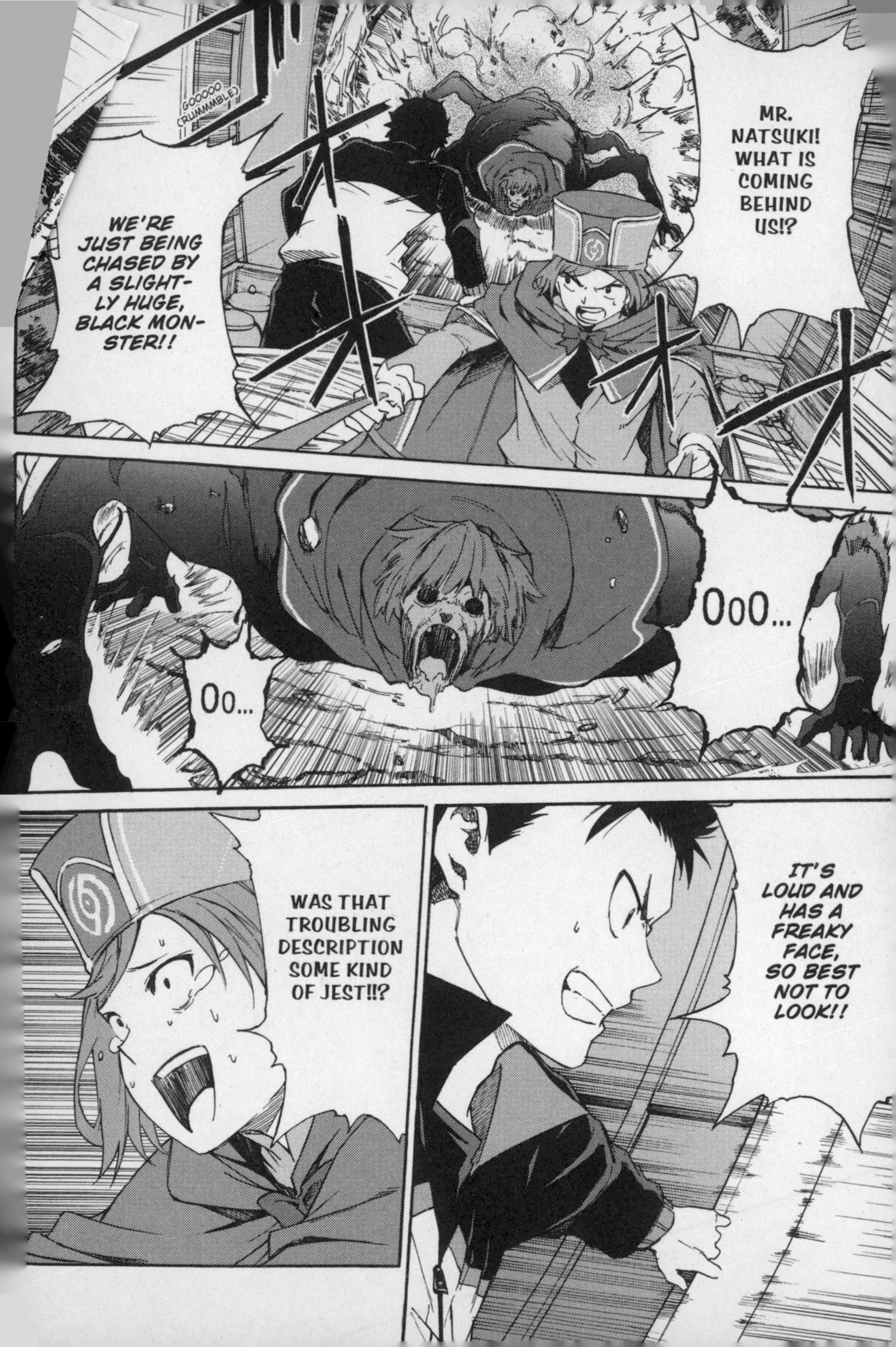
MR. NATSUKI! WHAT IS COMING BEHIND US!?
GOOOOO (RUMMMBLE)
WE'RE JUST BEING CHASED BY A SLIGHT-LY HUGE, BLACK MON-STER!!
OoO...
Oo...
IT'S LOUD AND HAS A FREAKY FACE, SO BEST NOT TO LOOK!!
WAS THAT TROUBLING DESCRIPTION SOME KIND OF JEST!!?

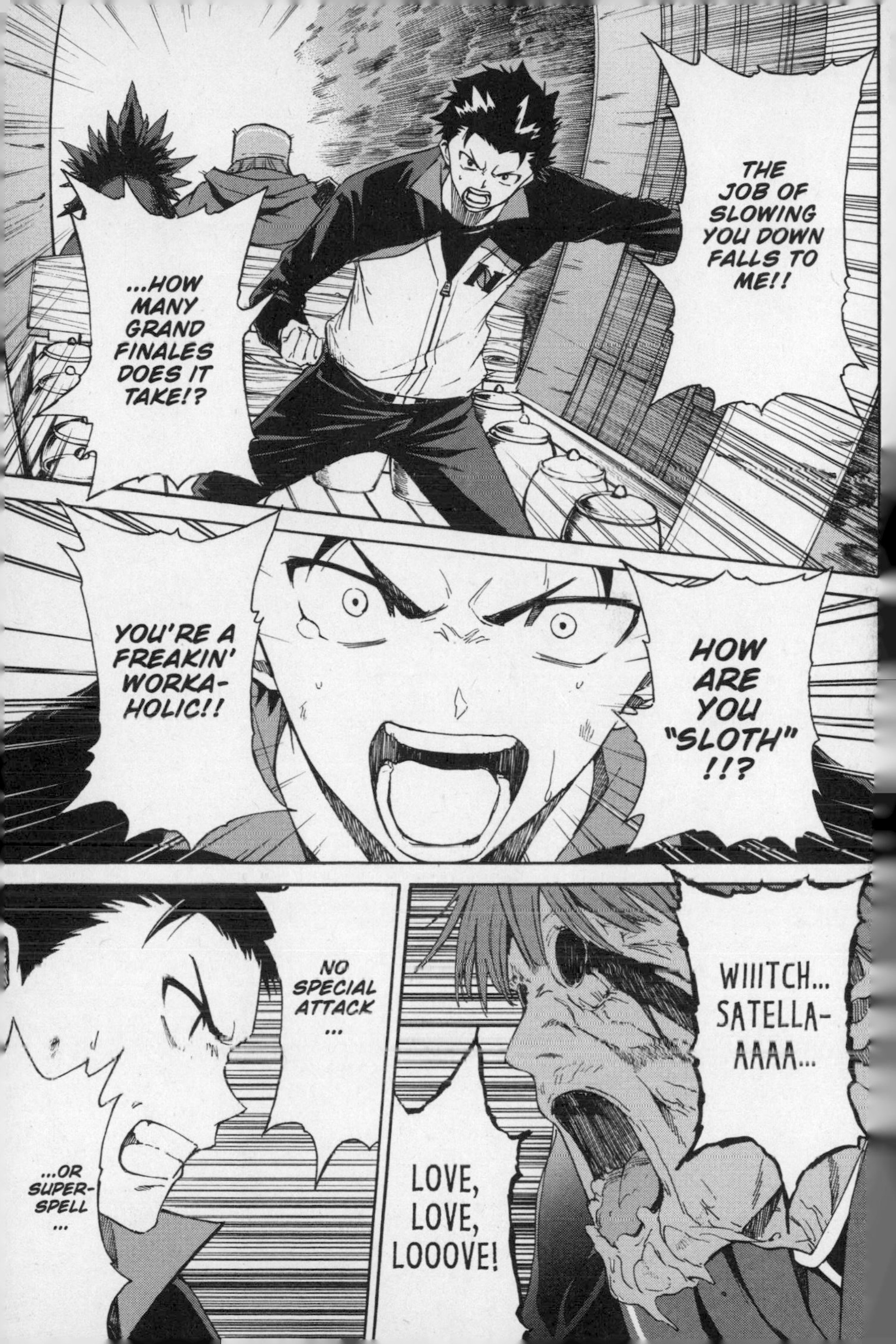
THE JOB OF SLOWING YOU DOWN FALLS TO ME!!
...HOW MANY GRAND FINALES DOES IT TAKE!?
HOW ARE YOU "SLOTH" !!?
YOU'RE A FREAKIN' WORKA-HOLIC!!
WIIITCH... SATELLA-AAAA...
LOVE, LOVE, LOOOVE!
NO SPECIAL ATTACK ...
...OR SUPER-SPELL ...

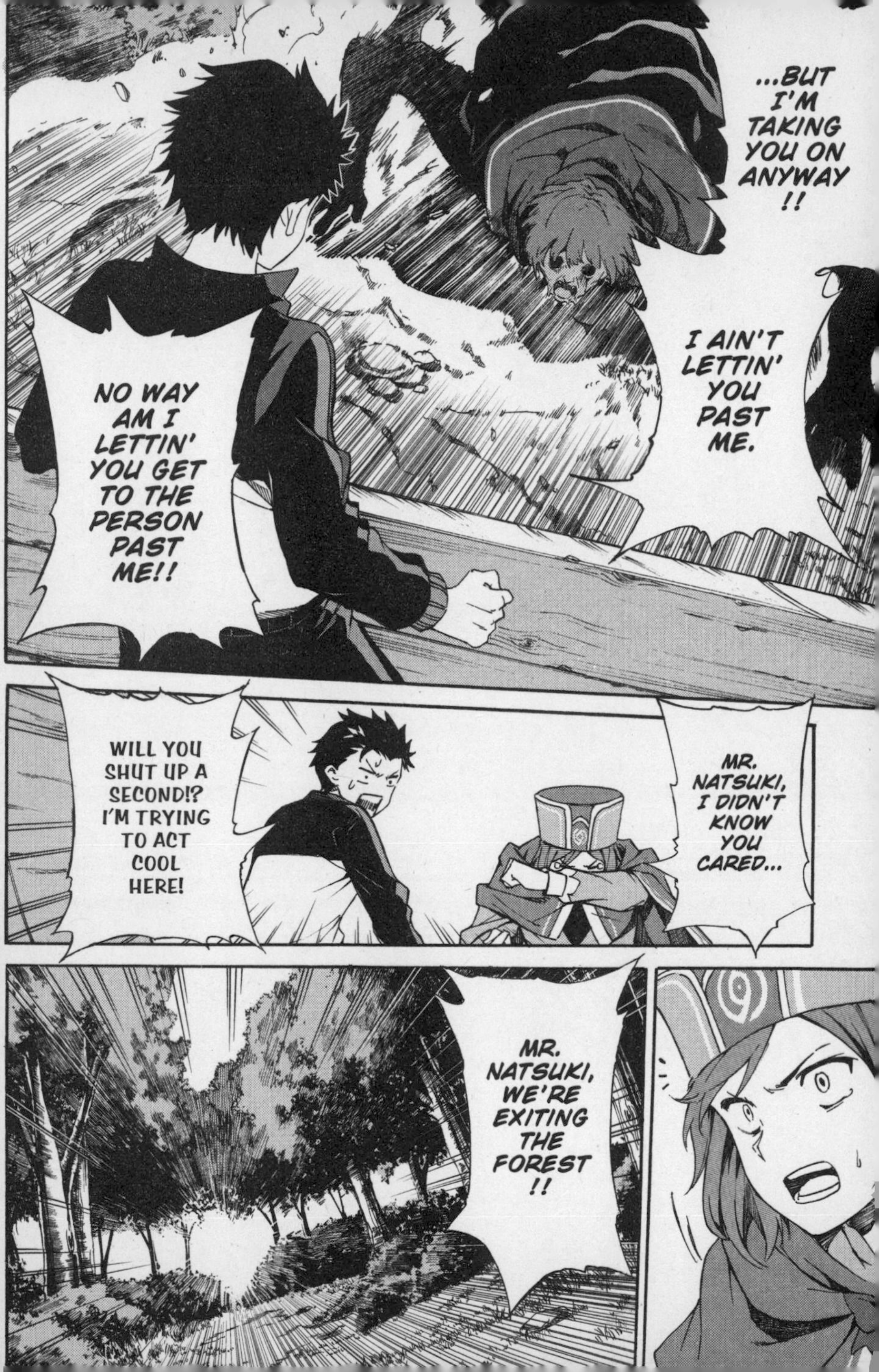
...BUT I'M TAKING YOU ON ANYWAY!!
I AIN'T LETTIN' YOU PAST ME.
NO WAY AM I LETTIN' YOU GET TO THE PERSON PAST ME!!
MR. NATSUKI, I DIDN'T KNOW YOU CARED...
WILL YOU SHUT UP A SECOND!? I'M TRYING TO ACT COOL HERE!
MR. NATSUKI, WE'RE EXITING THE FOREST!!

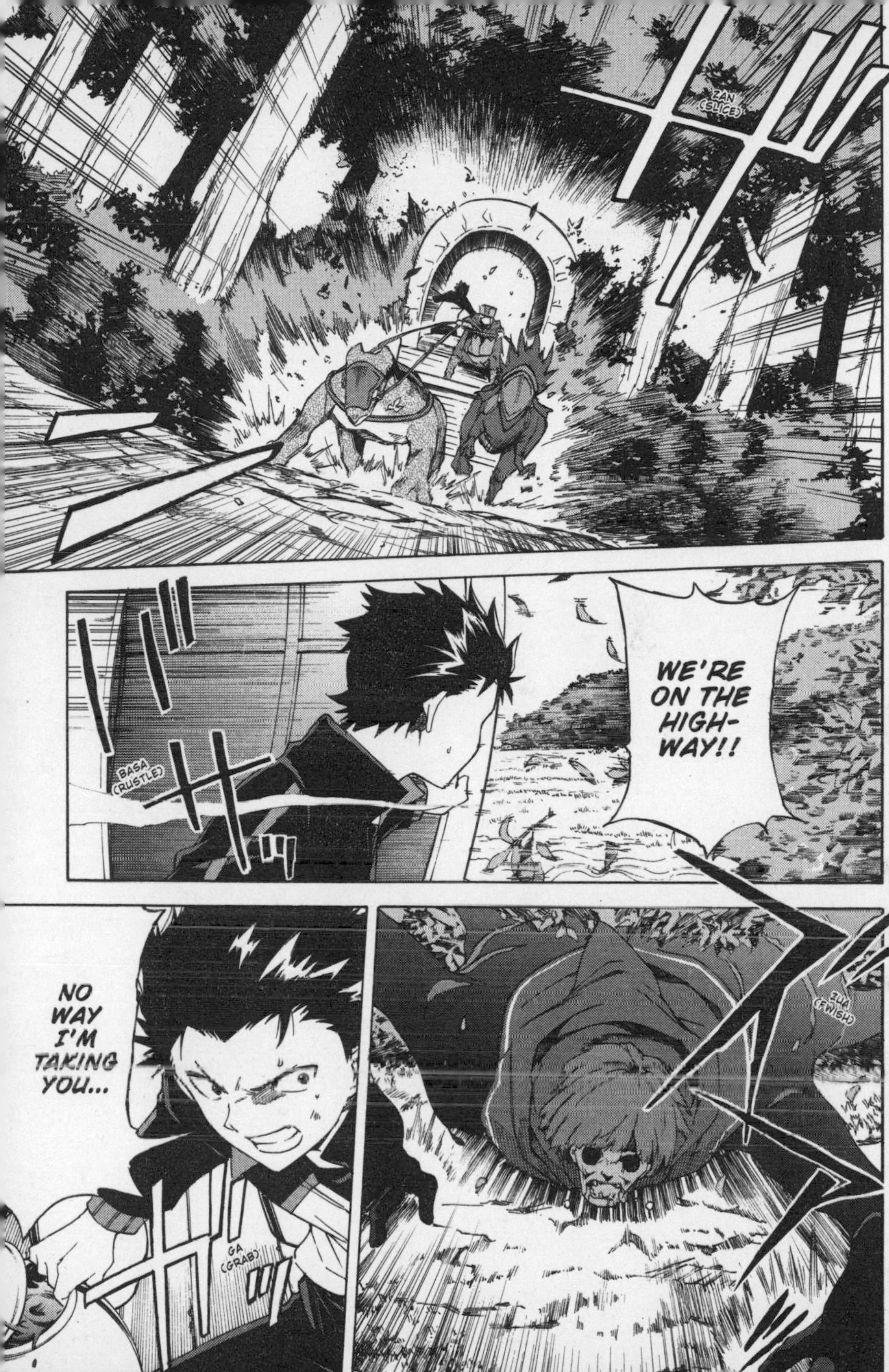
ZAN (SLICE)
WE'RE ON THE HIGHWAY!!
BASA (RUSTLE)
ZUA (FWISH)
NO WAY I'M TAKING YOU...
GA (GRAB)

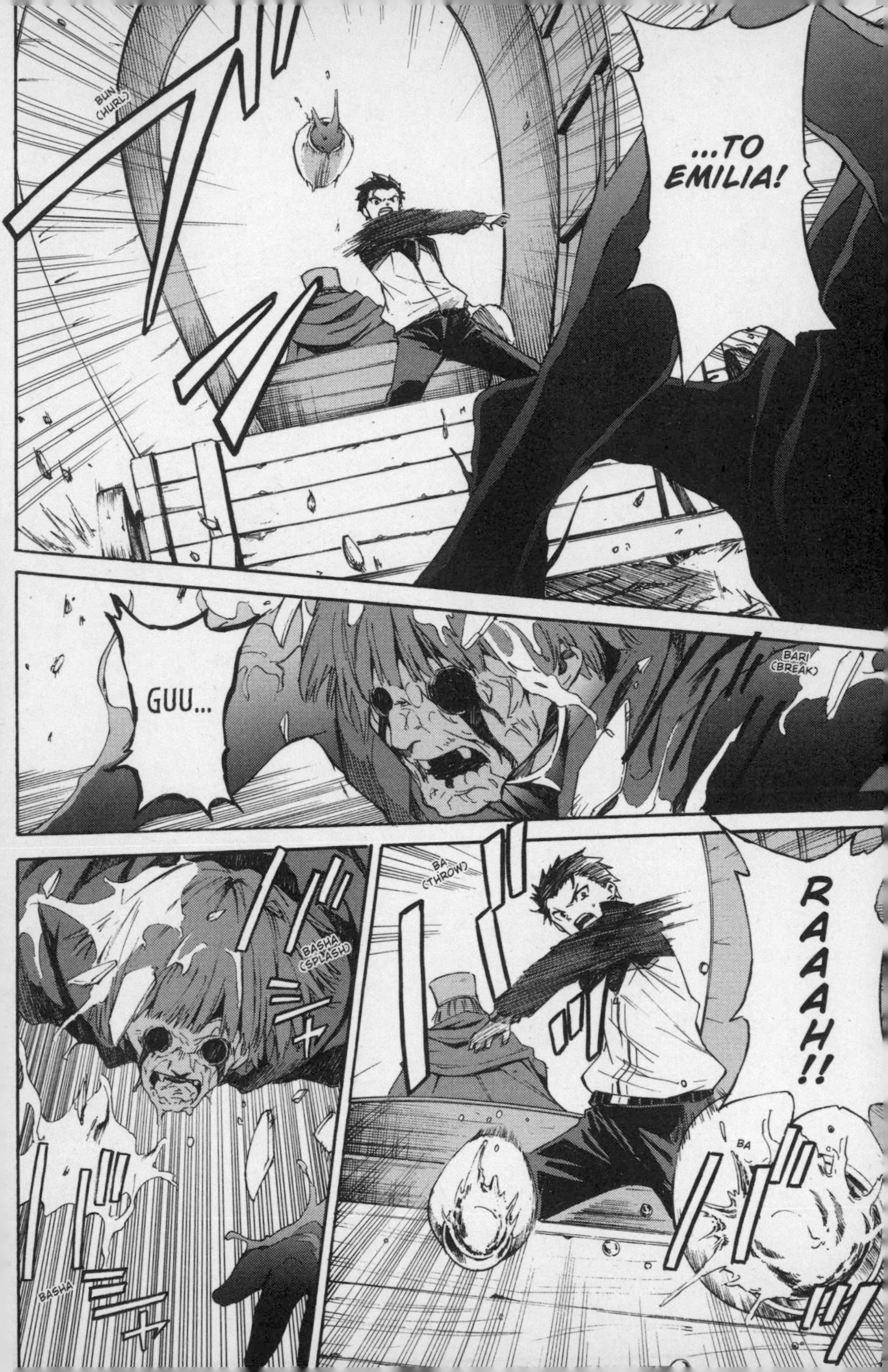
...TO EMILIA!
BUN (HURL)
BARI (BREAK)
GUU...
RAAAAH!!
BA (THROW)
BA
BASHA (SPLASH)
BASHA

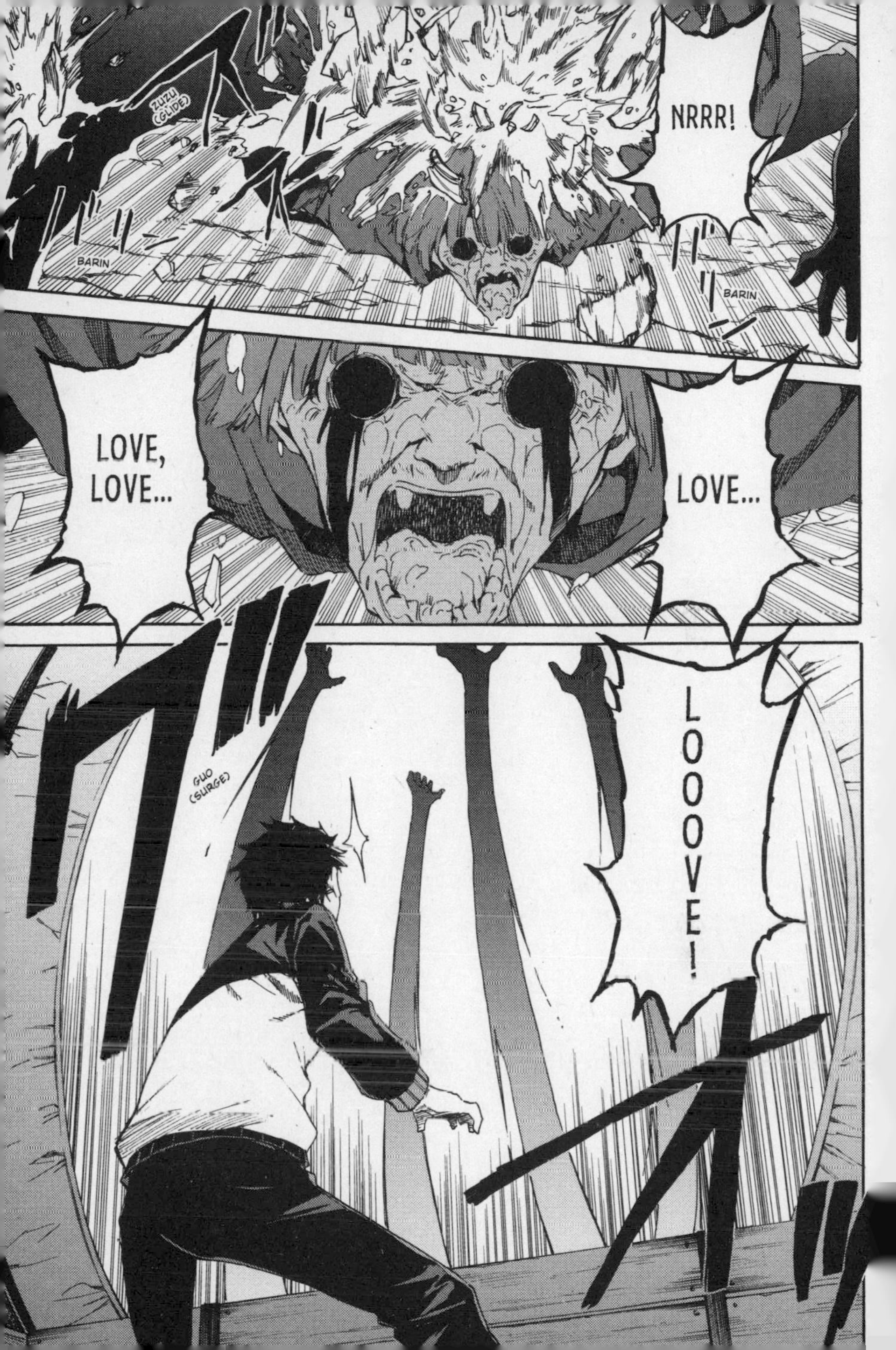
NRRR!
ZUZU (GLIDE)
BARIN
BARIN
LOVE...
LOVE, LOVE...
LOOOVE!
GUO (SURGE)

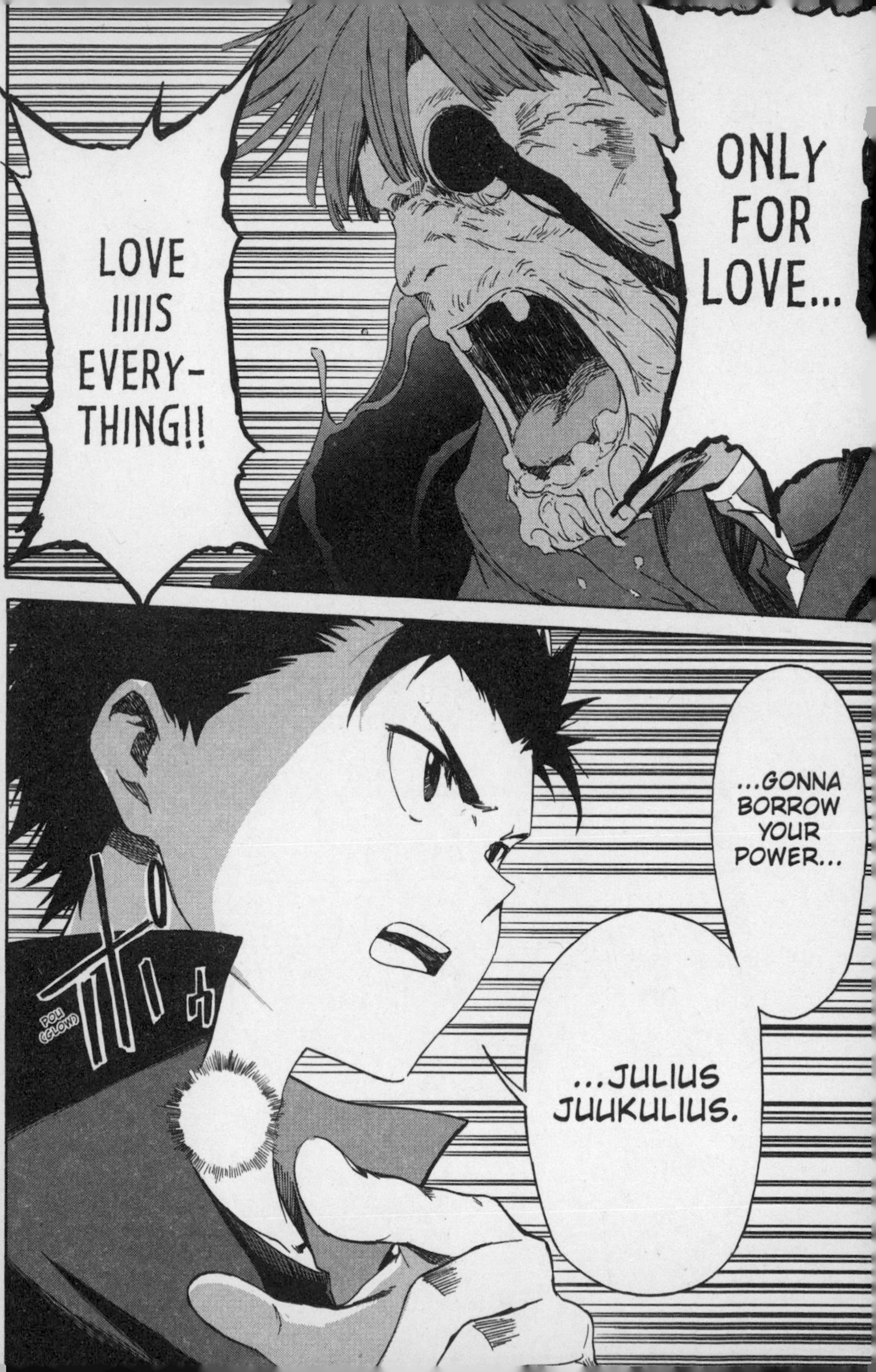
ONLY FOR LOVE...
LOVE IIIIS EVERY-THING!!
...GONNA BORROW YOUR POWER...
...JULIUS JUUKULIUS.
POU (GLOW)

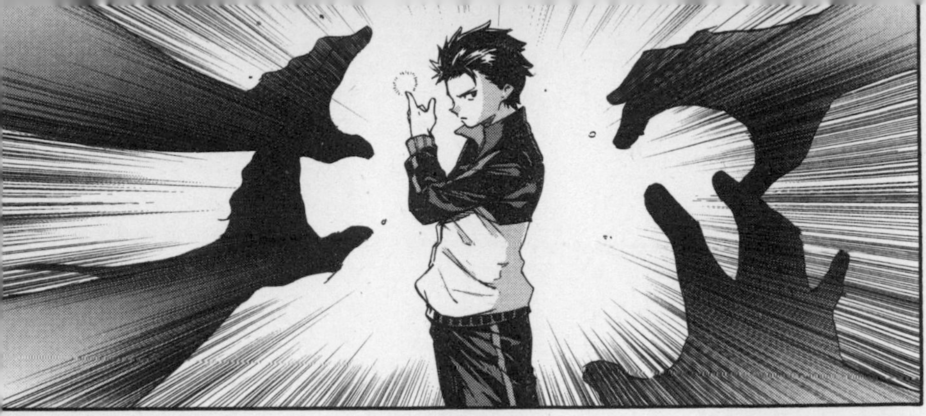
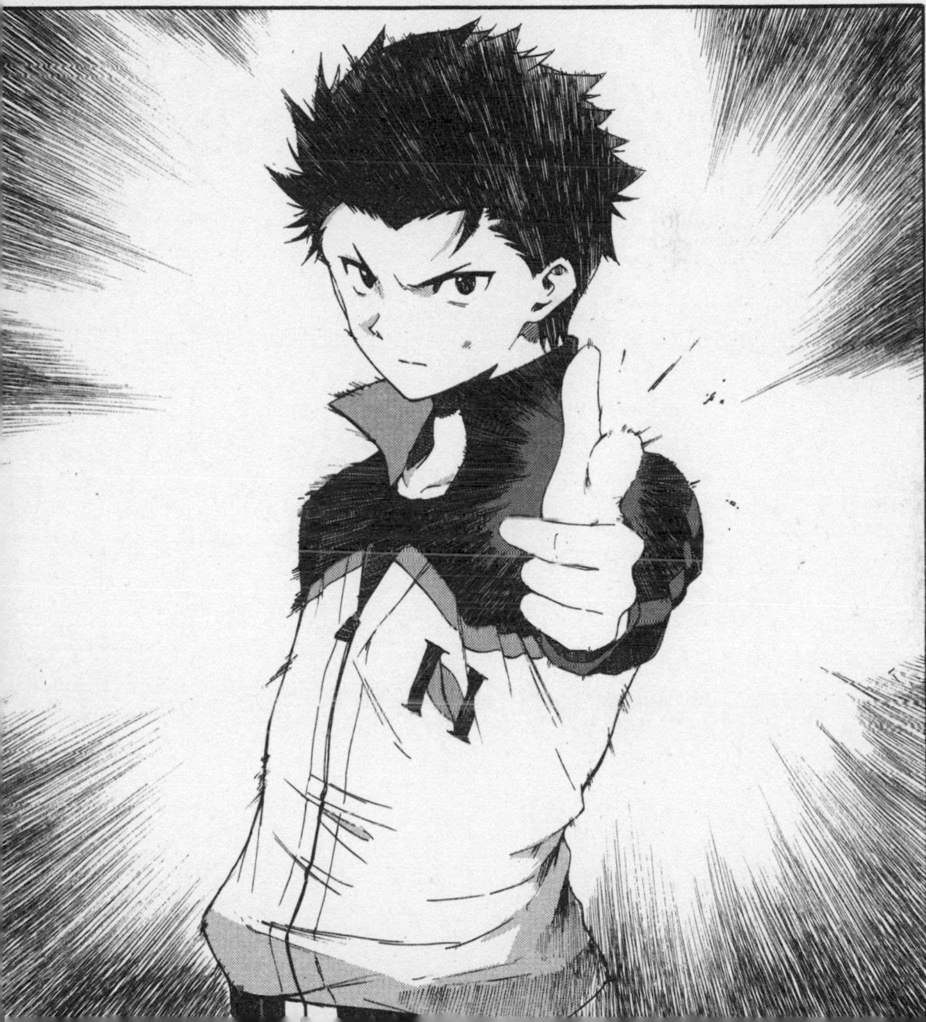

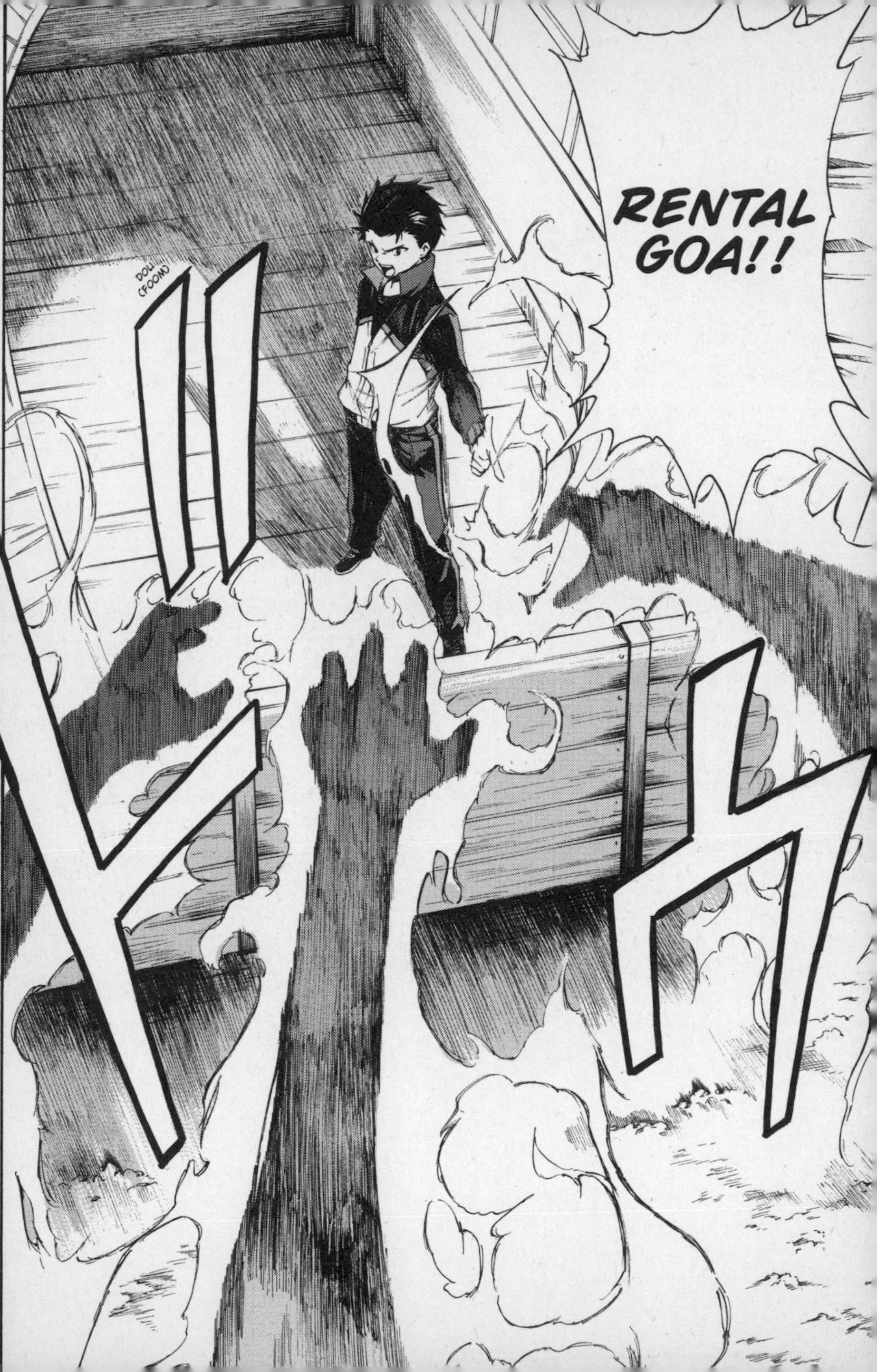
RENTAL GOA!!
DOU
(FOOM)

Re:ZERO -Starting Life in Another World-

The only ability Subaru Natsuki gets when he's summoned to another world is
time travel via his own death. But to save her, he'll die as many times as it takes.

Truth of Zero

The only ability Subaru Natsuki gets when he's
summoned to another world is time travel via his own
death. But to save her, he'll die as many times as it takes.

Re:ZERO -Starting
Life in Another World-

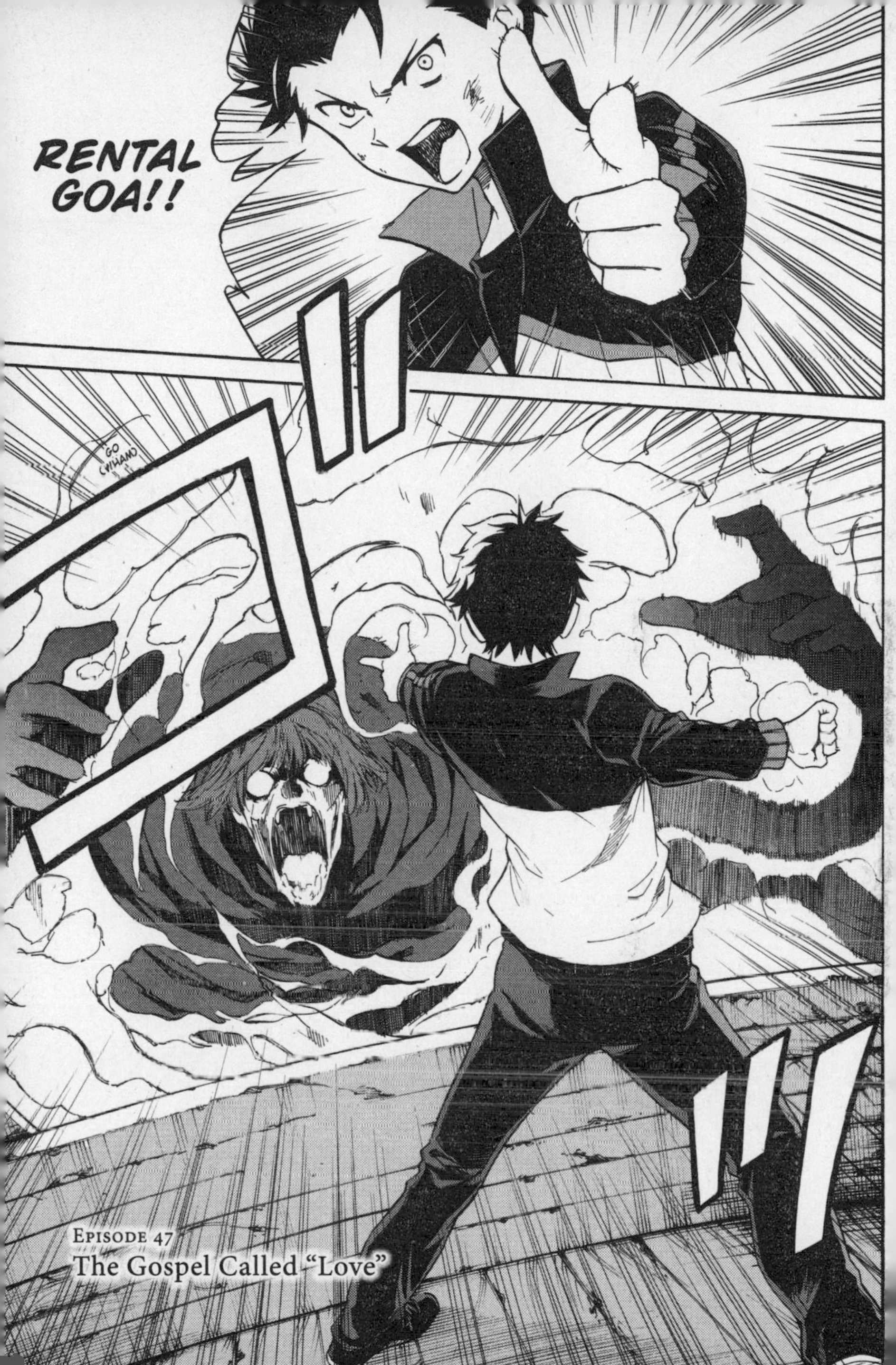
RENTAL GOA!!
GO (WHAM)

Episode 47
The Gospel Called "Love"

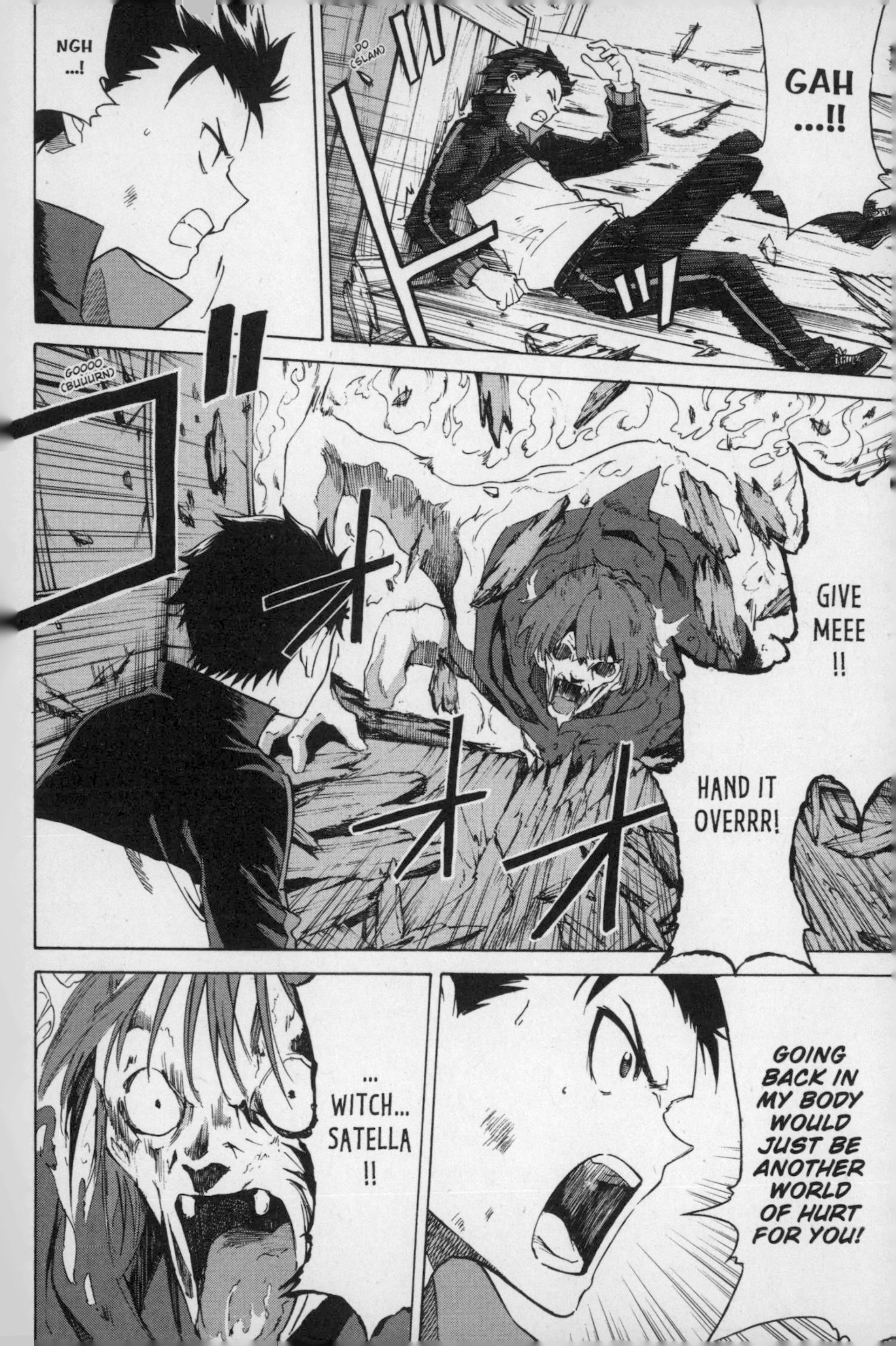
GAH ...!!
DO (SLAM)
NGH ...!
GOOOO (BUUURN)
GIVE MEEE !!
HAND IT OVERRR!
GOING BACK IN MY BODY WOULD JUST BE ANOTHER WORLD OF HURT FOR YOU!
... WITCH... SATELLA !!

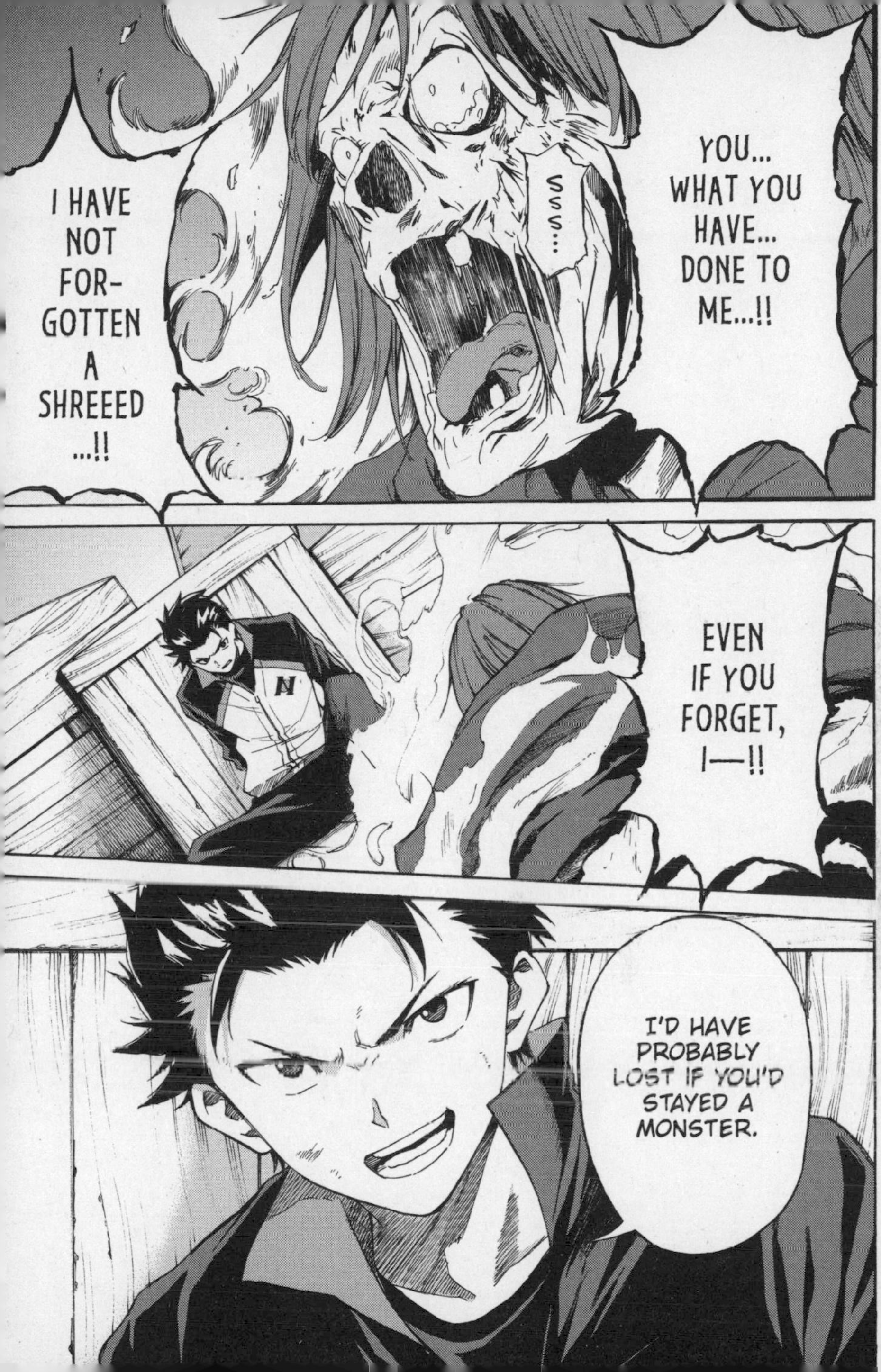
YOU... WHAT YOU HAVE... DONE TO ME...!!
SSS...
I HAVE NOT FOR-GOTTEN A SHREEED ...!!
EVEN IF YOU FORGET, I—!!
I'D HAVE PROBABLY LOST IF YOU'D STAYED A MONSTER.

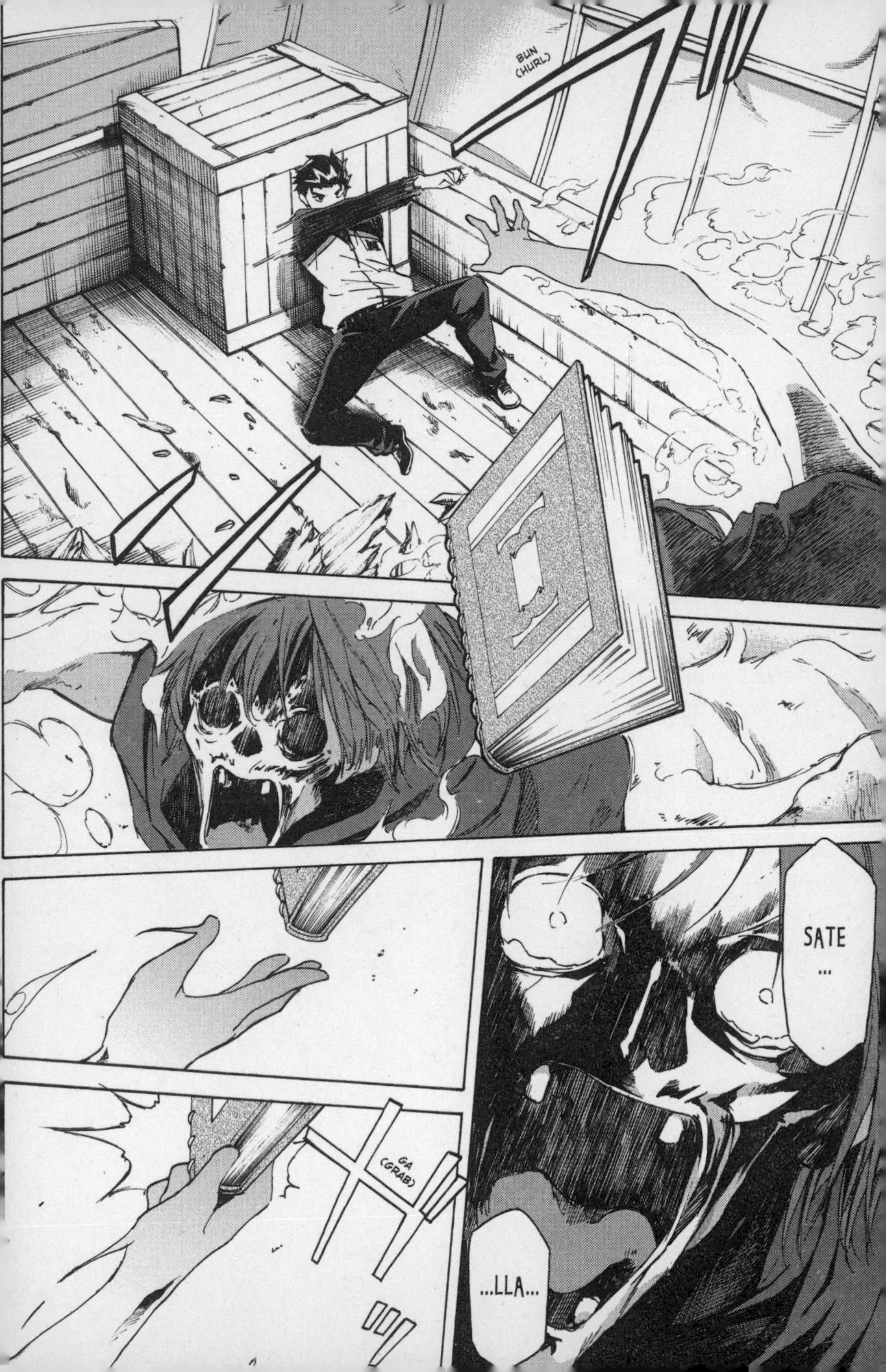
BUN
(HURL)
SATE ...
...LLA...
GA
(GRAB)

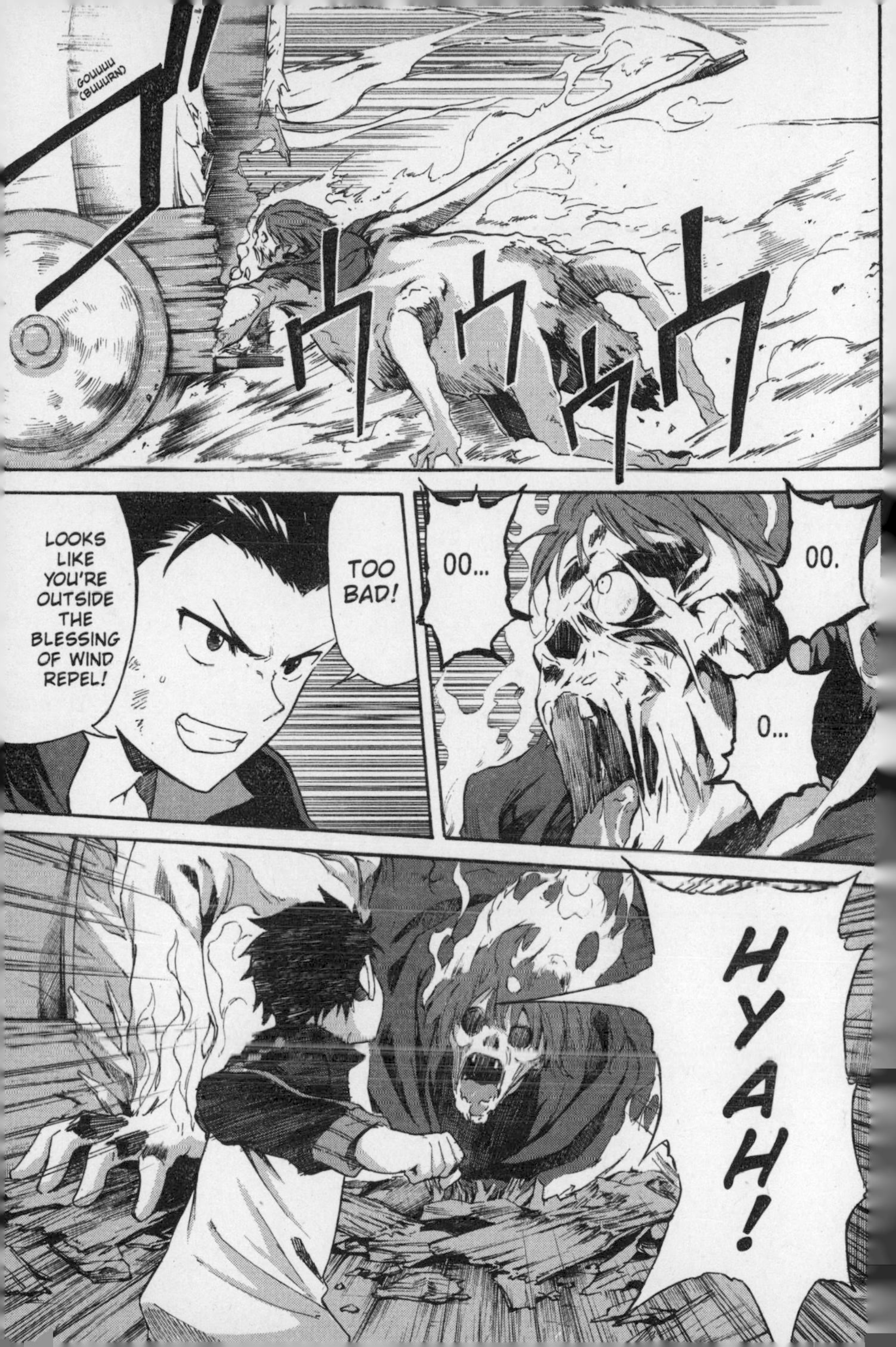

GOUUUU (BUUURN)
OO.
OO...
O...
TOO BAD!
LOOKS LIKE YOU'RE OUTSIDE THE BLESSING OF WIND REPEL!
HYAH!

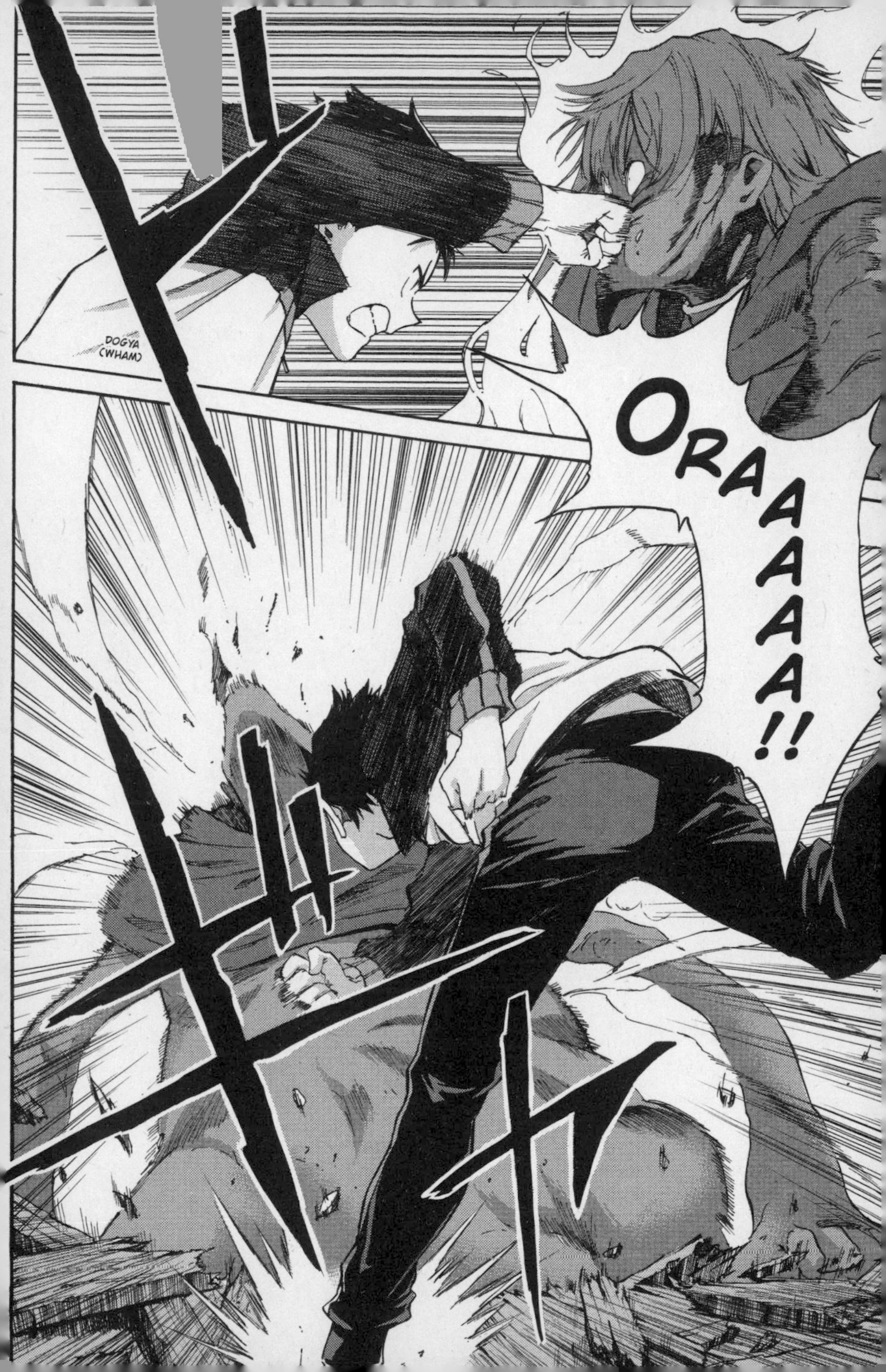
DOGYA
(WHAM)
ORAAAAAAA!!

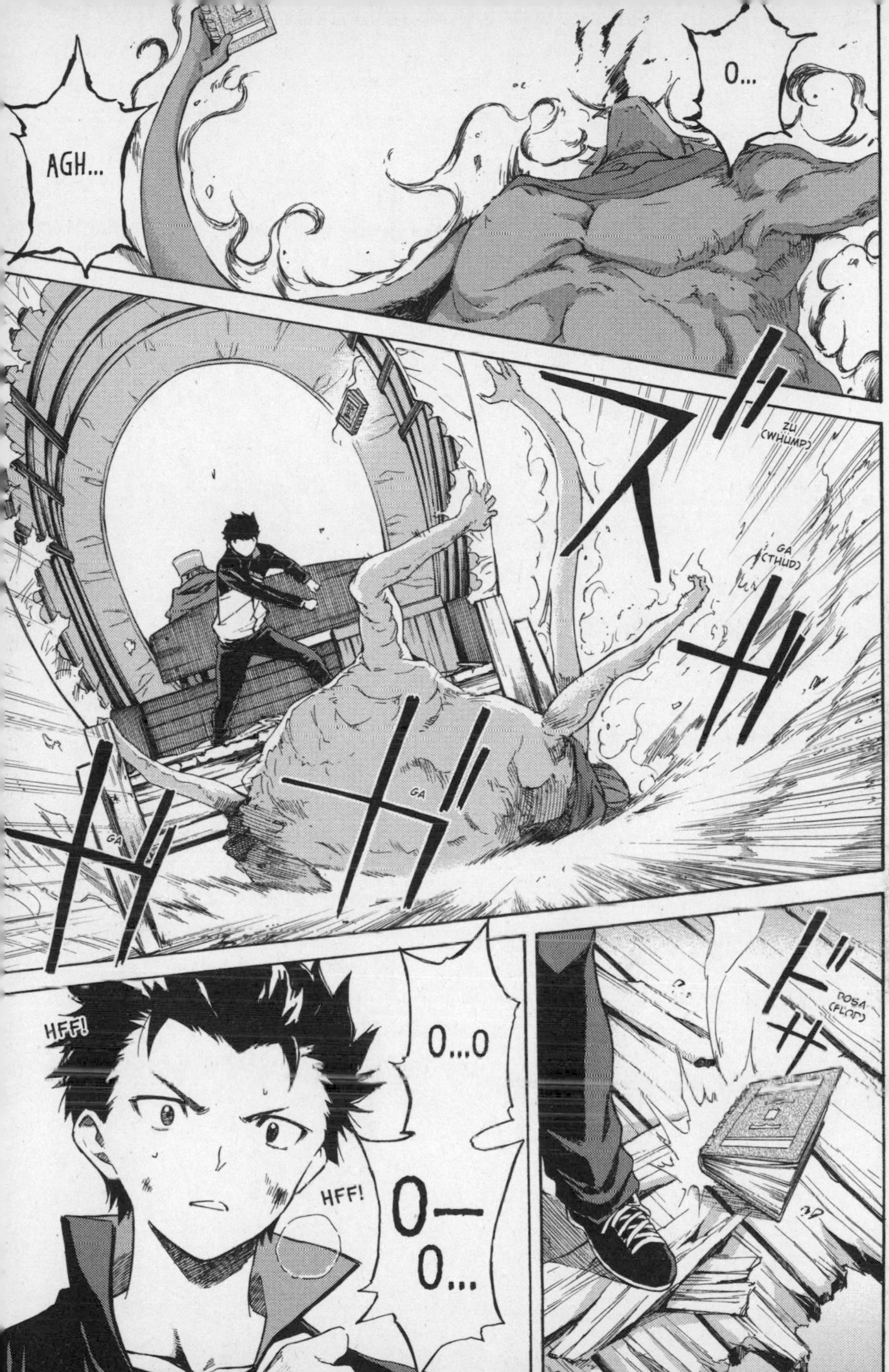
O...
AGH...
ZU (WHUMP)
GA (THUD)
GA
GA
DOSA (FLOP)
O...O
HFF!
HFF!
O— O...

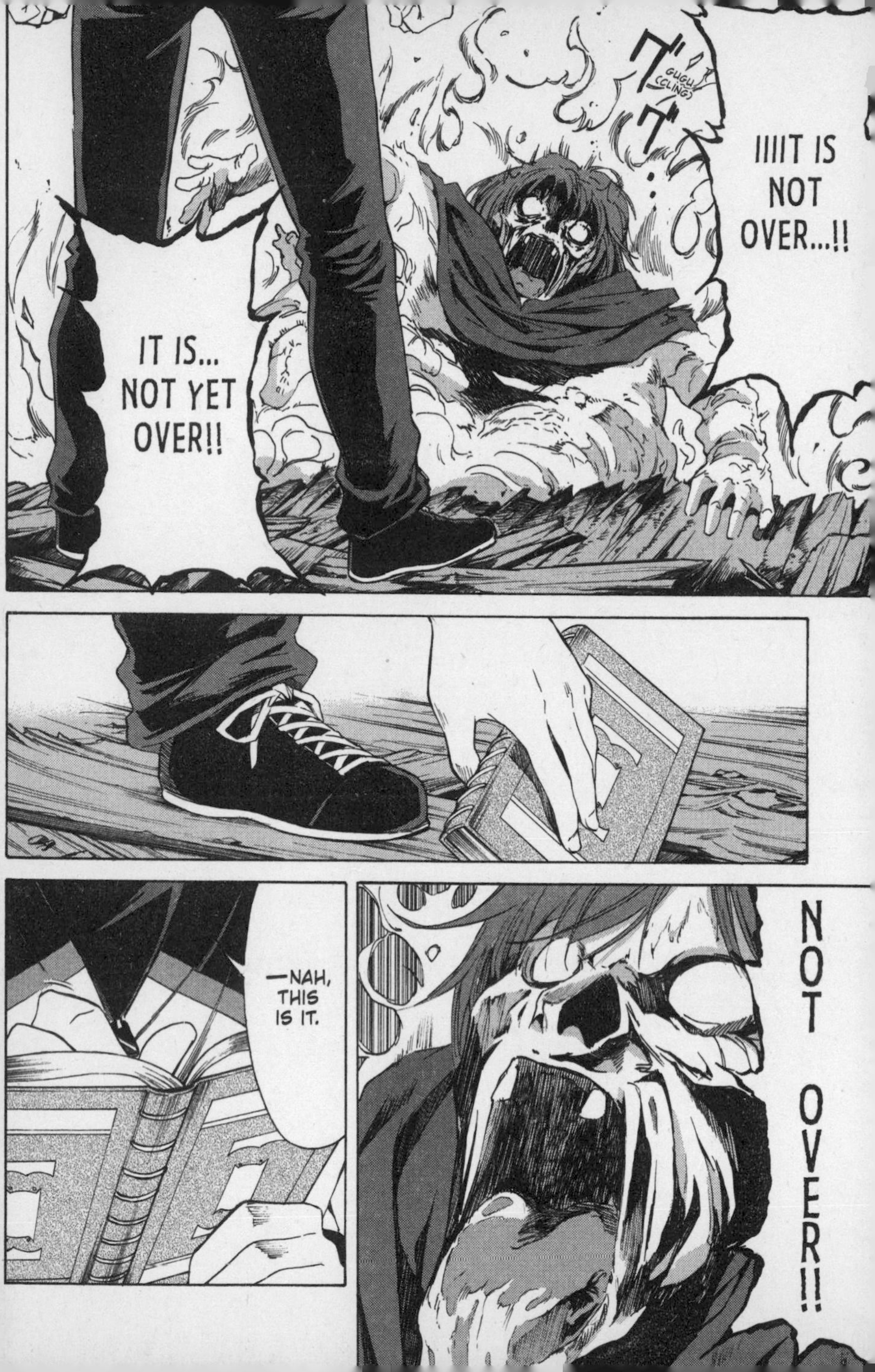
GUGU (CLING)
IIIIT IS NOT OVER...!!
IT IS... NOT YET OVER!!
NOT OVER!!
—NAH, THIS IS IT.

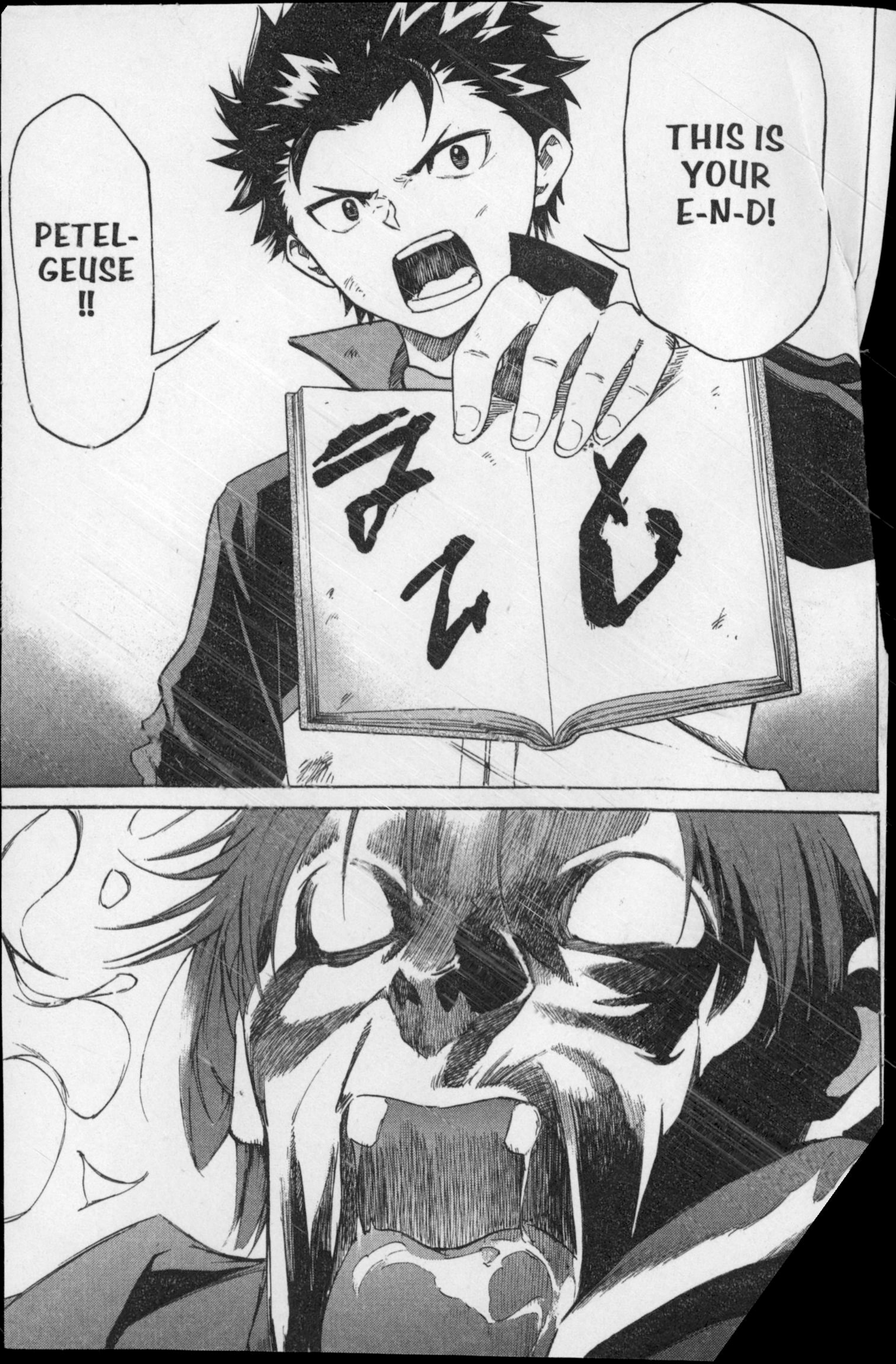
THIS IS YOUR E-N-D!
PETEL-GEUSE!!

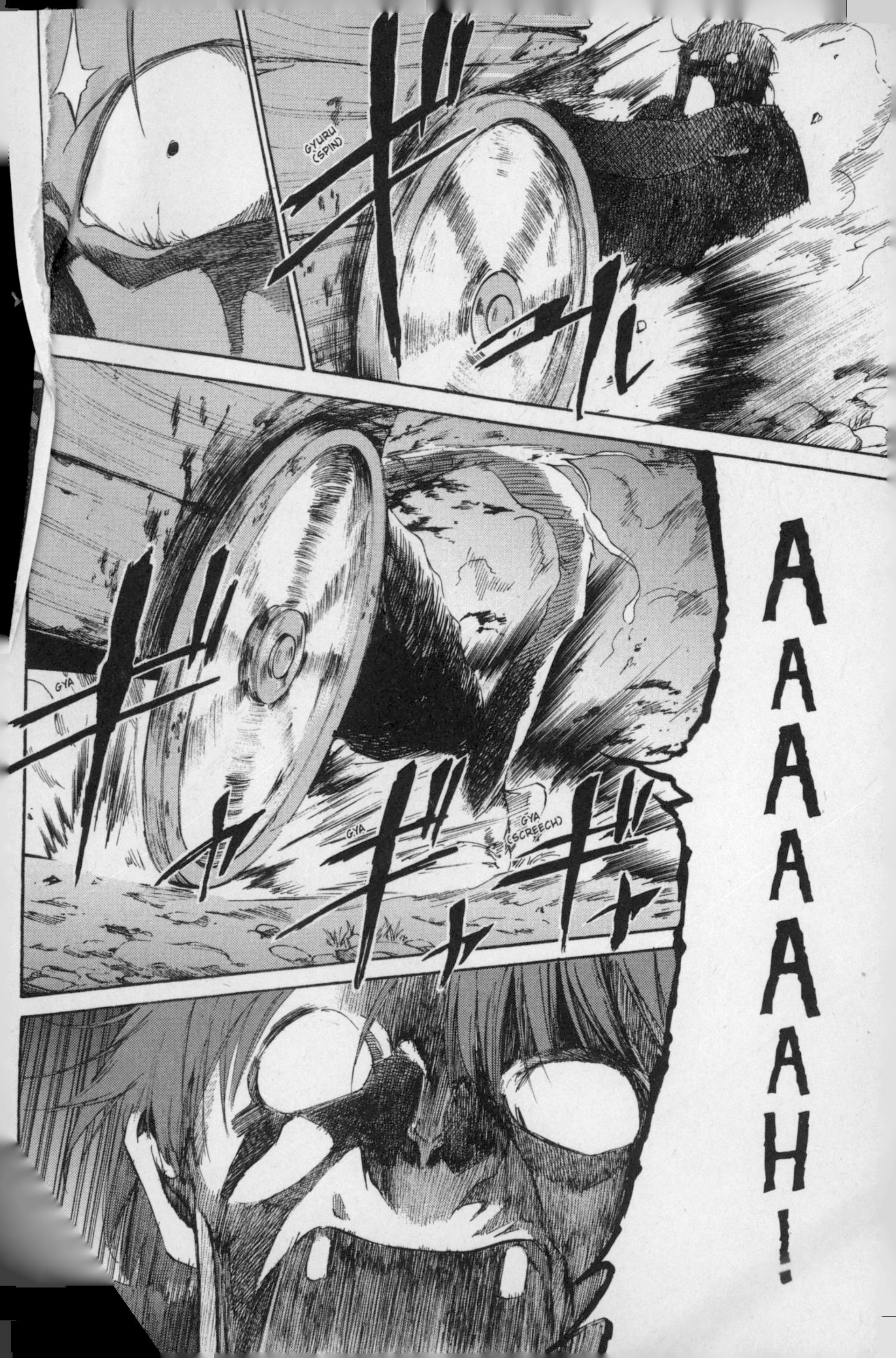
GYURU (SPIN)
AAAAAAAAH!!
GYA (SCREECH)
GYA
GYA

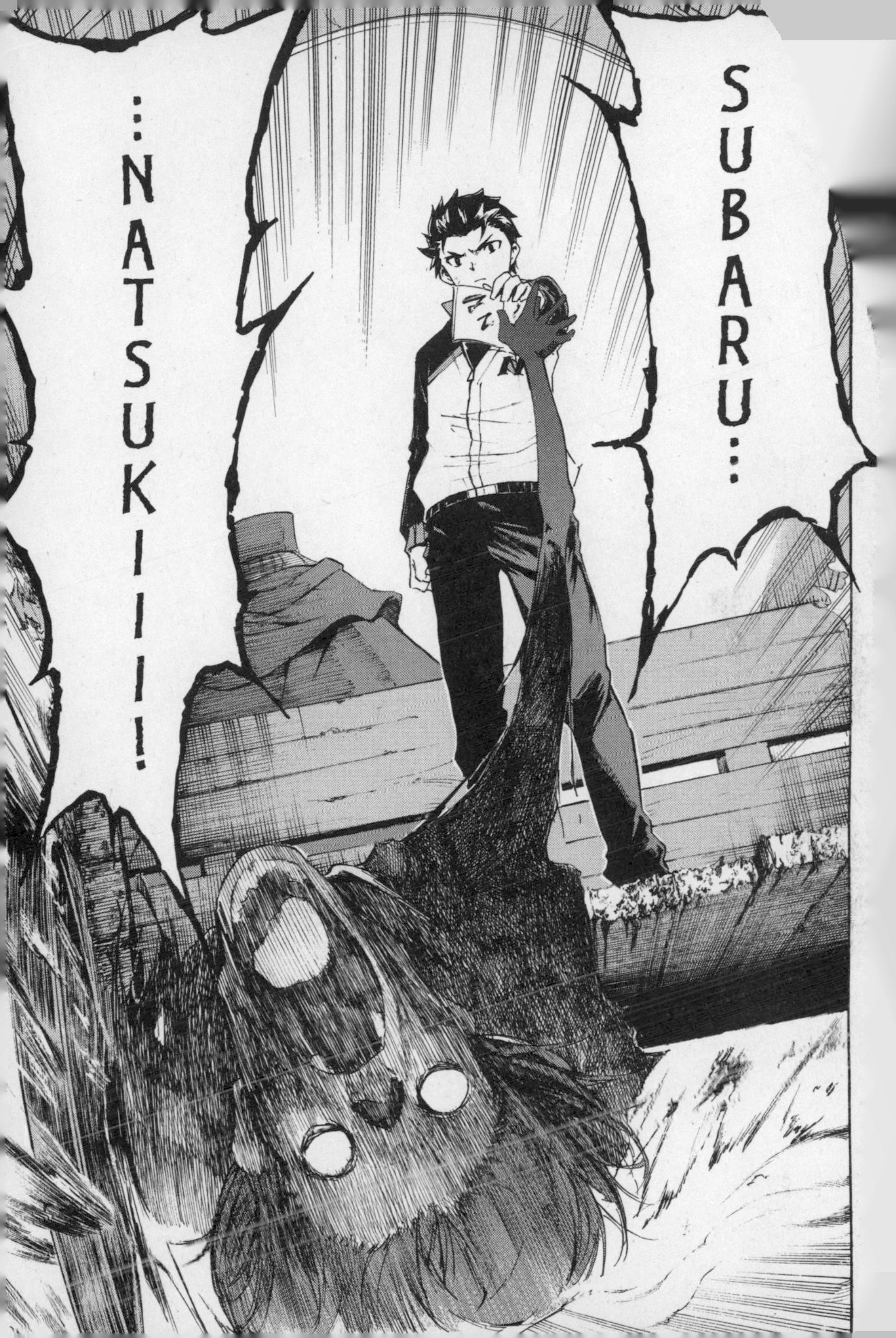
SUBARU...
...NATSUKIII!

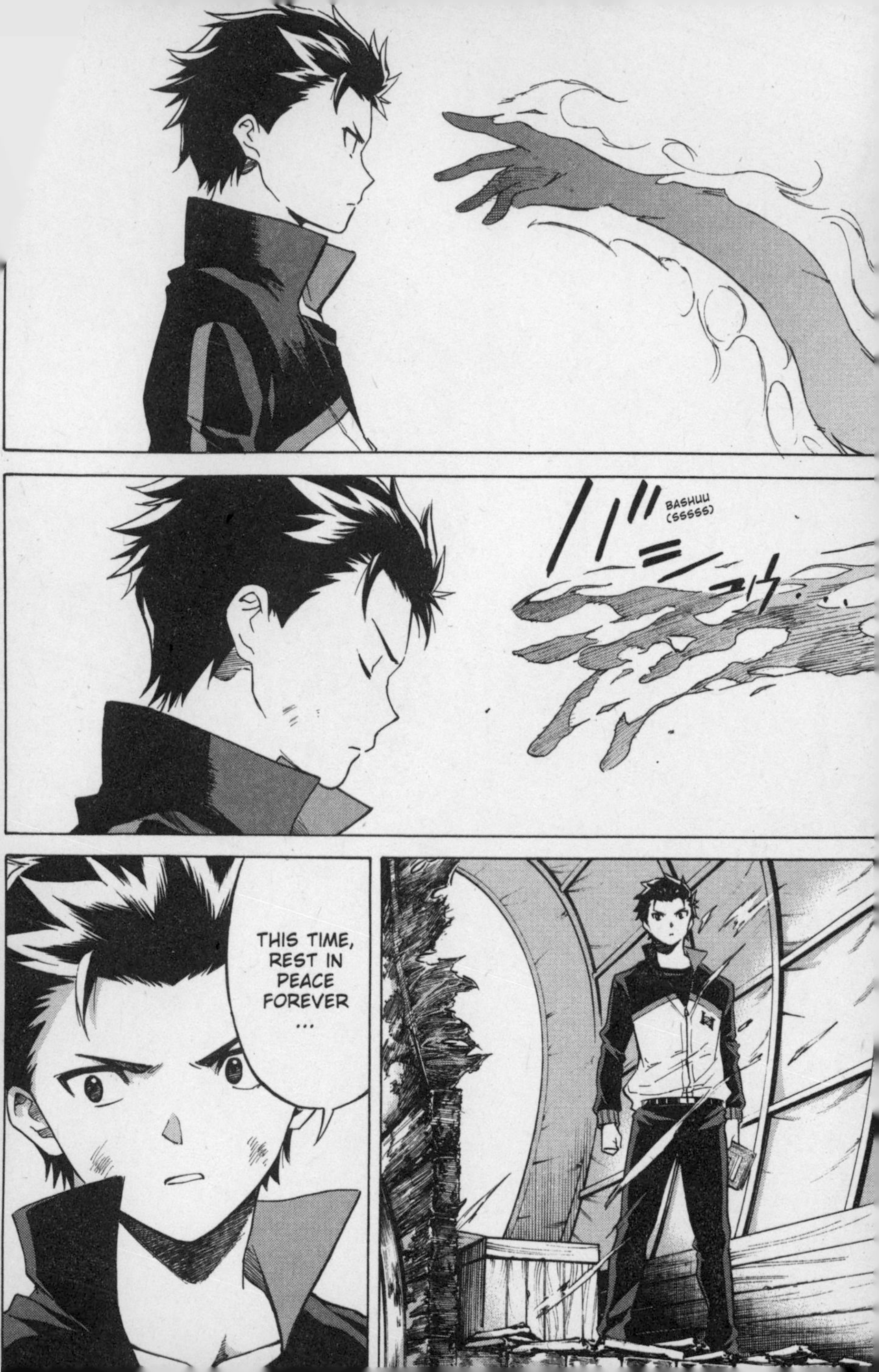
BASHUU (SSSSS)
THIS TIME, REST IN PEACE FOREVER ...

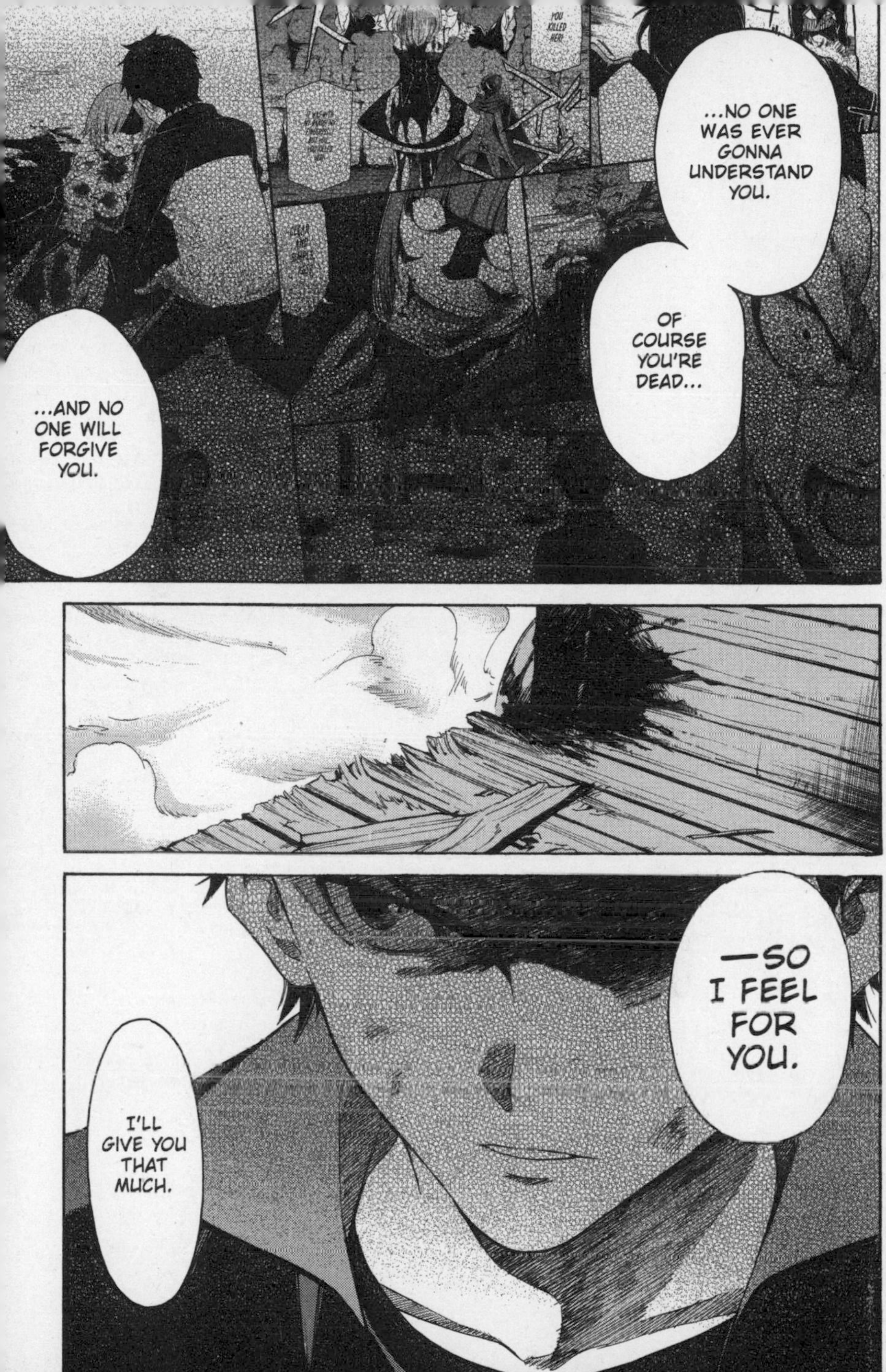
YOU KILLED HER!
...NO ONE WAS EVER GONNA UNDERSTAND YOU.
OF COURSE YOU'RE DEAD...
...AND NO ONE WILL FORGIVE YOU.
—SO I FEEL FOR YOU.
I'LL GIVE YOU THAT MUCH.

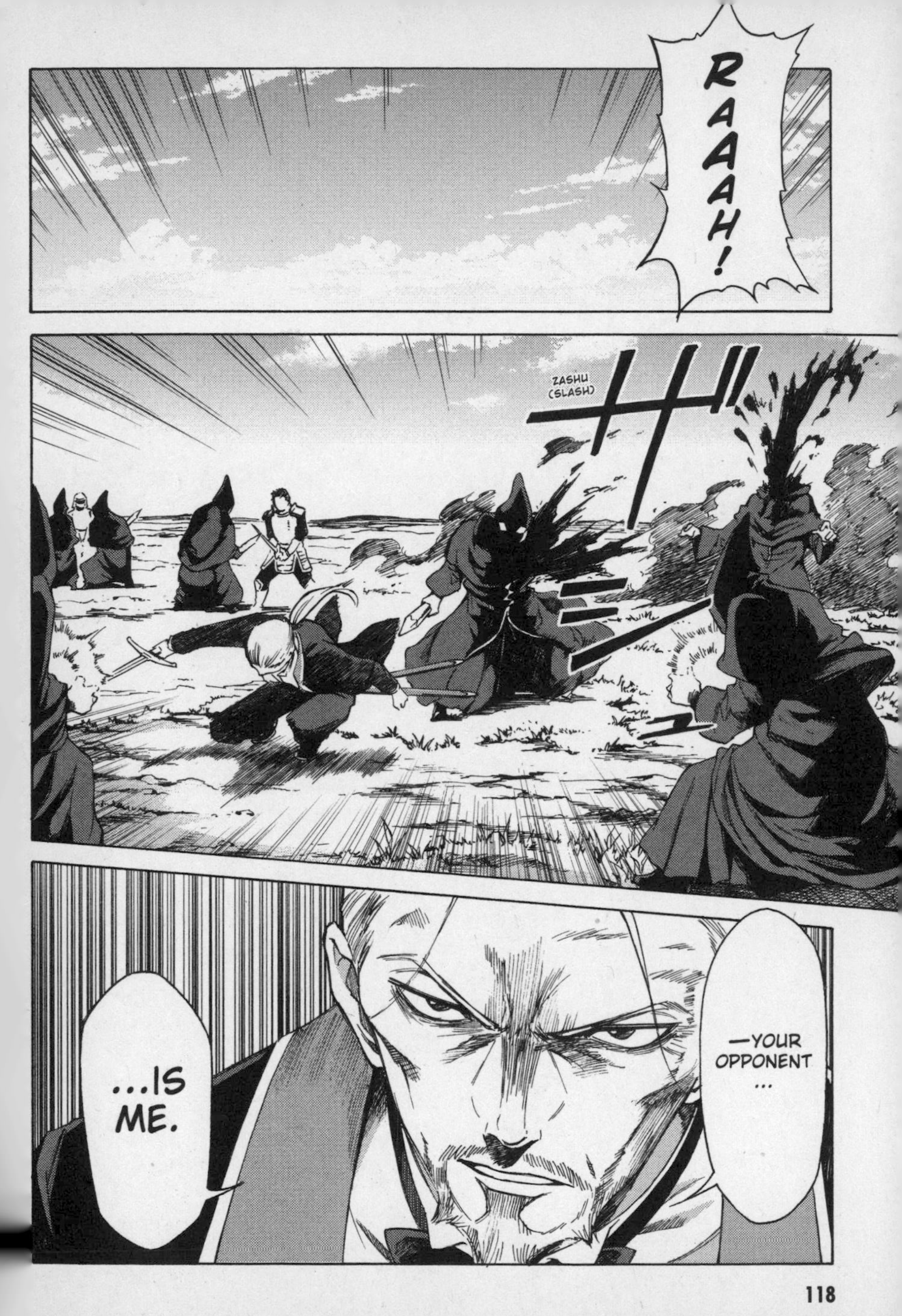
RAAAAH!
ZASHU (SLASH)
—YOUR OPPONENT ...
...IS ME.

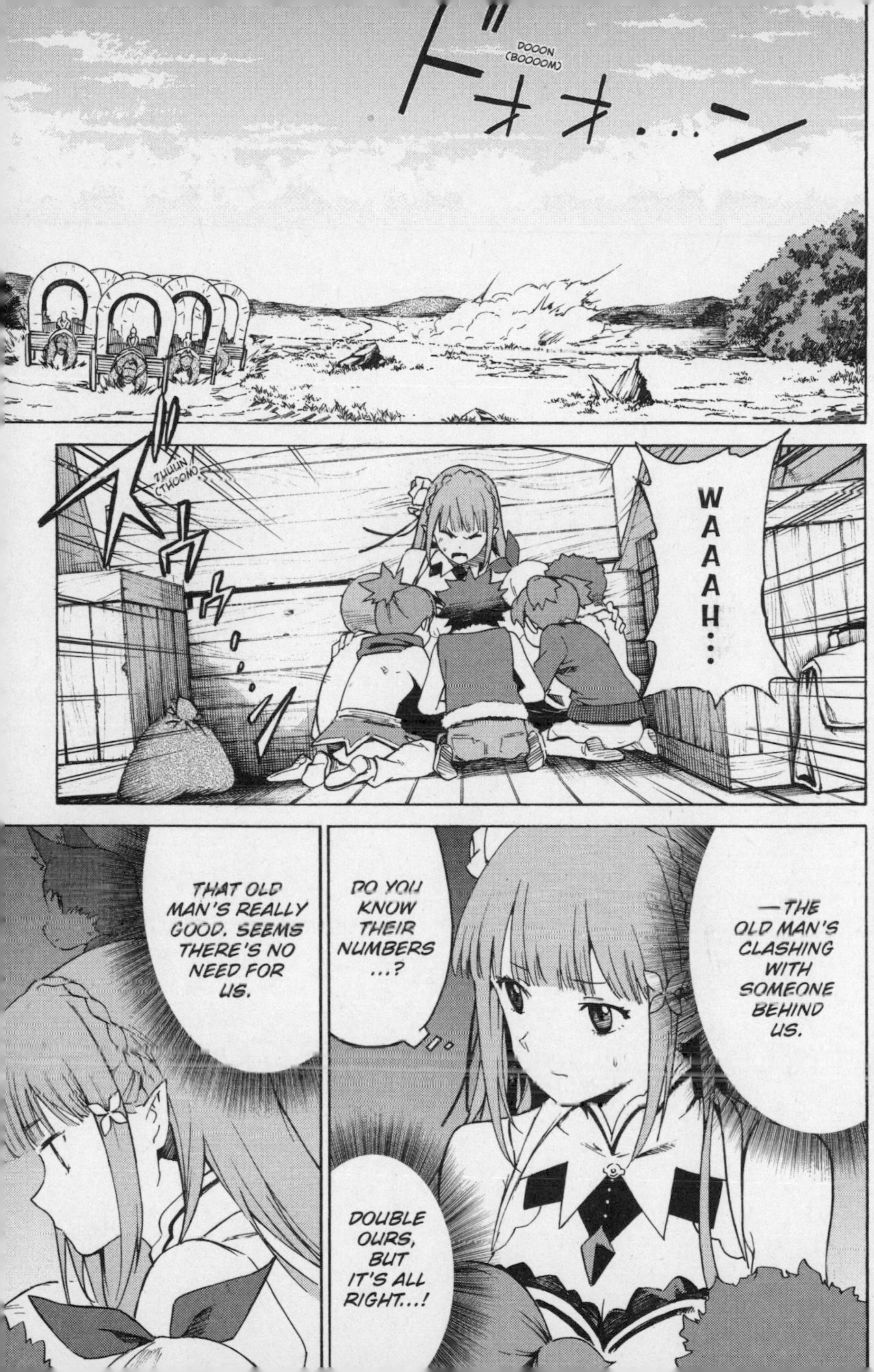
ドォォ…ン
DOOON
(BOOOOM)
ズン
ZUUUN
(THOOM)
WAAAAH…
—THE OLD MAN'S CLASHING WITH SOMEONE BEHIND US.
DO YOU KNOW THEIR NUMBERS …?
DOUBLE OURS, BUT IT'S ALL RIGHT…!
THAT OLD MAN'S REALLY GOOD. SEEMS THERE'S NO NEED FOR US.

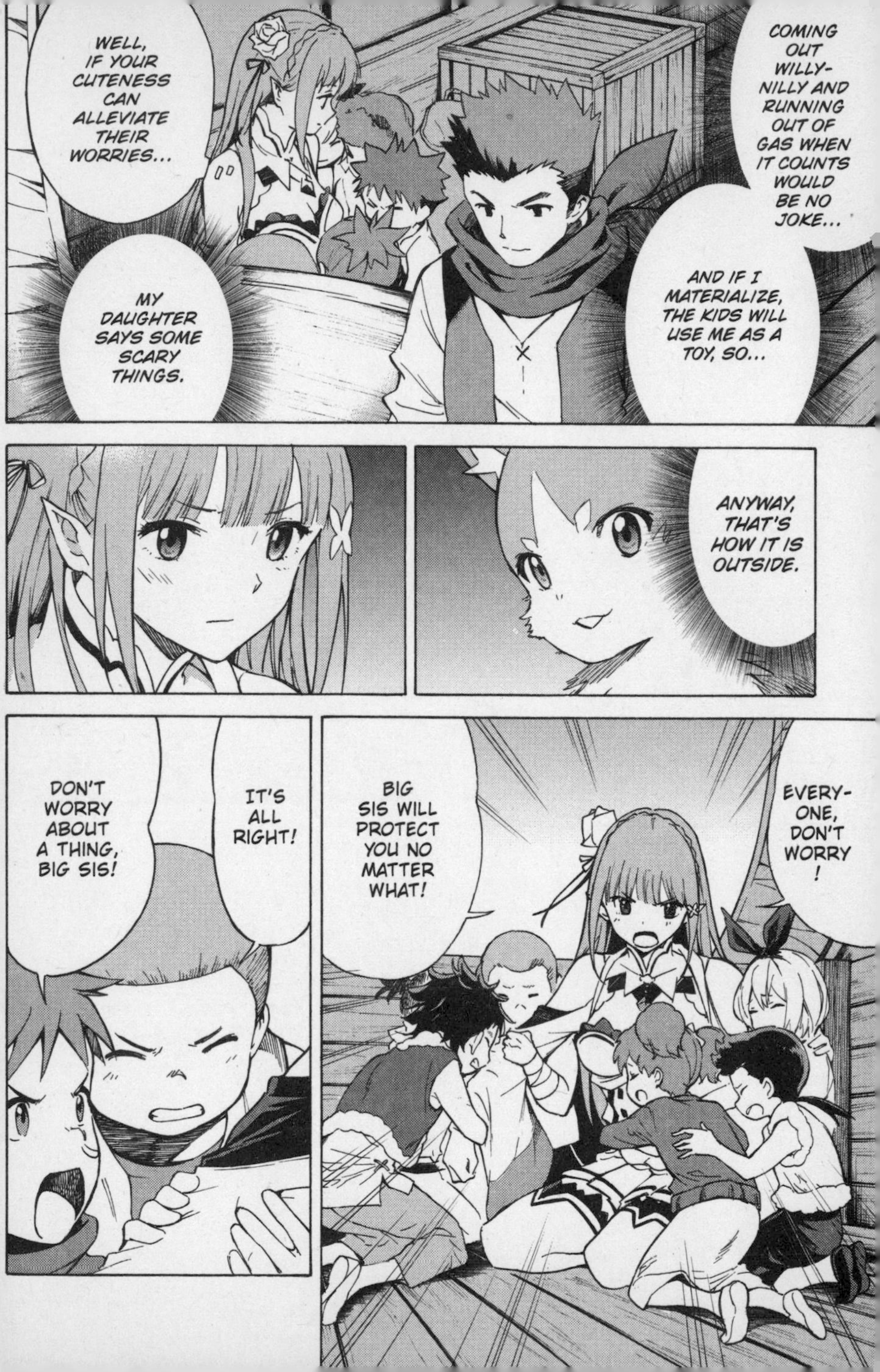
COMING OUT WILLY-NILLY AND RUNNING OUT OF GAS WHEN IT COUNTS WOULD BE NO JOKE...
AND IF I MATERIALIZE, THE KIDS WILL USE ME AS A TOY, SO...
WELL, IF YOUR CUTENESS CAN ALLEVIATE THEIR WORRIES...
MY DAUGHTER SAYS SOME SCARY THINGS.
ANYWAY, THAT'S HOW IT IS OUTSIDE.
EVERY-ONE, DON'T WORRY!
BIG SIS WILL PROTECT YOU NO MATTER WHAT!
IT'S ALL RIGHT!
DON'T WORRY ABOUT A THING, BIG SIS!

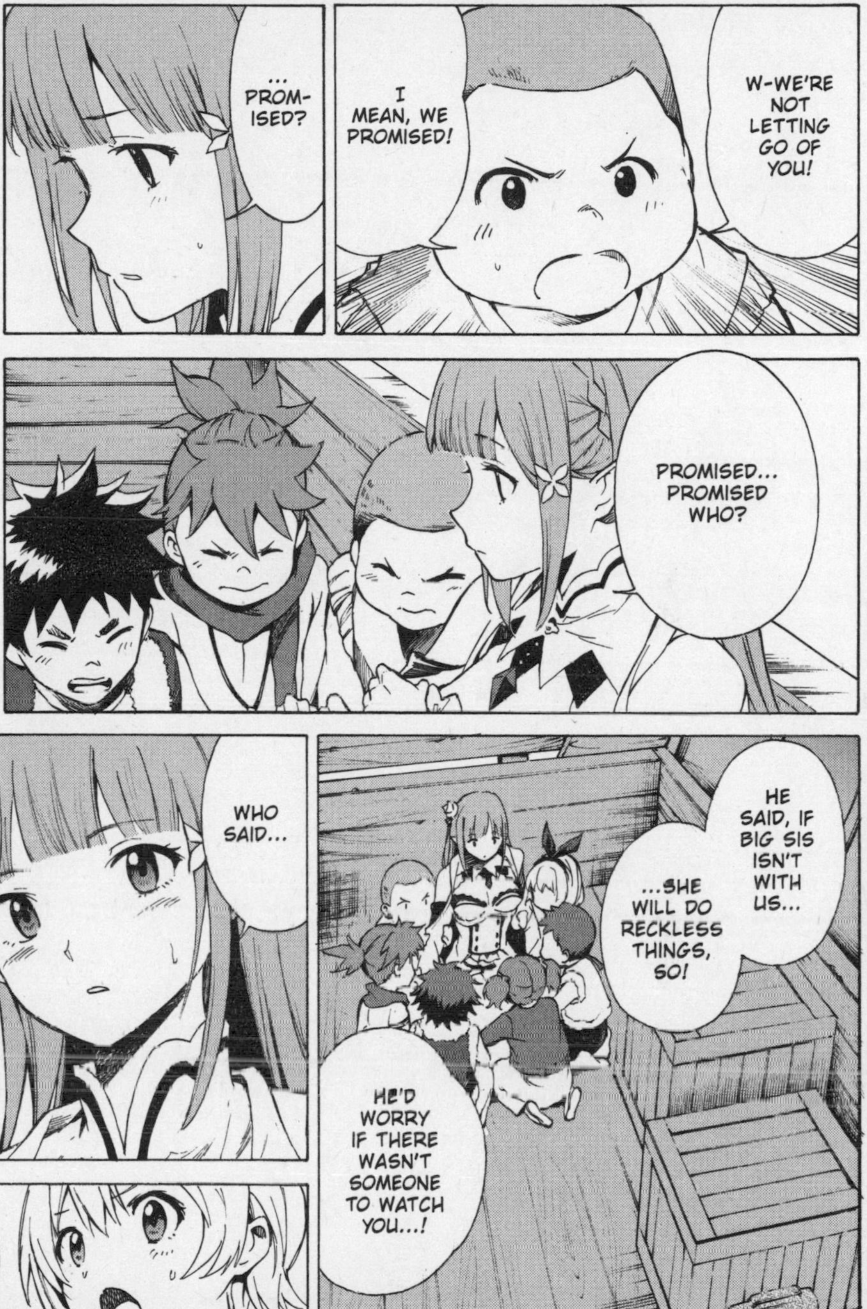
W-WE'RE NOT LETTING GO OF YOU!
I MEAN, WE PROMISED!
... PROM-ISED?
PROMISED... PROMISED WHO?
HE SAID, IF BIG SIS ISN'T WITH US...
...SHE WILL DO RECKLESS THINGS, SO!
HE'D WORRY IF THERE WASN'T SOMEONE TO WATCH YOU...!
WHO SAID...
...THAT...?
AH...

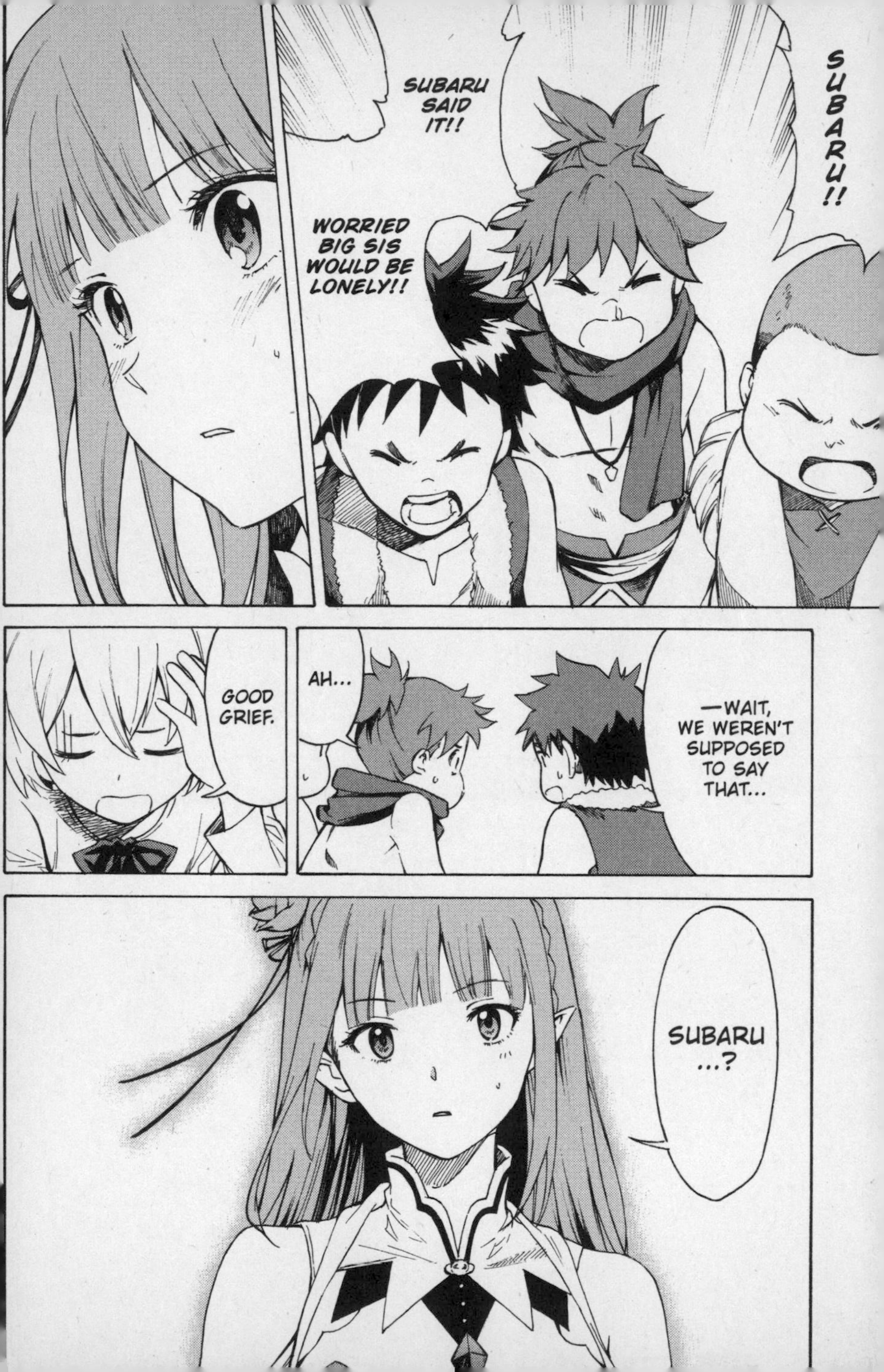
SUBARU!!
SUBARU SAID IT!!
WORRIED BIG SIS WOULD BE LONELY!!
—WAIT, WE WEREN'T SUPPOSED TO SAY THAT...
AH...
GOOD GRIEF.
SUBARU ...?

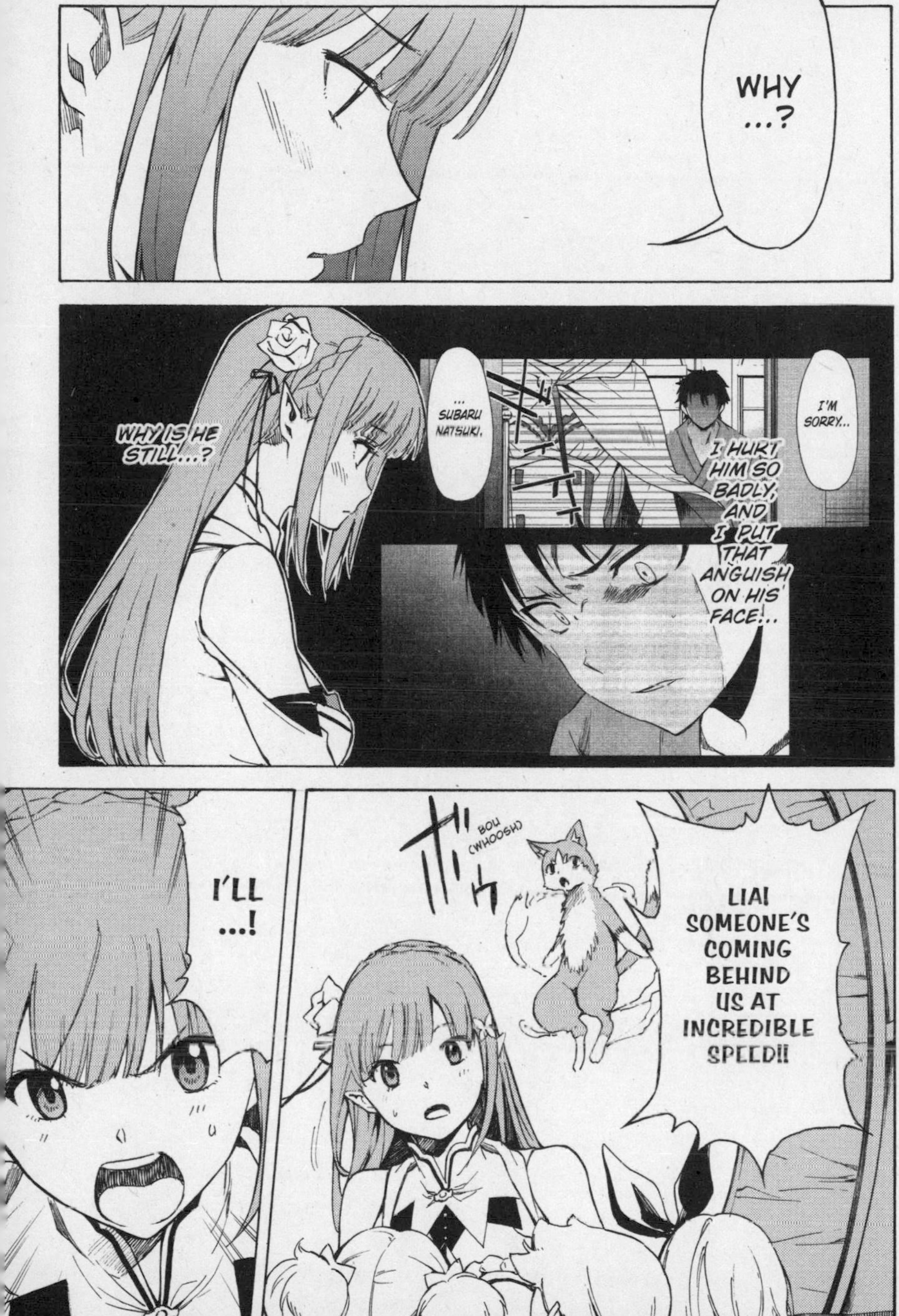
WHY ...?
I'M SORRY...
... SUBARU NATSUKI.
I HURT HIM SO BADLY, AND I PUT THAT ANGUISH ON HIS FACE...
WHY IS HE STILL...?
LIA! SOMEONE'S COMING BEHIND US AT INCREDIBLE SPEED!!
BOU (WHOOSH)
I'LL ...!

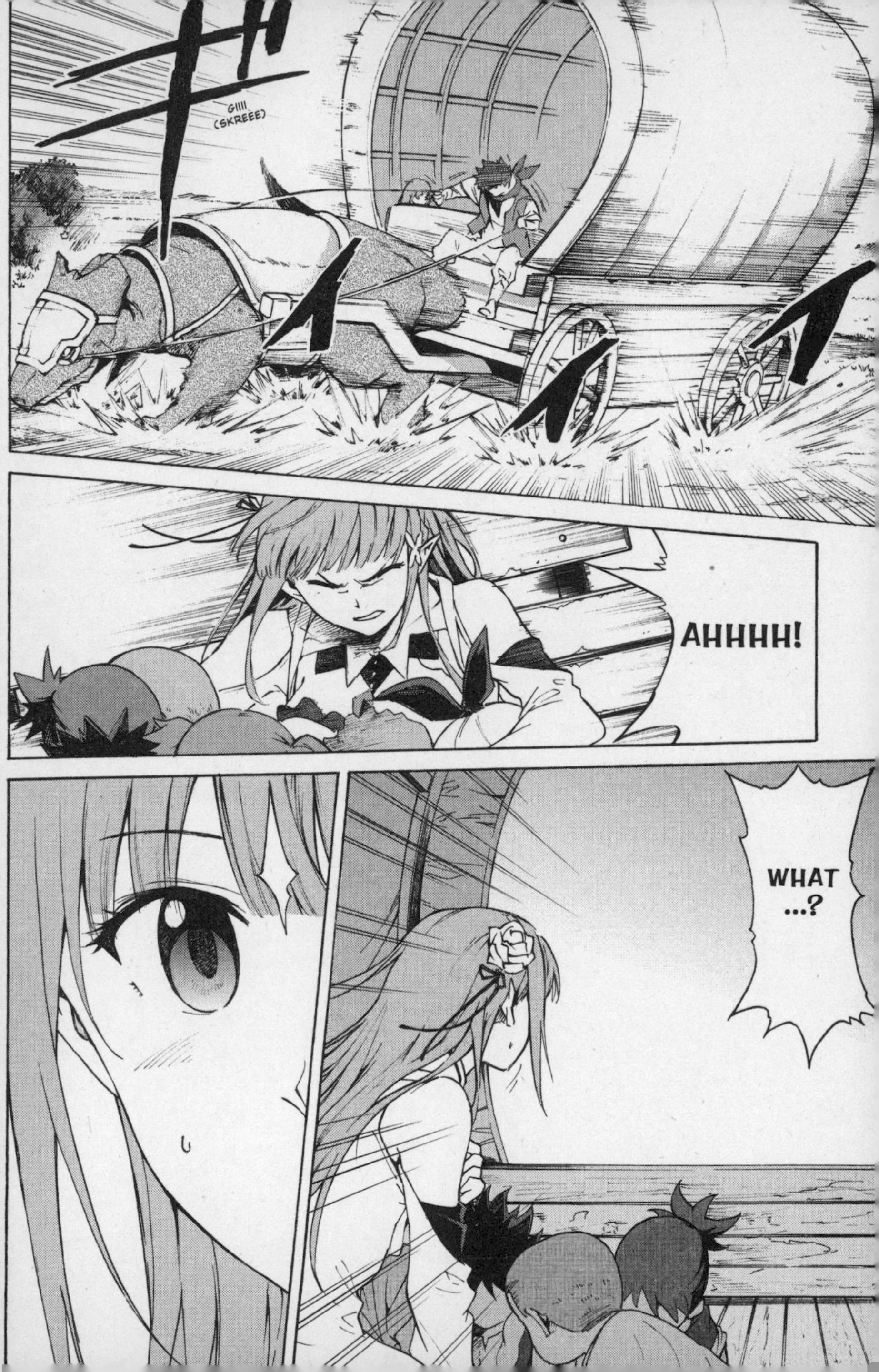
GIIII (SKREEE)
AHHHH!
WHAT ...?

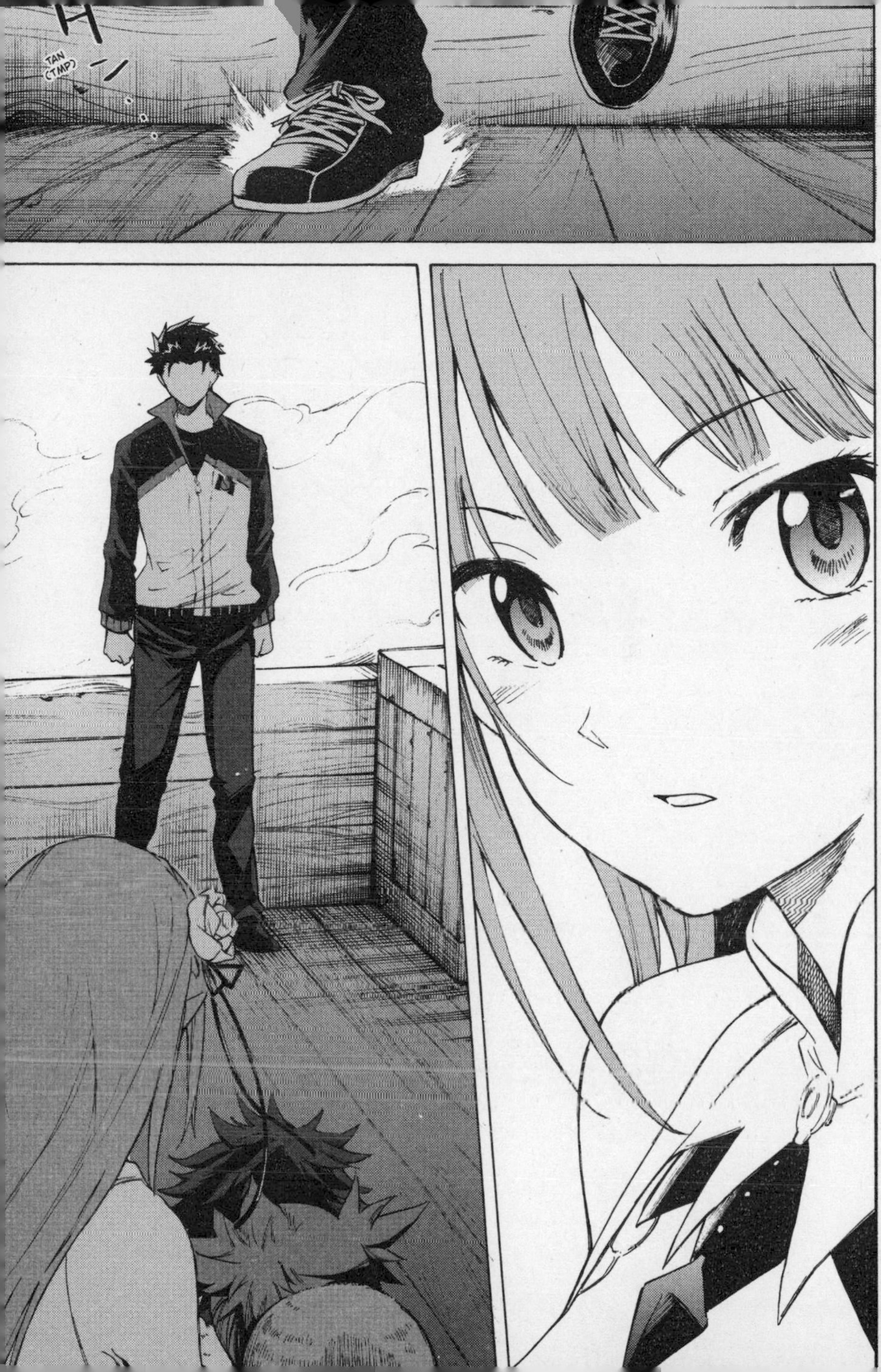
TAN (TMP)

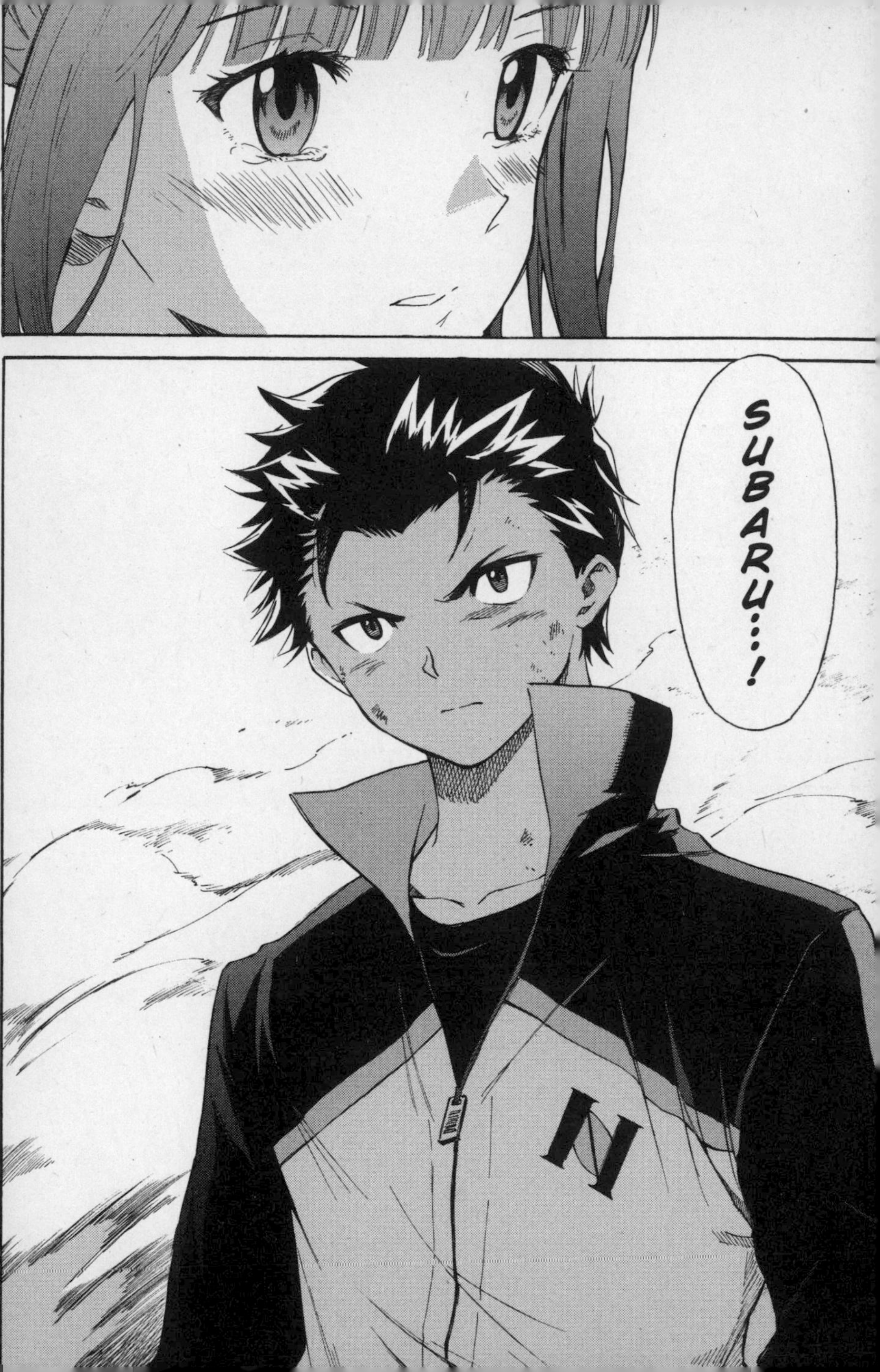
SUBARU...!

Truth of Zero

The only ability Subaru Natsuki gets when he's summoned to another world is time travel via his own death. But to save her, he'll die as many times as it takes.

Re:ZERO -Starting Life in Another World-

The only ability
Subaru Natsuki gets when
he's summoned to another
world is time travel via his
own death. But to save her,
he'll die as many times
as it takes.

Re:ZERO -Starting Life in Another World-
Truth of Zero

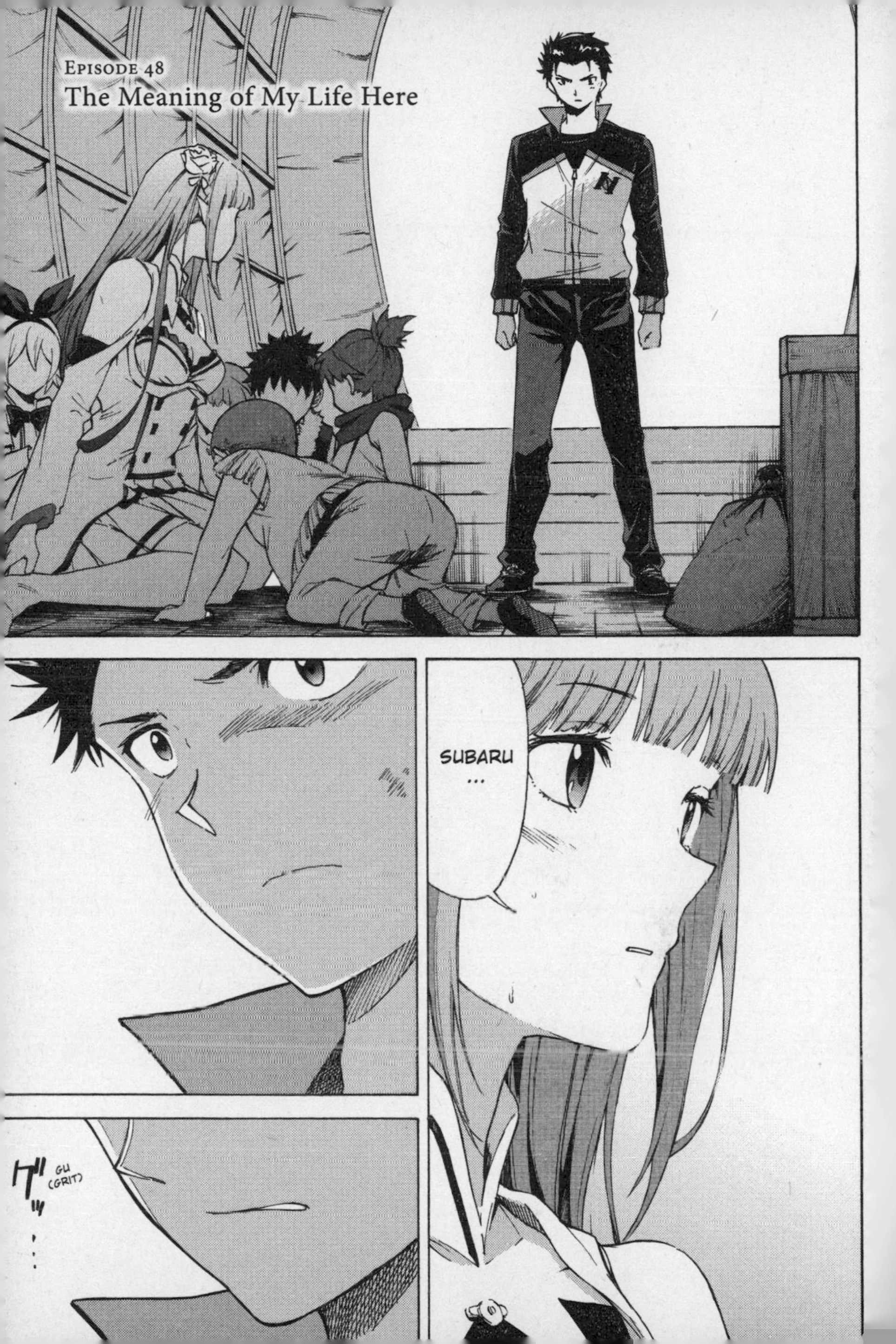
Episode 48
The Meaning of My Life Here
SUBARU ...
GU (GRIT)
...

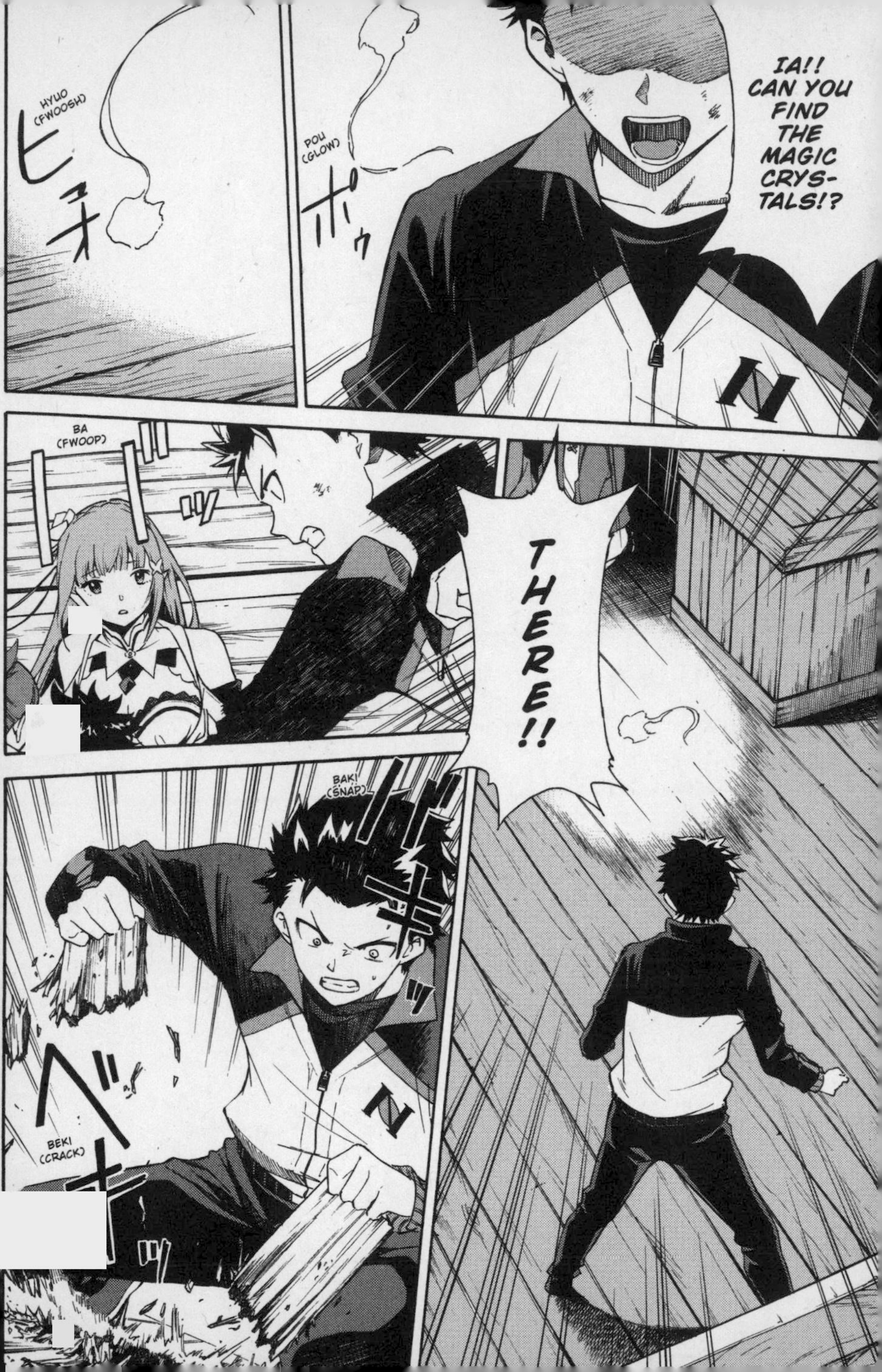
IA!! CAN YOU FIND THE MAGIC CRYS-TALS!?
POU (GLOW)
HYUO (FWOOSH)
THERE!!
BA (FWOOP)
BAKI (SNAP)
BEKI (CRACK)

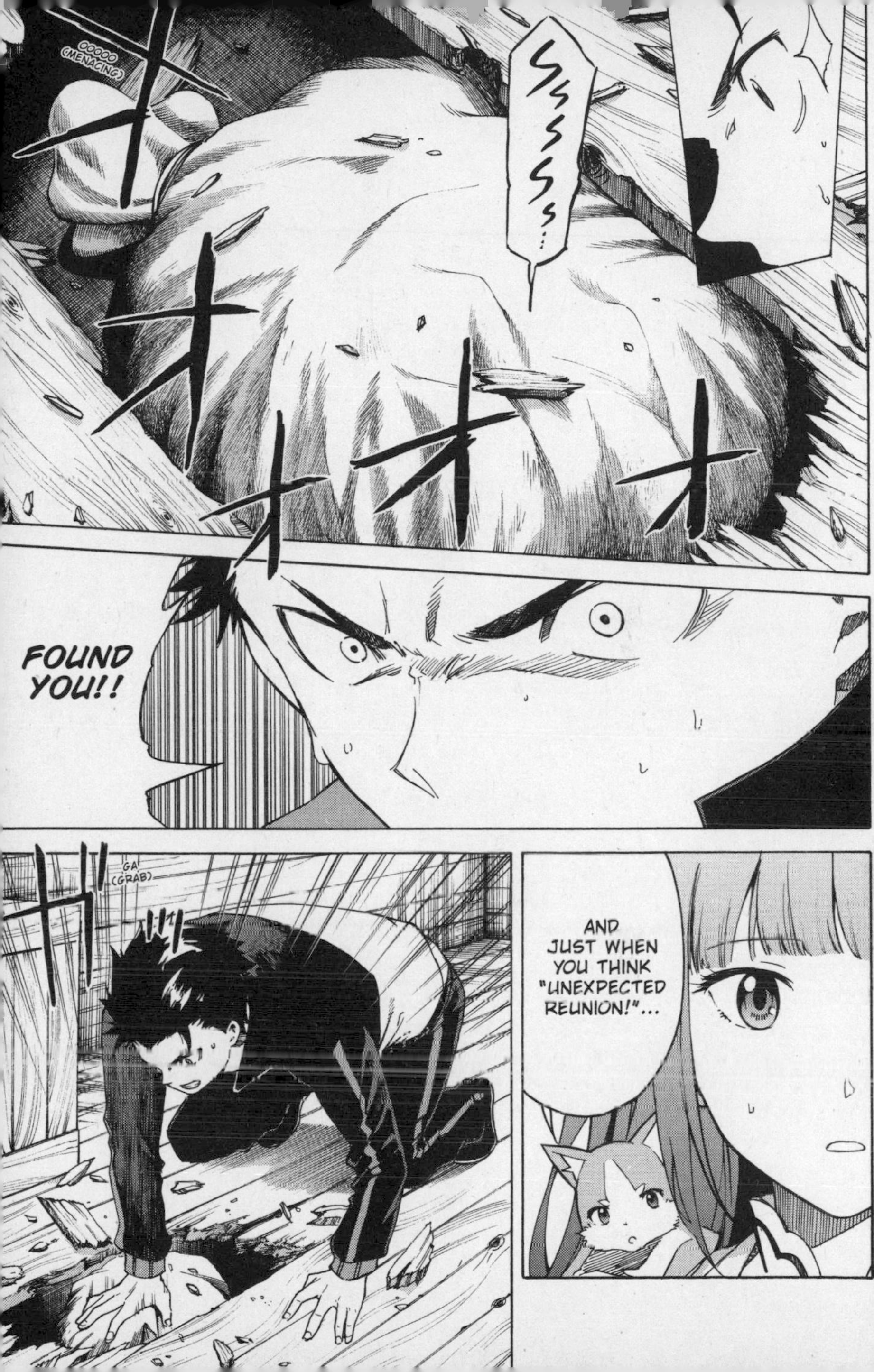
SSSSS...
OOOOO (MENACING)
FOUND YOU!!
AND JUST WHEN YOU THINK "UNEXPECTED REUNION!"...
GA (GRAB)

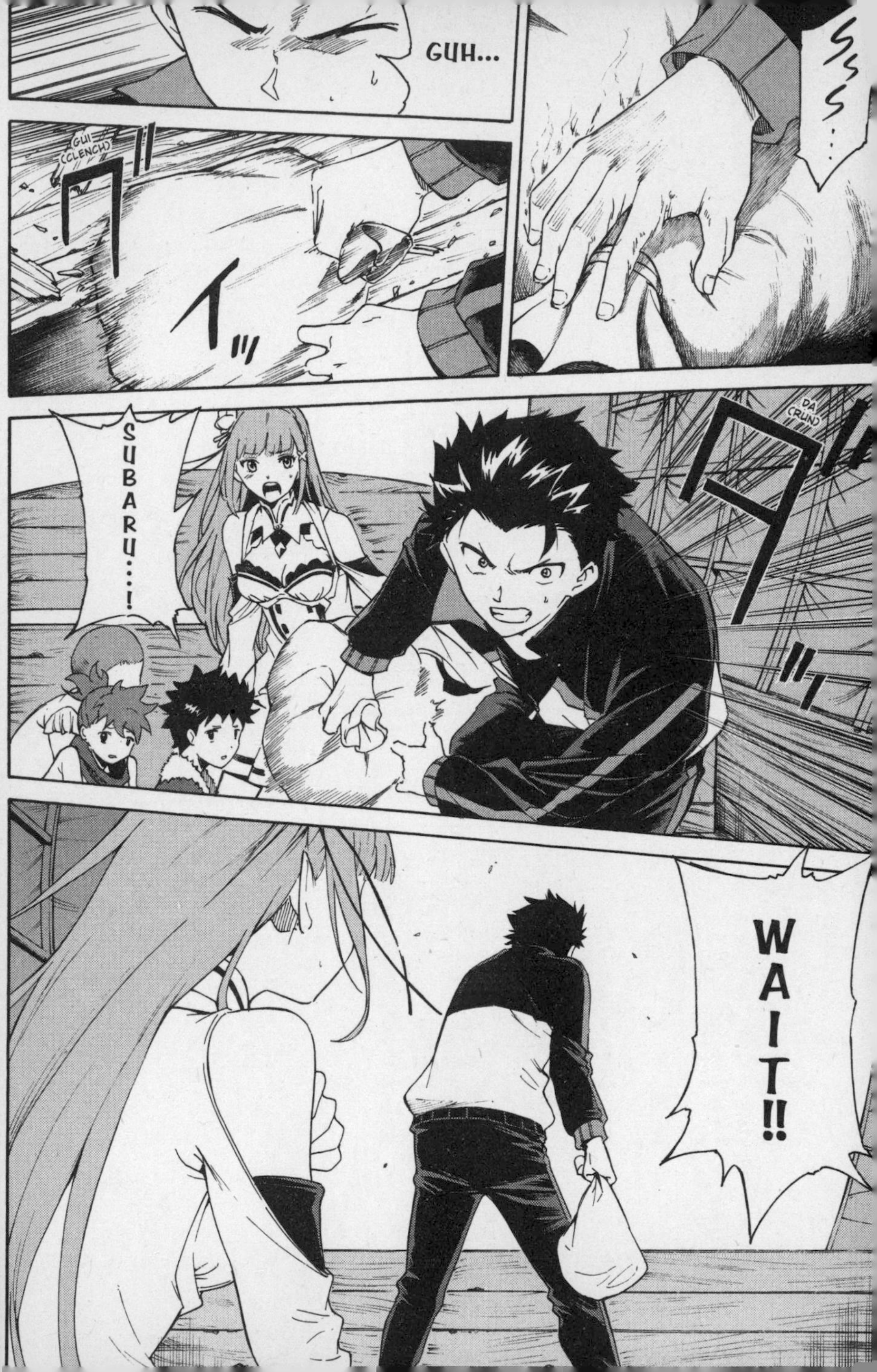
SSS...
GUH...
GUI (CLENCH)
DA (RUN)
SUBARU...!
WAIT!!

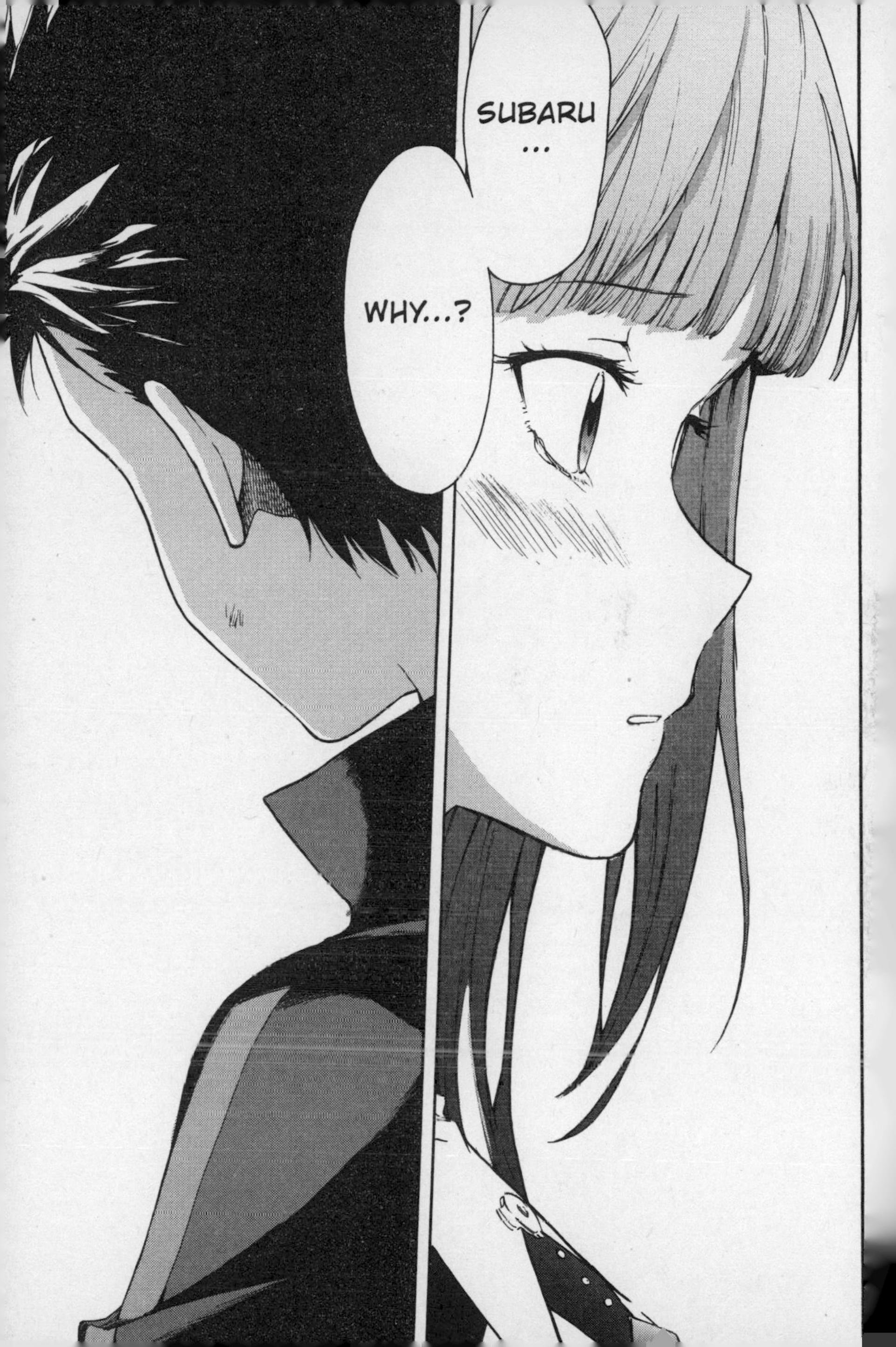
SUBARU
...
WHY...?

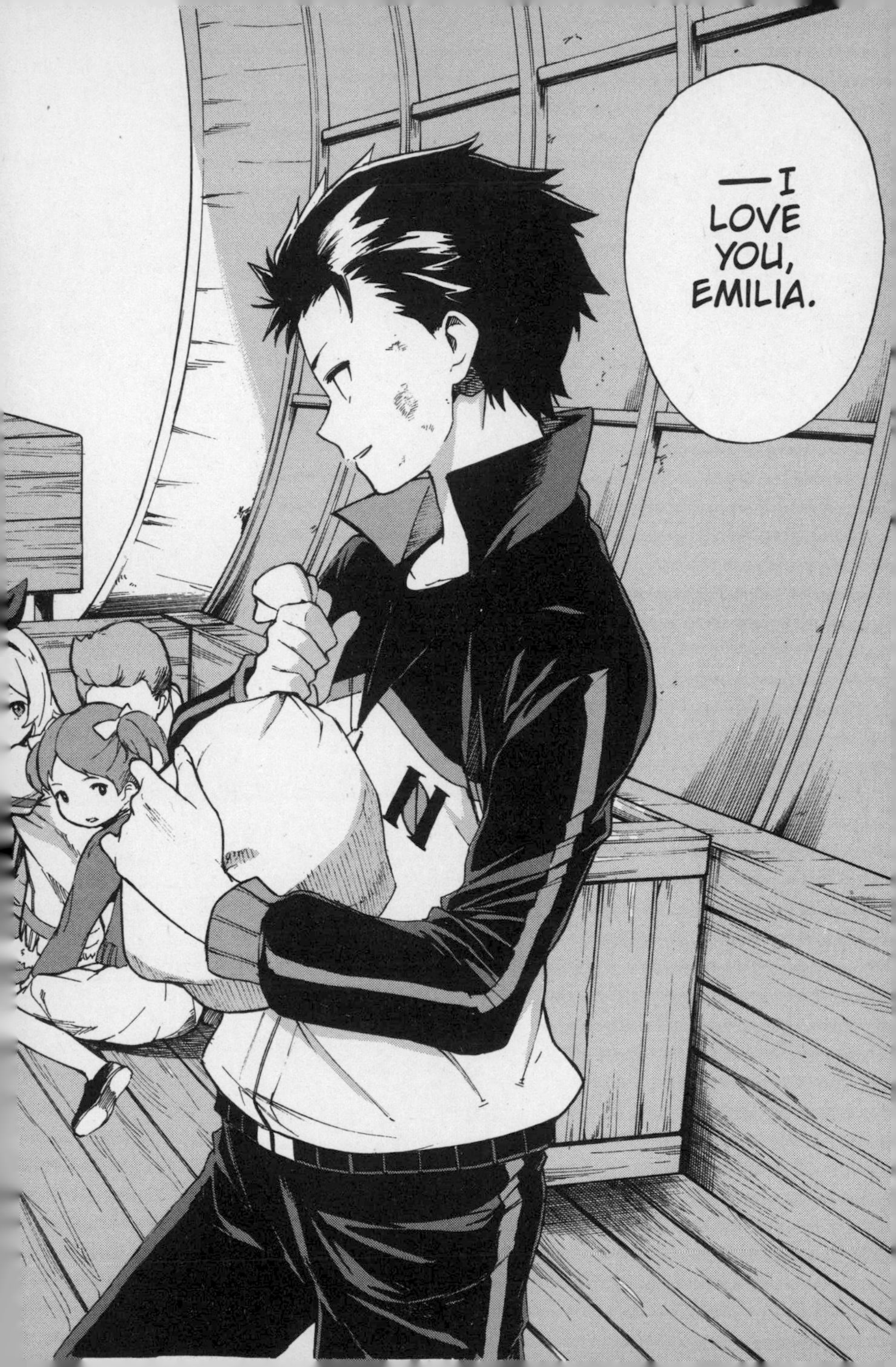
—I LOVE YOU, EMILIA.

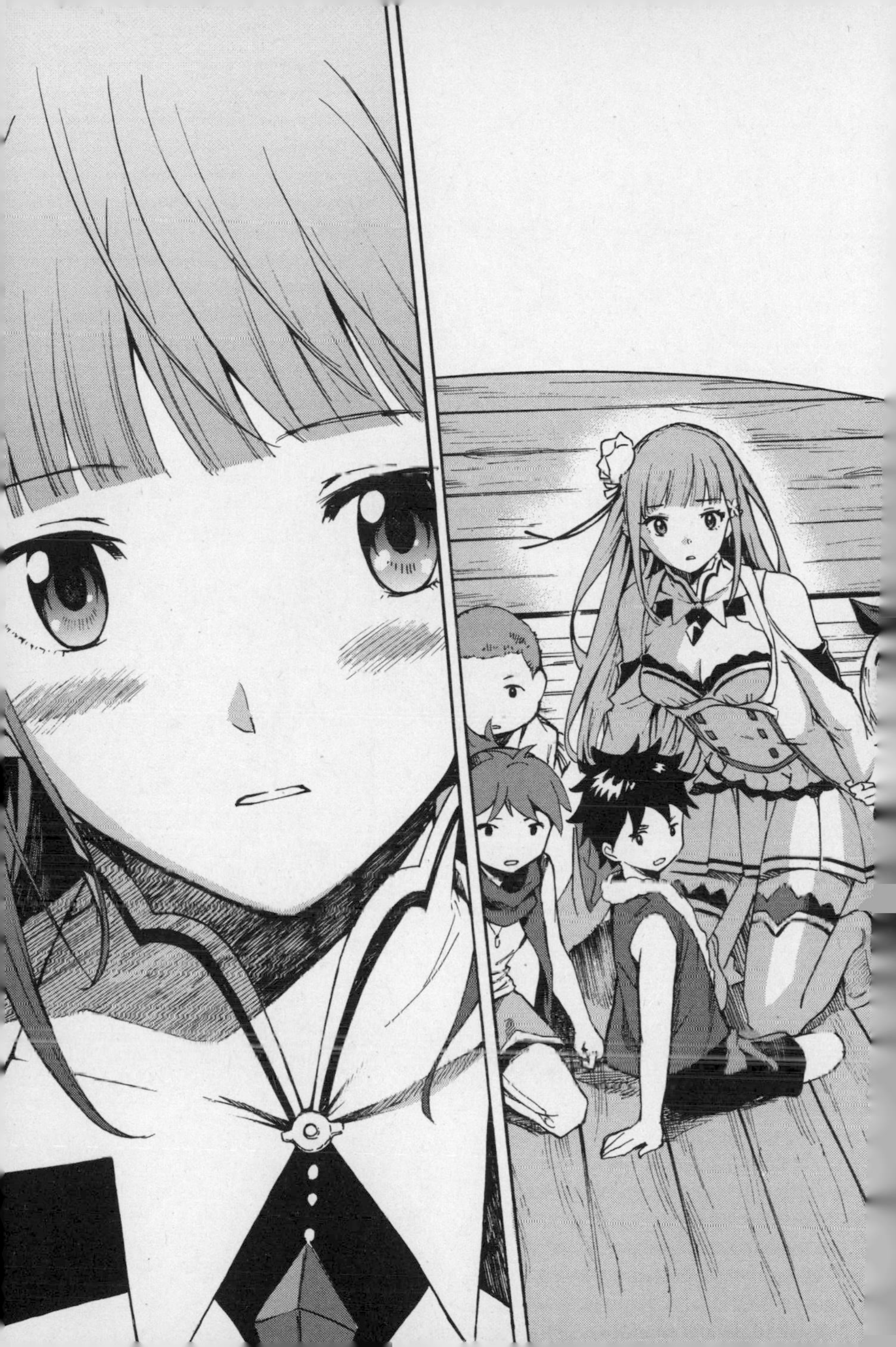

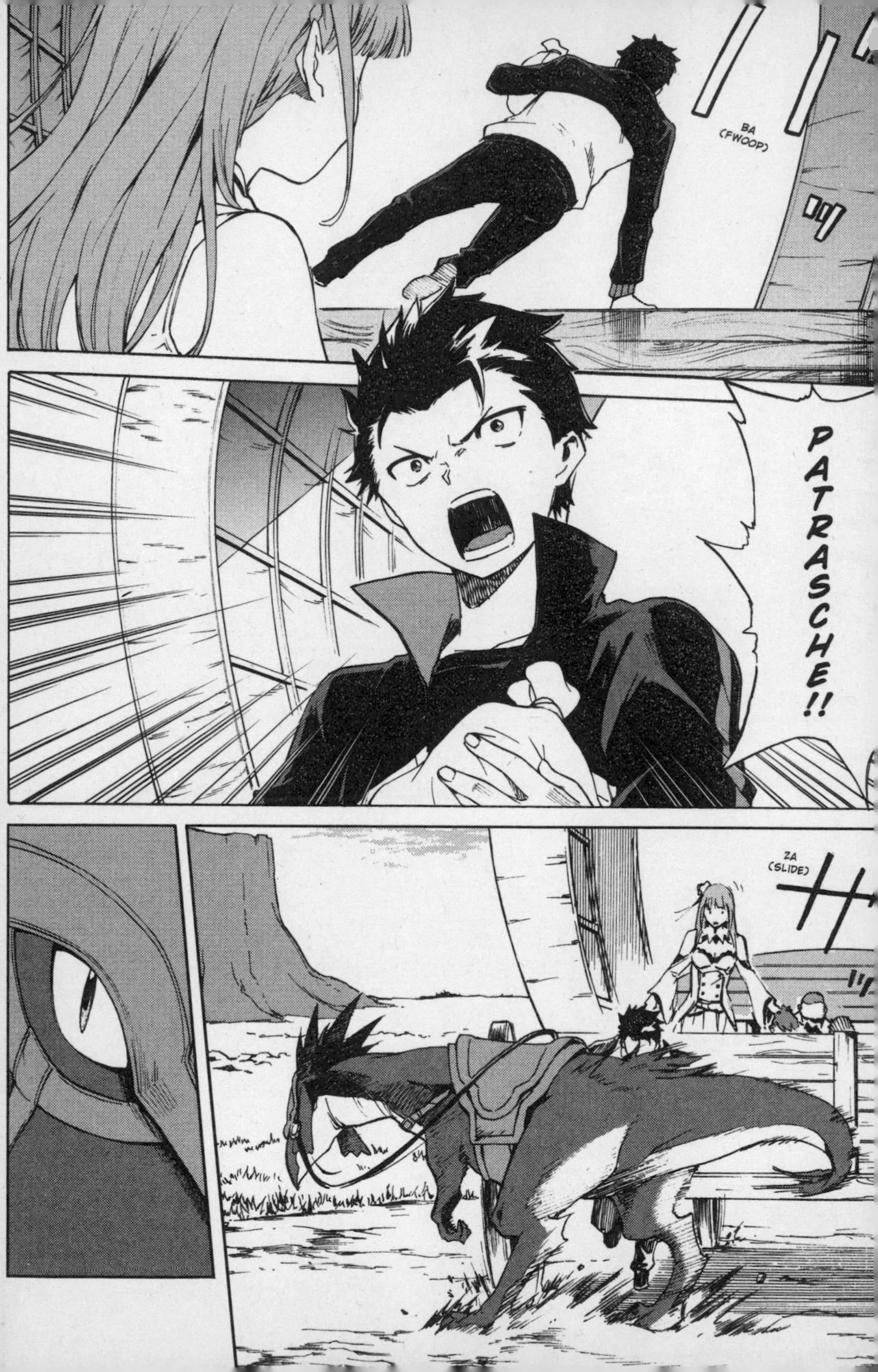
BA
(FWOOP)
PATRASCHE!!
ZA
(SLIDE)

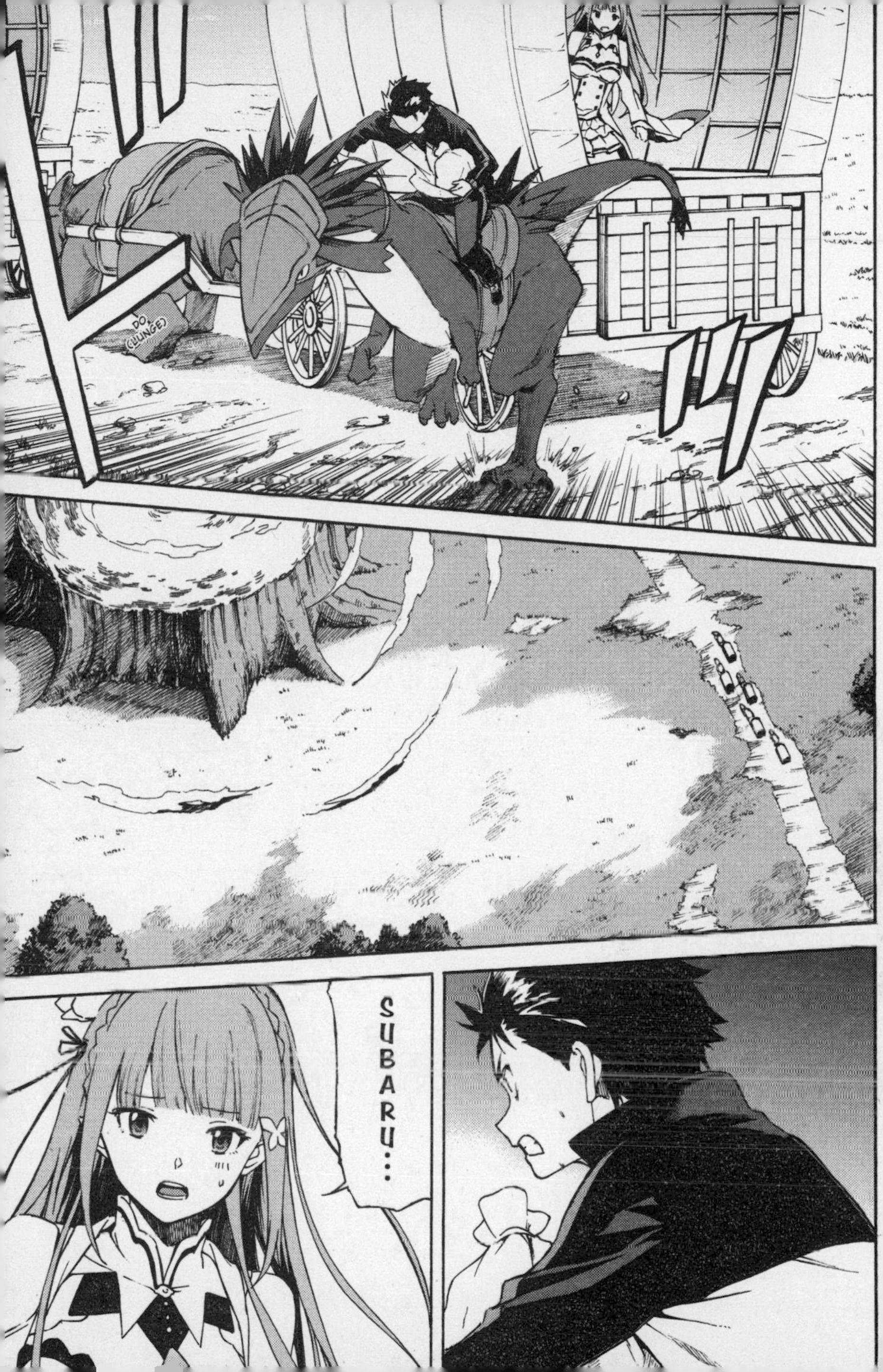
DO (LUNGE)
SUBARU...

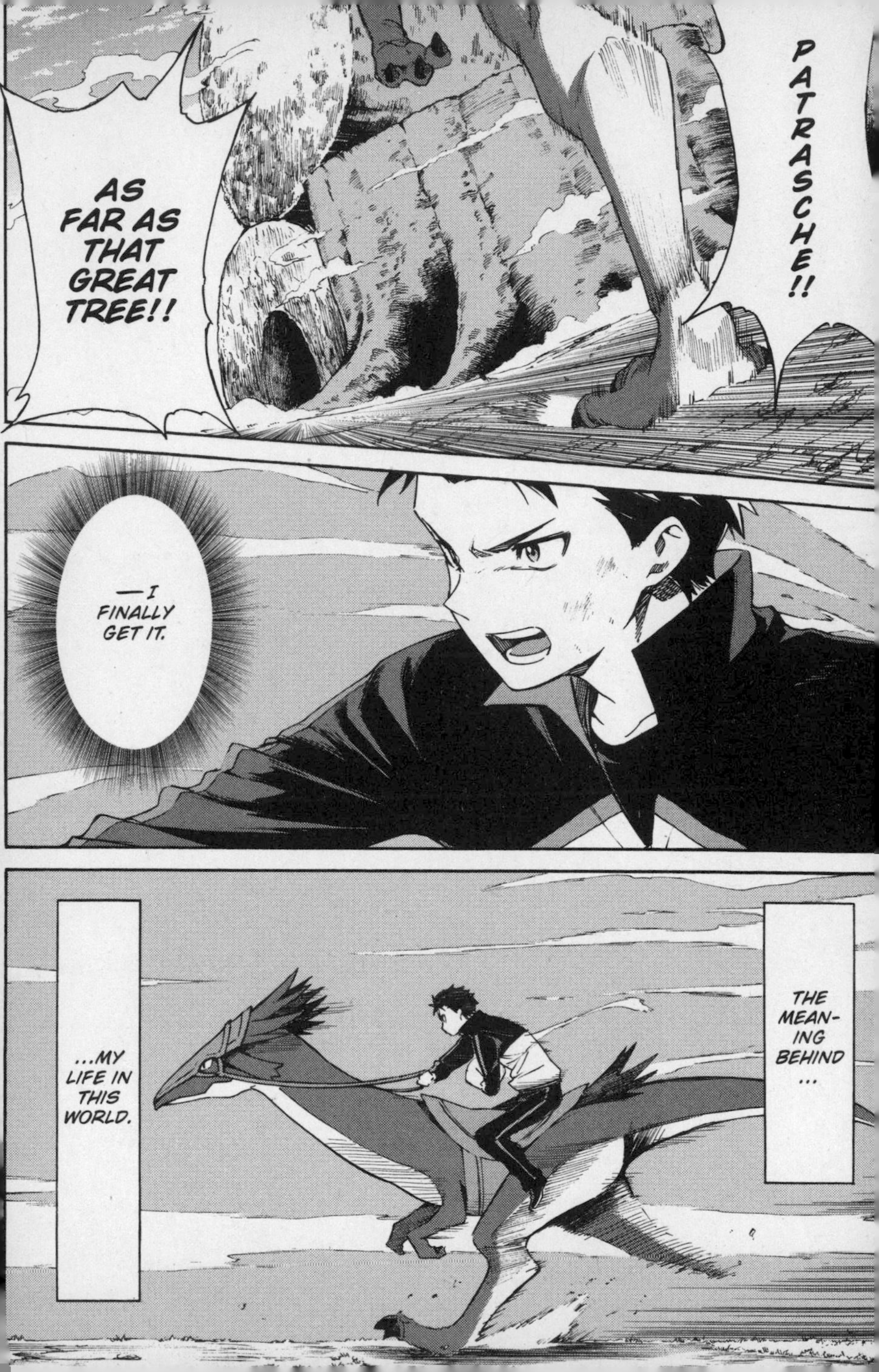
PATRASCHE!!
AS FAR AS THAT GREAT TREE!!
—I FINALLY GET IT.
THE MEANING BEHIND...
...MY LIFE IN THIS WORLD.

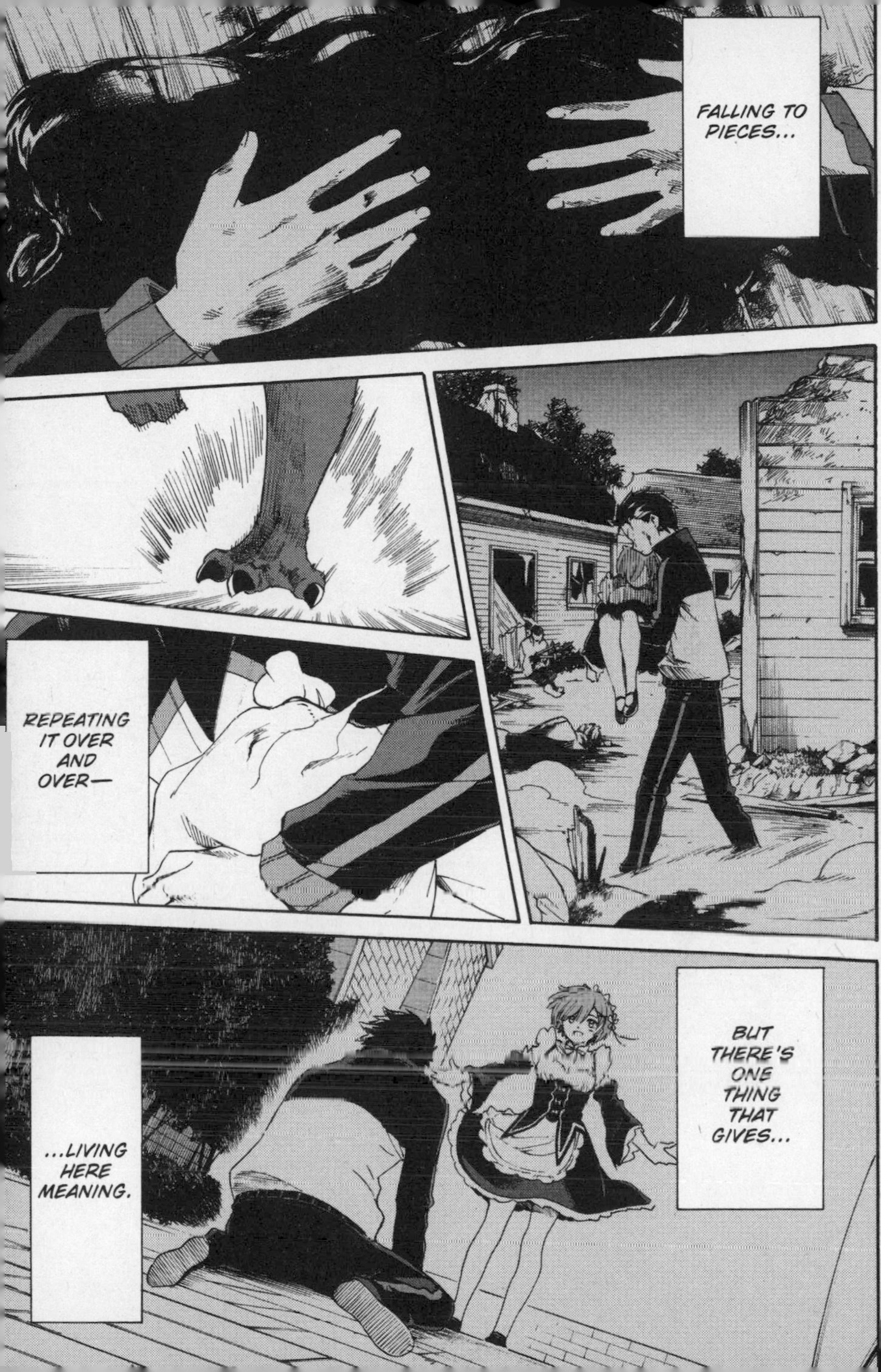
FALLING TO PIECES...
REPEATING IT OVER AND OVER—
BUT THERE'S ONE THING THAT GIVES...
...LIVING HERE MEANING.

...EMILIA.

JUST EMILIA.

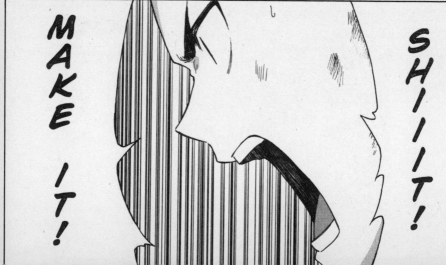

MAKE IT!

SHIIIT!

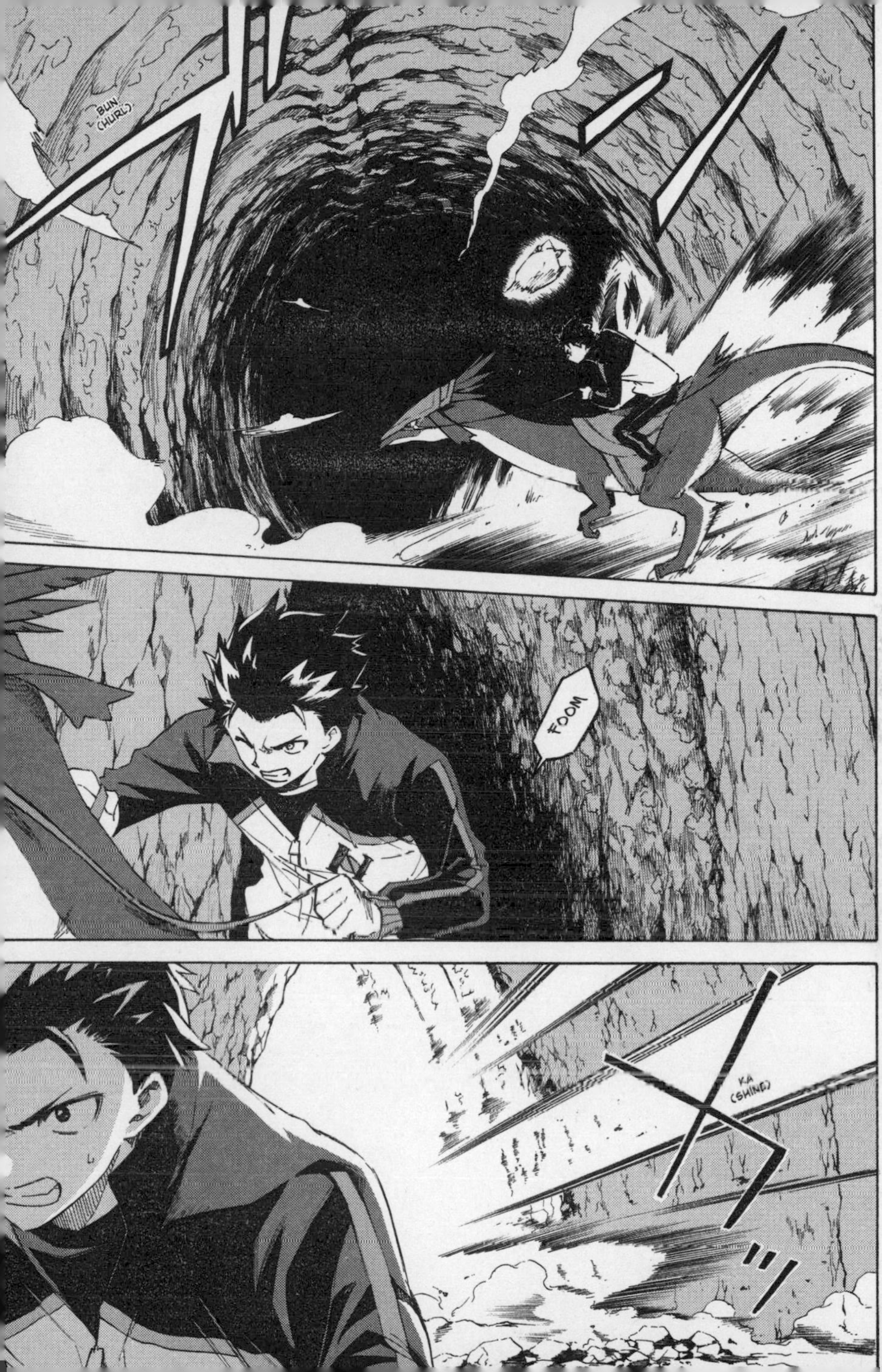
BUN (HURL)
FOOM
KA (SHINE)

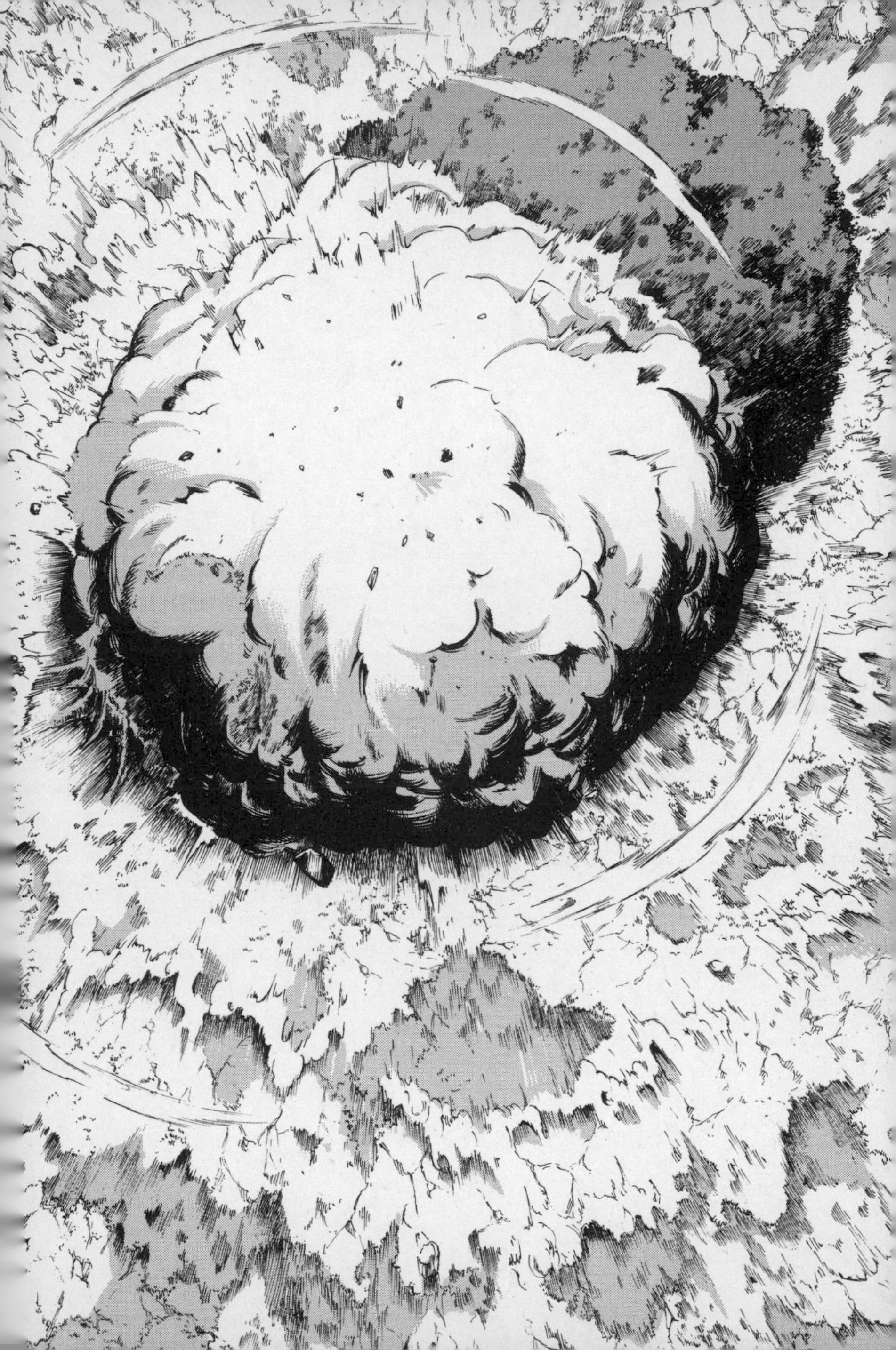

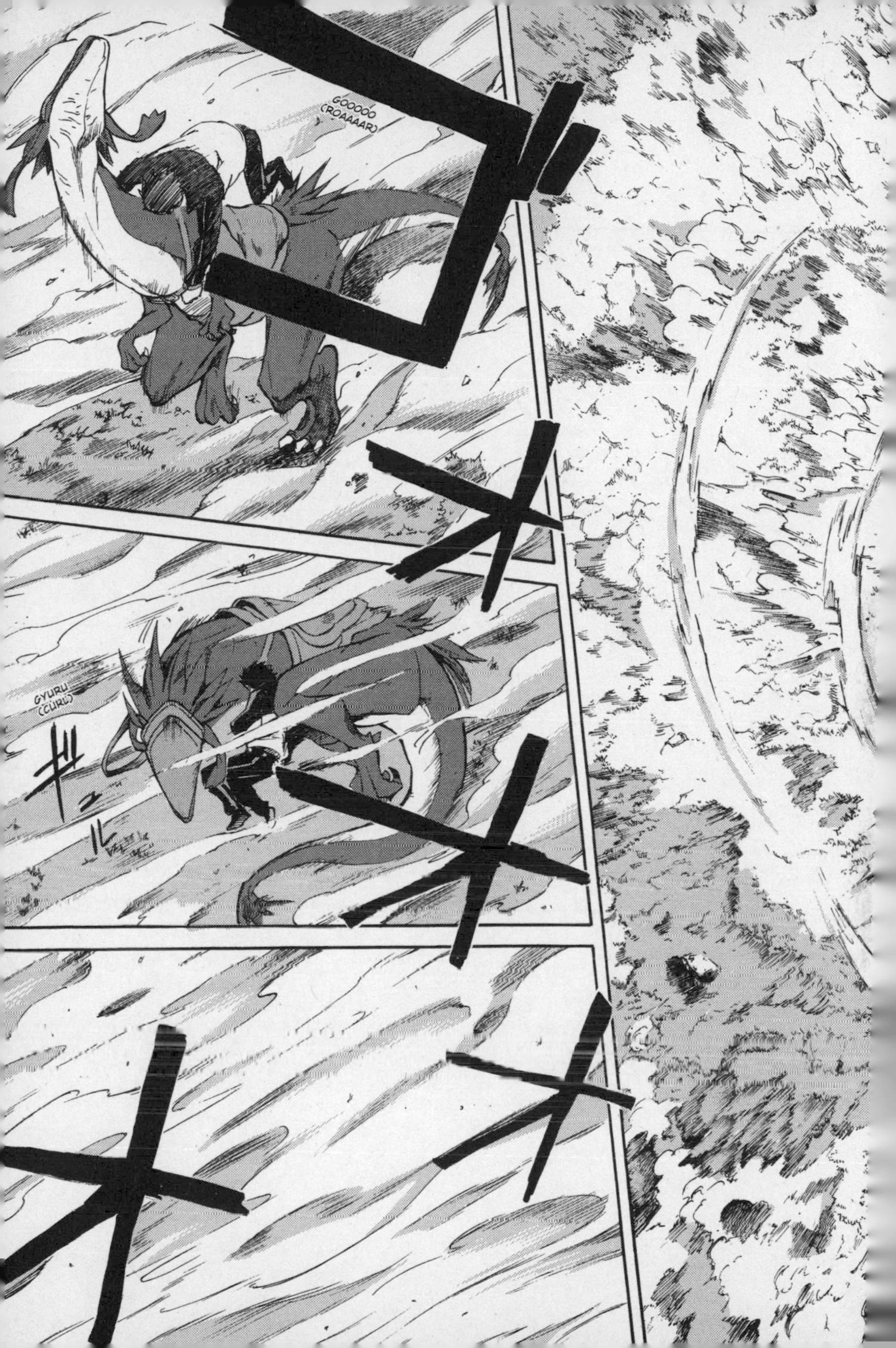
ゴオオオ
GOOOOO
(ROAAAAR)
GYURU
(CURL)

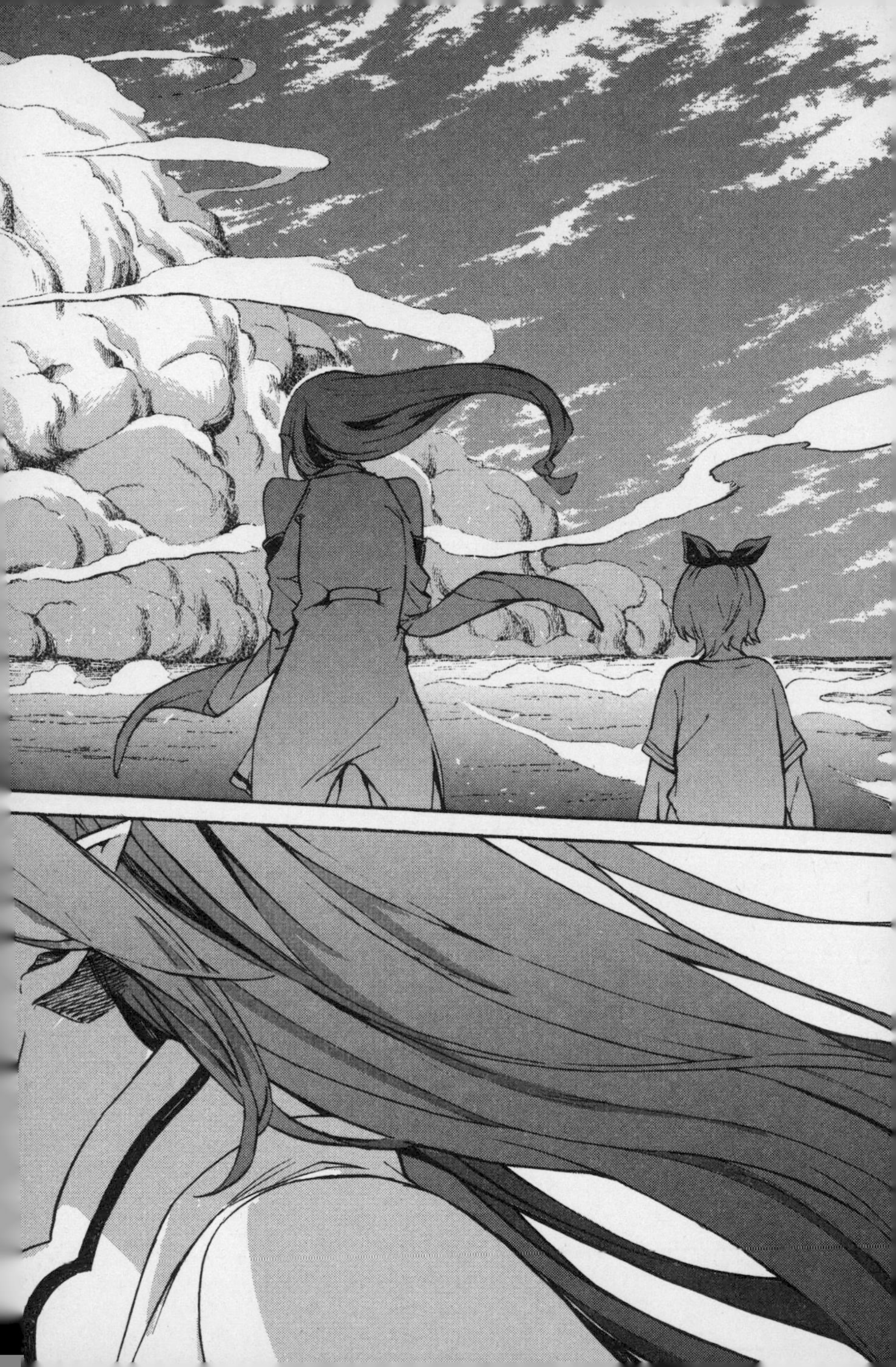

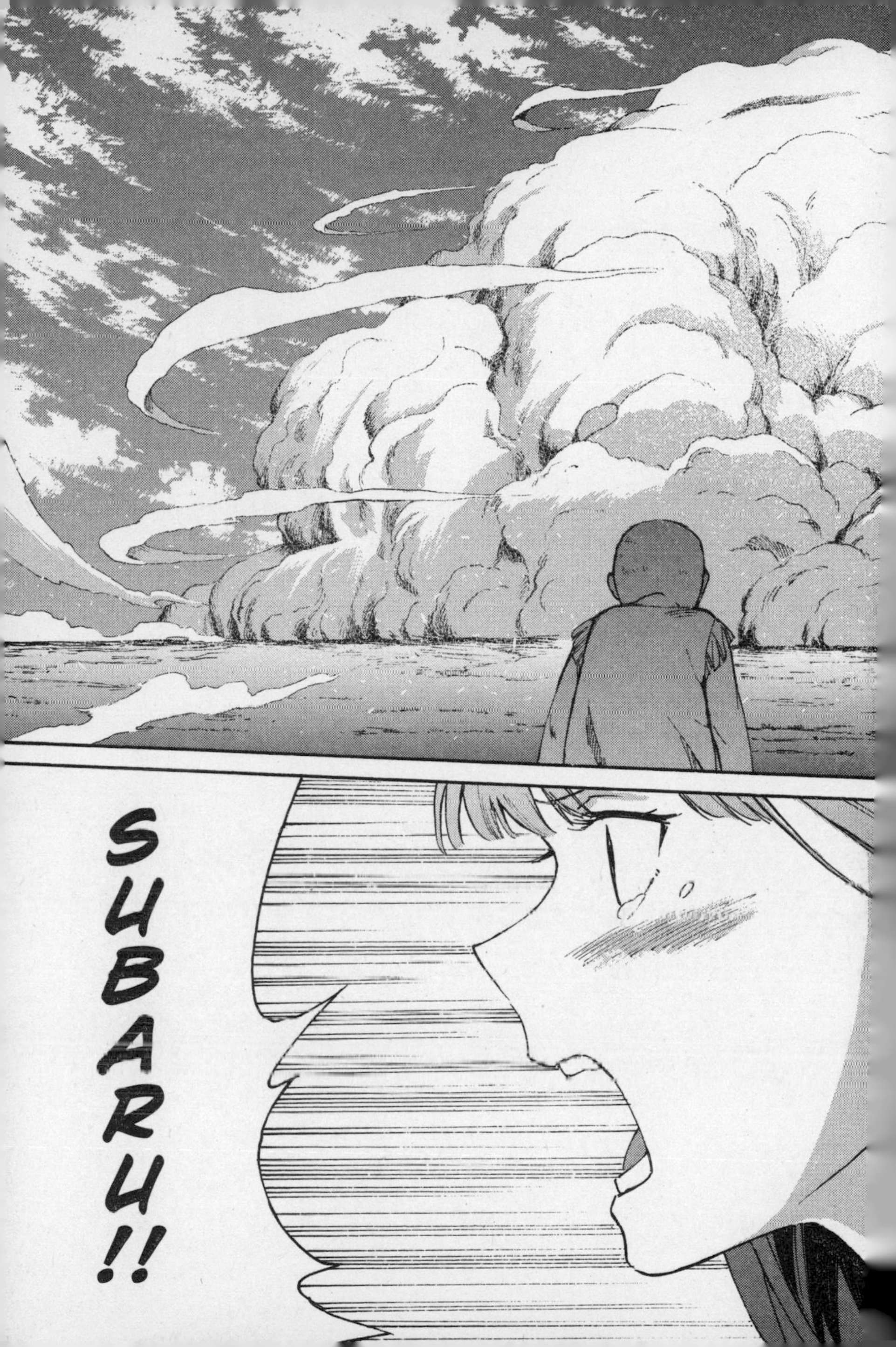
SUBARU!!

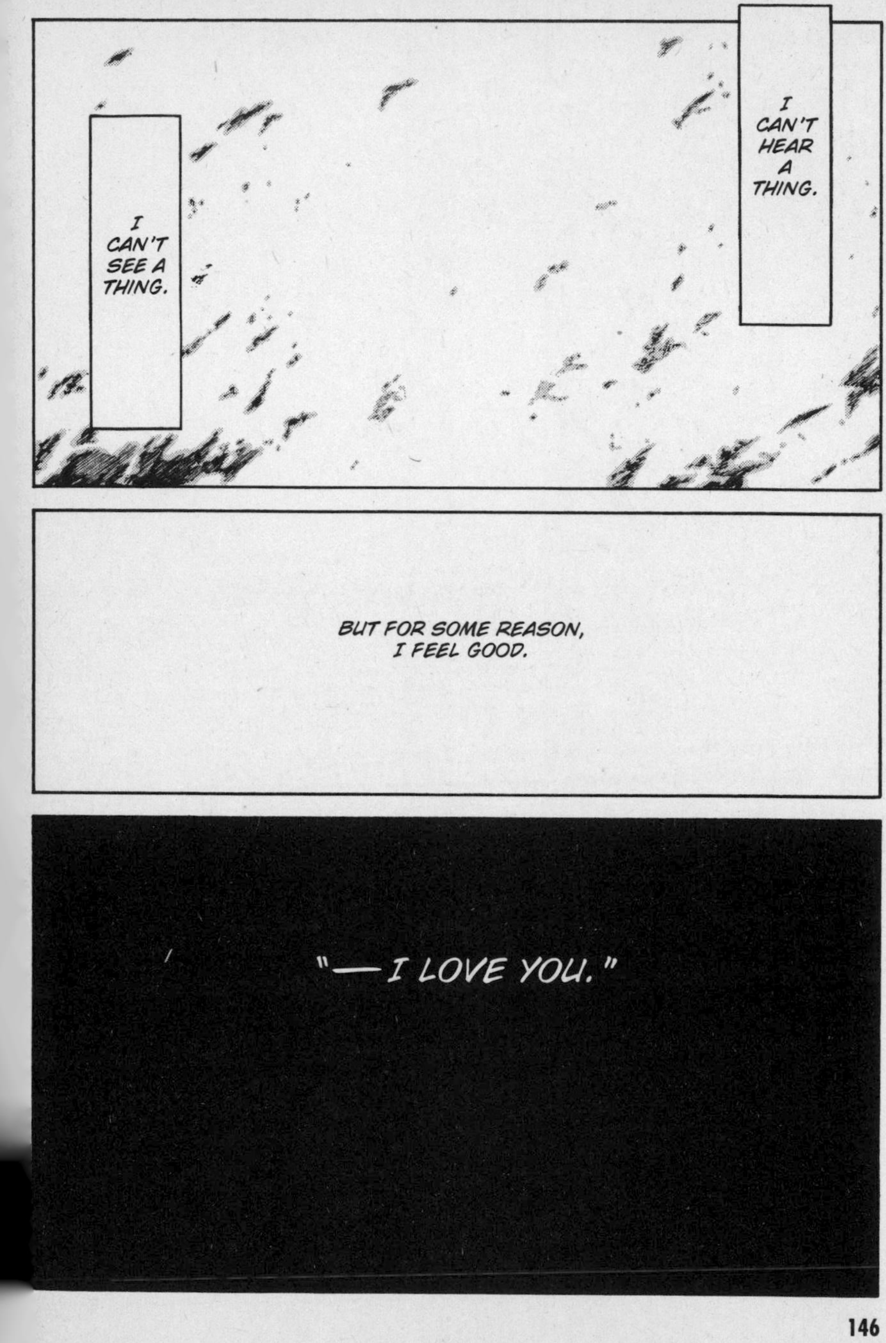
I CAN'T HEAR A THING.
I CAN'T SEE A THING.
BUT FOR SOME REASON, I FEEL GOOD.
"—I LOVE YOU."

Re:ZERO -Starting Life in Another World-

The only ability Subaru Natsuki gets when he's summoned to another world is
time travel via his own death. But to save her, he'll die as many times as it takes.

...BARU!
...SUBARU!

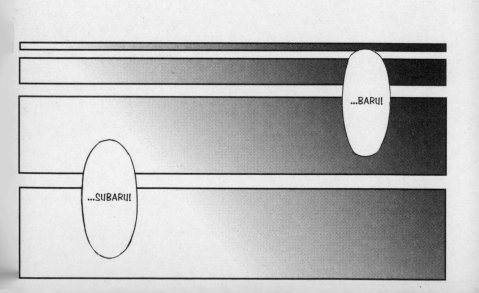

Episode 49
—It Was That Simple a Story

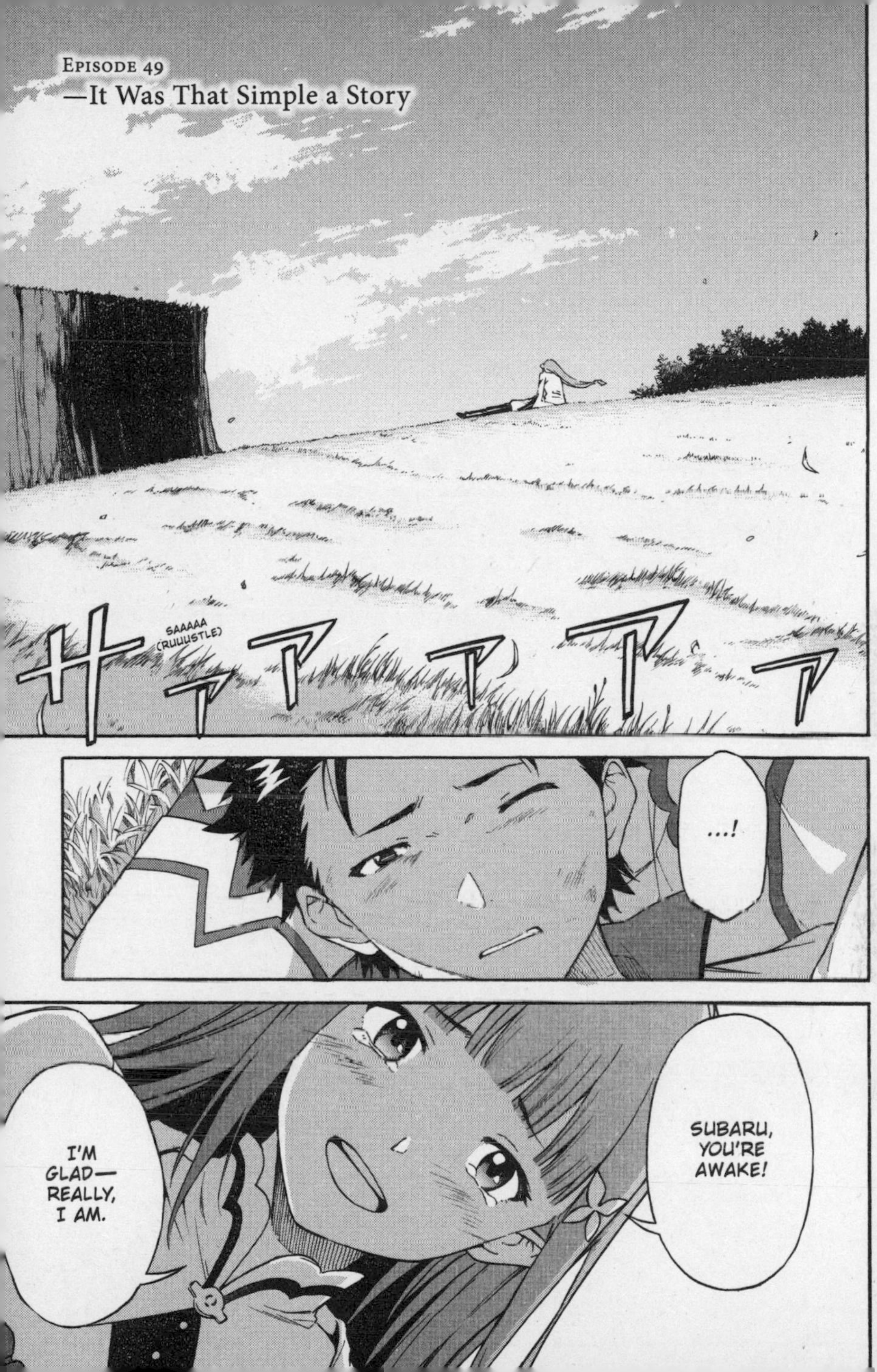
SAAAAA (RUUUSTLE)
...!
SUBARU, YOU'RE AWAKE!
I'M GLAD— REALLY, I AM.

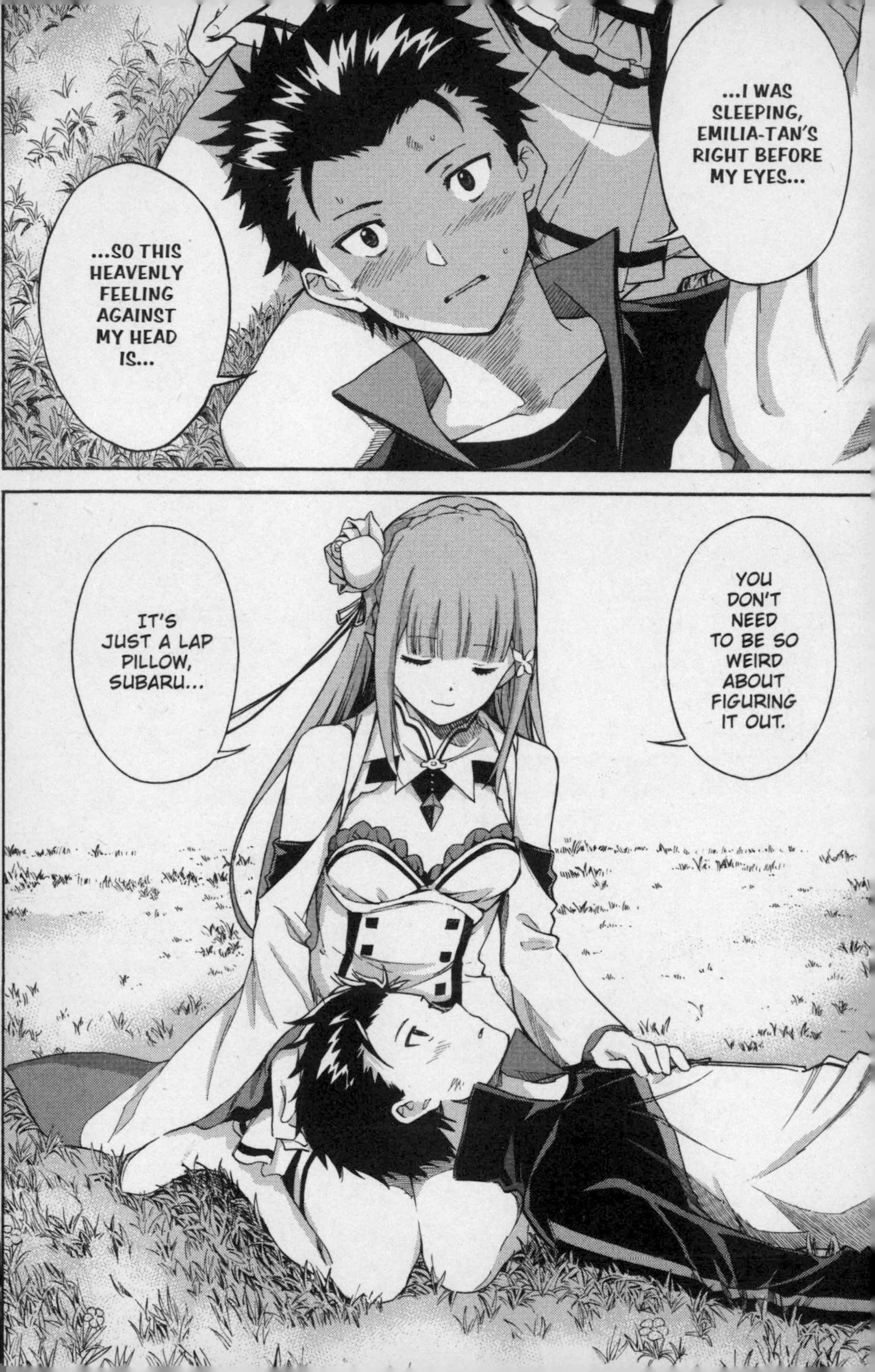
...I WAS SLEEPING, EMILIA-TAN'S RIGHT BEFORE MY EYES...
...SO THIS HEAVENLY FEELING AGAINST MY HEAD IS...
YOU DON'T NEED TO BE SO WEIRD ABOUT FIGURING IT OUT.
IT'S JUST A LAP PILLOW, SUBARU...

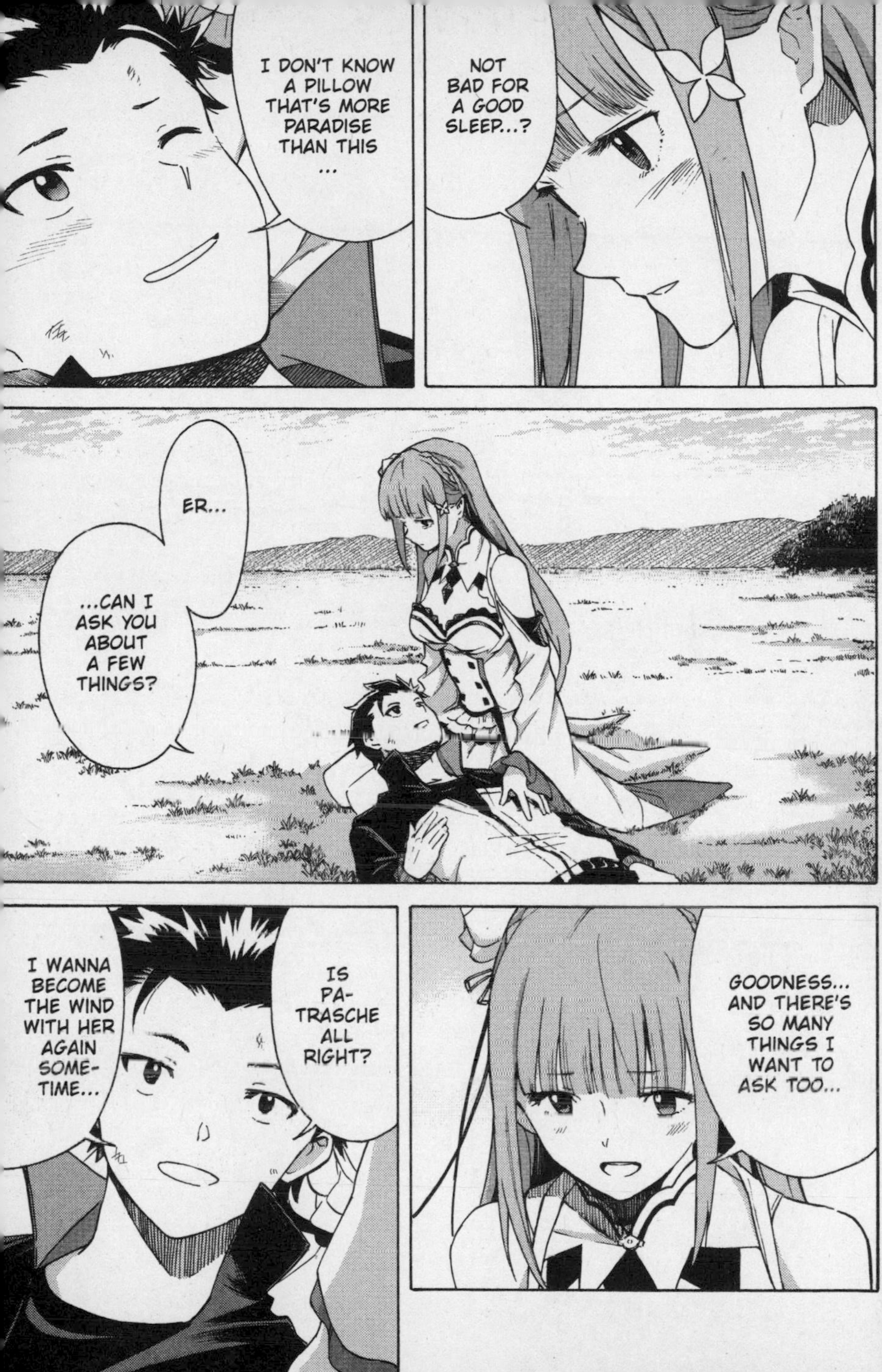
NOT BAD FOR A GOOD SLEEP...?
I DON'T KNOW A PILLOW THAT'S MORE PARADISE THAN THIS ...
ER...
...CAN I ASK YOU ABOUT A FEW THINGS?
GOODNESS... AND THERE'S SO MANY THINGS I WANT TO ASK TOO...
IS PA-TRASCHE ALL RIGHT?
I WANNA BECOME THE WIND WITH HER AGAIN SOME-TIME...

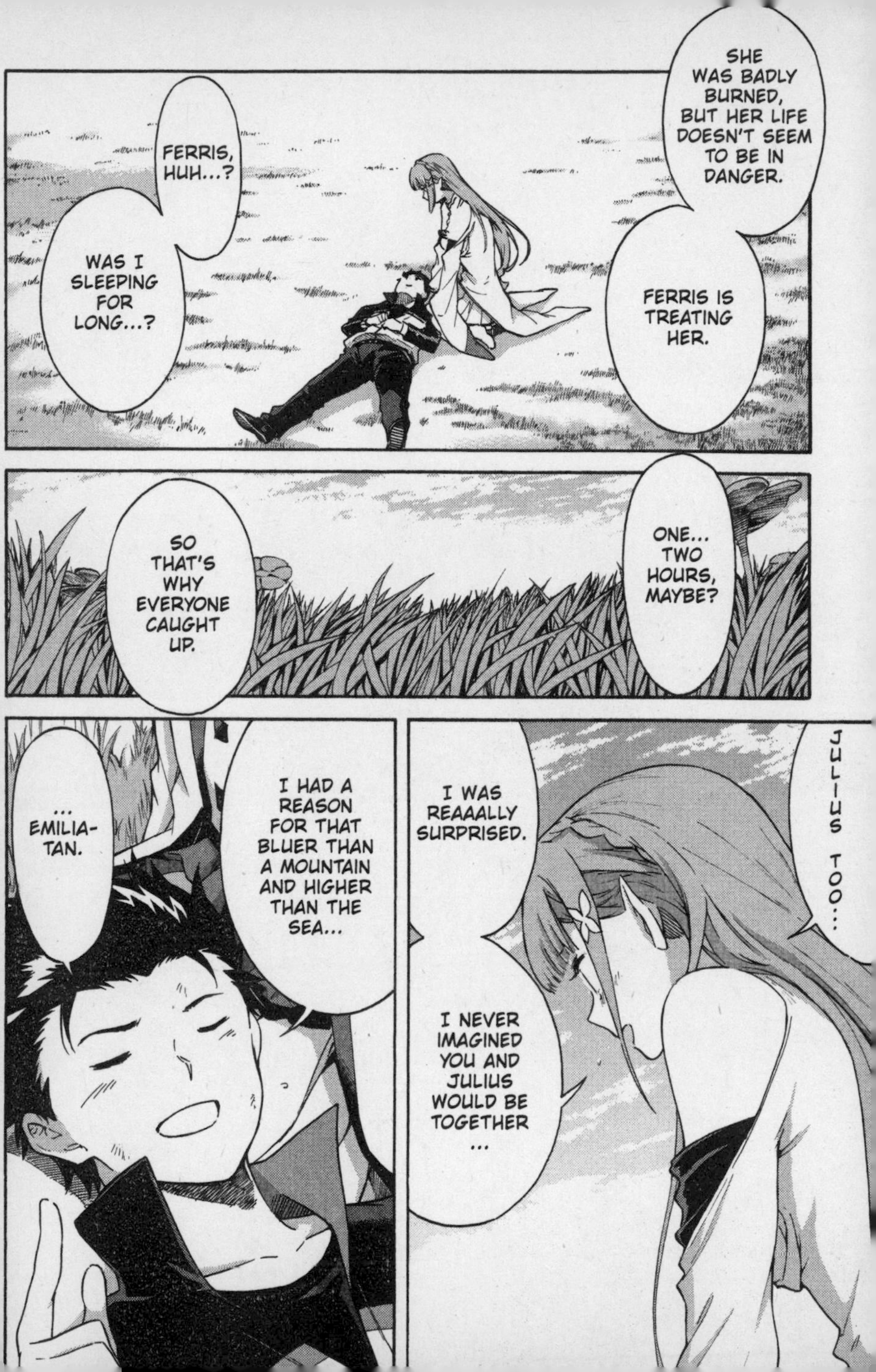
SHE WAS BADLY BURNED, BUT HER LIFE DOESN'T SEEM TO BE IN DANGER.
FERRIS IS TREATING HER.
FERRIS, HUH...?
WAS I SLEEPING FOR LONG...?
ONE... TWO HOURS, MAYBE?
SO THAT'S WHY EVERYONE CAUGHT UP.
JULIUS TOO...
I WAS REAAALLY SURPRISED.
I NEVER IMAGINED YOU AND JULIUS WOULD BE TOGETHER...
I HAD A REASON FOR THAT BLUER THAN A MOUNTAIN AND HIGHER THAN THE SEA...
...EMILIA-TAN.

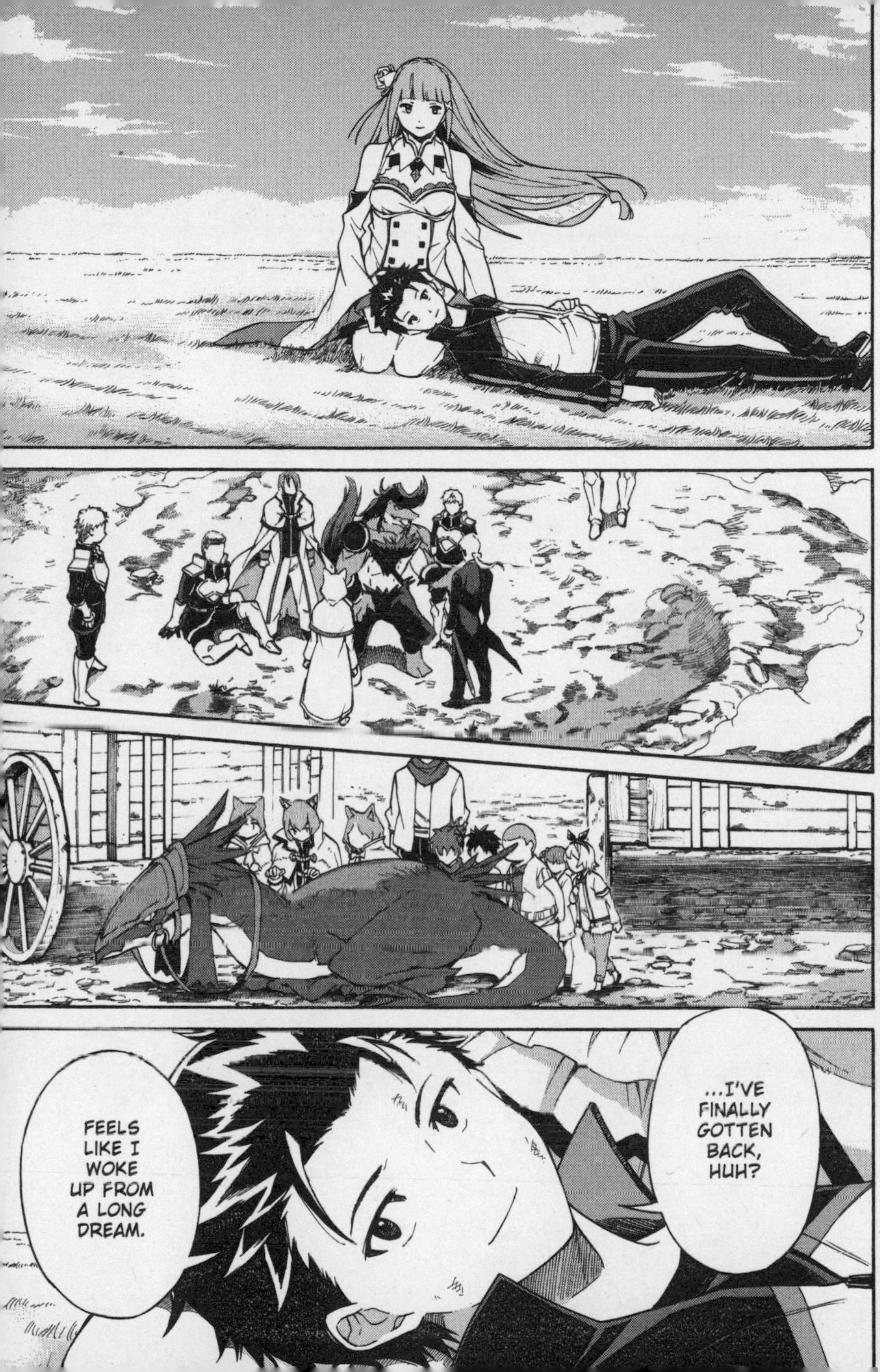
...I'VE FINALLY GOTTEN BACK, HUH?
FEELS LIKE I WOKE UP FROM A LONG DREAM.

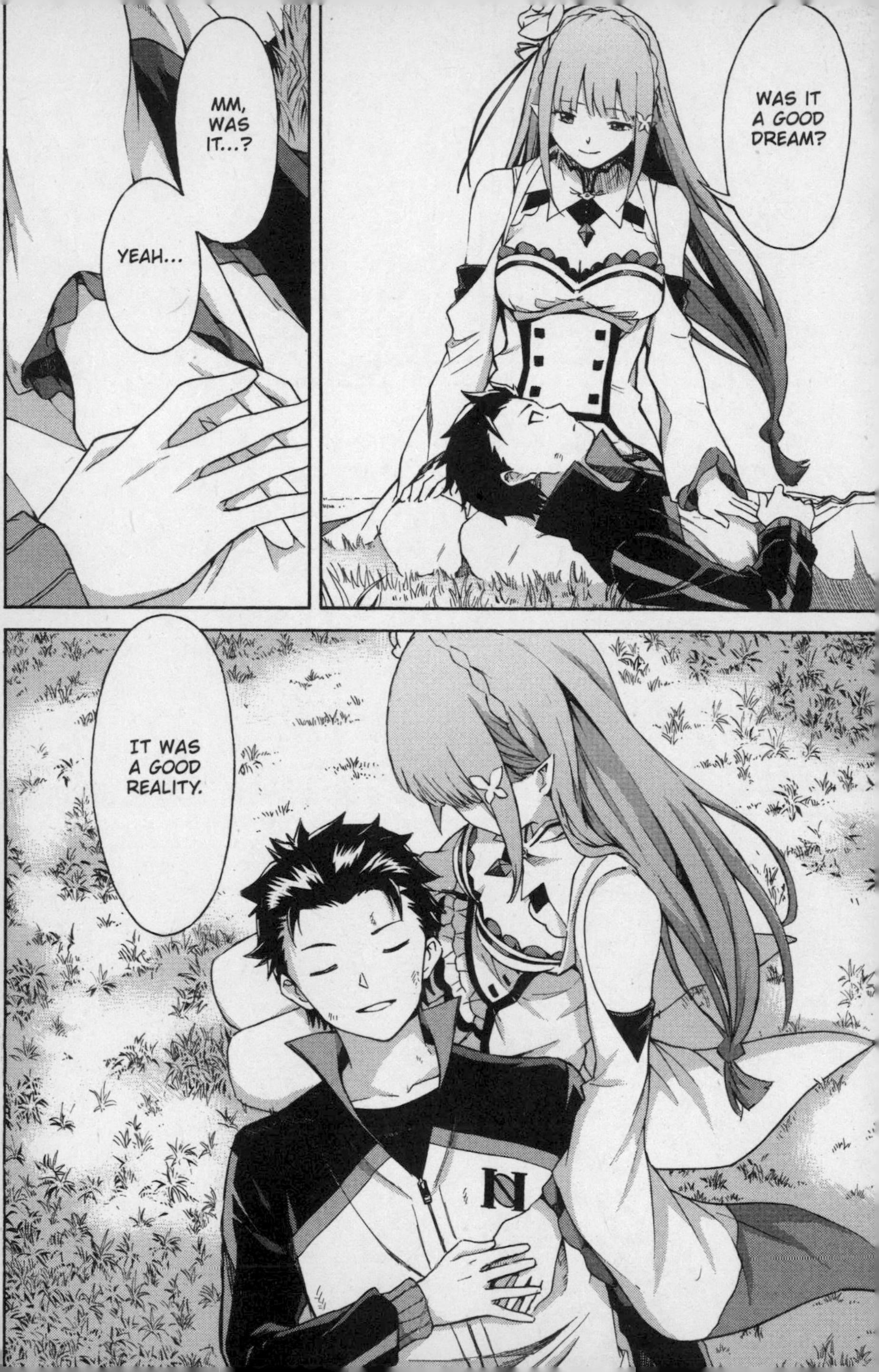
WAS IT A GOOD DREAM?
MM, WAS IT...?
YEAH...
IT WAS A GOOD REALITY.

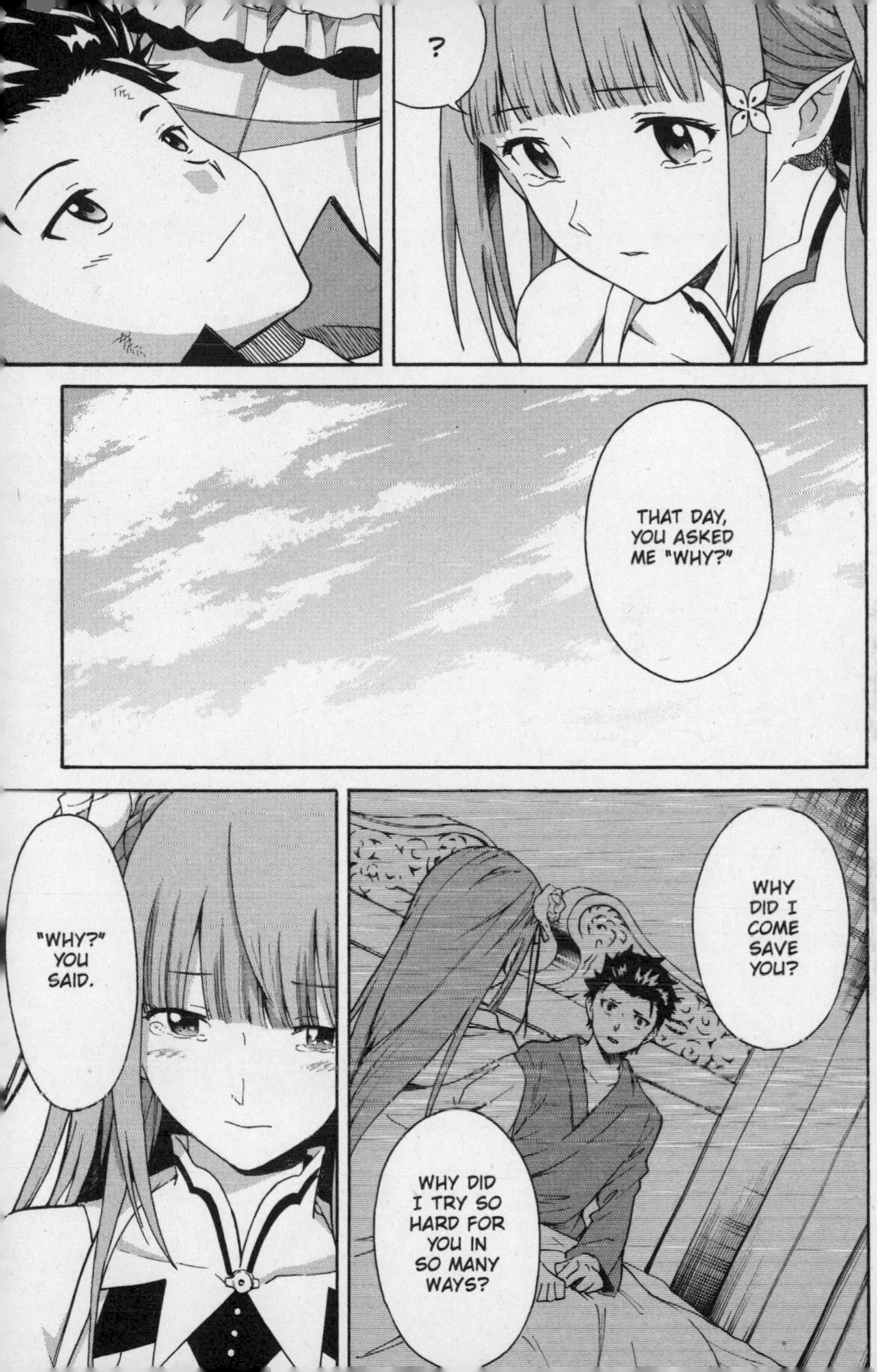
?
THAT DAY, YOU ASKED ME "WHY?"
WHY DID I COME SAVE YOU?
WHY DID I TRY SO HARD FOR YOU IN SO MANY WAYS?
"WHY?" YOU SAID.

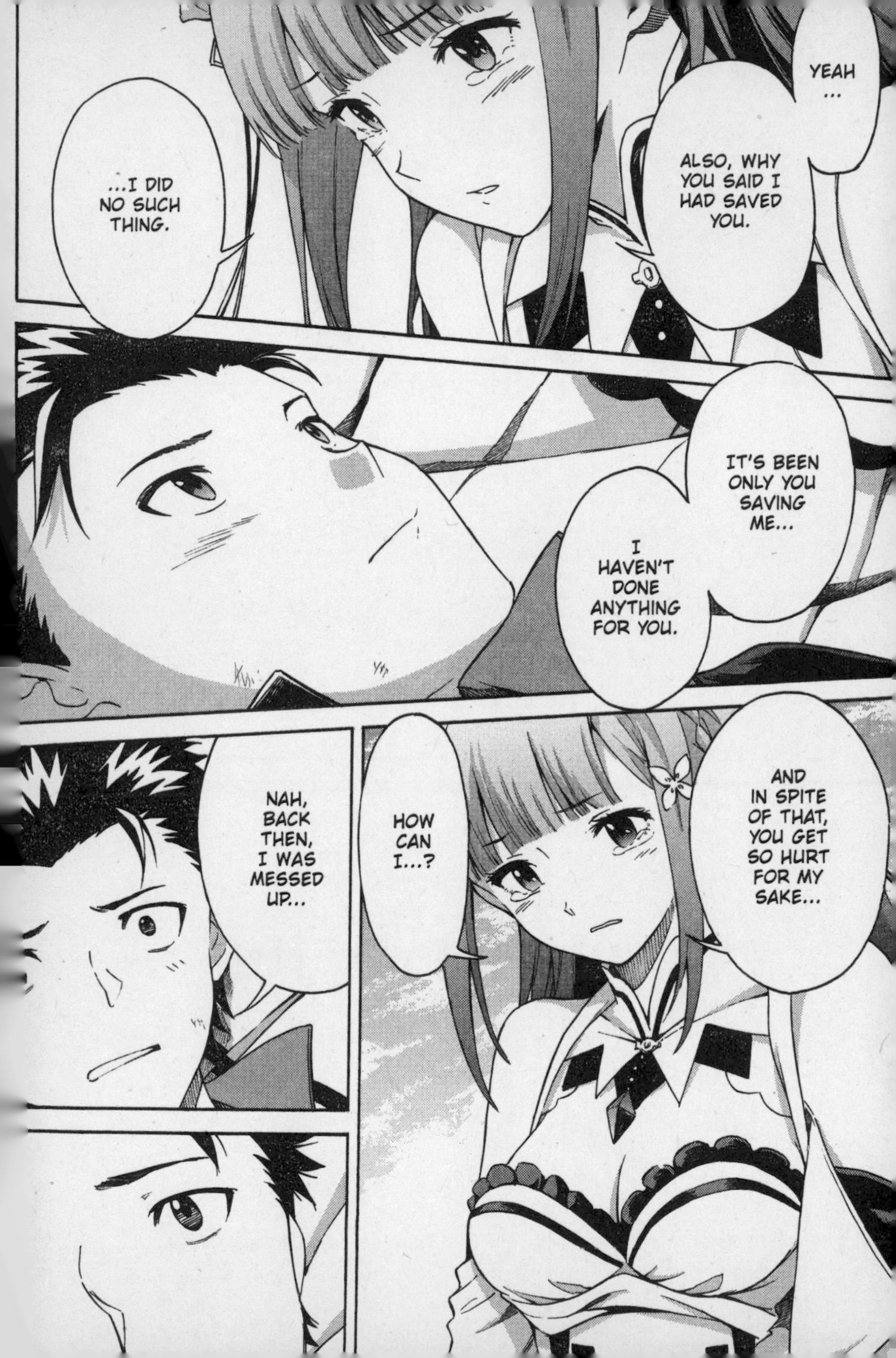
YEAH...
ALSO, WHY YOU SAID I HAD SAVED YOU.
...I DID NO SUCH THING.
IT'S BEEN ONLY YOU SAVING ME...
I HAVEN'T DONE ANYTHING FOR YOU.
AND IN SPITE OF THAT, YOU GET SO HURT FOR MY SAKE...
HOW CAN I...?
NAH, BACK THEN, I WAS MESSED UP...

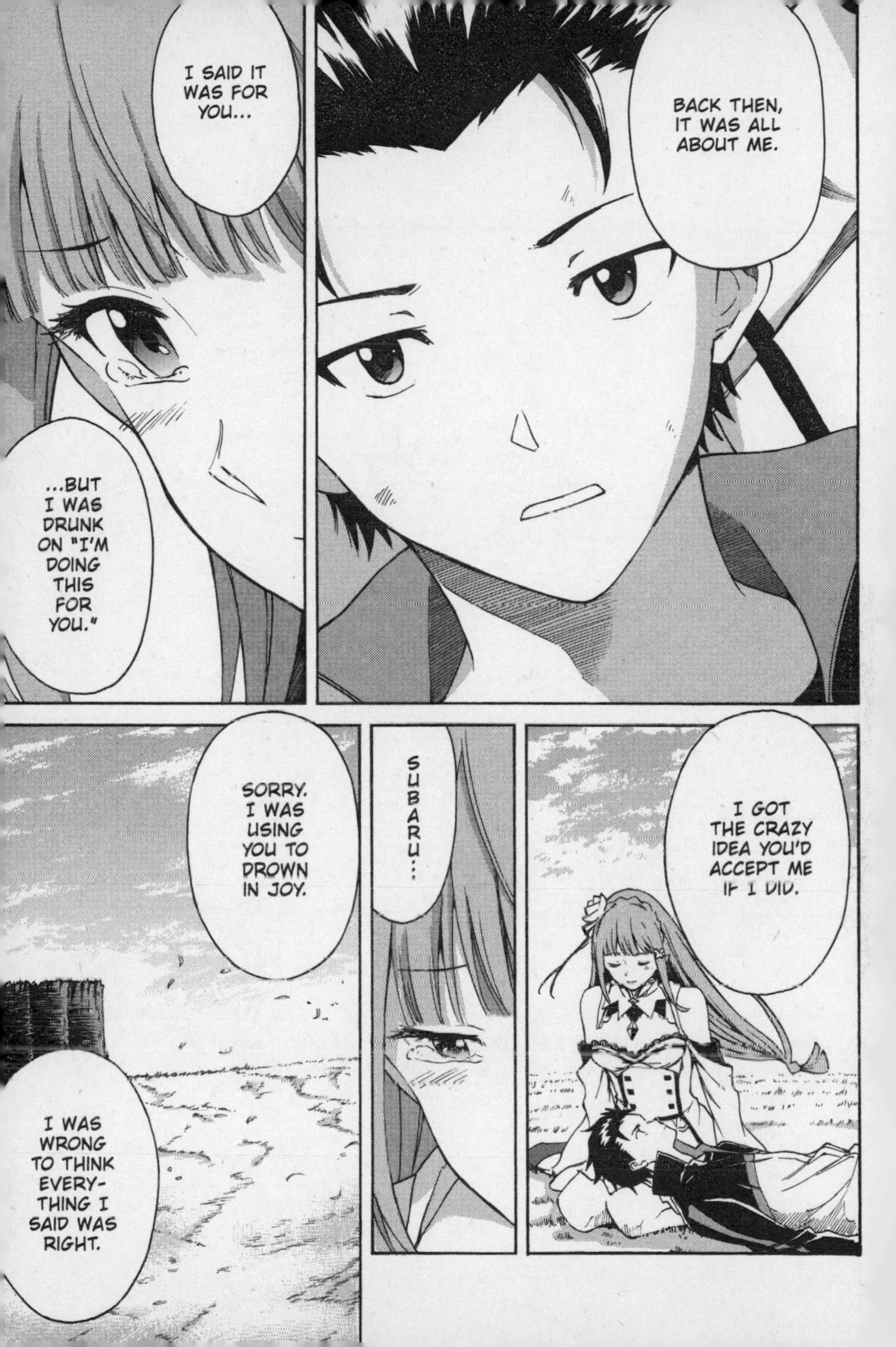
BACK THEN, IT WAS ALL ABOUT ME.
I SAID IT WAS FOR YOU...
...BUT I WAS DRUNK ON "I'M DOING THIS FOR YOU."
I GOT THE CRAZY IDEA YOU'D ACCEPT ME IF I DID.
SUBARU...
SORRY. I WAS USING YOU TO DROWN IN JOY.
I WAS WRONG TO THINK EVERY-THING I SAID WAS RIGHT.

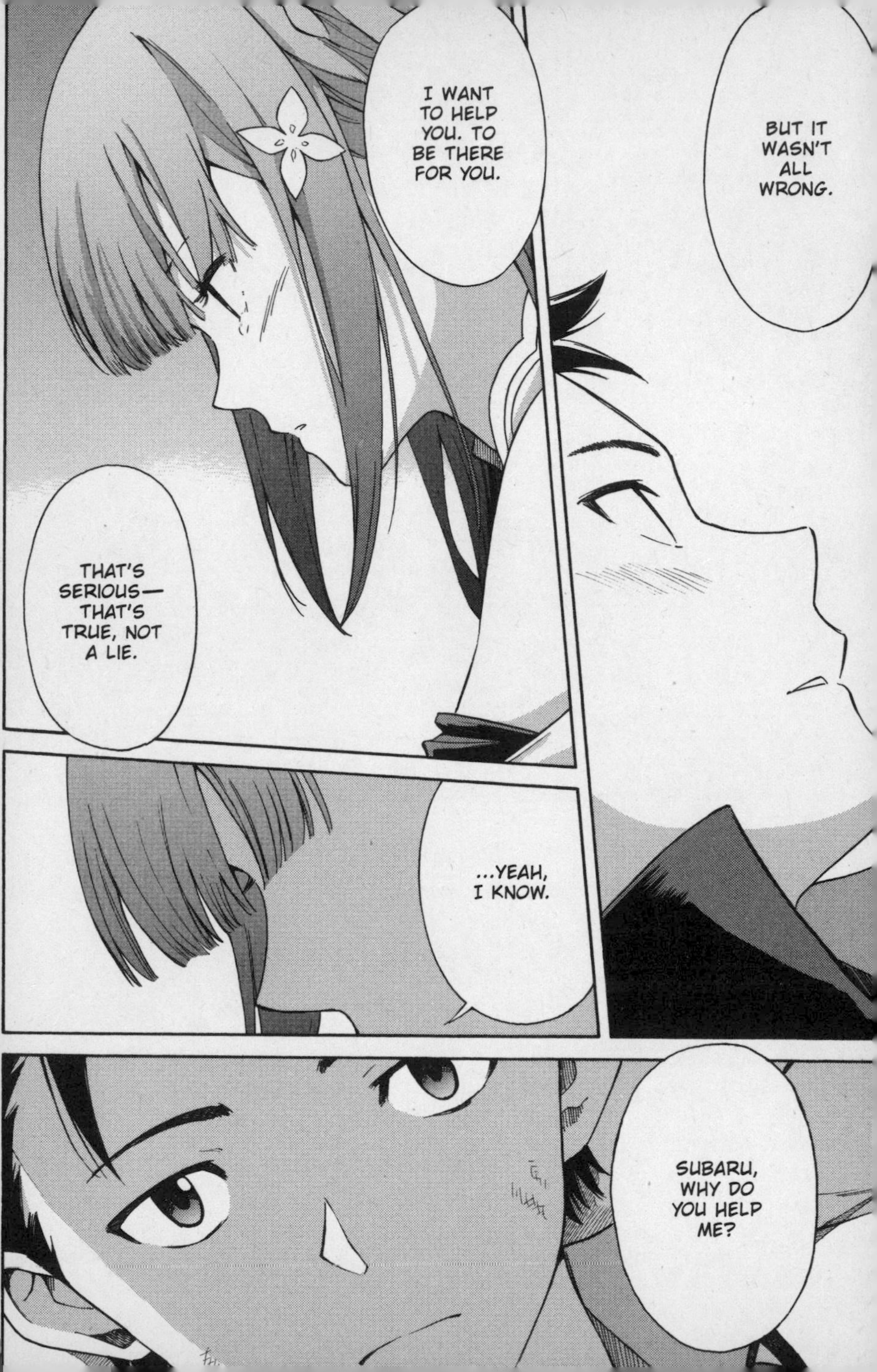
BUT IT WASN'T ALL WRONG.
I WANT TO HELP YOU. TO BE THERE FOR YOU.
THAT'S SERIOUS—THAT'S TRUE, NOT A LIE.
...YEAH, I KNOW.
SUBARU, WHY DO YOU HELP ME?

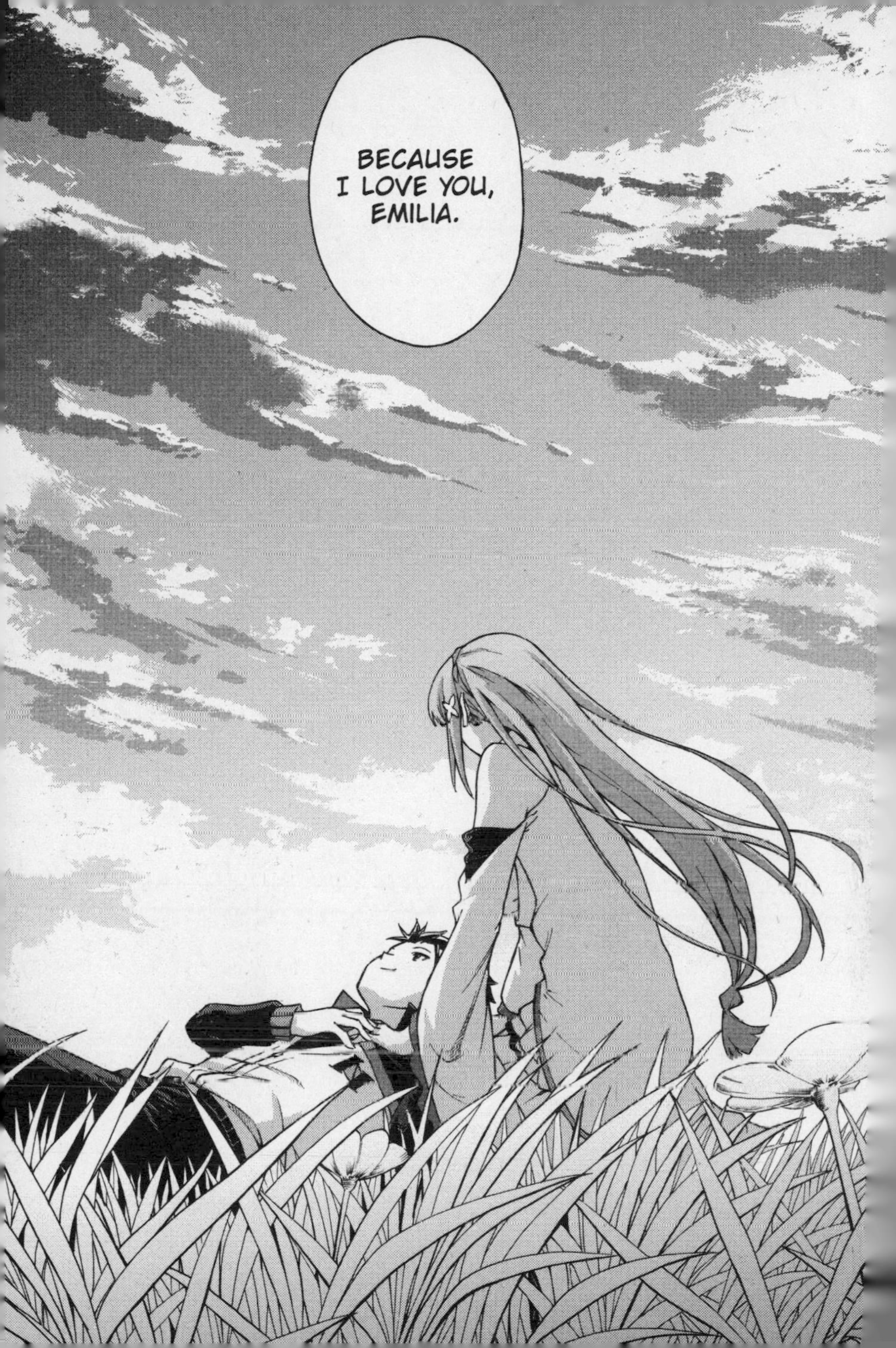
BECAUSE I LOVE YOU, EMILIA.

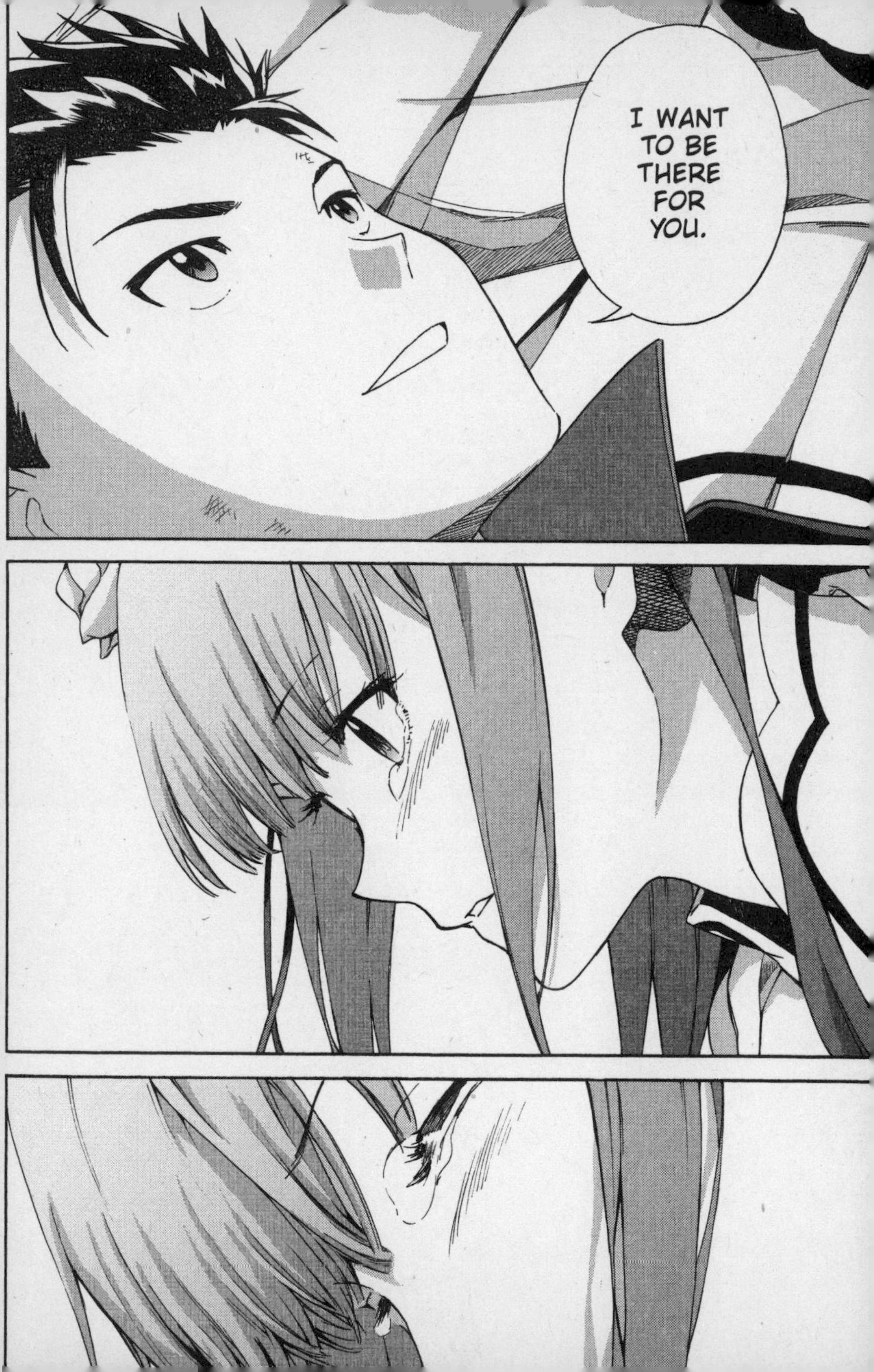
I WANT TO BE THERE FOR YOU.

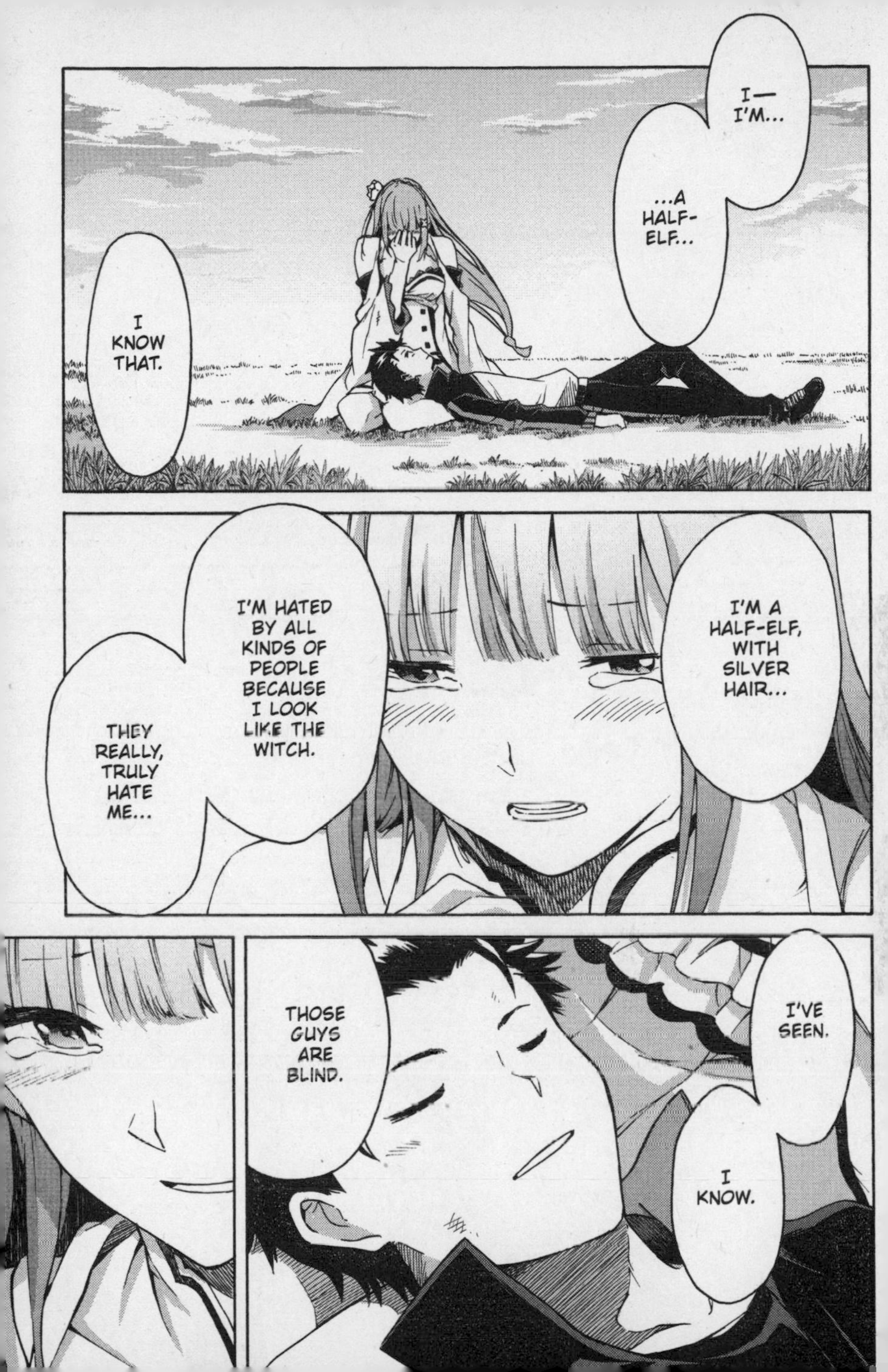
I— I'M...
...A HALF-ELF...
I KNOW THAT.
I'M A HALF-ELF, WITH SILVER HAIR...
I'M HATED BY ALL KINDS OF PEOPLE BECAUSE I LOOK LIKE THE WITCH.
THEY REALLY, TRULY HATE ME...
I'VE SEEN.
I KNOW.
THOSE GUYS ARE BLIND.

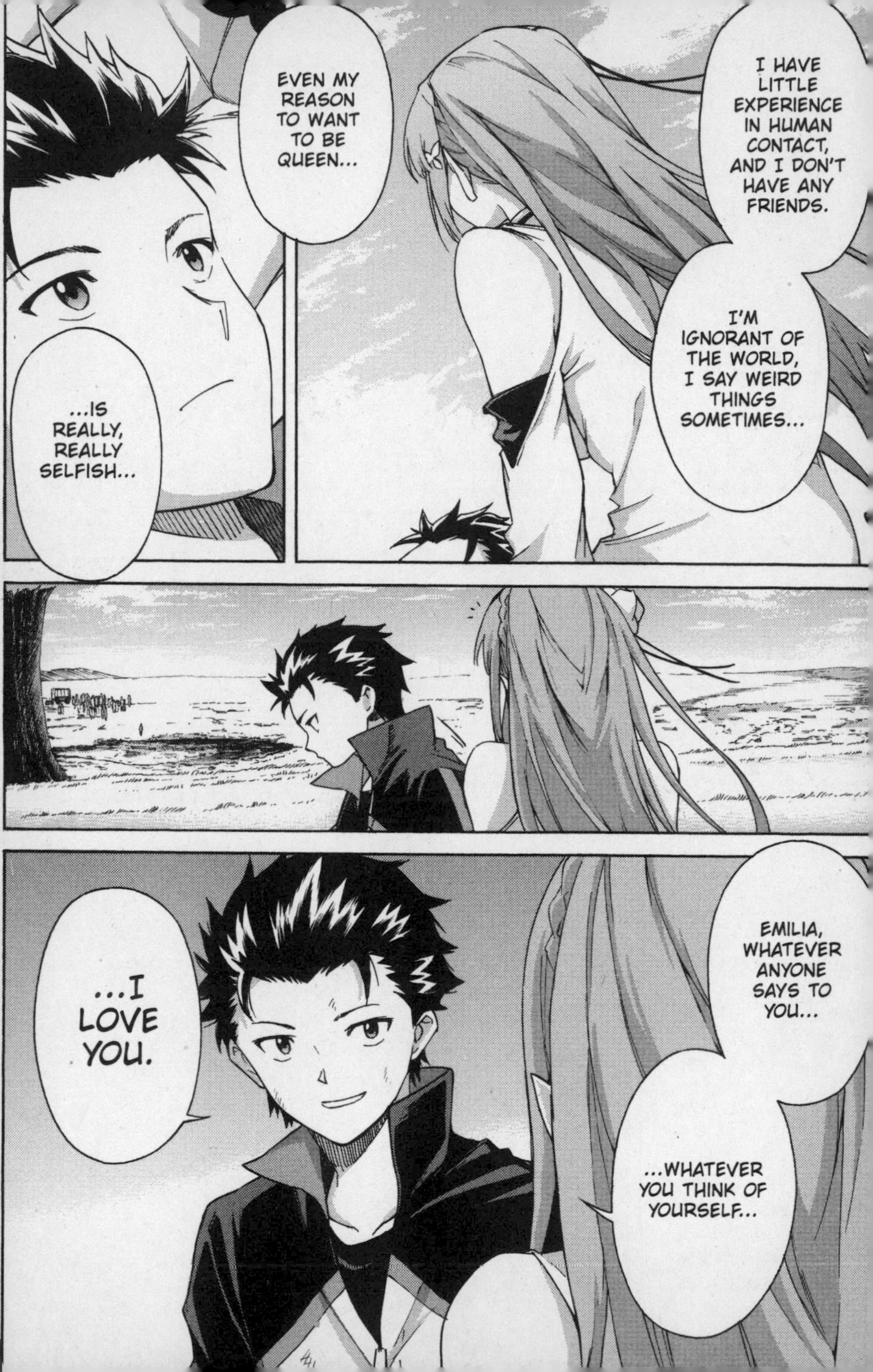
I HAVE LITTLE EXPERIENCE IN HUMAN CONTACT, AND I DON'T HAVE ANY FRIENDS.
I'M IGNORANT OF THE WORLD, I SAY WEIRD THINGS SOMETIMES...
EVEN MY REASON TO WANT TO BE QUEEN...
...IS REALLY, REALLY SELFISH...
EMILIA, WHATEVER ANYONE SAYS TO YOU...
...WHATEVER YOU THINK OF YOURSELF...
...I LOVE YOU.

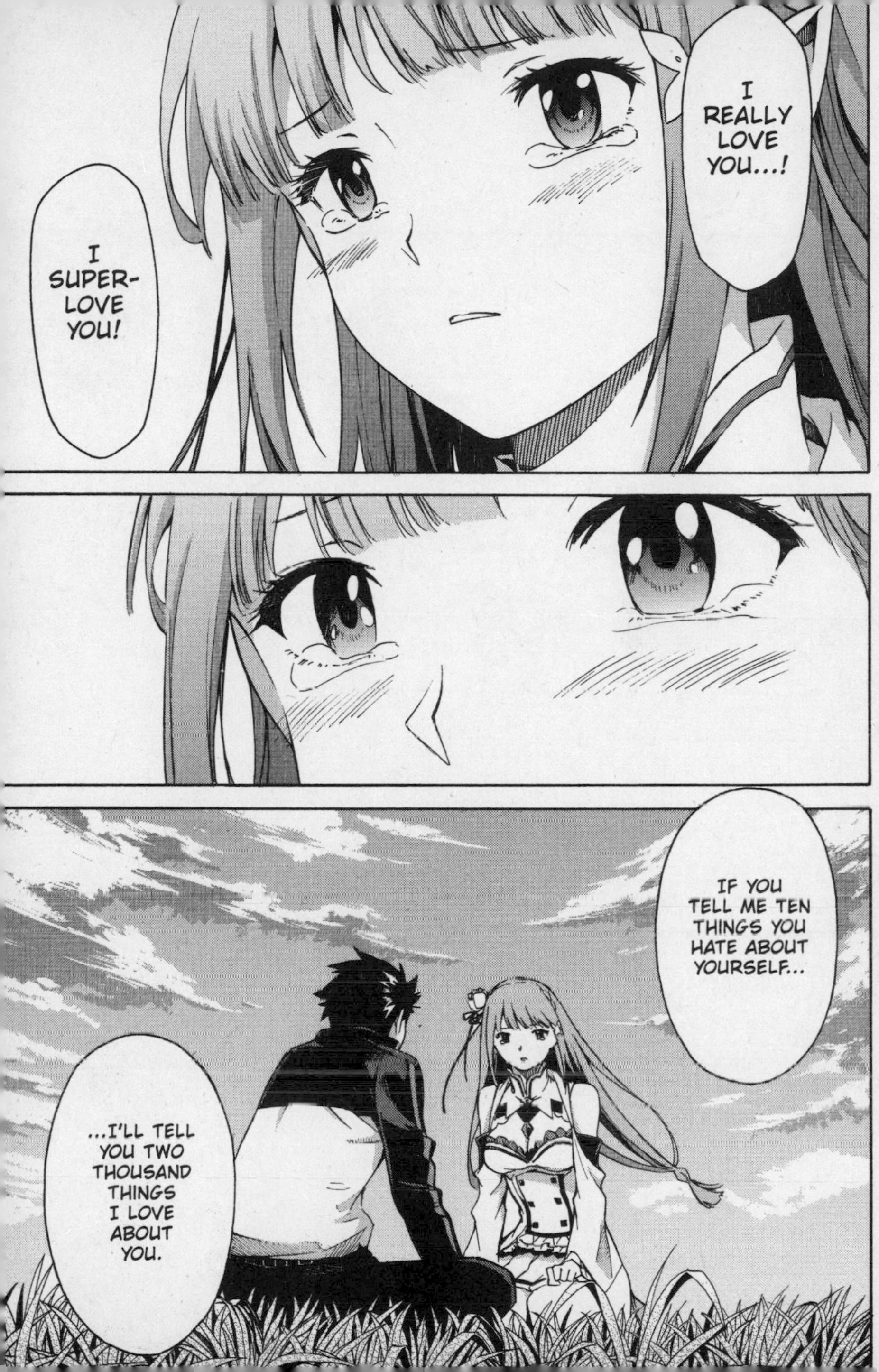
I REALLY LOVE YOU...!
I SUPER-LOVE YOU!
IF YOU TELL ME TEN THINGS YOU HATE ABOUT YOURSELF...
...I'LL TELL YOU TWO THOUSAND THINGS I LOVE ABOUT YOU.

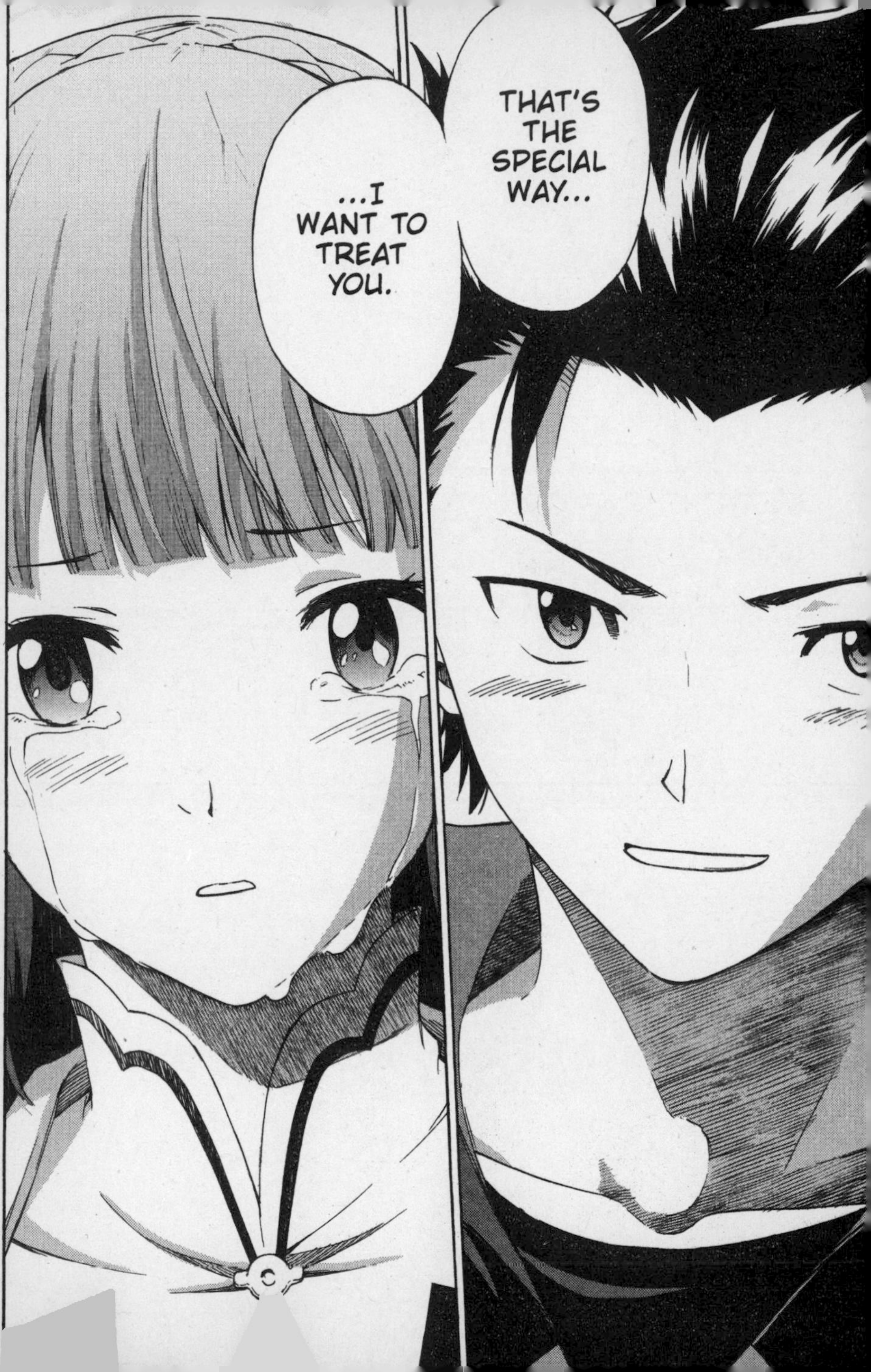
THAT'S THE SPECIAL WAY...
...I WANT TO TREAT YOU.

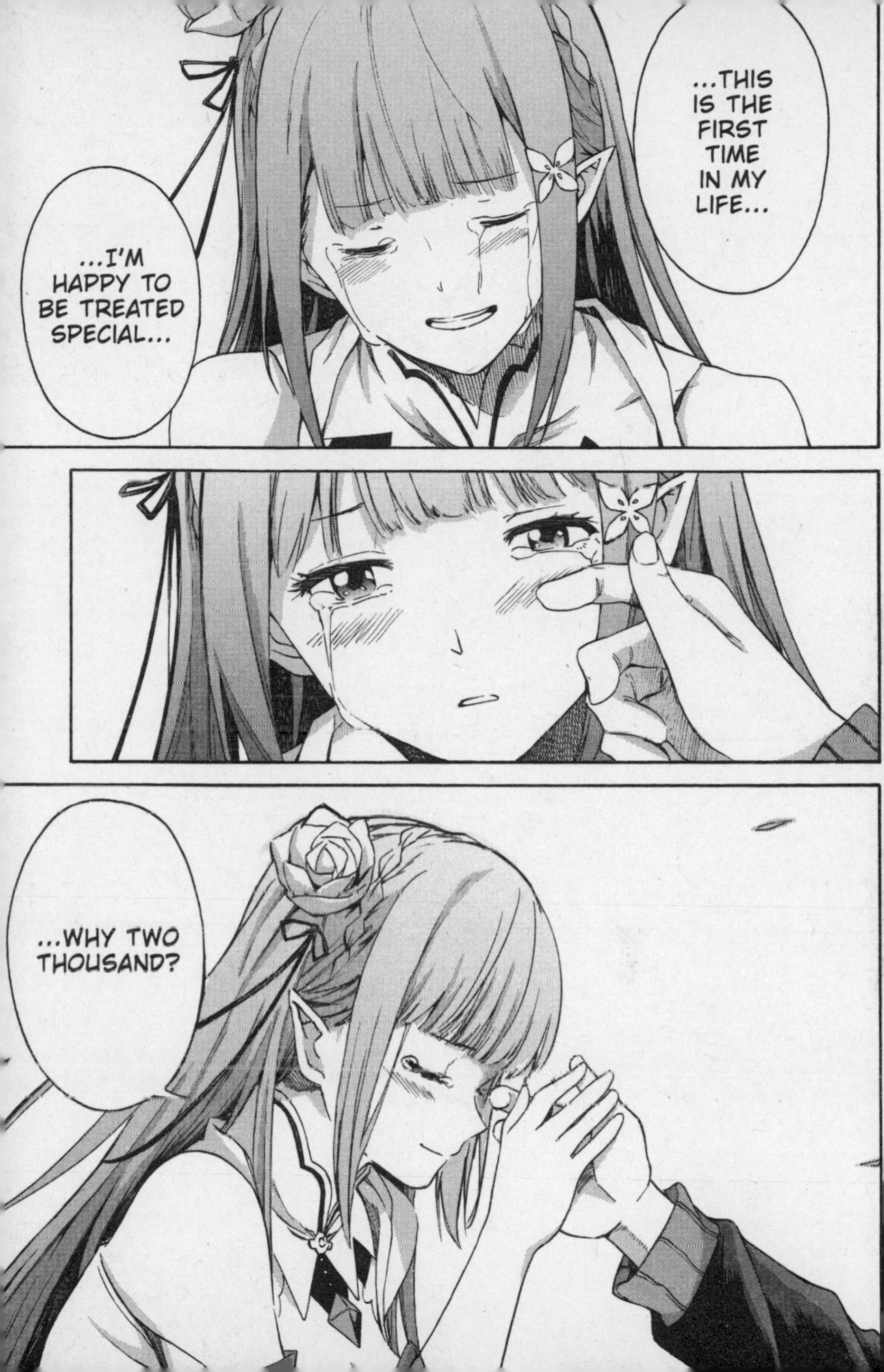
...THIS IS THE FIRST TIME IN MY LIFE...
...I'M HAPPY TO BE TREATED SPECIAL...
...WHY TWO THOUSAND?

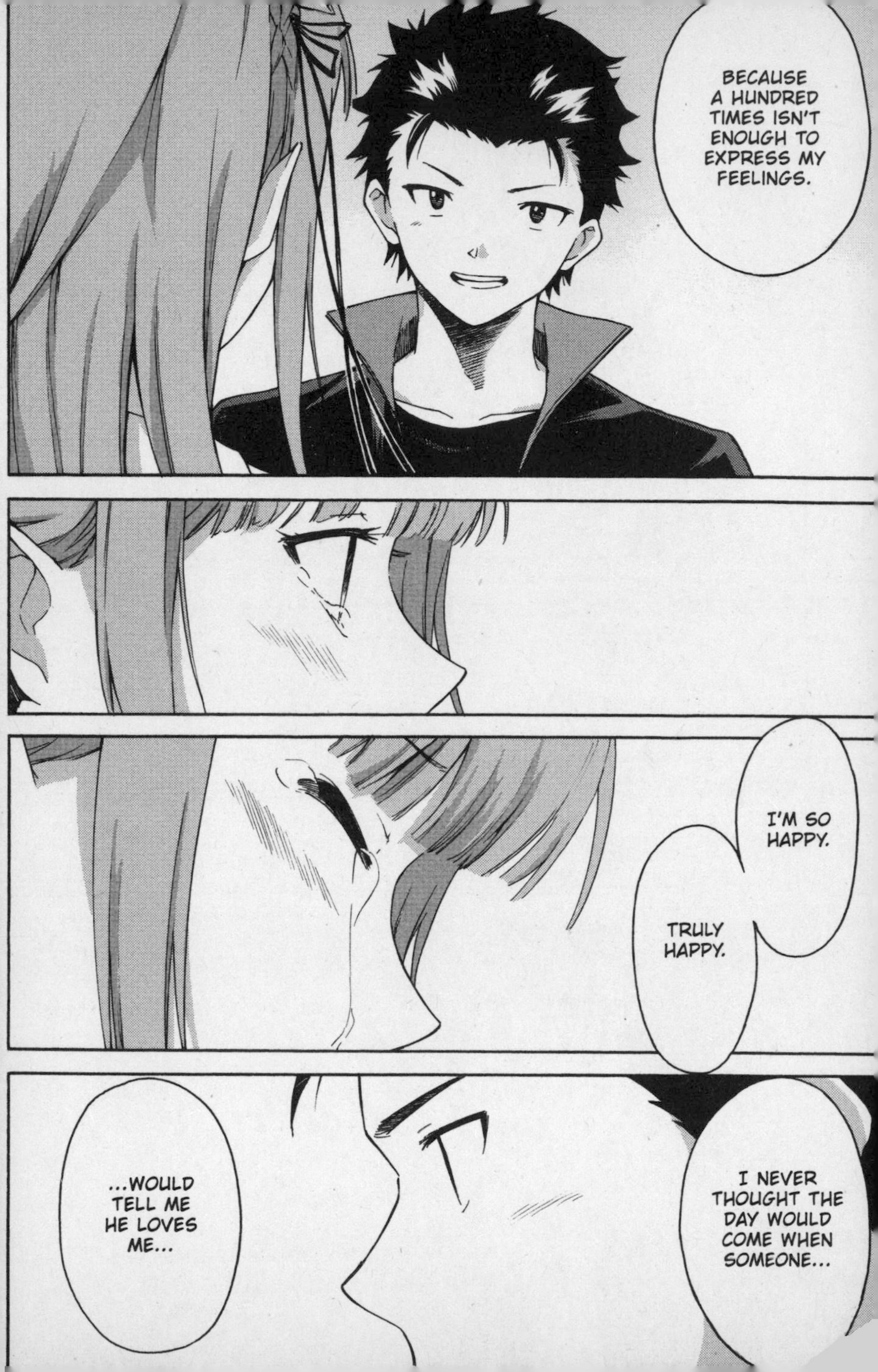
BECAUSE A HUNDRED TIMES ISN'T ENOUGH TO EXPRESS MY FEELINGS.
I'M SO HAPPY.
TRULY HAPPY.
I NEVER THOUGHT THE DAY WOULD COME WHEN SOMEONE...
...WOULD TELL ME HE LOVES ME...

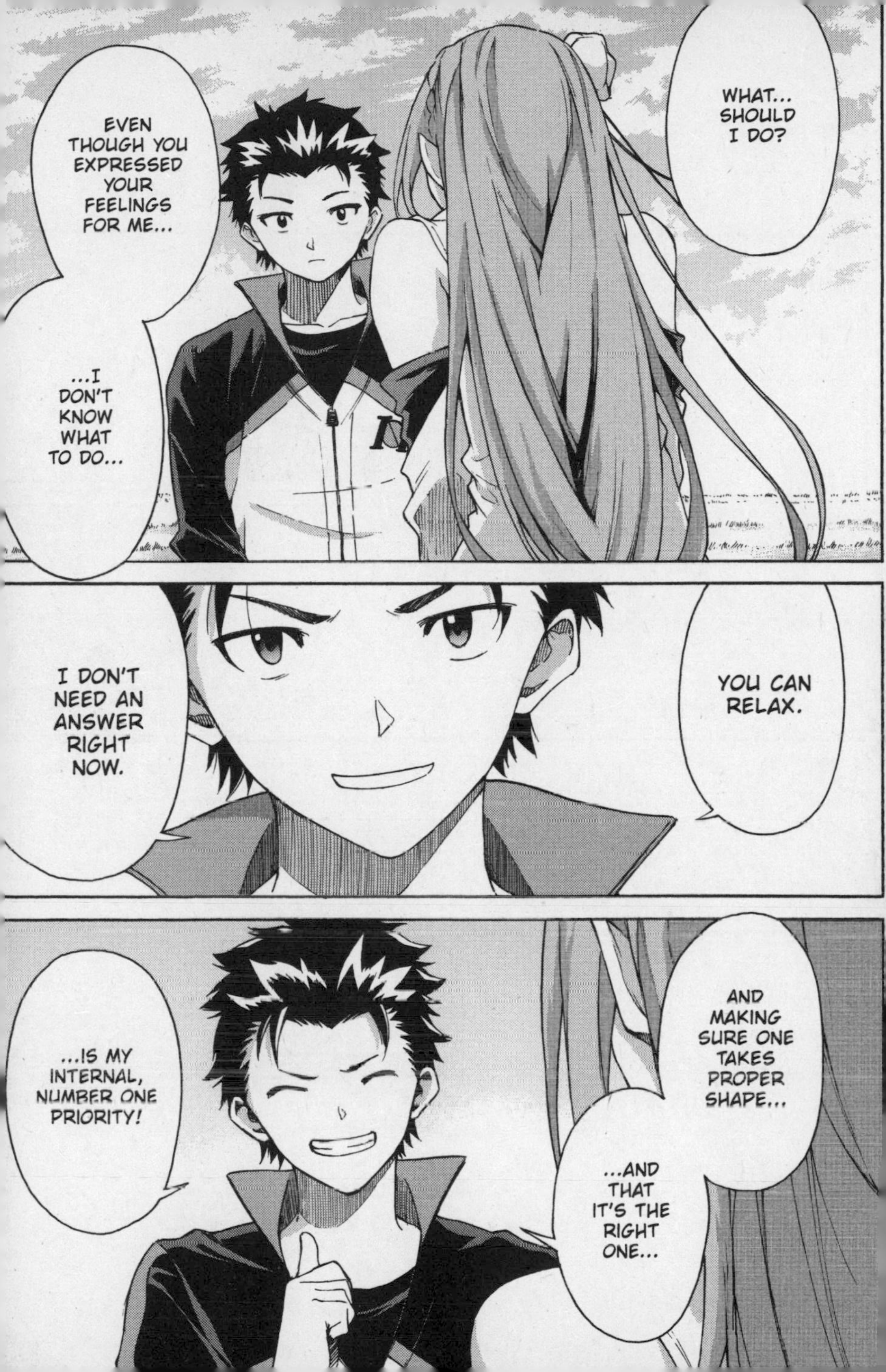
WHAT... SHOULD I DO?
EVEN THOUGH YOU EXPRESSED YOUR FEELINGS FOR ME...
...I DON'T KNOW WHAT TO DO...
YOU CAN RELAX.
I DON'T NEED AN ANSWER RIGHT NOW.
AND MAKING SURE ONE TAKES PROPER SHAPE...
...AND THAT IT'S THE RIGHT ONE...
...IS MY INTERNAL, NUMBER ONE PRIORITY!

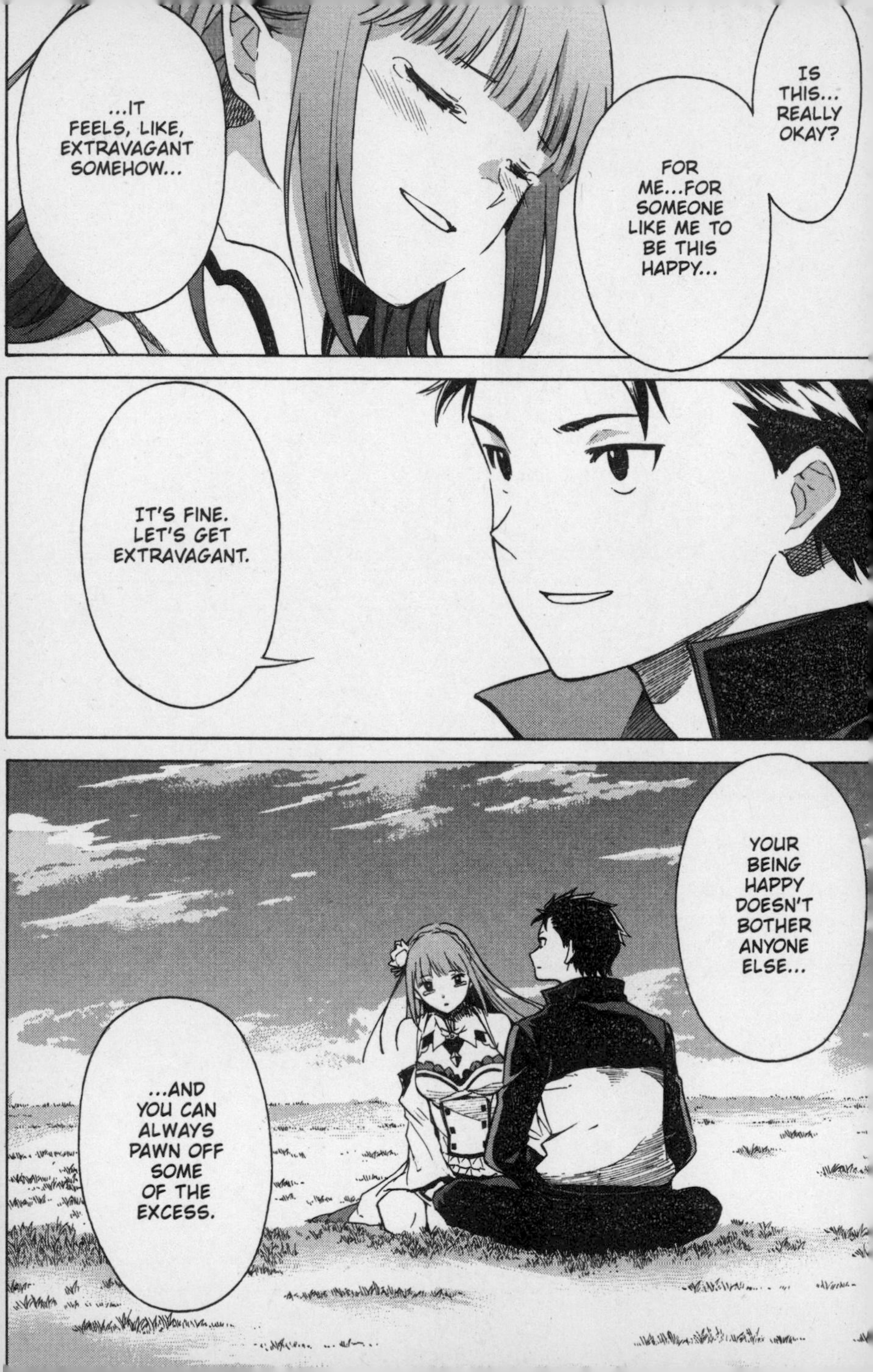
IS THIS... REALLY OKAY?
FOR ME...FOR SOMEONE LIKE ME TO BE THIS HAPPY...
...IT FEELS, LIKE, EXTRAVAGANT SOMEHOW...
IT'S FINE. LET'S GET EXTRAVAGANT.
YOUR BEING HAPPY DOESN'T BOTHER ANYONE ELSE...
...AND YOU CAN ALWAYS PAWN OFF SOME OF THE EXCESS.

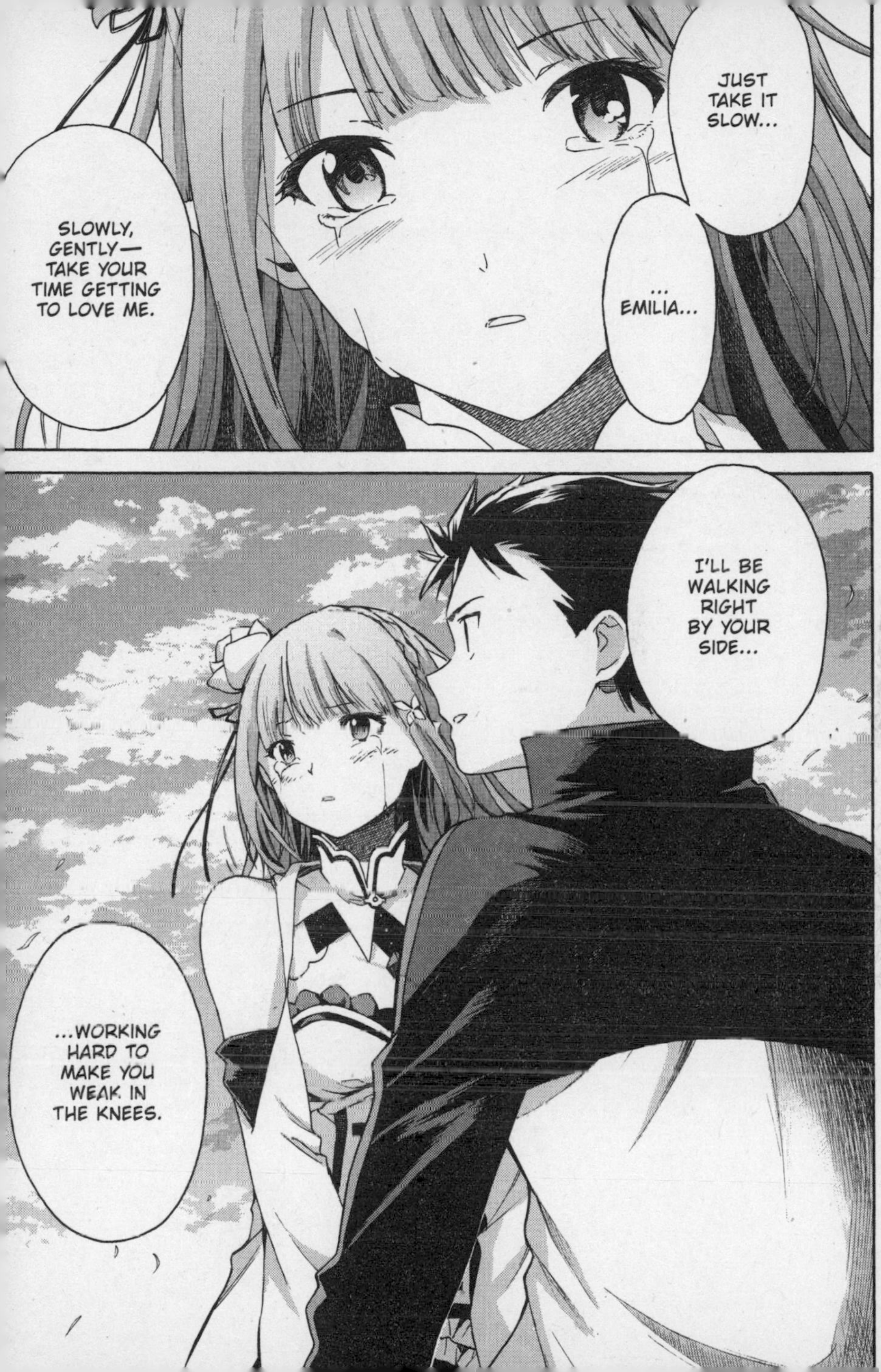
JUST TAKE IT SLOW...
... EMILIA...
SLOWLY, GENTLY— TAKE YOUR TIME GETTING TO LOVE ME.
I'LL BE WALKING RIGHT BY YOUR SIDE...
...WORKING HARD TO MAKE YOU WEAK IN THE KNEES.

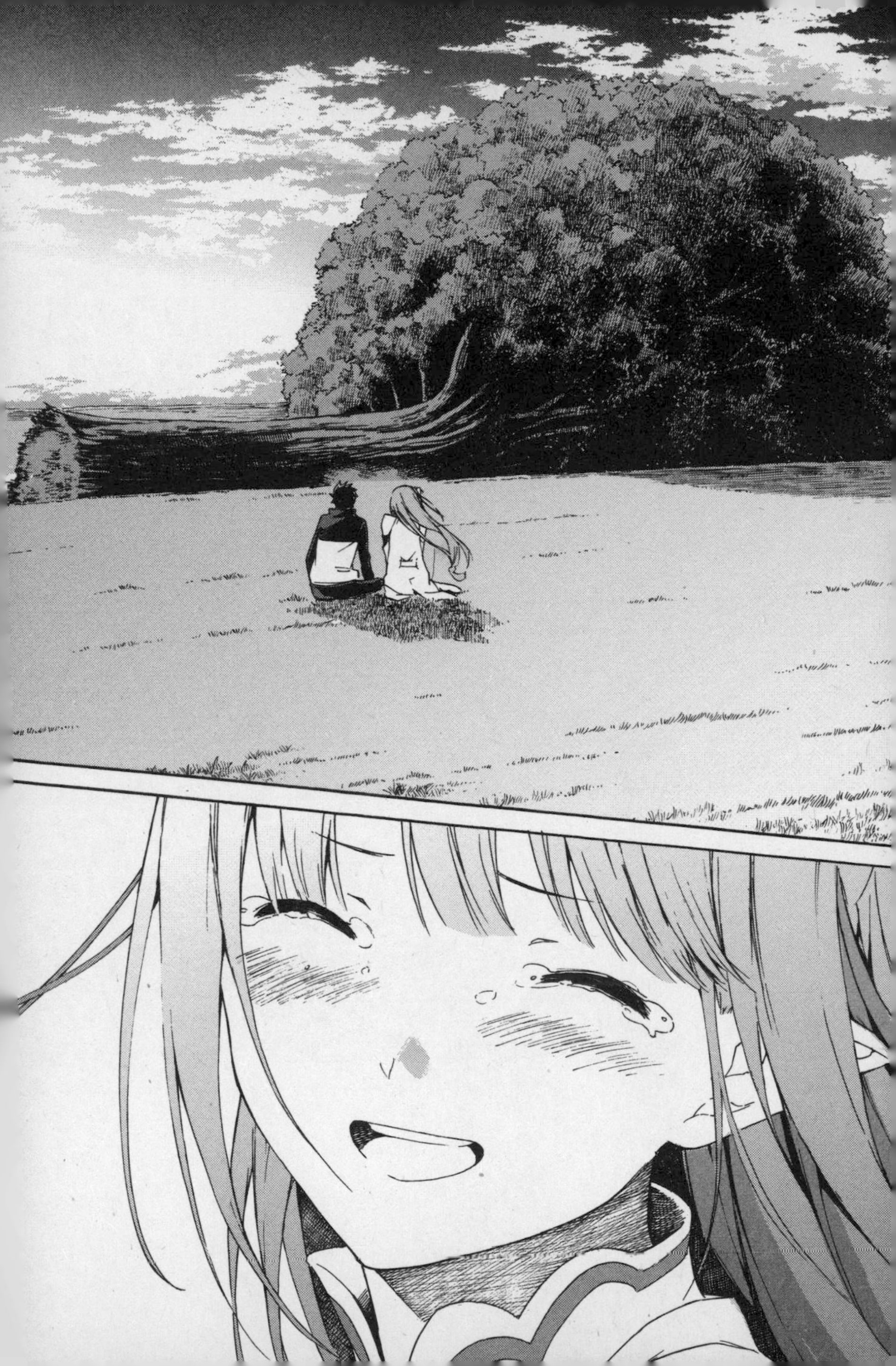

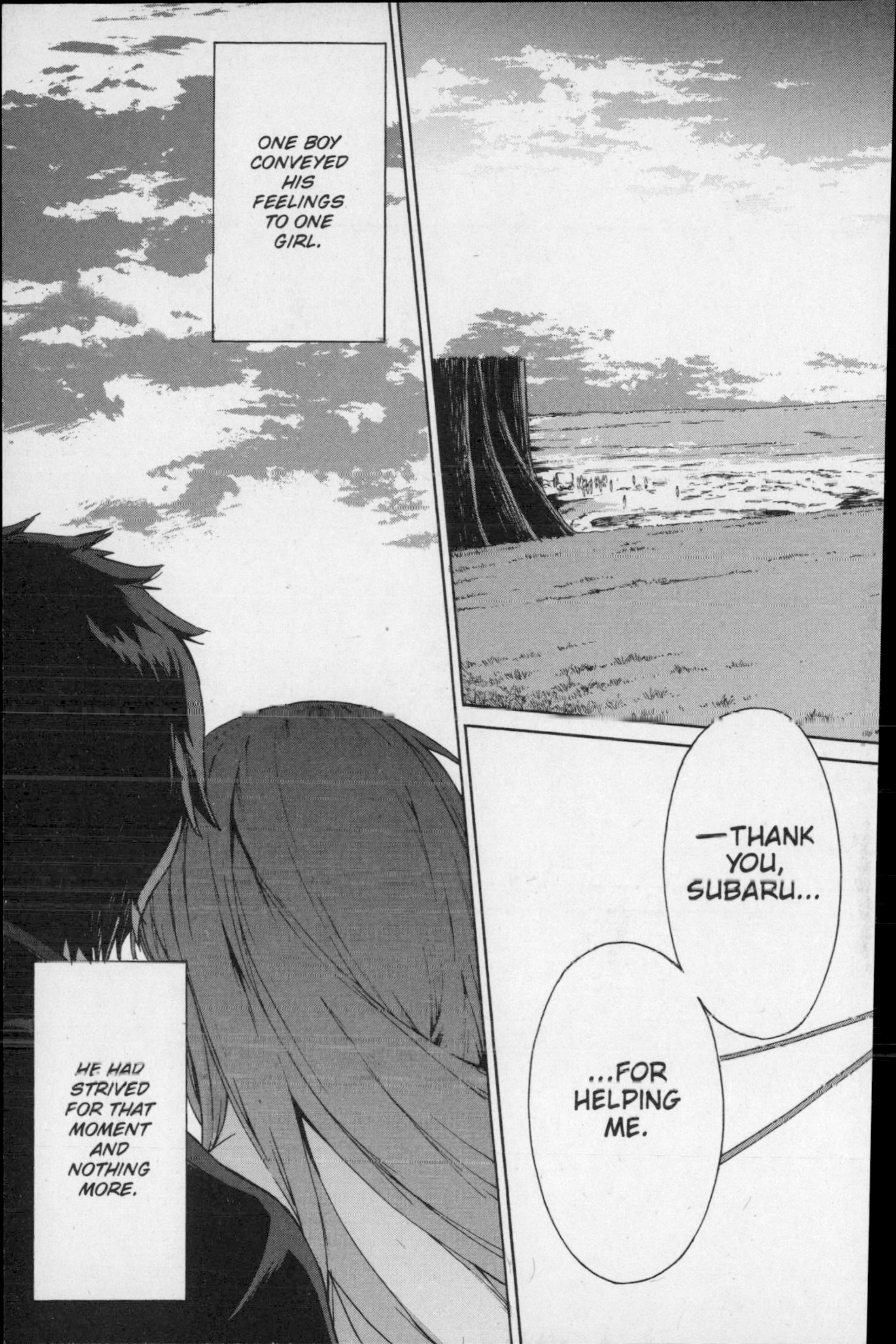
—THANK YOU, SUBARU...
...FOR HELPING ME.
ONE BOY CONVEYED HIS FEELINGS TO ONE GIRL.
HE HAD STRIVED FOR THAT MOMENT AND NOTHING MORE.

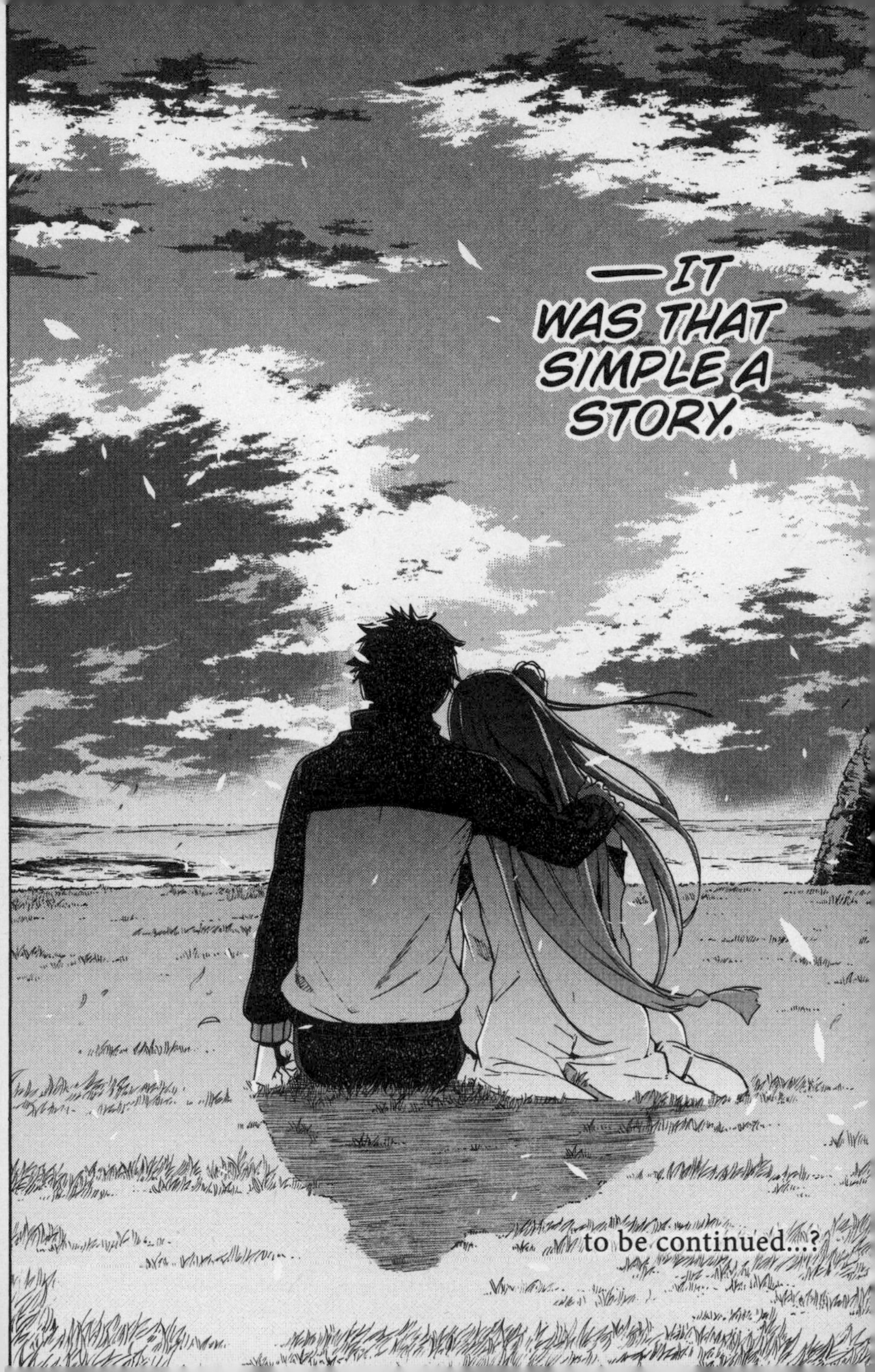
—IT WAS THAT SIMPLE A STORY.
to be continued...?

Truth of Zero
The only ability Subaru Natsuki gets when he's summoned to another world is
time travel via his own death. But to save her, he'll die as many times as it takes.

Re:ZERO
-Starting Life in
Another World-

Illustration by Shinichirou Otsuka
(Character Designer)

Re:ZERO -Starting Life in Another World-

Supporting Comments from the Author of the Original Work, Tappei Nagatsuki

Daichi Matsuse-sensei! Congratulations on Volume 10 of this *Re:ZERO* comic going on sale!

And with this, Chapter 3 has finally arrived at double digits in volumes! Incredible!

More than that, as everyone who has read to this tenth volume and watched the anime knows, we've finally arrived at where the anime ended!

Thinking back to the publication of the first *Re:ZERO* book, when I first worked with Matsuse-sensei, we've already been together quite a long time.

And while I had strong feelings when we hit "From Zero," I had a different kind of strong feeling the moment we hit "—It Was That Simple a Story."

Beginning with the breakup with Emilia in the royal capital, the subsequent appearance and rampage of Petelgeuse, passing through "From Zero," the battle with the White Whale, and finally the showdown with Petelgeuse—Having overcome all of this, Subaru finally reaches the point of "—It Was That Simple a Story."

I can firmly declare that when I actually read the chapter, I had absolutely no complaints about the comic edition whatsoever.

Matsuse-sensei, thank you so, so much. Matsuse-sensei, I am truly glad.

The comic edition has reached the final episode of the anime, but this is not yet the final volume. Matsuse-sensei's exquisite touch will reach ahead to parts not portrayed by the anime.

I invite everyone to enjoy with me the tale beyond the ending!

Re:ZERO -Starting Life in Another World-
Chapter 3: Truth of Zero

Artist Comments

AFTERWORD

THANK YOU FOR BUYING CHAPTER 3, VOLUME 10. WITH THE FINAL BATTLE WITH PETELGEUSE COMPLETE, SUBARU SUCCEEDED IN REUNITING WITH EMILIA! CONGRATULATIONS, SUBARU!
...HOWEVER, AS THOSE WHO HAVE READ THE ORIGINAL WORK ARE AWARE, CHAPTER 3 CONTINUES FOR A LITTLE WHILE LONGER! SO BEST REGARDS GOING FORWARD!

DAICHI MATSUSE
JUNE 2019

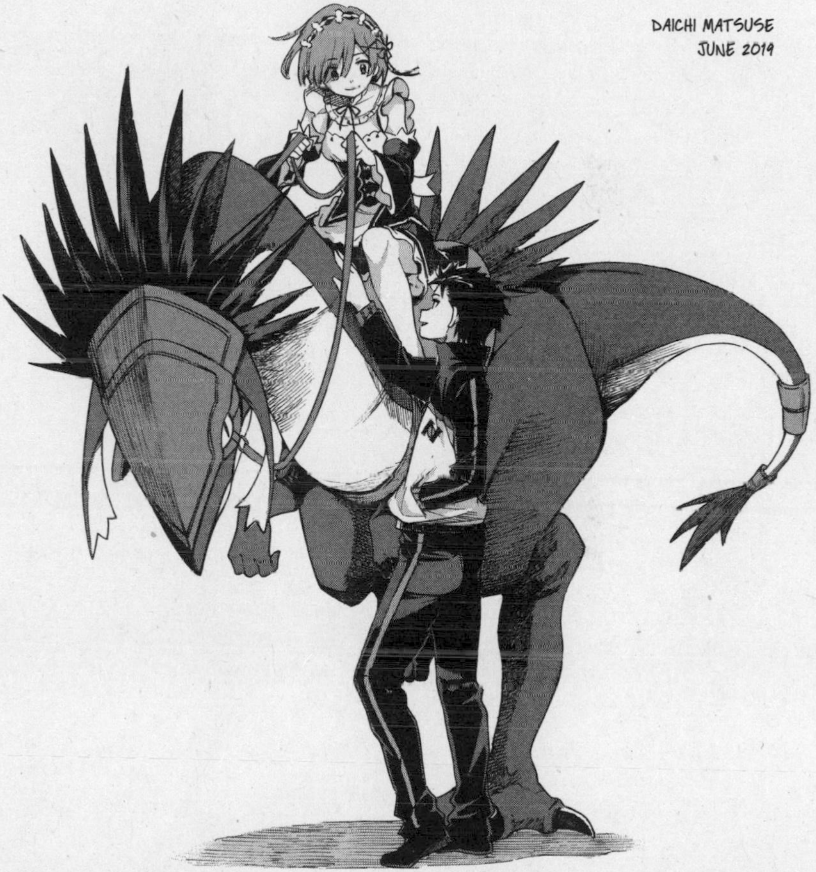

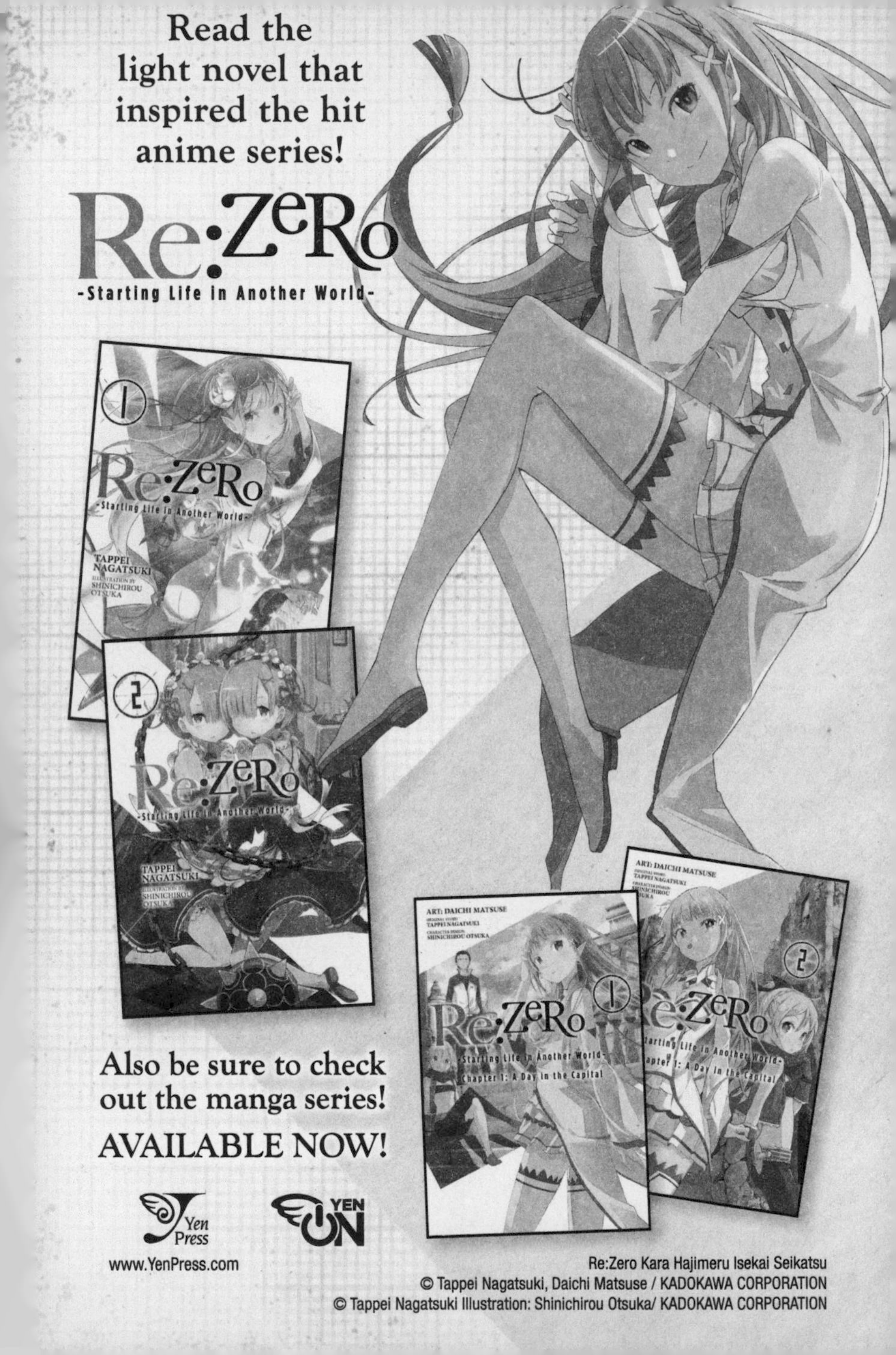
Read the light novel that inspired the hit anime series!
Re:ZeRo
-Starting Life in Another World-
Also be sure to check out the manga series!
AVAILABLE NOW!
Yen Press
YEN ON
www.YenPress.com
Re:Zero Kara Hajimeru Isekai Seikatsu
© Tappei Nagatsuki, Daichi Matsuse / KADOKAWA CORPORATION
© Tappei Nagatsuki Illustration: Shinichirou Otsuka/ KADOKAWA CORPORATION

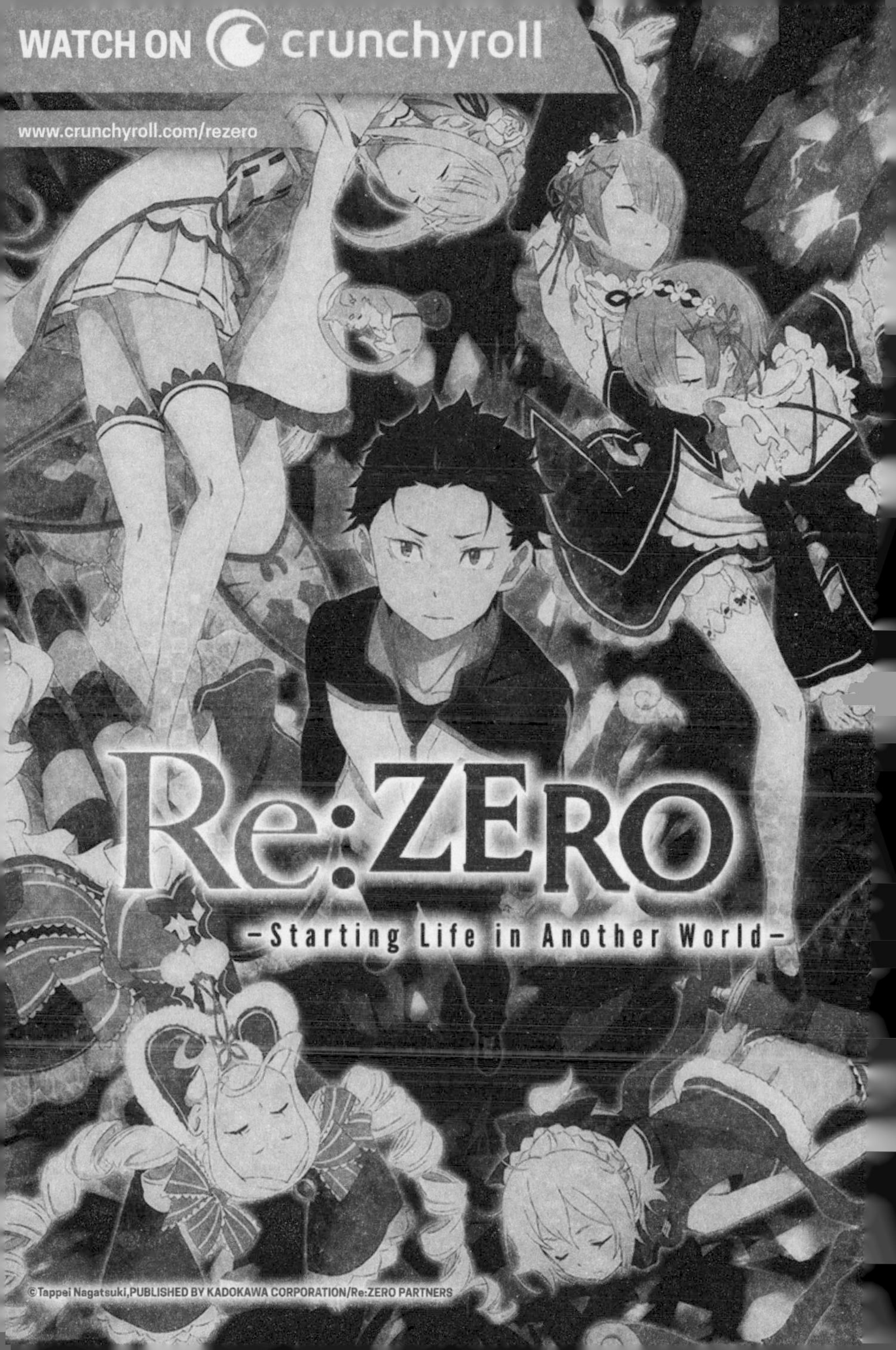

RE:ZERO -STARTING LIFE IN ANOTHER WORLD- ⑩
Chapter 3: Truth of Zero

Art: **Daichi Matsuse**
Original Story: **Tappei Nagatsuki**
Character Design: **Shinichirou Otsuka**

Translation: Jeremiah Bourque
Lettering: Rochelle Gancio

RE:ZERO KARA HAJIMERU ISEKAI SEIKATSU DAISANSHO
Truth of Zero Vol. 10
© Daichi Matsuse 2019
© Tappei Nagatsuki 2019
First published in Japan in 2019 by KADOKAWA CORPORATION, Tokyo. English translation rights arranged with KADOKAWA CORPORATION, Tokyo through TUTTLE-MORI AGENCY, Inc.

English translation © 2020 by Yen Press, LLC

Yen Press
150 West 30th Street, 19th Floor
New York, NY 10001

Visit us at yenpress.com
facebook.com/yenpress
twitter.com/yenpress
yenpress.tumblr.com
instagram.com/yenpress

First Yen Press Edition: February 2020

Yen Press is an imprint of Yen Press, LLC.
The Yen Press name and logo are trademarks of Yen Press, LLC.

Library of Congress Control Number: 2016936537

ISBNs: 978-1-9753-0809-4 (paperback)
       978-1-9753-0808-7 (ebook)

10 9 8 7 6 5 4 3 2 1

WOR

Printed in the United States of America